Arabic Short Stories 1945-1965

Arabic Short Stories
1945-1965

Edited by
Mahmoud Manzalaoui

The American University in Cairo Press

First published 1968 by the American Research Center in Cairo
under the title *Arabic Writing Today: The Short Story.*

113 Sharia Kasr el Aini
Cairo, Egypt

Fourth printing 1992

Dar el Kutub No. 4336/85
ISBN 977 424 121 5

Printed in Egypt by The American University in Cairo Press

CONTENTS

FOREWORD

by

H.E. Dr. Sarwat Okasha

Minister of Culture of The United Arab Republic

It is one of the commonplaces of comparative literature that national character is best expressed in literary forms which have grown organically out of the traditions and experience of a national environment. No national literature can be considered, with any degree of understanding, divorced from the modes of expression which it has chosen for itself. The Aristotelian divisions were the fruit of observation, not the prescriptions of a law-giver, and the main determinant of literary genius has been the shapes of its own intention. This is not to say, however, that national literatures are mutually exclusive and that forms evolved in one tradition are not valid for another. One may, indeed, draw comfort from the universal craving for self-renewal through commerce with other cultures. The borrowing of forms from areas of experience beyond one's own has invariably been one of the many ways in which mankind has come to terms with loneliness.

If the short story, in all its complexity and density, is one of the literary achievements of nineteenth— century Europe, it remains for many of us a compendious medium of expression admirably suited to the situations and introspections of modern life. And although the short story, modulated by the pens of Poe, Maupassant, James and Chekhov, became a remarkably elliptic rendering of significant moments in human experience, it remained nevertheless fundamentally European or American in moral climate.

Modern Arabic literature, however, seeking modes of expression which would, as it were, encapsulate the experience of living in a twentieth century in a world tending towards universalism, without loss of national character and intellectual roots, turned with eagerness to the short story. Distant heir to the tales and romances of oriental tradition, the short story was not too alien a mode of literary expression. It provided the discipline of concentration and brevity for prose fiction which the epigram and the short *qasida* had provided for poetry. It also fitted comfortably into the pages of the daily press, where so much of modern Arabic thinking and literary experiment had taken place since the last two decades of the nineteenth century. It had affinities with the ancient *maqama*, that repository of anecdote, Theophrastian character and essay writing, so much admired in Arabic letters. In short, it was, of western literary forms, one of the closest to Arabic tradition.

The purpose of this anthology, which, it is hoped, will be the first of a series which will be representative of most of the literary genres practised in modern Arabic, is to provide, both for the general public and for students of literature, a sampling of the variety of short story writing in the Arab world today. The editor of this volume, Dr. Mahmoud Manzalaoui, together with the editorial committee which assisted him, have shown discrimination and understanding in their choice, a choice which cannot have been easy to make, as the short stories were of necessity to reflect what was best in the profusion of modern Arabic examples, while being readily accessible to the literary sensibilities of the English-reading public. The problem of translating stories, where so much rests on economy of expression and on a context of shared assumptions, must have been very difficult. But I am confident that the English-speaking public will agree with me that the editor and translators of the stories have achieved a very high degree of readability in their English renderings. It only remains for me to commend their joint efforts and to wish well to a series which has been launched so auspiciously.

Cairo

PRESENTATION

It is a paradox that the intensification of cultural contacts between peoples widely apart in location and language, and, indeed, the spectacular rise of specifically modern achievements in an ever enlarging circle of literatures of ancient traditions and recently revived ambitions, have tended to separate rather than unite the readers of the world and to veil, one behind the other, the writings of too many language areas. The result of this screening has been, unintentionally but effectively, to obscure the creativity of regions as significant as the Arab world. Occasional translations and the almost haphazard acceptance of some great reputations in no way belie the isolation from the interested outside public of a development whose ultimate importance cannot yet be gauged but which bids fair to offer, if ever it becomes accessible, aesthetic enrichment as well as stimulation and insight into a universe imbued with thinking and feeling that are among the most intense and most varied of our time.

It may be too soon to identify with complete assurance the lastingly significant and even the lastingly influential; but there is no doubt that the time has come to identify for those not born to the Arabic tongue what, of the immense production of the recent past, appears most important in tendence and formal perfection to writers and critics concerned with the future development of Arabic literature. It is not for the outsider to determine the branch of literary endeavor in which the Arab public will recognize itself most readily, nor is it for him to select within that branch the individual works that are being experienced as the most representative and to which therefore the foreigner, writer, critic, scholar, and public at large should be exposed.

A distinguished group of connoisseurs has fastened on the short story as the first genre to be presented. The interested *arabisant* has been happy to accept their selections. Their judgment is most likely to be convincing to the English-speaking reader and most helpful to the student of comparative literature.

The American Research Center in Egypt has seen its function exclusively in suggesting the undertaking and in facilitating its completion. Credit and gratitude must go to the Committee that chose the texts and supervised the translations. In fact, the only valid mode of expressing our appreciation and our sense of indebtedness to the Committee is to present as effectively as possible to the Western reader these documents of a literature that has so much to give as art and as mirror of a society whose life it both reflects and shapes.

Los Angeles, 1967 **G.E. von Grünebaum**

INTRODUCTION

When it was decided to publish a representative selection of any one specific genre of contemporary Arabic writing, the choice fell perfectly naturally upon the short story. Not only because this enables one to present in a single volume a wide range of relatively brief texts, each of which is complete in itself, but rather because this form has shown a particularly interesting and vigorous development in the Arab world in the past few decades. The literary pages of the daily newspapers have often seen the first publication of stories which have later been collected into volumes, and a wide public has formed a discriminating taste for the form: some writers — such as Youssef el Sharouni — have made it their principal means of imaginative expression; some — such as Youssef Idris — have begun their literary careers with the short story; others — such as Mohamed Kamel Hussein — have turned to it after first venturing into other fields of activity, or have returned to it (as Naguib Mahfouz has done) after having made their names in other genres. The period during which the short story has been the dominant genre in Arabic literature, the one at which an aspiring writer would most normally try his hand, is the two decades which followed the Second World War; only in the last few years has the short story been yielding pride of place to the theatre. This flowering therefore coincides with the period with which we wish to acquaint the English-speaking reader : the mid-twentieth century, the generation which came after that of the founding-fathers of our modern imaginative literature, men such as Taha Hussein, Mikhaïl Naïma and Ibrahim el Mazni (some of these are still with us, and some, indeed, still active in our field, and have therefore been represented in this collection: we open with stories by Mahmoud Taymour and Tewfik el Hakim). While these outstanding precursors are gradually becoming known internationally, the Arabic literature of the second half of the century, the truly and immediately contemporary voice of the Arabs, is far less so.

This volume is a contribution to the attempt at bringing such intertraffic as thoroughly up to date as the mechanism of selection, translation, and publication in book form, can allow.

It will be seen that the period of the flowering of the short story in Arabic is later than its peak in western literature, yet not, as in the case, say, of the drama, later by many centuries : the time lag here is only one of two or three generations. By the 'short story' is meant here the modern genre of short narrative, in which the pattern is centripetal and not linear, in which the unity of theme and action is clear, and is basically dependant upon the unfolding of the subjective psychological predicament of one or more of its characters. The short story, properly so called, arose, surely, in the age of Gogol and Poe, reached maturity in the age of Maupassant, Chekhov and Conrad, and remained a dominant genre in that of Katherine Mansfield and of James Joyce. It is a form which has evolved largely in environments where the writer has wished to reach a newspaper-reading public which is a good deal larger than the book-buying public, a situation which existed in the United States and in Russia in the middle of the last century, and gradually arose in the Arab world in the decades that intervene between Poe's days and our own.[1] In modern Arabic literature, we may say that the taproot of the short story is formed by two twin fibres : the pre-existing western model, as developed since the mid-nineteenth century, and an indigenous need, felt by both the writer and the public, for this concentrated creative form, caused by socio-cultural changes which are analogous to those which made it arise in the west, and which have acted upon the Arab imagination from the closing years of the nineteenth century, up to the present moment.

But if these form the taproot of the modern short story, in Arabic literature as in the western tradition, the genre has innumerable fibrils nourishing it from the oldest indigenous forms of the short prose narrative. The Arab tradition knew the short narrative in several different

(1) I must here acknowledge a debt to Professor Lynn Bartlett of Vassar College, stemming from a conversation with him, which he will have long since forgotten.

forms. The *Koran*, although gnomic rather than narrative in its basic structure, contains one great chapter, the *Sūra* of *Joseph*, which is fully narrative in form. The anecdote-collection is given literary form by writers of the Golden Age: the *Kitāb-ul-bukhalā'* — *The Book of Misers* — of al-Jahiz springs to mind. The lives of the poets, especially of the lover-poets, as told by the belle-lettrists of the Silver Age (such as Abul Faraj al Isfahani, author of the *Kitāb-ul-aghāni* — *The Book of Songs*), have the verses of the poets embedded in them, and thus often develop into examples of the narrative form known as *cante-fable*. The *maqāma* was an Arabic genre both picaresque in its contents and euphuistic in its manner — indeed it has been surmised to have influenced (or even initiated) the two separate European *genres* of the picaresque, and of the euphuistic, romance. The animal-fable, the folk-tale, the professional story-teller's repertoire, are rich veins in Arabic literature, and, in the last of these three groups, the *Arabian Nights* were to attain the status of world-literature even before they received the accolade of official recognition as worthwhile artefacts, on the home ground of formal Arab culture. Renan and other western observers consider that the traditional Semitic scale of cultural values did not readily admit the indirect, concretized symbolic forms of the narrative (nor of the image, nor of the melody) to the same high seriousness of purpose as was recognized in poetry and in the gnomic directness and of the prose of statement. Certainly the initial unwillingness to assimilate the modern European genre of the short story is in fact an observable feature in the emergent phases of the modern Arabic short story, in what Abdel Aziz Abdel Meguid[1] has called its Embryonic stage (from 1870 to around 1914) and its Trial stage (from around 1914 to the mid-twenties); it also continued in critical opinion well into the period of Abdel Meguid's third, or Formative, stage (from the mid-twenties up to the early fifties, where his study concludes). In the earliest stage, stories often set out to be directly didactic and moralistic : perhaps the very earliest approach to the modern short story form, Selim Bustany's *The Shot that Nobody*

(1) *The Modern Arabic Short Story : Its Emergence, Development and Form*. Cairo, 1955.

Fired ('Ramya min ghairi rāmi', *Al Jinan*, Beirut), which dates from 1870, although it contains one character that is emerging into the round, is in fact a lightly-treated instructional anecdote about stinginess in domestic economy. Sometimes, the story is shamefaced at its being fictional and not based on historic fact : just as *Robinson Crusoe* had to override the criticism of those who were said to 'reproach it with being a Romance'. In the year 1898 we find both the translator of an English story, and the female author of an original story, taking pleasure in announcing that the tales they are telling actually took place in real life.[1] Even translations and adaptations of European stories, such as those carried out by Manfaluti, were sometimes pre-eminently stylistic and linguistic exercises, and the move away from the dominance of verbalism, towards the evolution of a pliant narrative style, was long and slow. As for the accusations of frivolity and immorality, it is as late as January 1937 that we find Mr. Ahmed el Zayyat, editor of *Al Rissala*, boasting that his weekly will not accept such trivialities — though, in his case, the *amende honorable* was not slow to come, for in the next year, he began to issue as an off-shoot of the parent-magazine, a periodical called *Al Riwaya* devoted exclusively to fiction[2]. The embryonic stage of the modern Arabic short story reveals an interesting phenomenon for the historian of literary forms : since the environment was not yet ready to accept the pattern and aims of this *genre*, it was converted back into the homiletic weapon and stylistic exercise which the public expected. When the environment grew ripe for the borrowed form, it was accepted and developed, and made fully its own. Even the early misapplication — or should one say 'indigenizing' ? — of the genre is perhaps not entirely without its positive advantage; for it left the Arabic short story freer, by a convention now native to it, to

(1) Nasib al Mash'alani, 'An-*najāh ba'dal-ya's* (*Relief after Despair*) and Labibah Hashim, *Hasanat al Hubb* (*The Virtues of Love*), both in the Cairo periodical *Al-Diyā*'.

(2) For this detail and many others in this preface, a debt is owed to an unpublished English lecture by Dr. Saheir el Kalamawi, entitled *The Short Story* (delivered in Cairo in the summer of 1965) which is a mine of information, particularly upon the earlier periods.

depart from the accepted architectonic pattern of its western counterpart in order to achieve its own literary effect, or for any further intention in the author's mind. Among the stories printed below, Ehsan Kamal's *Jailhouse of My Own* follows a simpler linear pattern than a western writer would attempt, while *Atrocity*, by Kamel Hussein, begins on the lines of the Theatre of Cruelty, and later launches into philosophical dialogue : perhaps these departures from the western norm should be seen as examples of an acquired freedom of manœuvre?

Many critics consider that the first true modern Arabic short story is Mohamed Taymour's *In the Train* — at least, in so far as Egypt is concerned. Certainly it formed a starting point for the central strand of the modern tradition. (This is true down even to its very setting, for beside the archetypal symbolism of travel and the chance meeting, a means of public transport in a country of divergent social patterns such as Egypt was then, is one of the few places where lives and habits converge : so that, in twentieth-century Arabic fiction, as in nineteenth-century Russian, the train journey—as well as the journey by service car or long distance taxi — was to become a recurrent theme : it is present in this collection in *The Night Train Home*, *A Jailhouse of My Own*, *Still Another Year*, and *Vostok Reaches the Moon.*) Recent research assigns the claim of priority in time to earlier works; one claim[1] goes back to 1904, to two collections of stories by Mohamed Lotfy Gomaa[2]. Certainly the translation movement which began in the nineteenth century increased in impetus in the field of the short story in the opening years of this century. In Egypt, we find periodicals of that time each specializing in translation from a specific foreign language : *Al Bayan* published translations of English (including American) works, *Al Sufur* specialized in French. The somewhat later *Al Fagr* produced translations from Russian, as well as encouraging original efforts in Arabic,

---

(1) By Mr. Mohamed Rushdy Hassan, in an unpublished M.A. thesis, presented at Cairo University, on the influence of the *maqama* on the rise of the modern Egyptian short story.

(2) *The Nights of a Perplexed Soul* (*Layāli-r-rūh-il-hā'ira*) and *In People's Houses* (*Fi Buyūt-in-nāss*) .

and around its editor, Khairi Said, gathered the so-called 'New School' of writers and artists, whose influence upon the twenties was considerable. The New School turned its efforts to the production of true short stories of the modern type, derived its themes from essentially Egyptian situations, and based its patterns upon genuine human tension, and not on an abstract concept; it recommended, and used, a 'middle' language which would have something of the immediacy of life, without losing the traditional dignity which had always been a cherished element in Arab writings. The group included Mohamed Taymour, his brother Mahmoud Taymour, who is represented in the opening pages of our collection, and Yehia Hakki, who figures prominently in the pages below. It is a pleasure to have the opportunity to do homage to Mahmoud Taymour by including, as we have done, one of his more recent short stories; for, with his brother, he was a pioneer in this field, and his output spans more than four decades of our literary history, often including the first experiments in each of the different types of story — realism, naturalism, symbolism and allegory and in such fields of exploration as the sympathetic understanding of the poor, and the delineation of the underworld — in all these directions he has led the way.

By the time we arrive at the opening of the year 1953, the short story is no longer in search of formal recognition as a serious art form. In January of that year, the literary periodical *Al Thaqafa* published a special Short Story number, in which prize-winning specimens of stories were printed. (It is pleasing to note that two of our contributors, Tewfik el Hakim and Kamel Hussein, appear in that number as established critics, while three more appear as prize-winners : they are Saheir el Kalamawi, Abdel Rahman Fahmi, and Farouk Khorshid). In the post-war years, immediately preceding this publication, the short story had played an important part in the intellectual, social, and political fermentation that was taking place[1]. From its inception,

(1) Here, and elsewhere in this introduction, I have quarried deeply, with the author's permission, in Dr. Shukri Ayyad's unprinted English lecture, *The Egyptian Short Story since* 1944, delivered in Cairo in 1965.

the Arabic short story as we have seen, had been directed towards didactic ends : ends concerned not only with personal morality, but with the problem of social and political injustice. In the twenties, the method of social realism had been making its way to the fore. These two tendencies merged together in those seminal years and made the short story a weapon of pamphleteering, partly relieving the feelings, partly calling for action, and, at the same time, not over-committing the writer or the newspaper editor who printed his work to any defined subversive position. If much that was produced was ephemeral, the movement was a forcing-ground which formed the generation now at the height of its literary powers : Youssef Idris and Abdel Rahman el Sharkawi may be mentioned in illustration. In this field, Dr. Taha Hussein, already by then the doyen of Arabic letters, worked as a pioneer when, soon after the Second World War, he began his collection of short stories and vignettes, *The Tormented of the Earth* (*Al-mu'adhabūna fil-'arḍ*), which, when eventually published in book form, was to bear the dedication "To those who yearn deeply for justice, and to those who are mortally afraid of justice I direct this discourse".

In the years that followed, an awareness of western explorations in technique, and of twentieth-century questionings around the human condition, has modified the attitude of most writers. The experiments of twentieth-century western writers have impinged fast and thick upon the awareness of Arab readers, so that, in something like fifteen years, the different attitudes that have revealed themselves in Europe over the last sixty years or so, have demanded assimilation by the younger Arab writers and thinkers. An accelerated rate of development, an accumulation of foreign models, jostled together by an appreciable narrowing of the time-lag, a continued search for indigenous standpoints, a preoccupation with both literary and non-literary anxieties, sometimes coming together, but often pulling in different directions — such has been the background which has formed our newer writers. A greater subjectivity, a blending of the fanciful and the real, an exploration of the non-rational in man, a growing freedom from the seriality of outward events, the use of symbolism and private mythology, the search for freshness in the linguistic tools— these can all be detected in the works which we have placed in the concluding portions of our collection.

In all but this most recent phase, one dominant characteristic is detectable in the modern Arabic short story : a romanticism of tone, deriving partly from the nineteenth-century European literature which nourished the genre at its birth, and partly from an indigenous stress upon the pathetic, the eloquently suasive[1]. The reverse side of this quality leads to sentimentality, to an adolescent over-emphasis on sensuality, to too many faultless heroes, to a melodrama of excessively wicked rich villains illtreating a preternaturally pure hero plunged in a life of poverty of so grotesque a pattern that it fails to move the reader's genuine sympathies[2]. But the obverse is one of the positive qualities enriching the genre of which it is an integral structural element: in its different manifestations it gives us the Byronic compassion of Tewfik el Hakim's *The Martyr*, the sympathetic feeling for the poor prostitutes in Naguib Mahfouz's *Mosque in the Narrow Lane*, the elusive sensuality of the heroine of Youssef Idris's *Peace with Honour*, the aristocratic bedouin code of Ghaleb Halassa's *Trial by Ordeal*, the gently nostalgic picture of childhood in a great house, in Saheir el Kalamawi's *Nanny Karima and the Hammam*. And by contrast with the effusiveness into which the genre sometimes fell in its earlier stages, a more careful craftsmanship has been cultivated of late, particularly by the national Story Club (Nadi-l-qissa), the Short Story associations found in Faculties of Arts, and the words of advice and criticism that were until recently given in his monthly column by the assistant-editor of *Al Qissa* (*The Story*) magazine, the short story writer Sarwat Abaza. A salutary dose of auto-criticism has been administred to itself by the Arabic short-story in the person of its doyen, Mahmoud Taymour, in

(1) See the discussion of this in Gaston Wiet, *Introduction à la Littérature Arabe*, Paris, 1966; p. 294.

(2) See some acute criticisms made in the second part of Abdel Kader el Qot's article, *Mushkilatāni fi-l-qissat-il-miṣriyyati-l-qaṣira* (*Two Problems of the Egyptian Short story*), *Al Shahr* nos. 1 and 2, 1958.

a series of public lectures organized by a cultural branch of the Arab League.[1] Taymour warns of the following salient dangers : over-direct moralism, alternating with descriptions of extreme depravity, an over-generalization that ignores specific truths, a tendency to neglect the contradictions in a single person's make-up, a wavering between excessive condemnation and excessive condoning of human weaknesses, the intrusion of the author's voice where his characters' voices should be heard, a neglect of image and atmosphere in favour of a bare narrative of information, an over-narrow range of subjects, a dependence on far-fetched incidents. To these criticisms may be added those which regret the rarity of humour and happiness in the genre[2].

To have devoted so much space in this introduction to this self-criticism requires a word of explanation, especially as I do not wish to be classified among those Arab critics who are taken to task by Professor Jacques Berque for being hypercriticial of our own contribution to modern culture[3]. It seems justified for two reasons. First, it is a sign of self-confidence, and faith in one's own cause, if one occasionally washes one's dirty linen in public. Secondly, I am convinced that the reader may find in the stories that follow, every one of the virtues that form the contraries of the listed faults. It is best to let the stories speak for themselves, but one might allow oneself a few passing remarks on them. *Peace with Honour* shows a sufficiently clean break with cut-and-

---

(1) *Lectures upon Fiction in Arabic Literature, Past and Present,* (*Muḥāḍarāt fil-qaṣaṣ fi 'adab-il-'arab, māḍīhi wa ḥāḍirih*), League of Arab States: Institute of Higher Arab Studies, Cairo, 1958; pp. 68-73.

(2) This criticism is made by Ghaleb Halassa (author of the story *Trial by Ordeal* given below) writing of Youssef Idris, '*The Philosophy of Neo-Realism in Arabic Literature*' (*Falsafat-il-waqi'iyyah-l-jadīda fil-adabi-l-'arabī*), *Al Adab*, Beirut, March 1962, and by both Taha Hussein and Amin el Alem, of the stories they are presenting respectively in the *Foreword* and the *Preface* of the collection *Specimen of the Egyptian Short Story* (*Alwānun min al-qiṣṣati-l-miṣriyya*) Cairo, 1956. The *Alwan* collection is defended against this charge, on the grounds of its commitment to a serious standpoint, by Dr. El Qot, in the article referred to on p. 22 n. 2 above.

(3) R. and L. Makarius, *Anthologie de la littérature arabe contemporaine. Le roman et la nouvelle*, Paris, 1964; preface by Jacques Berque, p. 33 n. 3.

dried moralism. It is not depravity, but the almost cosy quality of the evil in us all that is wrily portrayed in the *Brass Four-Poster*. The particular circumstances of time, place, or employment, are dealt with in their different ways, by *The Mosque in the Narrow Lane*, *A Jailhouse of My Own*, and *The Night Train Home;* those of peculiarity of character in *Just a Puppet* and *A Boy's Best Friend*. The draperies that conceal the inward struggle are ferociously excoriated in *An Empty Bed*. In *The Sneak-Thief* it is the thoughts and words of the hero, and the words of his visitor, which alone sketch the predicament to us, a neat blend of the direct — for we hear their spoken voices without comment, and of the indirect — for their own conversation never utters aloud what is in their minds. Atmosphere is persuasively conveyed, evocative images sought after, by Yehia Hakki and Shukry Ayyad. We are in the most typical everyday world of Egypt's town and country in the *Cheapest Night's Entertainment* and *A Boy's Best Friend*. There is enough humour in this last story, as in the other Cairene vignette, *The Master Milkman*, in the Syrian *Dearly-Beloved Brethren*! and in the Moroccan *Master Loaf the Cross-grained Oaf*, to counterbalance the grimness and pathos found elsewhere. As to the question of range, not only of theme, but of attitude, of geographical and social background, of scale of moral seriousness, of literary method, of the intellectual assumptions of the authors and of the 'height' or level of their 'brows', it is hoped that this collection has been as truly diverse and catholic as it is possible to be. No doubt a word of apology is due to those authors for whose work no space was found, and we are aware that the geographical coverage of the Arab world has not been complete. One can also think of tendencies one would have liked to represent, if space had permitted : the historical short story (such as those written by Farid Abu Hadid), the story for children, the use of *Arabian Nights* themes in a contemporary manner, the stories — and they might have been of particular interest to our readers — in which an Arab describes the western world as he has known it, a theme well handled by Hassan Mahmoud and Abdel Ghaffar Makkawi. (On another level, we might have included representatives of science-fiction, which has been enjoying a certain popularity in Cairo periodicals)[1]. It is perhaps of greater symptomatic importance, to note that few of the stories included are based upon any positively-held philosophical stand: our writers are in a period of intellectual questioning rather than at a stage of consolidation : perhaps alone among the contributions, those of Tewfik el Hakim, Yehia Hakki and Kamel Hussein are exceptions in that their stories imply the working-out of some form of philosophical conviction — though the element of faith would have been more strongly revealed if we had included a contribution by Ali Ahmed Bakatheer, or the Mauriac-like study of spiritual dryness and fulfillment which is Fathi Radwan's *Al-'ānis* (*The Old Maid*)[2].

A collection such as this will, without editorial planning, tend to represent the main preoccupations and tensions of the group of imaginative writers which it covers. Certain recurrent themes occur in the stories we have included. Inevitably, in the field of public affairs, the unhappiness caused by poverty looms large (see, for example *The Night Train Home* and *Three Men and a Dog*); the peculiarly Egyptian problem of overpopulation and overcrowding is the subject of *The Cheapest Night's Entertainment*, and is reflected in *The Crowd*. The Egyptian countryside, a love of it, and an anxiety over its problems are seen in a number of stories, of which *The Scorpion* may stand as an example; social and political conflicts are seen in the two short stories by Naguib Mahfouz. In the field of personal predicament, a good number of stories show a preoccupation with the problem of the family, both as concerns the relationship of husband and wife (*Just a Puppet*, *The Enemy*, *Vanity Box*), and the tension between parent and child (*The Crowd*, *A Boy's Best Friend*). I am not, I think, mistaken, in finding that a large number of stories deal with loneliness, the loneliness of the solitary (*By the Water's*

(1) For an astonishing combination in one author's work, of the charm of genuine pastoral 'primitivism' and of the themes of science-fiction, compare two works by the Tunisian Mohamed el Marzouki, *'Arqub ul-Khayr* (*The Tendon of Bounty*) and *Fi 'alami-dharrah* (*In the World of the Atom*), in the collection which takes its name from the first of these two (Tunis, 1956).

(2) *Al Magalla* cv, September 1965.

Edge), of the failure (*The Fortune Teller*), of the person of greater sensibility who does not establish a full accord with his environment (*An Empty Bed*, *The Futility of It All*, *Vestok*) : perhaps the nature of the short story lends itself particularly to a form of choric soliloquizing which is suited to the condition of the Egyptian intellectual (*In the Surgery*). One range of problems which are partly public and partly personal are those concerned with the peculiar Arab predicament of the twentieth-century : how to find a *modus vivendi* between innovations and inherited conventions, to what extent an individual should come to terms with either, or free himself from them as best suits his individuality. Conventions are satirized in *The Brass Four Poster*, and the comic hero of *Dearly Beloved Brethren* ! fulminates against innovations. But, in a more dramatic illustration of the problem, three stories with different environments — a Syrian city, a Jordanian bedouin tribe, and the Egyptian countryside show the principal characters partially or wholly rebelling against the cruelty of the *vendetta : Snow at Night*, *Trial by Ordeal* and *Peace with Honour* are deliberately juxtaposed in the pages below. Similarly, the condition of woman in modern Arab society is illustrated by the totally-contrasting halves of the dyptich formed by the Upper Egyptian *Jailhouse of My Own* and the Beiruti[1]: *Street Walker*.

The arrangement of the items, however, on the whole follows the chronology of their writers' births or of the actual writing of the story. The evolutionary sketch that emerges from this arrangement is in itself interesting, for it tells the reader something more of the development we have already discussed — even though all the stories have in actual fact been written comparatively recently, within the space of some twenty years. Tewfik el Hakim's *The Martyr* does not have the ordinary world of men as its setting, and its inspiration is European. It belongs to world-literature. Mahmoud Taymour's *The Enemy* and Kamel Hussein's *Atrocity* are deliberately denuded of local colour, in order to give them a direct universality. The stories that follow, and form the bulk of the collection, are realistic, making great use of local

(1) The writer is Syrian, but the environment and the tone are those of the Lebanese capital.

colour, and concerned with the problems of Arab communities. In the later pages, the centre of gravity is the inner predicament of the individual, and the method is more experimental, from the series of flashbacks which form *The Crowd*, to the totally oneiratic *Vanity Box*.

It is impossible to satisfy all readers in everything, and the task is made difficult by our conscious policy of trying to interest four types of readers. The western Arabist should find sufficient foothold in our collection to enable him to follow up his reading of it with a fuller study of the author's works in the original : at the back of the book, is a selected reading-list of Arabic anthologies and relevant critical works. The comparativist should find an adequate illustration of trends in modern Arabic fiction, and be able to note for himself which western models have impinged most effectively. It must be borne in mind, in reading modern Arabic literature, that, side by side with indigenous traditions and talent, the literature of the west (by which is meant Europe — eastern as well as western — together with America) has had the same powerful rôle of inspirer, model, catalyst, and admired rival, which classical literature played in Europe in the earlier centuries of modern times — and that it has given writers at one and the same time both a nourishment and a desire to free themselves from it. As Raoul and Laura Makarius write :[1]

> Cette littérature qui est une des plus jeunes du monde offre, par rapport à l'Occident, le double intérêt d'avoir été nourrie aux mamelles de son art, et de s'en différencier.

The main move in the centre of gravity of these influences has been away from the very strong early predominance of Maupassant, first to the subtler model of Chekhov, and then to the Joycean and Faulknerian. Each reader will want to make the connexions for himself, but, in the editor's opinion, he will feel the presence of Maeterlinck in Tewfik el Hakim, of Katherine Mansfield in *The Fortune Teller*, of Virginia Woolf's *Mrs. Dalloway* in *Dunya*, and of the fin-de-siècle prose-

(1) Op. cit.; p. 47.

poets in *Street Walker*.

The third category of reader we have in mind is those who, like ourselves, may read the fiction produced by another environment, not for its literary qualities, but in order to inform themselves about the life, thought, and feelings of different communities. This collection should satisfy their documentary needs : if they find certain portions of the Arab world, certain trends of Arab thought, not represented, it is because the stories chosen fitted the literary exigencies best. A restricted number of footnotes, designed to elucidate, but not to comment, have been supplied. The more seriously professional wing of this category will perhaps be social anthropologists and cultural historians, but the opposite wing will blend with the fourth, the largest and most important group we have in mind : intelligent readers of good modern fiction, who are also, at the same time, curious about their fellow human beings. These, we hope, will find in this volume a précis of the life and letters of a group of communities which, in many ways, resemble their own, and, in many others, are radically different.

This sameness within difference has been the prime factor in shaping the methods of translation that we have followed. The life and thought of the personages in thes Arabic stories can be so misleadingly similar to those of the characters in western fiction, that there is a temptation to assume that identity exists in the matter of what it is now the usage to call the *pragmatics* of the two cultures. Yet crucial moments occur in the stories, at which essential differences come to the fore. At these points, the tendency to reduce the differences, or to omit the offending cause, or to translate it in a style which clashes glaringly with its context, has to be fought against. In the opening lines of one of our stories, *A Jailhouse of My Own*, the heroine describes her future husband in terms which are lullingly similar to those a western heroine might have used :

> He was my father's partner in business in Alexandria when I first came to know and admire him, and he occupied the flat facing ours where we lived in Ramleh. What first made

me notice him was his consideration towards his neighbours.

But the examples of this consideration plunge the western reader without warning into another climate of living :

> For instance he would never embarrass my mother by remaining on his balcony when she was out on ours. Also, when he came to visit my father he would acknowledge the sacrosanct nature of the home, and always make a point of choosing a seat from which he could not see out of the drawing room into any other room; before leaving, he would wait until my father had cleared the way. If my mother or I happened to run into him, and greet him, he would return the greeting courteously, keeping his eyes respectfully averted.

If the style and vocabulary of the preceding passage had been made more familiar, these details would, by contrast, read as though they were the actions of a western 'in fancy dress'. While to translate the passage too specifically in the manner of traditionalist Islamic injuctions on the comportment of a stranger in the presence of his host's womenfolk, would be to drive a wedge between the two components of present-day Arab life and emotions, traditionalist and contemporary, and create an unauthentic cleavage in what is in fact a symbiosis. Only a relatively 'neutral' manner of translation can avoid such a pitfall. When, in *The Enemy*, the wife replies to her husband's accusation at the height of a quarrel between them, with the somewhat formal "I swear, my love, it's never occurred to me to be unfaithful", any more staccato style of translation, attempting the manner of the average western wife in such circumstances, would rob her words of the solemn and hieratic overtone which they hold for the reader of the original. Into the dying thief's mind, in *The Thief and the Watchman*, swims his fraternal wish to invite his killer home and give him 'coffee and milk'. This means he would like to ply him generously with alternate glasses (not cups) of coffee and of milk. Any translation which suggests a cup of *café-au-lait* removes the story to a higher and more Europeanized social environment, while an overfull translation, explaining the custom, as I have done in the preceding sentence, both holds up the story too long, and, risks, in western taste, the bathos of excessive preoccupation either with the stomach or with a host's protocol. We have therefore compromised, (and inverted) by writing 'He wanted to take him home, to offer him some milk, to offer him a glass of coffee.' The hesitation over the wording in this example shows a consciousness of the opposite danger to that of assimilation : the temptation to explain too much, to emphasize the exotic character of the texts, to overlay the real Middle East with a flavouring of the pseudo-orient of European tradition. In general, we have usually reduced oaths such as 'By Allah !' into some more casual modern English equivalent, into the 'Honestly' or 'Yes, indeed !' which is the pragmatic equivalent. But where a greater solemnity is indicated by the context, we have used such terms as "By God" or "I hope to God". When the mother in *The Brass Four-Poster* refuses to allow the family to give up the great bed to her and to sleep on mattresses on the floor, in, as we have written, 'the *sitting-room* or the hall', an annotated translation would have had the freedom to be more literal. For the author wrote '*drawing-room* and hall' and he is maliciously glancing at the habit of furnishing a room with gilded sofa and chairs, and leaving it closed and unused on all but the most formal occasions — a habit followed almost universally by the lower middle classes, however humble their circumstances, and however small this room may have to be. Without an explanatory note, 'drawing-room' would have surprised the western reader of the story of Adeela and her daughter, and, therefore, the more neutral sitting-room' was, with some regret, adopted. In *Vostok Reaches the Moon*, the habit of writing prayers of invocation upon the rear of taxis is altogether too unfamiliar to pass without a footnote, but in the text itself we have avoided the word 'invocation', which jars with the general stylistic tone, and have tried to make up for this, and find an equivalent in English pragmatics, by translating the invocation itself into the rhythm of *Hymns Ancient and Modern*. Occasionally, nothing but the fully exotic term has seemed sufficient : hence the *hammam* in the title of Saheir el Kalamawi's story, for neither *bathroom* nor *baths* would, we think, have suited.

The biggest problem, as all translators know, is that of dialogue. An attempt to sound colloquial must be made, without adopting any idiosyncratic dialecticism of the vehicle language; while informality, solemnity, illiteracy, archaism, must all in turn be somehow suggested. A particular difficulty in the case of Arabic, is the impossibility of conveying in English, the interplay between the literary and the colloquial languages which are both used in fiction. In general, in these stories, the dialogue is in colloquial Arabic, and the author's own description and comments are in the literary language. But in some stories (e.g. *The Enemy*) all is in the literary language, and one story (*Just A Puppet*) is in earthy Cairo colloquial from beginning to end. There are further subtleties : a few authors adopt a deliberately high style, but most a deliberately 'middle' style which will meet the colloquial dialogue half way; some authors intuitionally, use a pungent colloquial word at the high points of their literary narrative; some, especially Yehia Hakki, are painstakingly meticulous in choosing the *mot juste* and avoiding clichés; of those represented by two stories each, there is in Youssef Idris a marked move away from banality of vocabulary, to a more evocative and individual manner, between *The Cheapest Night's Entertainment* and *Peace with Honour*.

This compilation is in every sense a collective effort. The selection was carried out jointly by the members of the Editorial Committee. Each story was then given to one of fifteen translators : thirteen of these were Egyptians (mostly graduates in English), and two, Englishmen (both graduates in Arabic). Each translation was then revised by the editor, before being submitted for its style to a further reviser, deliberately chosen for having English (standard British English in all cases) as his mother tongue, and for knowing little Arabic or none — there were ten such revisers, almost all graduates in English Language and Literature, and teachers of this subject. It then passed to a final reviser, an Egyptian teacher of English. Before and after this stage, the editor intervened again. This experiment must be judged by its results. I realize now that in working it out I was influenced by the description of method given in the *Introduction* to the *New Testament* of the *New English Bible* (1961), and I note with pleasure that the identical method of 'double control' is recommended by an Anglo-Russian translator in *Soviet Literature Monthly*[1].

In some cases, the original title of the story struck us as unsuitable, and has been replaced : where this has been done, it is indicated in the note on the author, found on the opening page of the story.

There is method in my madness in the question of transliteration. In the parts of this book designed to serve as an instrument for scholars, titles of books and articles, and names of periodicals, have been given in a form as close as typographically possible to orientalist convention[2]. Elsewhere, names and transliterated words and expressions have been given in the form which is normally used today by an Arab writing in English : thus authors' and collaborators' names are given as they would spell them in English themselves in their everyday lives. Arabic names and expressions left in the translations, are transliterated in line with the use of each Arab country : the *hagga* of the Egyptian stories becomes a *haja* in the Jordanian contribution. The vocabulary of Englishmen living in the Levant has been used for local objects : e.g. *gharry* for the horse-drawn carriage. I am guilty of turning the spiced bean-rissoles known in Cairo as *taʿmia* into *falafel* whenever they occur: this is the Alexandrian name for it, but I do not use it out of provincialism, for it is also the name which English-speaking residents in Egypt habitually use.

One final word of apology to American readers. The editor and his

(1) Avril Pyman, 'On Translating Turgenev into English', *Soviet Literature Monthly*, X, 1966; p. 177-8.

(2) Even here, I have consciously departed from these conventions by writing *g* for *j* in the names of modern Egyptian authors and in certain proper names in the titles of their works. It seems out of place in a work exclusively devoted to twentieth-century writers, to use classical forms which they would never dream of using themselves when they read out their names and works aloud.

revisers are all familiar with British, rather than American, usage; a floundering attempt at American colloquialism would have been fatal. The linguistic habits, therefore, are almost exclusively British throughout : this applies to the spelling, in all but the title-page, where the *Centre* which is our host appears in its native garb as a *Center*. I hope the effort at mentally re-coding this translation into American shape will not be a heavy one, and our failure to do so not taken amiss. But if you choose a British-educated editor you must accept the consequences.

Mahmoud Manzalaoui

ACKNOWLEDGEMENTS

My debts are so many that an attempt to list them all risks both being incomplete and proving overlengthy for the reader. It is an honour to have a Foreword by H.E. Dr. Sarwat Okasha, who is doing so much for the cultural life of the U.A.R. The American Research Center has seen three Directors since this project was first mooted : Dr. Ray Smith was present at the conception, Dr. George Scanlon watched over the gestation, and Mr. John Dorman has presided at the birth. It has been a pleasure to collaborate with the other four members of the Editorial Committee — Professor Kalamawi, Professor Nur Sherif, Fr. Anawati, and Dr. Ayyad — for in spite of their very busy professional lives, they all made the project so much their own. Dr. Yehya el Khashab would have been one of our family, in any case, through his marital ties, but he has in addition given the scheme the particular kindness and interest one would show to a foster son. Without the practical efficiency, and never-failing buoyancy of our Business Manager, Mr. Z. Misketian, my task would have been many a score of times more difficult. To the skill, patience, and keenness of all the translators and revisers, whose names appear at the conclusion of each story, any success this volume has will be principally due.

For suggestions as to stories to be considered, I must thank Mr. Mohamed Ali Zeid, Mr. Fuad Zaki, and, to a quite particular extent, Mr. Raouf Riad, who first drew my attention to no fewer than eight of the items finally included, and whose suggestions have greatly enriched the Arabic Reading list which closes the volume. For information, encouragement, and help of every sort, I must at the very least express my gratitude to Dr. Afaf Loutfi el Sayyed, the Rev. Fr. J. Monnot, O.P., Dr. Mohamed Mustafa Badawi, Dr. O. Haddarah, Monsieur Charles Vial, Mr. Trevor Le Gassicq, Mr. Abdel Halim el Kabbani — friend and fellow-worker of so many of the writers here represented, and Mr. El Said Bayoumi el Waraki, whose suggestions extended my reading-list to almost unwieldly proportions. Mr. Helmi Heliel, with discerment and tact, saved us from many errors which had slipped through all the nets that had been cast before his own fine mesh. The editor of the *Arab Observer* and the authorities of the UAR Broadcasting Service kindly agreed to allow us to use four stories previously translated for them by Mrs. Nadia Farag.

Thanks are due from me to Mr. Denys Johnson-Davies, translator and editor of the admirable collection recently published by the Oxford University Press : his kindness extended to allowing me advance knowledge of the titles of the Egyptian items is his volume, thus saving us from duplicating his efforts by including Naguib Mahfouz's *Zaabalawi*, which we would certainly have wished to present to the English-reading public if he had not already done so. I am glad that chance has had it that we did not duplicate any of the non-Egyptian choices he made.

To all authors included I feel grateful; those with whom I have had personal contact I feel particular happiness in being able to thank. To those whom we would have liked to include, my apologies. I was especially anxious to have the Sudan represented by an item by its distinguished short story writer Tayyeb Saleh, but his untranslated work was not accessible to me, and my letters to him remained unanswered. I cannot omit the staff of the American Research Center in Cairo, of the Central Library of Alexandria University, the libraries of the Alexandria Faculty of Arts, and the American University in Cairo, and of the Dar Al-Maaref Press.

Finally, but above all, my thanks go to Professor Gustave von Grünebaum, on whom I have leant so heavily throughout. Not only is this volume his brain child, but he has watched over it at every stage, and descended from time to time to effect its fortunes favourably, in the true tradition of the *deus ex machina*.

M. A. M.

THE MARTYR

Tewfik el Hakim

TEWFIK EL HAKIM is the leading imaginative writer of the contemporary Arab world, and is one of the few Arabic writers whose works have been translated into several European languages (English, French, Italian and Russian), and have been adapted for broadcasting in the west. Born in 1898 of a well-to-do family, he studied law and literature in Cairo, before continuing his studies in law in Paris. He came to know the rural life of Egypt well through working as public prosecutor in the provinces. Subsequently, he worked in the Ministry of Education, but in 1938 decided to devote himself to his writings. He had already in 1935 written a novel (*'Awdat ur-rūḥ*: *The Return of the Soul*) which reflects his thoughts upon social problems, and his nationalist feelings. He may be considered as the creator of the modern Egyptian (and Arab) literary theatre.

His works are, mostly, cosmopolitan in spirit, He is influenced by the various movements of European literature, particularly symbolism, realism, and, latterly, surrealism (His play *Yā Ṭāli, ash-shagara* — *The Tree Climber* — has been translated by Denys Johnson-Davies, and its date and manner connect it with the Theatre of the Absurd. But the preface he has written for it reveals that he was familiar with the Dadaist theatre of the twenties, and that he decided to wait until the sixties before he felt that the time was ripe for such a work to be attempted in Arabic). Some of his early work deals with the problem facing the educated Arab who returns to his native country from the west. El Hakim is equally at home in the novel, the drama—full-length and short — and the essay. But his output, which covers fifty volumes, includes short stories.

The Martyr appeared in a collection of stories published in 1954 and bearing the title *Arini-llāh* (*Show God to Me*), with the sub-title *Philosophical Tales*. It is to early twentieth-century French radical positivism, and not any other source, that we must go for the origins of the imaginary worldly Pontiff and Grand Rabbi who appear in this story.

The church bells rang in Christmas; their resonance vibrated through the very being of Rome as holiness echoes through and through the being of a pious monk. At that moment a stranger descended upon the city and headed towards the Vatican. His ears were intent upon the words of the Gospel that were being intoned from all directions around him. "And She shall bring forth a son, and thou shalt call his name Jesus : for he shall save his people from their sins." On the winter wind came the music of Handel's *Messiah* and Bach's *Christmas Oratorio :* the master works of religious music were hailing Jesus Christ who brought mankind, laden with the burden of its own selfishness, His message of love that would wash away all sins.

The Gospel readings came to these words : "And the devil said unto him, If thou be the Son of God, command this stone that it may be made bread. And Jesus answered him, saying, It is written, that man shall not live by bread alone, but by every word of God . . And the devil, taking him up into an high mountain, shewed unto him all the kingdoms of the world, in a moment of time. And the devil said unto him, All this power will I give thee, and the glory of them : for that is delivered unto me; and to whomsoever I will I give it. If thou therefore wilt worship me, all shall be thine. And Jesus answered and said unto him, Get thee behind me, Satan : for it is written, Thou shalt worship the Lord thy God, and him only shalt thou serve".

And here the stranger sighed, and exclaimed from the depths of his heart, "I wish I had obeyed him then."

He reached the palace of the Pope, where he asked to be granted an immediate audience. It was not easy to stand in the way of such a person : his eyes had the gleam of a power that could not be challenged. No one, neither priest nor cardinal, dared block his path. The doors were open before him and he entered, with his head humbly bowed, into the throne room of the head of the Church.

The Pope looked fixedly at his visitor, as he stood before him in the image of man and his voice trembled as he exclaimed, "You ?"

"Yes, it is I."

"And what do you seek of me ?"

"To enter into the haven of faith."

"What are you saying, you cursed creature ?" The Pope spoke in a whisper, lost in bewilderment, but the visitor said in a voice ringing with truth and sincerity :

"I no longer deserve to be called the Accursed. I have come to you in repentance, and misfortune it will be for me should you mock me or even doubt my intention. Everything has an end. Surely the day had to come when I should see the truth and return to the paths of righteousness ? Was it not inevitable that one day I should yearn for the bosom of God, and tire of this long, futile war, that I should want to abandon my stubborness, shun the banquet of evil, and long for the taste of good ? Yes, take of me what you will, submit me to the most abhorrent of tortures, inflict your severest punishment upon me, but in the name of the Lord of all the heavens do not deprive me of the taste of good for a moment longer. What is the taste of this thing which you call Good, this thing which you hold in your hands and which you deny me ? I have been living since time began; I have forever been arrogant and vain, forever I have held on and held out, always claiming that what I possessed was all, that I was self-sufficient, needing nothing further for myself or for my followers in my Kingdom. There is no one, no one at all, who has not followed me for some portion of time. My subjects are everywhere, even here within these walls, in spite of the monastic robes and the crosses. But what use is my fabled kingdom as long as I feel only deprivation ? Save me, in the name of your God ! Let me, if only once, know the taste of Good, and then throw me down into hell. I have laid down my arms and renounced the struggle. I am a believer and nothing else : this is now my greatest wish — to become one of those faithful worshippers at this moment crowding the churches, kneeling before God and singing hymns of praise to Him, rejoicing in the birth of Christ, repeating His words and hailing His deeds . . O Your Holiness, O Vicegerent of Christ, I have come to kneel at your feet for you to baptize me with your own hands and for you to receive me into the faith — and you shall find me one of the truest and best sons of your church."

The Pope was visibly stirred by this fervent plea, yet he could not overcome his surprise, nor prevent himself from exclaiming : "You ?

You, Satan ? Now you want to embrace the faith ?"

"And why not ? Did not Christ say, 'I say unto you, that likewise joy shall be in heaven over one sinner that repenteth, more than over ninety and nine just persons, which need no repentance' ? Did Christ ever draw a distinction between one person and another ? Are we not all equal before forgiveness and redemption ? Why do you wish to shut the door to redemption in my face ? I am forsaking sin. Take me into the faith. Hear the cry of faith that now comes from my heart."

The Pope was greatly perplexed. He shuddered at the idea, overwhelmed by it. He exclaimed, as though speaking to himself, "No .. no .. This I cannot do".

At that moment the room filled with the strains of Palestrina's *Missa Papae Marcelli*, and the Pope's imagination soared with the melody. If Satan should enter the faith, then where will the glory of the Church lie after that? What is to become of the Vatican, its museums and treasures and magnificent religious monuments ? Everything stands to lose its meaning and its splendour and be left without purpose for the rest of time. The Sistine Chapel with Michelangelo's frescoes .. the Temptation of Eve .. the Prophets .. the Flood .. the Last Judgement .. And the murals of Raphael in the halls and chambers .. *Fiat Lux* .. the Expulsion from Paradise .. the Baptism of Jesus ..

The fiend is the pivotal point in the Holy Bible, Old and New Testaments alike. How could he be eliminated without destroying all the symbolism and legend, even the teachings about good and evil that quicken the hearts of the faithful and stimulate their imagination ? What significance would the Day of Judgement have if the spirit of Evil were wiped out of Man's world ? Would the fallen angels who had followed Satan be brought to judgement ? Or would their own sins be expunged, since Satan's repentance would have been accepted ? Then how would the world fare without evil ? The wars that made Christian Europe the mistress of the world ? And these spiritual rivalries, the mental and material conflicts which set off the spark of thought and produced the light of knowledge through their friction ? No, that would be a very grave matter. The Pope ought not to make a binding decision upon it. To demolish Evil, to raze it off the face of the earth, would cause an explosion so great that the mind could not grasp it.

The Pope raised his head, looked at Satan, irritated and embarrassed.

"Why did you choose to come to me ? Why did you choose Christianity and not one of the other religions ?"

"It is the Christmas celebrations which have made me reach my decision."

"Listen.. I do not know by what name I should call you .. Do you see the predicament ? Even what name you should have after your conversion causes quite a problem. No : the Church cannot accept your request. If you wish, try one of the other religions."

And the Pope turned his back upon him.

* * *

Disappointed and humiliated, Satan left the Vatican. But he had not lost hope. There were many gates which led to God. He would try another. And he turned his steps towards the Grand Rabbi.

The religious Head of the Jews received him in the same manner as the Christian Pontiff. He listened patiently to Satan's wish. Then he asked him, "Do you wish to become a Jew ?"

"I want to reach God".

The Grand Rabbi pondered carefully upon what Satan had said. If God were to grant Satan forgiveness and wipe Evil off the face of the earth, what would **then** distinguish one people from another ? The Jews are the chosen people of God. But if this were to come about, there would no longer be any justification for regarding them as a people apart, a people especially favoured. Even the supreme mastery of finance which had been theirs for generations would disappear with the disappearance of Evil out of men's hearts, with the annihilation of greed and avarice, with the total elimination of selfishness. Satan's finding of faith would make the structure of Jewish privilege collapse, and destroy the glory of the sons of Israel.

The Rabbi raised his head, and said in sarcastic tones; "It is not our habit to conduct missionary work. We have never sought to persuade any others to embrace our faith .. even if he who asks be Satan himself. So, be gone from here, and seek for yourself another religion".

* * *

Satan came away from the Rabbi crestfallen, but he did not despair. There was still one gate left open before him : the religion of Islam. He made straight for the Sheikh of El Azhar.

The Sheikh received him and listened to what the Fiend had to say. When he had understood what he was seeking, he said :

"For Satan to find faith is a good thing, but .."

"But what ? Have not people the right to enter God's religion in their masses ? Does it not say in His Holy Book 'And Praise thou the mercy of your Lord and seek His forgiveness, for He is the redeemer' ? So — here I am, praising the mercy of God and seeking His forgiveness. Wholeheartedly and in all sincerity, I want to enter His faith, to become a Moslem, a truly good Moslem, and the best example for others who are seeking the Faith."

The Sheikh of El Azhar considered the consequences. If Satan were to become a Moslem, then how would the Koran be recited ? Would people be able any longer to recite : "I seek God's shelter from the cursed devil" ? And if this verse should be abrogated then it would follow that the same would have to be done to most other verses of the Koran .. Comminations of the devil, and cautions against his evil and his temptations occupy a great part of the Book of God. How could he, the Sheikh of El Azhar, accept Satan's conversion without weakening the entire structure of Moslem faith ?

And the Sheikh of El Azhar raised his head, looked at Satan and said :

"You have come to me about a matter over which I have no power .. this is a matter too great for my capacity and far beyond my authority. What you seek is not in my hands. You have not turned to the right quarters by coming to me with such a request."

"Who should I turn to then ? Are you not the head of all religious teachers ? How then can I reach God ? Is this not what anyone who is seeking to approach God should do ?"

"Yes, but you are not like others . ."

"Why not ? I do not seek to mark myself out from others. I do not ask to rise immediately to the high heavens and converse with the angels and meet the prophets. This I could have done; but I did not wish to base any appeal on my special powers, and take pride in my own personality. I do not seek to knock at the gates of Heaven with my sceptre like a king . . even though it should be the King of Evil. I have not asked that the heavens should resound with my clamour, nor that the skies should tremble at my voice whilst I lay down my sword and surrender my arms, and submit as one crowned head should submit to another . . I seek to enter the gates of religion a poor and humble creature . . to crawl on my knees, to heap the dust of humiliation on my royal head, and beg for forgiveness and guidance from all temples, churches and mosques, like the most miserable and weakest of mortal men."

The Sheikh of El Azhar bowed his head for a moment, scratched his beard and said :

"Certainly a good intention . . but . . all the same . . let me speak to you quite frankly : my calling is to advance the word of Islam, and to preserve the glory of El Azhar. It does not involve putting my hand in yours."

"Thank you."

* * *

Satan said this meekly and humbly, and he left in despondency. He walked about the streets aimlessly; he gazed at the innocence of children with his heart longing tenderly for all that is pure and innocent; he saw kindness in the deeds of good people and burned with desire for all that is good; he looked into the hearts of the faithful as though he were looking at a window display . . and saw exhibited in them all that goodness and faith could produce; he reached out for them with an impotent hand . . To be incapable of good — that is the supreme torment which the devil has to endure.

Satan let forth a cry of pain that scattered the clouds and pierced the heavens. He could no longer keep patient; he shook with the violence of someone about to render up his soul. But he mustered his courage and mounted to the skies.

With his fists he pounded at the gates of heaven and pummelled at its bastions, for his calm reasoning was gone, and he was now like a starving beggar knocking on a door at sunset to ask for a morsel of bread.

Gabriel appeared to him :

"What is it that you seek ?"

"Forgiveness."

"At this time ?"

"Am I too late ?"

"On the contrary; you are too early. This is not the time to change the established order. Go back to where you have come from, and go on with your life upon earth as you have been living it."

"You too ? Oh .. I cannot any longer .. allow me only a taste of Good."

"To you Good is forbidden .. you are not to come near it."

"A forbidden fruit ?"

"To you, yes .. and you shall not find anyone to help you break that order .. as Eve did once, when she tempted Adam to taste of the fruit of the tree."

"Is there no mercy, no forgiveness ?"

"The order of the creation may not be upset by mercy and forgiveness."

"I am only a humble creature .."

"Yes .. but removing you from earth will be removing its foundations and shaking its walls. The features of the earth will be unrecognizable .. its colours and shapes will be wiped away. Virtue has no meaning without sin .. truth has no meaning without error .. there can be no righteousness unless evil exists, no light without darkness : mankind cannot see the light of God save through your own blackness .. your presence upon earth is needed for as long as earth continues to be the seat of the supreme gifts which God has bestowed on mankind."

"My presence is necessary for the very existence of Good ? My dark soul must remain as it is for the glorious light of God to shine against it?" Satan paused, but went on to say, "Then I shall accept my terrible fate so that Good may continue to be, and God's radiance to shine down in all its brightness. But will I be bound forever in this affliction ? Will this curse lie upon my name forever ? Will there be no regard to my intentions, which you can see are noble and good ?"

"Yes, you must remain outcast to the end of time. If your doom were lifted then everything else would be dismembered."

"Mercy, oh my God ! Why should I bear this terrible burden ? Why is it that this dread fate has been written for me ? Why wouldst Thou not now make of me one of Thy meek angels, to whom is granted the supreme joy of entering into Thy love and the love of Thy Light, and who are requited with Thy loving-kindness and with the praise of men ? Here I stand with unequalled and unsurpassed love for Thee .. A love that requires a sacrifice hitherto unknown to angel-kind or mortal man .. a love for the sake of which I put on the cloak of disobedience to Thee .. to appear as a rebel against Thee .. a love for which I must bear Thy curse and the curse of men .. a love which does not allow me even the distinction of claiming it .. nor the joy of affiliation to it. If an anchorite held such love within him, it would fill his heart with a blinding light : yet though I hold it close to me within my breast, the light refuses to penetrate my heart .."

Satan wept ..

His tears fell down to earth .. not as raindrops but as dark meteorites and as falling stars ..

Gabriel, alarmed, sought to appease him :

"Steady now, steady. They are raining down upon the faithful, who do not deserve to suffer this."

Satan immediately held back his tears and said in a painful voice as though addressing himself :

"Yes .. even my tears turn into catastrophe for others."

He held back his tears.

"Try and bear your destiny," said Gabriel to him, speaking now in a gentler tone. "Do your duty and carry on with your task, without grumbling, complaining or rebelling."

"Rebelling ? If I had really wanted to rebel I would have revolted, broken my loyalty, defied my orders. I could have declared my disobedience simply by keeping my silence for a moment, by holding back my hand for a mere instant .. just one minute without my inspiring evil and the earth would have found itself, as you say, Gabriel, with every corner in ruins and its foundations crumbling .. But I love, and I seek not to revolt; my love for God is the secret strength by which the structure He has made of earth holds together. It is the secret of the harmony of His laws and His order."

"Pay heed to my advice and return to your work."

"I shall return, wearing the cloak of my curse and not knowing when I shall shed it. Actors upon earth sometimes undertake the rôles of treason and treachery, but they know that at a certain hour they shed them, and have their honesty and honour restored to them in their fullness. But, for me .. ?"

"Go down to earth, and bear with your sufferings; he who loves must endure his sufferings."

"I do more than that. He who dies in battle in the name of God is enrolled in His book as a martyr. But for Him I suffer more than death. I wish it were a battle. I wish it were death. I wish I were one of His soldiers. I must exist to disobey the One I love: I despise myself, and I curse myself at every instant of my being. I cannot die or I could have killed myself or got myself killed in the name of God. But I subject myself to measures of hatred and wrath far more fearsome than killing, yet I have no right to hope for mercy or to aspire to forgiveness, nor even to cherish the idea of joining the ranks of His soldiers some day."

Gabriel noticed tears beginning once again to glisten in Satan's eyes.

"Shed no tear," he said to him hurriedly. "Shed no tear. Do not forget that your tears are catastrophes — and your laughter a calamity.

For the sake of human beings, do not give way to your emotions. Go now; be patient and moderate your feelings."

Satan paused lengthily, with his head bowed, and thought over Gabriel's words. Finally he stirred : "You are right," he said almost in a whisper.

* * *

And he left heaven submissively and descended upon earth. But a stifled sigh burst out from him as he winged his way down through space; instantly, it was re-echoed by every one of the stars as though all were joining with him to cry out in agony :

"I am a martyr — I am a martyr."

Translated by David Bishai; revised by Ronald Ewart.

THE ENEMY

Mahmoud Taymour

MAHMOUD TAYMOUR (b. 1894) is the doyen of Arabic short story writers, and no anthology would be complete without a contribution from him. His first collection was published in 1925, and his stories have been appearing continually ever since. *The Enemy* was published in the monthly magazine *Al-Hilal*, in August 1965, though its manner links it perhaps to an earlier generation. The importance of Taymour cannot be shown by one example of a story written late in his career, since it lies in the fact that he has been a pioneer in almost every type of short story, and has been the most considerable single indigenous influence upon all the writers who have appeared since the mid-twenties. His brother Mohamed Taymour is often regarded as the first genuine artist in the *genre*, in Egypt, but his early death cut his career short. His aunt Ayesha Taymour was a distinguished poet. He had the advantage of belonging to a family which was not only wealthy, but deeply interested in learning and writing. As with all the older generation of Egyptian writers, his work is greatly influenced by the European models which he read and by his firsthand knowledge of European life and thought. In addition to short stories, he has published plays (mostly of a symbolist nature) and criticism; in his short stories, paradoxically, and in contrast to the general tendency, his growing interest in the problem of writing in classical Arabic has made his dialogue increasingly literary, and decreasingly colloquial, in form. Until it ceased publication in 1966, he was editor of *Al Qiṣṣa*, a monthly magazine devoted to the short story. A collection of his short stories in an English translation by Denys Johnson-Davies was published in Cairo in 1946, but copies of this are exceedingly rare.

Taymour has published some fifteen volumes of short stories, seven novels, a number of plays, and several works of criticism.

The present story first appeared in the monthly *Al-Hilal* for August 1965 : its doppelgänger theme returns to the questionings about true identity which recur in some of Taymour's major works.

He had lived alone since they separated; he could not bear anyone to share his house. He no longer trusted any relation, companion or friend and he did without anyone to help him in his affairs. The rooms in his house remained locked — except the bedroom, where he made his own bed for himself; he took his meals — morning and evening — in a restaurant, a bar or club.

Nevertheless, he used to wonder whether this was enough to make his life secure and free from hurt.

There was a powerful enemy continually on the watch for him, wanting to destroy him, so as to clear the way to her — the wife who had left him for good. He had taken pains to obtain a revolver and took care to keep it permanently loaded and to carry it with him night and day. It was war between him and his enemy, but covert war — all apprehension, caution, stratagem — and inevitably its outcome would be the death of one rival at the hands of the other.

No, he would not fall into the trap — rather his enemy would. To leave his wife a prey to the hunter was inconceivable. He would have to put up with her until he had dealt with the enemy : after that would come the time to settle accounts with her.

He remembered how one day he had asked her,

"Why are you deceiving me, Sulwan ?"

"I swear, my love, it's never occurred to me to be unfaithful!"

"Liar !"

"Darling, calm down. Let's try to understand this thing intelligently."

"You call me 'Darling' . . I wonder what you call him ?"

"This jealousy of yours is quite without foundation ! I have no right to call a man anything when I'm not even aware of his existence."

"You go on denying it . . I shall find out all about him, and with one shot of my revolver I'll bring him down dead before your eyes. You'll have to confess everything then."

"A good thing if you did," she laughed, "Then, at least, I'd know what he looked like."

"What a two-faced liar she is," he muttered to himself.

However, there was always a picture of her on his bedside-table; it stood close to his head, and from it he took in her sweet breath and sank happily into sleep with dreams of passion. When he awoke in the morning, he snatched the picture from its place and tore it up into little shreds. Then, when night fell, the picture made its way back to him, settling down on his bedside-table, and he filled his eyes with the brilliance of hers.

The photographer kept him supplied with copies of the picture, so that whenever a set ran out, another took its place.

He had heard a lot about incurable addiction. Was her picture the drug to which he was enslaved ? Had she become the indispensible elixir of his life ? He could not allow himself to be made a fool of, nor could he submit to the humiliation that was imposed on him. He gathered all the remaining pictures he had of her and threw them into the fire. He watched them burning .. saw Sulwan — his wife — as flesh and blood being eaten by the fire; he smelt the smoke that came from her burning body and grew intoxicated with the odour, as a worshipper with the fragrance of incense. He spent a black night in tearful repining.

A few days later the picture was back in its chosen place — it was as if the darkness of that night had been swept away by its return. No, no, — he had to put an end to this torment — he could not leave things as they were .. he would uncover her treachery and annihilate his rival with one shot of the revolver he kept in readiness.

The revolver became all-absorbing : he busied himself with it assiduously for whole hours at a time and never failed to polish it and keep it in trim, sometimes checking its loading, at other times trying a shot into the air. Once he pointed the revolver at her picture and said, jokingly, "Careful, Sulwan. You'll find death sweet at my hands : it's your penance for your devotion in deceiving me; but believe me, I shan't kill you without putting an end to *him* first .. my enemy, down to the marrow."

"Darling, I know of no enemy of yours. So I shall never suffer harm at your hands."

"Trying to deceive me with sweet words ! Hiding your guilt !"

"Whatever you do, you will never hurt me, you're too obsessed with your love for me, you're almost crazy with it."

"Shut up ! I hate you ! I loathe you !"

He rushed to the clothes-hanger and seized some of her blouses which were permeated with the smell of her body. Furiously, he tore them to pieces, ripping them with his nails and biting them with his teeth as if it were her flesh which he were attacking. When he had done he collapsed over the shreds, rubbing his face in them, sniffing at them avidly.

* * *

Deep down he acknowledged that Sulwan was not all evil; how many brief, unforgettable hours of happiness he had spent, held in her arms, feeling her gentle finger-tips stroking his hair, her eager breath lingering on his face and her warm lips rubbing over his cheek ! So many times she had rocked him as a loving mother rocks her child, and had sung her sweet songs so touchingly that he had imagined himself in the happy childhood which he had experienced only in daydreams.

He had been devoted to his mother : when death took her, his grief was shattering. Without her, life was barren. He found no substitute for the companionship and sympathy he had lost .. Then one day he met Sulwan, and recognized in her another mother. The resemblance was uncanny .. it was as if they were twins. She was startled to hear him call her 'Mother', but she instantly smiled back at him with understanding. From that moment he sensed a firm bond between them and it seemed inconceivable that he should part from her.

He married her. His life with her was the life of a captive lover, consumed by his passion; it was not the life of a husband whose wife's companionship enabled them to confront life together. Time went by. Then came this business.

No, — Sulwan was not all evil ! Just as he was not all good.

He felt in his reveries that something stirred in his being, a thing repugnant, nauseating, lying in the bottomless depths of his soul. For this thing he felt an unmatched hatred which he wanted to pluck out by the roots and to hurl far away from him. Be that as it may, he was faced with the fact of her guilt, and it was up to him to settle the matter and to be rid of this oppressive nightmare.

After she left him, she chose to live in a fine villa in the suburbs .. it was a good choice — a suitable place to meet her lover, the one whom he was really up against. A distant retreat in an unfrequented spot, a quiet place to help her carry out her deception.

But her trick did not work. It was not long before he discovered her hideout and engaged several agents to observe her every movement, and to send him long and detailed reports. Those who recorded doubts and heaped suspicion on her were generously rewarded, but those who cleared her behaviour of any taint were paid little and their reports rejected. They soon realized this, and began to fill their reports with particulars which indicated a bad reputation and shameful behaviour. Often the reports were lavish in revealing the ingenious ways the rival used to sneak to the love-nest.

The function of these intermediaries was now over and the time had come to take the task upon himself and to lay bare the truth.

He used to prowl around the villa for a good part of the night, following tracks as if he were a diligent and tireless hunting-dog. How many times he had stood under the window of her lighted bedroom, watching, his eyes following her as she came and went behind the transparent curtains. Hidden in his corner, he used to whisper to her in words of tortured longing, in the silence, unaware of the passing of time.

He was sure after close watching, night after night, that the rival came to see her and that she made him welcome in her room. It came to the point where he saw with his own eyes the shadow of his rival in the darkness, creeping to her villa through a concealed back door. He found out the time of assignation and the path the lover took to carry out his disreputable purpose. He had assembled all the evidence, he had passed sentence — it remained only for him to execute it.

On the chosen day, he spent the time in the company of his revolver, practising his hand and eye .. He left his house at the appointed hour, reached the hiding-place at the right time and waited for his rival's appearance at the expected moment.

He was in full control of his nerves and was gripping the pistol in his clenched hand, but he felt his heart beating like a drum; his eyes, however, kept wandering as if under the influence of a hidden magnet.

Finally, the dark shadow of the rival appeared, hovering before his eyes, cautiously taking the path to the back door. The husband followed him, moving mechanically until he drew near, then he shouted :

"Stop ! tell me who you are. .. I'll kill you ! I shan't hesitate !"

The rival turned round, his face becoming clear for the first time. To his amazement he saw what he could never have imagined : a looking-glass reflexion of himself.

Without his realizing it, the gun went off with a loud explosion. The husband collapsed on the ground with blood gushing from his head.

For several days he lay in hospital hovering between life and death.

Finally, he began to come out of his coma, his eyelids flickered, and he murmured :

"The light disturbs me .. cover it !"

And the curtains were drawn. Moments went by as he continued mumbling, his eyes trying to find out where he was.

"Where am I ?"

He felt a soft hand touching his and heard a gentle voice saying, "Don't worry yourself about anything .. you're safe and you'll be better soon."

"Have I been ill, Sulwan ?"

"You're well .. just keep resting, darling."

He gripped her hand tight.

"You won't leave me ?"

"I'll always be with you; I shan't leave you."

He drew her hand to his mouth and kissed it, fervently, as if it were the hand of a holy man. He closed his eyelids; tears flowed down his cheeks and before long he was soundly asleep.

Next day he asked her, "What brought me here ?"

"You're being treated for a wound in your head; it's almost healed now."

"Wound in my head ?" he mumbled, "From a revolver shot ?"

"You rival fired it in a fight between you."

"My rival ?"

"You finished him immediately : that was the end of the rival."

He concentrated his thoughts and tried to see the details clearly, but his memory did not help, and he could not. There was, however, one thing he was able to recall out of everything that had happened .. that an unknown person had lain in wait for him and had wanted to snatch her from him .. snatch her .. his very dearest .. from him."

He heard her as she went on :

"You shot him dead, that scoundrel who pursued me so hard .. you killed him in my defence .. you rescued me from him .."

The doctor was near the two, listening to this conversation, and a smile of approval appeared on his face for a moment. The wife exchanged a significant glance with him .. and the couple were lost in a long, hungry kiss.

Translated by Anthony McDermott; revised by Leonard Knight and David Kirkham.

ATROCITY

Mohamed Kamel Hussein

MOHAMED KAMEL HUSSEIN (b. 1901) is a distinguished surgeon and scholar, a member of the Arabic Language Academy of Cairo, a former Rector of Ein Shams University, Cairo, and former President of the Egyptian Academy of Sciences. He studied medicine and surgery in Egypt and England in the twenties, and it was as a country doctor that he started his professional career. He is very familiar with European thought, and was one of the circle of thinkers and artists who were especially active in the twenties in the search for new directions for Arabic literature and thought. He has produced a history of Arab medicine and written reflexions on human knowledge and history: *Wiḥdatul-ma'rifa* (*The Unity of Knowledge*), *At-taḥlīlulbiūlujī lit-tārikh* (*A Biological Analysis of History*), 1955, but is best known for his novel *Qarya dhālima* (1954) — which has been translated into English as *City of Wrong* by the Rev. Kennett Cragg, and has also been turned into French and into Spanish. The work consists of a set of dialogues debating the problem of conscience, and the central event around which this Moslem thinker ranges these discussions is the Crucifixion. As with the present short story, Dr. Kamel Hussein's novel is a set of reflexions in the garb of fiction: one would not classify Kamel Hussein among the Egyptian novelists, in the usual sense of this term, but describe him as perhaps the one Egyptian writer who has achieved final intellectual depth in making use of the novel as vehicle. There is a full study of *City of Wrong* in the article 'Jésus et ses juges d'après "La Cité inique" du Dr. Kamel Hussein', by Fr. G. Chehata Anawati, a member of our committee, in MIDEO (*Mélanges de l'Institut dominicain d'études orientales du Caire*), 2, 1955 (pp. 71-134). The present short story, the only one known to us to have been written by the author, appeared under the title *Jarīma shan'ā'* (*An Atrocious Crime*) in the Cairo monthly *Al-Hilal* for April 1961).

The members of the jury asked one another whether they were entitled to recommend to the judge, if it were at all permissible, that the criminal should be burnt alive. The judge declared that never in his life had he condemned any man to death — no matter what the nature of his crime — without a sharp pang and a deep melancholy: but today his mind was at rest. Indeed, he added, he might even say that he was happy to sentence this criminal to death, in order to wipe away the shame which mankind bore because of this atrocious crime.

The accused was a young man of twenty. Nobody in the small town knew who his father was : he himself had not known him. His mother was a loose woman with a fierce temper, who had lived her life in wretched squalor and poverty.

In misery, she had taken up with a foreign sailor in a distant town; he soon deserted her, leaving her with this son. She had spent her days in a constant struggle to find food for them both, until he was old enough to work. She had made him forage for his own food then, threatening to drive him away if he ever felt too tired or ill, and never sparing him even if he could not find any work.

He was working in a nearby coalmine : and this was a time when coal-mining was a harder lot than slavery. His misery was all the greater because no one showed him any sympathy. What they knew about him and his mother made his workmates distrust him.

He himself was not an easy person to get on with : it was not in his nature to show any friendliness, and he did not join in his mates' talk; a pariah, he was fond of none of them, and was liked by none. The same was true in his relations with older people, and with those placed over him; they gave him the most difficult and most exhausting tasks. He was too poor to buy new clothes: what he wore was so tattered that it no longer even covered him decently. His shoes could no longer protect his feet from winter cold and the filth of mud. He had no supply of water easily at hand, and he would go for months without a wash. People who saw him in this condition, were not sorry for him, but took it that this squalor was his by choice. Indeed, he had become so used to living like this that he no longer cared about improvement, and people assumed that he relished loneliness, dirt and poverty.

He grew into the habit of spending most of his time, summer and winter, sitting upon a stone block in front of the church. It made a cold and painful seat, and he had no covering thick enough to make him comfortable, yet there he always sat until he was too tired or too cold.

This church had become his only link with humankind; yet he did not dare enter it when there were people within. He knew that neither the congregation nor the priests could bear to see him among them; though their religion unambiguously commanded them to accept people such as he, they perhaps judged that this could only be carried out to the letter by those who had the faith of a saint, and that God would pardon them if they refused to make a place for him amongst them.

Once he plucked up enough courage to enter the church on a feast day. As he went in fear that people's repugnance for him was so strong that they would drive him out, to have done as he did was an act of the highest courage. Once inside, he stood in the remotest spot possible, alone in a dark corner, where he was almost invisible to the congregation.

After that, he began to frequent the services, and this was noticed by one of the priests in charge, who considered that it was sufficient Christian charity to allow him to remain in his corner : he neither drove him away, nor gave him any encouragement. Once, during the offertory, the young man came forward with a hand that shook with fear and added to the plate the single penny which was all that was left to him that day. The priest felt pity for him but did not like to return the tiny amount on the grounds that the donor would need it more than anyone else. The priest almost let a tear fall for this man whose misery and poverty had not made him fail in his duty towards the church. He realized that the single penny was a truer sign of faith than the pounds which a rich man gave. The wretched young man now had the beginnings of human sensibility. He felt that he was becoming a man, that he had so far been an animal that knew only how to eat and drink and perform other animal functions, with nothing to distinguish him from the dogs he saw around him. His attendance at church, giving a penny to the priest from time to time, created this new feeling.

When his anxiety had passed, and he was no longer afraid of being thrown out, he grew to appreciate the beauty of the church, and of the lights that shone in it; now he could listen to the organ and his heart was transported by it, as though he had not heard it before. A second feast day came round : he watched the priests in their beautiful, bright vestments, the women worshipping in all their finery, with their most fragrant perfume : he noticed that the men were considerate towards the women — that with one they were polite and gallant, and with another they let her see that they found her attractive.

This drew him with a yearning he had never known in himself before. He became aware that music moved him, that the beauty of a woman stirred him as much as it stirred the rich, and that he could admire the splendour of the church, and pay reverence to it, just as much as a fortunate man could. This consoled him : whenever he withdrew into himself in this church, he found a haven from the storms of the world, which he had suffered all his life. Then there came round a holiday in the city. He had not been aware of holidays before, and had no notion when they fell : to him all days seemed to be of the same pitch black colour. He sat on his stone in front of the church : the doors were closed, and everyone had deserted it on that dark night. People came and went in front of him, looking their best in their fine clothes. Most of them were making for one of the most splendid houses in the town, where an all-night celebration was being held. Most of the guests had already arrived when one young girl realized that she had forgotten to put on the prettiest of her jewels, and so she slipped home on her own to put the finishing touches to her appearance, then hurried back towards the entertainment. Her path lay in front of the church. As she drew near, he was overpowered by the attractive scent she used, and he found himself stepping up to her, and saying with unwonted daring, "Come and sit with me for a little while."

The girl went pale : she panicked at finding her way blocked by the unkempt creature and was nauseated at the very sight of this person who was asking her to join him.

"Get away from me, you filthy beast," she said.

He paid no attention to her cry, but drew her to him by her arms. She screamed. He had to stop her screaming. So he put his right arm round her neck, and his hand over her mouth. This made her struggle more violently. He had to keep her quiet by a blow in the stomach : a blow which he meant to be a warning tap that would frighten her into keeping quiet, without doing her much harm. Her muscles went limp. He found himself holding her up by his right hand, which was around her neck. He felt the full weight of her body; carrying her away from the roadway, to a dark corner, he deposited her on the ground.

As he drew his hand from beneath her head, his fingers brushed through her silky golden hair : he had never before touched a softness and loveliness like this. He combed her hair with his fingers, gently, with great happiness : he did this again and again, fascinated. He had not realized that such beauty existed in the world. The scent she used enraptured him : he had caught a breath of such perfumes at a distance, but now, at close quarters, he abandoned himself to it, breathing it in with intoxicated delight.

In this enjoyment of her hair and her perfume, he continued for what seemed to him a long time. Then he switched on the little torch which he used to light his way : it lit up a sweet and engaging face. He had never been so near to such a beautiful face. Her red lips and her fine complexion struck him : the brightness had not left her eyes. He saw his reflexion in the fine pupil of her eye, and was sorry for her sake that her pretty eye should carry his own repellent image : he had not realized before that if you came close enough to another person's eye, you would make your reflexion appear in it. He felt her soft complexion with his rough fingers,the tenderness and smoothness astonished him. He sent his hands wandering over this skin as though it had made him forget her hair. He wanted to enjoy the softness of this skin to the full, and so he drew her cloak off her shoulders, and uncovered a silk dress which he pulled away from her body. It drove him almost mad with joy to feel the dead softness of the silk sliding over the live softness of her flesh. Ecstatically happy, he continued in this unimagined pleasure. It would have been better for him if he had found this happiness enough : but this sensation was so delicious to him that he went on and partly uncovered her breast and her belly. In his horny hand he seized a good fistful of this flesh, and squeezed it hard. He could feel the texture of the flesh, filled out and firm : it seemed to carry, hidden in it, a violent force which he could not fathom, a strange force which there had not been in the flesh of her face. At that instant the male instinct took a grip on him for the first time. It swept away the gentle happiness he had felt since he had begun to comb her hair with his fingers and since her perfume had overpowered him, and since he had looked into her face, and since he had felt her silk dress slipping down off her smooth breasts.

He was now overcome by a passion he could not control. He had not experienced its violence before, so that his resistance was weak. He held himself still, his eyes wide open and his teeth chattering; he could hear the hammerstrokes of his heart, violent, and painful. Fumbling, he began to unbutton his own clothes. The dirt had caked them hard as leather, and the buttons did not undo easily. Irritated, he tore his clothes apart, so as to be rid of the buttons. He no longer knew what he was doing; he was not thinking rationally : this was an eruption that nothing could control. And yet as he undressed her, he took care not to uncover more than need be : there were parts of her body that he ought not to look at. But when he was down to those underclothes that clung the closest, he raged like a wild tiger, tore them off violently, and threw them aside. His frenzy did not prevent his noticing the differences between his body and the girl's, which almost made them into creatures of two separate species. Her body was not yet cold, and so he was able to enjoy her warmth and softness. It was as though the whole world had opened up in front of him, offering him all of its delights. Then came the great moment; his heart beat to it, and then as his muscles finally relaxed, he almost wept with joy at a sensation of which he had never dreamed.

He was calm for a while. He realized that he had enjoyed the greatest of the physical delights that are known to glutted pleasure-seekers. He knew that in that instant he had put himself on a par in his experience with the richest and most important people whom he only saw at a distance, and whose pleasure he could only imagine.

Two feelings beset him. That he had now risen up to the full status of a human being, realizing that until then that he had been more lowly than the least of humans. And that he had taken his revenge upon mankind, who had deprived him of everything until then : in these few minutes he had snatched from them all that they had denied him. He stood up, and began to arrange his clothes, not knowing what he was doing. He did not mind what happened to him after that. As he stood there, he felt a strong hand seize him violently by the scruff of the neck, while a voice exclaimed, "What ! So near the church, and in the public highway, you animal !" The young man did not pay much attention to this newcomer, but went on setting his clothes in order, in something of a trance. The newcomer looked at the woman who was lying at their feet, and made as though to kick her.

"As for you, you —"

When she made no attempt to escape, made no movement at all, he bent over her, and discovered to his astonishment, that she was a lifeless corpse.

The man stared at them both, dumbfounded. It was inconceivable. Then he noticed her clothes, torn to shreds, and cast down beside her, and he realized what must have happened. If he had been able to, he would have killed the young man then and there. But fear paralyzed him. He tried to scream, to run away; he imagined that he was face to face with the fiend himself, in the shape of a squalid-looking human being.

At that moment, a policeman appeared. Both he and the passer-by realized what had happened, but neither could believe himself. Encouraged by the arrival of the policeman, the passer-by would have pounded the life out of the young man, but the policeman intervened. It was not for an individual to settle accounts with a criminal. The young man was dragged away to police headquarters. When he was alone with his commanding officer, the policeman told what he had seen, and gave his opinion. The officer, astonished, stepped out to take a look at the accused, expecting to find a criminal of the roughest type. He had come across a number of notorious rogues in his life, and he knew the stamp of one : but this was a young man who looked mild rather than vicious, simple-minded rather than criminal.

The officer gave orders for the man to be locked up, and hurried off to the scene of the crime, where it was his duty to carry out the investigation.

The policeman took his young prisoner to the cell. When he threw open the door, he hurled him in very violently. The young man hurtled against the wall opposite; his forehead received a blow, so that blood spurted down his face, and he wiped it away with his dirty hand.

He found himself in a narrow, dark, cold room, bare except for some rough bedding thrown on the floor. The room did not depress him; it was not very different from the room where he had spent all the nights of his life — narrow, dark, and cold; nor was the bedding very different from his own bedclothes at home. His new situation did not upset him : he had borne greater destitution and hardship than this; he did not feel the loss of any affection; he did not feel he had lost a freedom he had been enjoying. There was nothing in his existence which he would miss by being imprisoned.

He was not alarmed by the blood which his grimy hand was wiping away as it continued to flow out of his wound : it did not make him suffer as much as the tears he had wiped away with the same dirty hand when, as a child, his mother had beaten him. He sat down on the cold floor in a corner of the cell, not dejected, not in despair.

The event of that day rose in his mind. It was not yet an hour old : an hour ago he had been leading his accustomed life, with no notion that it might any day be different. He now knew that he could come face to face with something which seemed a small matter at first, but it could turn out to be of supreme moment. All he had wanted was to spend a few minutes sitting with a pretty girl, and then have no more to do with her. But things had followed one another fast. He had not been able to prevent them from leading up to a culmination as unexpected as it was pleasurable. He was not sorry, though, at what he had done. Yesterday, he had been an animal, merely eating and drinking, knowing nothing of the things for which others lived. Now he had enjoyed a wonderful beauty, enjoyed it at close quarters, where before he had only seen it at a distance. Now he had given every one of his senses a pleasure of a kind that was new to him, — new to his sight, new to his smell, new to his sense of touch. For the first time, it seemed, he had known the joy of human existence, a joy which a human being can never know on his own, a joy which drew all its wonder from a oneness between *two* human beings. He remembered the overpowering force which had mastered him when he had laid his hand on some particular parts of her body. When that had happened, he had no longer known what he was doing — but he had determined not to let slip this occasion which might never come again, determined to hold in his grip for an instant all that was enjoyed by the happy and the well-to-do in the midst of whom he lived.

Two moments in his life he recalled with rapture. The first time was when he had given the priest a penny for the church : he had thought his gift would be turned down, but the priest had accepted it. He could even remember very well that the priest had said, "Thank you" to him : a word no one had ever said to him before. That had been the first occasion when he had been conscious of his human nature. The second time was the great moment which had been the climax of the joy and beauty his senses had enjoyed, when he had come to know the supreme pleasure in the life of human beings, so that other people were no longer superior merely because they knew something which he did not. This moment he held to be so great, not because of its loveliness and the thrill of it — though these had been supreme — but because it had raised him at once to a level on which he could think of himself as a human being.

Until then, he had not known why his mother had brought him into this world. Now he knew the secret of this, and he could excuse her. No longer did he reproach her for what she had done : perhaps when she had been miserable and dejected, she had met a man who was miserable and dejected like her, and together they had planned their revenge upon the world and its miseries, decided to get to know this pleasure which others already knew, the only pleasure which the poor and wretched can enjoy in much the same way as the rich, their only way of making themselves the equals of those who would not even deign to look at them. For the very first time, he stopped hating his father and his mother.

* * *

There reached the house where the entertainment was taking place, the news that the pretty young girl whom everyone expected to have been the queen of the evening, had been murdered on her way there. Those who brought the news kept silent about what had happened to her after her death, for they did not want to add a sullying horror to the suffering of those who were close to her. Her family were prostrate : others, who hurried to the scene of the crime found that the police had removed her body into a special room, and had forbidden anyone to approach either the corpse or the murderer.

The discretion of the first announcements proved useless : in the morning, the news spread that she had been killed by a monster of depravity in order to assault her sexually : her family now bore both the bitterness of sorrow and the shame of scandal. A crowd tried to rush the prison in order to lynch the criminal. The police officer had to move him hastily, after nightfall, to a distant prison, so that the citizens might not gain the upper hand over the officer, break in, and carry out their intentions.

Into the new prison went the young man : there were a number of notorious criminals there, who were enraged against him when his news was reported to them. Though they were seasoned in crime, they were disgusted that they should have among them someone so depraved as to have committed what he had done; he had brought upon crime and upon criminals a shame which they could not accept.

He would not answer any of the questions which the investigating officer put to him. He paid no attention, did not even listen to his words for he wandered off into a daydream in which he was recalling the joy which his action had led him to experience.

"Your silence is a confession," said the investigator to him, "There's only one thing we want to know; the rest doesn't interest us. How did you kill her ?"

"What ? Was she *dead* ? Ha ! ha ! ha !"

He laughed uproariously in a tone that was not human — laughed as though a djinn possessed him and was making him laugh — laughed for a long time and then abruptly stopped, and fell into a dejection of spirit. During all this, the investigator tried in vain to find out what was going on in the man's mind.

"So she was dead ? So I still haven't fully enjoyed the pleasures they'd deprived me of.. I thought I'd had the greatest of them, thought I'd become a human being .. but I'm still below them all, every one of those swine who live in bliss .. if all that pleasure can spring out of the beauty of a corpse, then what must it be like for those who can enjoy living beauty ?"

A few weeks later he was brought up for trial. The public crowded in to learn the truth about the story that a man had killed a girl in order to rape her. They imagined that they would see a wild beast glowering at them from the dock. There were so many people in the courtroom that the guard was doubled. The defendant was brought in: he was a frail young man with a wan complexion and a sallow, meaningless smile.

The Public Prosecutor rose and addressed the court :

"I do not know, in the annals of our lawcourts, of a case which resembles the one before us today. In it, the prosecution finds itself in a peculiar position. We stand on easy ground with clearly demarcated features. No one is in any doubt as to the events which occurred. No one is in any doubt as to the significance of these events. And yet my task is a difficult one, painful and distressing. As concerns the events : they have been ascertained beyond doubt. The Medical Examiner asserts that the victim died a virgin, that she was deflowered after death. To establish this is a simple matter, since it is an attested fact that a wound inflicted after death does not bleed. The victim has been found to have been suffering from no disease such as might cause sudden death, so that it cannot be argued that she fell down dead and was subsequently found by this man. Such a supposition cannot in common-sense be maintained. If we are to accept the opinion of this expert — and there is nothing before us to cause us to question his expert opinion — our common-sense makes us surmise that this man killed her as she was walking along the public highway, and that he then carried her into the dark corner where she was found : it was not a spot she would have gone to of her own accord, upon such an evening, when she was expected at an entertainment where she knew she would be the centre of attention.

"The Medical Examiner has not been able to give a definite opinion as to the manner in which the victim was killed. Knowledge of that lies with the young man, and he refuses to divulge it. Did he give her the sort of knockout punch in which the assailant does not intend to kill his victim ? A blow of that nature requires technical skill. Nobody knows him to have practised boxing, and so to have learned to give such a punch. In any case, the accused cannot be permitted to conceal himself behind this silence. He cannot be permitted to make use of this silence as a means of escaping punishment. Let me pause over his words to the Investigator : 'Was she dead ?' We cannot take this as proof that he did not kill her, or even that he did not intend to kill her. He thought those words up as a stratagem. He has gone too far in claiming that he did not know she was dead : this itself is a point which stands against him. Is there anyone so ignorant that he cannot tell a dead person from a live one ? If you were to ask a child — younger than he, with less knowledge than he, with less experience — he would not hesitate in distinguishing between a lifeless corpse and a living girl. A baseless allegation; there might have been some plausibility in his defence if he had not nullified it with his plea of ignorance.

"If he killed her, he killed her deliberately, with the object of attaining an end which he knew very well he could not have reached if she had a breath of life in her. He had no previous acquaintance with her : and had no motive for killing her except this one end. Her torn clothing indicates that he did not achieve his purpose until after she was dead. If it were a question of violence which unintentionally led to manslaughter, then surely her death would have held him back, and he would not have persisted in his design ?

"So much for that part of my task which I find light. But when I contemplate the next step that falls to me to take, I do so with a heavy heart. What species of a human being is this that you have before you ? Is he in fact a human being ? I cannot persuade myself that he is. Not a stray dog, not a wild one, not a rabid one, would ever set upon a bitch if she were dead. We do not know of any beast that approaches a dead female of its species. How then can a human being do so ?"

The courtroom was held in awe. Gazes shuffled backwards and forwards from the Prosecutor to the accused as the one of them drew this contrast between the other and an enraged dog.

A middle-aged woman was sick on the spot, violently, audible to all. The murmuring public was hushed as they watched her being carried out. Nobody doubted that her nausea had come about by her visualizing this murderer raping the pretty young girl. But it was not upon this that her imagination had worked. What had sickened her was her memory of her wedding night. She had been young and tender : her husband confronted her with the violence, the coarseness, of an ogre.

To her, he was nothing but a gorilla, lumbering out of the jungle to seize into his brutish grasp the most cherished of her feelings and the most delicate fibres of her being. And by what right was he treating her in this way ? Was it by right of marriage ? She had not yet realized how extensive and demanding these rights were. Her breath was almost stifled : and then she had vomited, just as she was vomiting now. What disgusted her was not the man whom people could see in the dock : it was that much-respected man, her husband, who was sitting next to her, and who was showering her with attentions. Time had not made her forget that one night in her life. Nobody else in the courtroom had the least notion of what she was feeling.

When the woman had been helped out of the court, and the public had quietened down, the Prosecutor continued.

"Some beasts are so inflamed by their natural desires that they wander far and wide in search of a female, impelled by an overpowering force to which they give themselves up completely. But does a single one of them ever satisfy its desires upon a dead body ? This man has debased himself far lower than a cur, in order to satisfy a bestial desire which has dragged him down to the lowest depths."

* * *

The judge listened to all this, listened to the repeated references which the Prosecutor was making to dogs, and remembered what had happened to himself the night before. He had come home to find that his wife had, all for him, made herself as alluring as possible. They had gone to their soft, warm bed; she had been as enticing as she could, but he had responded to her eager demands with a certain hesitation. She found his lovemaking disappointing; when it was over, he turned away from her with a coolness that did not please her. She gave him a kick. There was a rose in a vase on the bedside table; she tossed it at him. She was trying to show a mingled vexation and playfulness. She told him he made love the way dogs do. She laughed : he laughed too, imagining himself on all fours, with his tail up in the air. They both laughed aloud together at this picture. He recalled all this now. He, the dignified and respected judge, had last night been "making love the way dogs do". Now, the Prosecutor, who knew nothing about this, was speaking of it as though it were the very lowest of crimes. The judge smiled at his recollection, then remembered that he was face to face with a solemn and sad matter, that these musings of his did not fit the present moment. He rapped at his table with the end of his pencil several times over, and cried out :

"Silence, please !"

There had not been a single sound from the public. The Prosecutor had paused for a moment, to allow his oratory to affect his audience, intending it to make them shudder at what he had put forward.

The public were astonished at the judge's exclamation. People concluded that he had been as shaken as they were by the account which they were listening to; he must have been as overcome as the woman who had been carried out in a fit of nausea. It enhanced their respect for a judge whose duties normally called upon him not to be influenced by anything but the most rigorous logic.

No one was more astonished than the Prosecutor. He thought at first that the words might be an order to him to cut his speech short. But the judge turned to him and said :

"Please go on."

A loud moan was heard : a young woman collapsed in a faint, her breathing spasmodic and painful. A case like this, said people to each other, should not have been tried in public. Peoples' nerves could not stand the strain. The young woman's husband was next to her. He had noticed that she had been averting her eyes so as not to see the accused, only occasionally stealing a glance at him, and turning her face away again. When she did so, she had pressed her body against his own, as if reassuring herself that his presence would protect her from such an iniquitous monster.

She had been married for about a year. She was highly passionate in her desires : her young husband was obviously less sensual than she. He found it shameful for a young woman to be eager. And so his wife had to conceal her real temperament from him. Attending this trial, she could not bear to look at the accused — not out of disgust, but frightened at her desire for him. She snuggled close to her husband's body in fear that the strength of her desire might make her blurt it out. She forgot that he had killed, that a young girl had died: she kept only in her mind that here was a man who had so passionately wanted a woman that he had risked execution. There were men so little impelled by this urge that they would not lay down a newspaper they were reading — nor break away from a trivial conversation they were listening to, nor put off joining a crony with whom they had arranged to have a cup of coffee or a glass of wine. Her fantasy grew stronger : she imagined herself in the criminal's arms — he was hugging her live body to himself more fiercely than he had ever held the dead body.

She fell into a hysterical fit. The public saw it, and heard it, but guessed nothing of the truth.

One of the jurymen, an army man who had reached the position of an instructor, kept an unwavering stare upon the dock. He looked as if he were trying to penetrate the secrets that lay behind this man's deed. The juryman was not attracted to women. He was cruel to his soldiers out of spite. The men knew this, and, to get their own back, they overdid their accounts of their sexual adventures when they spoke to him. As he stared at the criminal, there was envy in his heart, and delight, and astonishment, that any man should have the strength to do what this man had done.

One jury-woman fidgeted restlessly in her chair. She kept up a compulsive movement in which she continually ran her finger under her dress at the shoulder, and snapped the tape of her slip again and again upon her right shoulder, irritating everyone around her. She too stared at the accused without pause. She was saying to him, "Just wait for me to give my opinion about you. I'll have my own back on you and your kind. *He* was one of your sort. The other one. The brute who turned my daughter's head. Made her forget me. Forget her people. And run off with him."

And so the public sat through the trial together, separate in their reactions, parted from those who sat next to them, and from those who were nearest to them outside the courtroom, by a thick curtain which hid the feelings of every one.

The Public Prosecutor continued :

"This young man was a human being before he perpetrated his outrage. But God's wrath fell upon him — why, we cannot tell — and it turned him into a swine, or into something lower than that. Look at him ! Does he look sorry for what he has done ? Does he look aware of the horror of it ?"

Everybody turned to look at the young man. Some of the women shifted their glance away, covering their eyes in disgust. He was telling himself that the truth was the opposite of what the Prosecutor had said. Until that night, he had been a pariah dog with no human feelings . .

in those few moments, he had come to know the life that lay within him — when he seized her in the grip which aroused his vigour and drew him on to complete his delight by the greatest of man's sensual pleasures . . it was in those moments that he had turned into a human being. As this came into his mind, his face showed his satisfaction. And this made the public angrier and more disgusted with him.

The Prosecutor continued :

"Look at him : he is almost smiling ! You would think something pleasant were happening to him ! What are you to make of him ? Is he so insane as not to be responsible for his actions ? I cannot recall any insane man who ever calculatedly carried out what this man has. He is on a lower plane than any madman can be. I do not think that you will accept insanity as a defence. And if it be that madness causes a man to kill a young girl in order to assault her dead body, then, I say, let the retribution for such madness be death."

Here the accused interrupted :

"I didn't know that she was dead."

These were the first words the public had heard from him, and they came to them as though they were spoken by an evil spirit. Both the Prosecutor and the public took him to be merely denying that he had meant to kill her. This seemed inadmissible as a plea. No one could have understood what he really meant. *I didn't know that she was dead.* He was arguing with himself, justifying what he had done as a means of attaining the greatest human pleasure, defending his crime as a way of realizing his human nature. It did not disturb him to think that he had committed even the greatest of crimes, since it had led him to the greatest of joys. But to be told that she had been dead . . that he had not reached the summit of human feelings . . he had to wipe the notion out of his mind. There was one way to do this. To remind himself that he had not known that she was dead . . that he had not realized that he was tussling with a lifeless body.

The Defence did not attempt to say much. The only plea it put forward was that the accused was insane, and not responsible for his actions.

The judge summed up the case for the jury in these words :

"Ladies and gentlemen of the Jury, you must not allow the disgust which you have felt to make you bring in any verdict unless you are thoroughly convinced that it is the right one. Do not let emotion sway you in determining facts. It is your duty to disregard your feelings, and to decide in the light of the evidence brought before you whether or not the accused is guilty of what he is charged with. Do not take it for granted that the account which the Prosecution has given of events must necessarily be the true one, merely because the account is at one and the same time horrifying, yet easy to believe. It is possible that a less likely account may be the true one.

"It may be easier for you to reach a decision upon the second of the two counts with which the accused is charged. The medical expert firmly asserts that the victim was deflowered after her death. If it is your opinion that there is no circumstantial evidence which conflicts with the opinion of the expert, then you must say so clearly.

"To turn back to the first charge in the accusation, it is that of murder. You must consider this with the greatest of care, and examine the facts minutely. The cause of death is still not established."

The judge re-stated the Prosecutor's claims that the victim had been in good health, and that although a skilfull punch might have accidentally killed her, without leaving any revealing bruise, it was not likely that the young man should have given her a blow of this sort. "In my opinion," he continued, "you must determine whether this young girl died as a result of an action taken by the accused (even if we do not know the exact nature of such an action), or whether she died of natural causes for which he is not responsible."

"It will help you in determining what took place, and in reaching a verdict, if you enquire into the question of a motive for killing her. They had not previously known each other, and I can see no motive for murder unless we posit a determination to assault her sexually. If your opinion is that he lay in wait in order to waylay any girl whom he could, and carry out his purpose upon her, then this constitutes a predetermined intent, even if his intent were not directed specifically against this particular victim. If you believe that he gave her her deathblow without intending it to kill her, then was carried away into assaulting her sexually, this would constitute manslaughter.

"Your duty will no doubt become clearer to you if you ask yourselves, Did he kill her in order to rape her, — or did he kill her and then decide to rape her ? If he killed her with the intention of assaulting her sexually, then this is wilful murder with predetermined intent. If you believe that she died at his hands in the course of a struggle with him, and that he then proceeded with his sexual assault, this is manslaughter rather than murder. If you are in any doubt, then, of course, the accused should have the benefit of the doubt."

* * *

The jury retired to consider their verdict upon the two heads of the accusation. The tension in the courtroom relaxed, and people spoke to their neighbours in low tones. The defending lawyer was sitting next to the medical expert.

"What do you think of this young man's sickness ?" he asked him.

"He isn't sick."

"Do you think anyone of sound mind would do what he did ?"

"What you call his 'illness' is simply the slipping of the reins through his fingers. Myself, I call it *unmuzzling*. When that comes about, there's nothing to stop natural instincts from gaining their ends. There are two things that normally stop people from surrendering to the full force of their biological natures. One is their human qualities. And the other is the restraining influence of civilization. Every civilization has its own particular restraints which it imposes upon the instincts. Now, have we put into that young man enough humane qualities and enough civilization for you to hope that he should restrain his instincts ?"

"Isn't that what you people call *repression* ?"

"No, it's what we call *deprivation*. Repression is the tension between what ought to be and what oughtn't to be. The layman's idea of sexual repression as something that disappears as soon as that particular passion is satisfied is a false one. It's led to a lot of corruption, and given rise to an ugly permissiveness which people claim has its basis in psycho-analysis. The truth is that repression is a tension. It may be that it is the committing of what oughtn't to be done, and not the restraining of yourself, that increases the tension which gives rise to the trouble. This young man is not suffering from repression : but it is we who have withheld from him all the factors that make restraint possible — and so he gave his instincts their head."

"So much so that he was unconcerned about death — about killing ?"

"The death only came into this affair as an incidental — it has no essential link with the true crime. And that was that this young man grew up in total deprivation, and was never accorded the powers of restraint which can never be found apart from the very fullest humanity and civilization.

"As for sexual crimes, it's true that our experience has shown us that they rise, in men, out of being deprived. But human beings know how to grapple with this. They certainly do think that this urge ought to have a great deal sacrificed to it : but most of them don't go so far as to risk prison, and indeed, capital punishment. They realize that, however strong the urge is, it isn't beyond their ability to turn their attention away from it for some time.

"As for women, when they commit a crime of passion, it rises out of their despair at ever realizing the daydreams that it's in their nature to indulge in at a certain age. They dream of happiness as something which can only be found by falling in love. When they realize that this was a mere illusion and that the truth is quite different from their daydreams, they grow very disturbed. Most of them suffer depths of misery through the ignorance of their menfolk. And most of them end by reconciling themselves to a life different from the one they had hoped to have. But not those whose despair forces them into committing a crime."

The jury were away for only a short time. When they had returned, the judge asked them if they had reached a unanimous verdict.

"Yes," replied the head juror. "We find the accused guilty on both counts."

The public were satisfied at this verdict. The judge accepted the decision of the jury, and condemned the accused to be hanged by the neck till he were dead.

The young man had thought that his sentence would be solitary confinement or hard labour, neither of which held much terror for him. He was stunned when he learned that he was to be executed : his mind was drained of all feelings and thoughts.

Some time later, he was brought to the gallows in a state in which he felt nothing and was unaware of what was taking place. The prison chaplain gave counsel to him in words which were meaningless and savourless. The young man looked at him as he spoke his exhortation, and turned his face away. The priest himself hurried through his own words, which he was repeating automatically to a person whom he could see was making nothing of them. The young man was hanged by his neck until he was dead.

There came and knelt beside his body the city priest who used to see him in church, and who had accepted the pennies he had offered.

"My son," he murmured, "the judge forgot, or deliberately omitted, to ask for God's mercy upon your soul, as judges have asked for all ages : this was because he was horrified at your crime. So now I pray for God's mercy upon you, for His mercy is more generous than the justice of men. You were not evil, my son. You had the seeds of good in you, but they would not allow them to take root. Evil did not grow in you : but they left you barren of all good, and so you were a prey to the evil that chanced upon you. They deprived you of everything that distinguishes a human being; and then they were surprised to find that you should show no concern for those very things which make men human. Perhaps no one could really have understood you, but I am convinced that what you were trying to do was to feel in yourself some of the human sentiments that we had denied you. God will understand you where we could not, and He will have mercy upon you. The wrong that your fellow-creatures did you is greater than any harm you have done."

The prison chaplain turned to him :

"Are you asking for mercy for such a man ?"

"I feel very deeply that God will forgive this man whom you have put to death with your own hands without knowing whether what you do is pleasing to God or not. Some of us are very close to Hell, though our faces are set towards Heaven, and though we are very anxious to reach it. Some of us are very close to Heaven, even though we have no aspiration for it, and our faces are set towards Hell."

"And in which of the two groups do you place this man whose lust brought him to his death ?"

"It was his deprivation that brought him to his death. You and I and everyone else are to blame for that."

Translated by Mahmoud Manzalaoui; revised by Ronald Ewart.

THE BRASS FOUR-POSTER

Yehia Hakki

YEHIA HAKKI is one of the most distinguished literary figures of Egypt; too meticulous a writer to have produced more than a sparse amount of publications, his short stories and critical writings are outstanding in themselves, and have had a profound effect upon younger writers. Hakki was born in Cairo in 1905, into a literary family: his uncle was a writer, his brother edited the magazine *Sufur*, in which the stories of Mohamed Taymour appeared. The family circle was familiar with English as well as Arabic literature : Yehia Hakki himself was later to be influenced by Russian nineteenth-century fiction, but declares that he owes a debt to both Lytton Strachey and Virginia Woolf. Hakki graduated in law in 1925, and has worked as a lawyer, a civil servant in the provinces, and a diplomat in the Middle East and in western Europe. He is at present editor of *Al Magalla*, the leading cultural monthly of Cairo. He has, since the twenties, played a prominent part in literary and cultural movements, and his help and advice to younger writers has been seminal. Some of his critical works are mentioned in the Arabic reading-list at the end of this volume. Hakki's first story was published in 1925. He is perhaps best known for his long short story *Qindil Ummi-Hashim* (*The Lamp of Sayyeda Zeynab*), 1944. It is difficult to sum up the characteristics of Hakki : but he has a genuinely sympathetic, if ironic, humanism of outlook as a thinker, which, in many of his stories, emerges in a sharply wry form. The present story is taken from his collection *'Antar wa Juliette* (*Antar and Juliet*), 1960, in which the title story is in a totally different vein from *The Brass Four-poster* (*As-sarīr un-nuḥāsī*), being a prose poem about a rich dog and a poor one. Hakki is an exceptionally meticulous artist, and it is not easy to show in translation the great care he shows in the choice of words.

Zeinab found shopping for her future home as irksome as it was pleasurable. Her cup of joy was not unmixed with tears of a flavour that was new to her. These were sometimes tears of tenderness and joy, mingled with shame at seeing her mother wear herself out to provide her with all that she needed. It was her mother who thought of the jug and basin, the clogs and the bathroom stool. She even bought her two brooms, one long handled, the other short. But Zeinab's tears were sometimes tears of rage, not unlike those of a spoilt child. This was the case whenever her mother drew Zeinab's attention away from natural to artificial silk, saying :

"My dear, this is just the beginning. We still have more important things to buy."

How the mother would have loved to shower gold and jewels upon her daughter — but if wishes were horses, beggars would ride.

Theirs was a modest family whose fortunes had declined after the father's death. *El Sit*[1] Adeela had refused to remarry for fear of what her only child might suffer at the hands of a stepfather. Highly esteemed in the neighbourhood, she was a woman for whom men would rise to their feet, lowering their gaze in deep respect, as she passed by with her face hidden behind a veil that almost smothered her. In her hometown, Damanhour, Adeela led a life of self-sufficiency through the sale, by piecemeal, of the five feddans which were all that was left to her. Her daughter's fiancé insisted very firmly that she should live with them in Cairo, but she refused, saying that she did not wish to be suspected of sponging off a stranger; and she went on to declare that she would remain, until her dying day, in the house where she was born and where she had lived since her marriage. From that selfsame house, her body would be carried out, and her coffin would find its way, unguided, to the grave.

"How can you say such a thing, mother ! I'd give my life for you."

"We all have to go one day, dear girl," said the mother.

Zeinab grew up under her mother's wing, ignorant of all else in life. To that very day, they shared the same bed, and at night she would fold her arms around her mother and lay her head upon her soft breast. "Dear God, how fragrant her breath was, how sweet !" There wasn't another soul in the whole world who enjoyed such peaceful sleep. She was proud of her mother who had never in her life uttered

(1) Colloquial shortened form of 'al Sayyida': a title or mode of address, meaning 'Madame'.

a shameful word, nor ever hurt her daughter's feelings.

Zeinab's fatherless state had developed in her a hypersensitivity Which clearly displayed itself on the death of the schoolmate who had sat next to her in class. Zeinab mourned her at home, and refused to go back to school unless the headmistress agreed to move her to another desk, even if it meant ber sitting right at the back. So sensitive was she that her distress at having drawn attention to herself was no less than her grief at the death of her classmate.

This, then, was Zeinab, whose love for her mother bordered on worship, a passion which roused in her a mixed thrill of joy and apprehension alike. And yet now she was trailing her mother behind her from one shop to another for her purchases. When her own feet grew hot and swollen, she forgot to ask the old woman, who would be panting for breath, whether she, too, was tired — happiness, like misfortune, blots out all else.

Zeinab wanted to buy a wooden bed she had seen in a furniture shop. What she liked about it was the design on the front, which was repeated on the wardrobe. This motif, common to both pieces of furniture, particularly appealed to her, as it meant that she would be buying a complete suite, not simply two entirely different independent units. She was highly impressed also by the fact that at the head of the bed there were two bedside tables fixed one on either side. She could already imagine her great pleasure as she lay in bed, reaching out her hand for something in the drawer. She would be able to do this, whenever she had neither the inclination nor the time to get up and look for things in some remote corner of the room. She wanted to be 'modern', not like her mother who stuffed everything away between the mattresses.

But *El Sit* Adeela firmly refused to comply with her daughter's wishes.

"Do not be deceived by appearances," she said to her. "Look under the shiny veneer, and you will find nothing but ordinary deal wood which will crack in a couple of summers. It'll never stand the wear and tear of moving house and rough handling in general."

"The bugs will nest in the wood", she went on to say. "And why let yourself in for all that ?"

In spite of the tears that streamed down her daughter's cheeks, trickling almost into her mouth, Adeela bought her a magnificent brass bed, not nickel-plated with low angular posts in the modern style, but an old-fashioned brass bed with thick cylindrical posts, all four reaching up to the ceiling. On the top of every post was a huge domelike capital. The front of the bed, like the railing round a saint's shrine, was covered all over with an interlacing design of large and small circles, fixed together with nails whose bald heads gleamed brightly. This was the kind of bed to warm the cockles of the heart. It betokened the true gentility of the owner's origins. Only on such a bed could the body find rest. When *El Sit* Adeela had sewn a green jacket for the miniature Koran which was to hang from the top of the right hand post, she said to her daughter :

"Now, tell me, if you please, where would we have put it on that stunted wooden bed ?"

The brass four-poster was witness to Zeinab's wedding night, and to the birth of her first son and daughter, and of the twins that followed, not to mention her numerous miscarriages. Summer after summer passed,and time began to leave its mark on the brass as it does on wood. The domelike capitals fell off and the tops of the posts now looked like gaping drain-pipes with jagged ends. The shine had tarnished, and lost its lustre. Some of the rings had fallen off, leaving the general design incomplete, and baring the sharp fangs of nails which hurt you if you touched them. But the genteel never lose caste, despite the ravages of time. The posts of the brass bed, no longer upright, stood at an angle, like the legs of a horse that is making water, and the bed jingled as one got in and out of it; but, in spite of the scars and the aches and pains, the bed proudly held itself together, and remained welcoming, generous and spacious. Zeinab and her husband with one child between them, all slept together in the bed — and any of the other children would join them if he was sick. And if you lifted the corner of the mattress, you would find heaps of paper and old rags along with the housekeeping money for the month. Like mother, like daughter, when all is said and done.

This bed was Zeinab's refuge, the retreat where she found rest after a hard day's work which began at dawn and continued well into the night. Whenever she surrendered her huge tired body to the bed, she felt as light as a feather, gently falling into the palm of a hand open to receive her. She would pin up her hair and gather it in an embroidered headcloth, ready for sleep, and, before she dropped off, her features, at the idea of repose, would be transformed, and turn into the features of the graceful young girl she had once been, as she slept in her mother's arms. The lips of her wide mouth would pucker up, as though she were sucking a sweet; the tired expression on her face would change to one of innocence and total resignation; and the tone of the voice, murmuring — lullaby to her children, would become tender and gentle, as it never was in the daytime. During the long restless nights when her husband stayed out later than usual, the brass bed provided ample room for her tossing and turning, in her vain search for sleep. Zeinab could not have gone on living if she were ever deprived of that bed. Even on her visits to Damanhour, when she slept in her mother's arms, she still longed for her own bed.

El Sit Adeela was in the habit of visiting her daughter at feast-times. How delightful those visits were; the children shrieked with joy for them. She used to come laden with baskets of loaves, biscuits, pies, large fresh eggs and a dressed duck whose rich fat was like amber. At night, the mother would sleep on the sofa in the hall, for *El Sit* Adeela assured everyone that she liked the sofa because it was suited for all purposes : for sleep, for relaxation, for a siesta and for resting tired legs. If ever a visitor turned up while she was lying down, a slight move to shift the pillow from the head of the divan to the middle was all that was required, and she was ready to receive the newcomer with all due decorum, seating her next to her. There was also a special spot on the sofa for the coffee tray, and the breakfast, lunch or dinner tray if her feet hurt her and she was unable to get up for meals. But why try to justify her liking for the sofa ? The fact is that Zeinab's home contained only one bed which stood there in all majesty, and never would *El Sit* Adeela consent to the whole family's giving it up for her to sleep in alone, while her dear ones slept on mattresses on the floor in the sitting-room or the hall.

Two days after her arrival on her last visit, *El Sit* Adeela had her dinner on the sofa. She ate what was left of the pie, which had turned dry and leathery; for dessert, she had some molasses. Soon after, she felt a heaviness, as though the food were pressing down upon her. Maybe the molasses had been on the turn. She asked for a glass of water with a drop of orange-blossom essence in it, to give her relief; then she dozed off. The next morning, she could not lift her head off the pillow, and when Zeinab felt her forehead, she found her feverish.

"It's nothing to worry about" said *El Sit* Adeela in a feeble voice, "I've just caught a bit of a chill."

Aspirin, tea with lemon, bean soup — nothing helped. That evening, her temperature rose and her body was all of a sweat. Her answers to her daughter's questions grew more hesitant and, at times, they were incoherent.

After a while, she lost consciousness. Tossing and turning, her body, as if on fire, was overcome by a fit of violent excitement. She would have taken flight, but was chained fast. Her head, in continual motion, turned from right to left, as though she were one of a circle of dancing dervishes, and her hands swept upwards and downwards, one after the other, now on her chest, and now dropping heavily by her side like stones. She was in great agony. Zeinab stood pale-faced and dazed, and would have burst into tears if she had not imagined that her mother, although unconscious, was aware of everything around her. If only her mother would scream; that would be easier for Zeinab to bear, than to see her dear one so silent.

Then the tears began to stream down her cheeks, as she saw her mother's hands reaching to tear off her clothes, as though she wished to strip herself naked. *El Sit* Adeela, who had lived all her life pure and untainted by any hint of scandal, to strip her body naked !

She must move her mother to the brass bed at once. That was the only place worthy of her. In any case, she was in danger of rolling off the sofa. Zeinab blamed herself for having delayed in paying due respect to her mother, but, then, she had never thought that the illness would overcome her so rapidly. She would sleep with her husband and children on two mattresses on the sitting-room floor. When her mother recovered — and that would be quite soon, she hoped — Zeinab would climb into the brass bed and lie next to her; with her head on her mother's breast, as she used to do in days gone by.

"If God wills it ! If God wills it !"

Zeinab called her husband, and, between them, they carried *El Sit* Adeela, like a slaughtered lamb in convulsions, and laid her on the brass bed. Zeinab's heart sank for she imagined that, this time, the bed's jingling sounded solemn and mournful. *El Sit* Adeela's body occupied only a narrow strip which formed a hollow beneath her in the bed. Yet, in spite of its spaciousness, the brass bed seemed tailored for her. This is how it always in when the worthy and the noble meet together.

But there was something unusual in the air of that room. Could it be the foot of the bed that seemed to have taken on the appearance of the railings of a grave ? Or could it be the Koran dozing inside its dusty green jacket ? Was it the gloom of evening ? Or the owl that had deserted the district for days, and had now chosen this particular night, as though by special appointment, to send forth its ominous hooting once again, squatting on the fence of the neighbouring waste ground ? Nobody knows exactly what it was that filled the room with the feeling that the brass bed was getting ready to perform, with nobility and majesty, a rôle that was new to it : it was to receive the angel of death, to witness the departure of a soul, and to house a dying body as it turned cold, its pale flesh going wax-yellow, then indigo-blue in parts — a live body with a warm radiance almost iridescent in the dark, springing out of a dynamo that hides its secrets behind closed doors, and that is being transformed into something with a damp rancid smell like wet plasticine, very soon turning to a putrid stench, the most abominable on earth. To this day, the brass bed had been a refuge and shelter, and here it was, now, preparing, without any sign of protest, to become a mausoleum.

The doctor came the next day in the afternoon and diagnosed the sickness as meningitis, saying that the following night would be critical. If day broke and the patient was alive, the danger would have passed. What he meant, in fact, was that she would be dead before sunrise. All the same, he gave her an injection of streptomycine, to comfort her family, to clear his own conscience and to justify his fee. He had hardly left, when the death-rattle started up, and Zeinab — poor soul — as usual when she was overcome by fear, suffered an attack of diarrhoea. This had always happened to her during air raids. Now she shunted back and forth between her mother and the lavatory, her tears streaming down her cheeks which she wiped with her wet fingers. She was in a state of unutterable fear, as though a knife were at her heart-strings. She could not believe that her mother was dying. The death-rattle developed into a snore, and grew louder, like the wrenching of a saw caught fast in the heart of a tree, whose bark had petrified at the sign of danger.

Zeinab went about the house, wringing her hands in utter bewilderment, as though demented. A voice in her heart whispered, "The smell of your mother shall remain in this bed, and it will be with you for the rest of your life. Will you have the heart to sleep on the bed where your mother died, and still enjoy repose ?" Should she sell the bed ? But who would buy it ? And where would she find its like, even second-hand ? Should she leave her mother on the bed, refusing to believe that she was dying ? Or should she move her off it in pity for her own self, in thought of her future nights on the bed — and so judge her mother dead before daybreak ? Could she, with her own hand, sign her mother's death certificate before it was due ?

She roamed about the house until she had almost lost her senses. The tears streamed down her cheeks, a heavy torrent which blunted her sense of taste, and peeled the skin off her inflamed eyelids. Before daybreak, the snoring became fainter, less marked; now it was the patter of running footsteps, gradually growing lighter before they cease altogether, as they reach their destination. Zeinab called her husband, and asked him to help her carry her mother to the sitting-room, where she had laid a mattress for her.

"What is the point ?" he asked. "Why disturb her at this hour ?"

"You fool," her heart cried out, "do you think you could have more feeling for my mother than I have ?"

What she actually said to him was, "I've got to do it — don't let's argue about it — it's taken hold of me.."

It was as though some other person had spoken, for neither she nor her husband understood the gist of her words.

Just as they had carried *El Sit* Adeela from the sofa to the brass bed, so they carried her off the bed once again, and laid her on the mattress in the sitting-room. Zeinab wept incessantly, and wailed, as her body bent with the weight of the mattress.

"God make you well again, mother. God make you well — and a thousand times over !"

With loving care, she spread a big eiderdown over her.

"To hell with the eiderdown ! The undertaker will take it with him anyway."[1]

She sat by her mother's side all night while her husband slept. Just before dawn, a mysterious energy surged through the body of the dying woman, enabling her lifeless arms to raise the heavy eiderdown, and to lift her right hand from under it. She held out her forefinger, while her lips remained rigid and her eyes closed. *El Sit* Adeela did not want to die before she had uttered the two *Shehadas* of the Creed.

* * *

All the neighbours and relations were agreed that Zeinab infused the wake with a show of feelings more fit for a bride who had died on her wedding night, than for an old woman who had had her fill of life.

---

(1) The quilt off a dead person's bed is taken away, by tradition, by the undertakers, as their perquisite.

She slapped her face with such ferocity that she tore the flesh out with her nails, as though she were taking revenge on an enemy. It was strange that people did not say, as they usually do on such occasions, "Don't take on so for your mother," but rebuked her with the words, "Stop torturing yourself".

Translated by Nur Sherif; revised by Josephine Wahba.

AN EMPTY BED

Yehia Hakki

The second story by Yehia Hakki which we print here, is in an exceptional position. The author refuses to include it in any volume of his collected stories, and was reluctant to have us include it in this collection. He feels that the story was written as an act of mental therapy, and that it should not be thrust upon the general public. The members of our committee all agree that it is one of the most striking and powerful of recent short stories, and that its portrayal of human degradation is a thoroughly serious one, which has produced a story that deserves to be known to a wider public abroad. The hero's surrender of his will is an illustration, in the obverse, of Hakki's recurrent stress upon the will as the source of virtue. *Al-firāshu-sh-shāghir* appeared in the first number of the review *Al Katib* (April 1961).

When the original of this story appeared in the magazine Al Katib *it was preceded by an editorial note which read as follows : —*

ART AND NIHILISM : The negative attitude can lead to malignancies of every kind, and draw its victim down into the lower depths. It is the arch-enemy of society, and it destroys an individual's self-respect.

Lean over the brink for a moment, and you will realize the full horror; this prophylactic experience will stimulate your ability to share your life with others, and make you appreciate the beautiful things in life. It is invigorating to breathe fresh air after stifling in a noxious hiding-hole.

The most effective way of conveying this experience is the use of symbol. Arabic literature in its current stage of development must not fear to learn the use of every manner of expression.

If you turn out of the Imamein Square into El Rihan Street, and take only a few steps forward, you will come, on your left hand side, to a small shop which you will not notice as you walk past, for it is one of a close-set indistinguishable row of shabby shops, marching exactly in step with the narrow, dilapidated pavement, in every one of its twists and turns, and every one of its straight runs. This shop and its companions are enveloped in a tattered web of murkiness, woven by a spider long-since dead, and since lodged in, first by confidence and prosperity, then by sloth and by hard times. The springs that set the puppets in motion behind the shop-fronts have grown rusty. A head hangs down upon a breast. A pair of eyelids move like cumbersome door-bolts, pulled upwards by cords and then falling heavily back into place. A hand trembles as it shunts from the task of receiving small coinage to the task of handing over a customer's purchase, and then to driving away the flies which are trying to drink their fill of the saliva that dribbles down between the lips, and the rheum at the corner of an eyelid, and the ropy fluid with the attractive glossy colour, which ouzes out of the channel of an ear.

If you raise your eyes slightly as you walk past this particular shop, and you catch sight of the signboard above it, it will dispirit you : you will avert your glance and hurry onward — even if you are someone who can walk in scarcely anything more then a decrepit shuffle. Worried, you will exclaim to yourself, "This cursed employment, squeezing itself in among shops that are carrying on the sort of decent trades that are praised in the Holy Book and praised by the Prophet, shops whose owners you wouldn't hesitate to shake hands with and sit down with to a meal. It's all wrong that this shop should be here : a pimple on a smooth cheek, a whore among chaste women, a leper in the harem of an oriental potentate — one who, as though his mere presence were not bad enough, gets drunk on fresh milk handed to him by a noble-blooded pimp."

Luckily for you, your fit of depression will be driven away by your pride in your own powers of deduction; you will think yourself the first passer-by sharp enough to have noticed that the signboard must originally have hung over another shop that was broader in its frontage, for it juts out left and right over the two neighbouring shop-fronts — a comparatively modest form of encroachment upon them on its part, for its shadow covers the whole stretch of ground below. Leaning forward slightly, and with a very pronounced list to one side, the signboard might be on the verge of tumbling down; and yet it has hung there throughout the years.

The shop to the right is a small grocery stores that supplies local produce. Just inside is a dusty counter of blistered wood on which you can see some pickled aubergines; every one of them has overripe seeds spilling out of its guts, while the decomposed flesh of the vegetable is falling apart in shreds, making the mouth of a customer water if he is of the vulture or of the hyena kind.

The shop on the left belongs to a leather-worker who makes bags, a craftsman in the left-overs of the butcher's trade, for the lid on one bag is the flank of a cow, the body of the next is the belly of a goat — suitcases made for separations, bags to hasten departures; strewn over railway platforms, squeezed into luggage racks, they roam the earth like homeless souls.

A donkey-cart lumbers past, giving off a faint odour of toddy; a chicken-coop without a roof or sides, crammed with black-garbed women[1], every one of them brooding upon her egg — and God help her if it does not hatch out, for they are, every one, involved in a race against a thieving kite, forever voracious, ever hovering patiently to swoop down upon their chicks. The donkey that draws the cart is bony and underfed; you can tell that the driver, although he is short of wind, is an insatiably avaricious person.

You glance back at the signboard once more before it passes out of your sight, at the sprawling, ornate *thuluth.*[2] letters of its inscription, daubed on in white paint which is full of cracks that give it a tortoise-shell pattern : UNDERTAKER FOR WHOLE OF IMAMEIN DISTRICT.

The master-undertaker's apprentice leaves the shop entrance for the inner depths, a dark cave inside which the glances of a passer-by

---

(1) In the cheaper quarters of Cairo, donkey-carts are sometimes still used, especially by women, as a form of public transport, each passenger paying a small fare, as in a service car.

(2) An ornate calligraphic style, used for inscriptions.

dissolve in thin air : he returns carrying on his shoulder a brand-new coffin together with its wrapping cloth, and hangs them both up on a nail upon one flap of the shop-door. Then he sits down, and polishes his nails by rubbing them against his striped *gallabiyya.*[1]

* * *

Opposite the shop there have lived for a long time a small family : the father, the mother, and their only son — for the firstborn had also been the last. The neighbours do not know much about them. They realize that the family wish to lead a retired life and believe that people who withdraw in that way want to conceal very great happiness, or else very deep grief, either of which is a mortifying stigma for any unobtrusive person to live with. Those who say that there is happiness behind the veil of privacy claim that you can sense this; in any case, they add, it is plain to your own eyes when it bursts into view on saints' days and at feasts, for on those occasions there stream down from the windows of that home a festive blaze of lights and a reverberating laughter that have no equal in the entire quarter.[2] Those who hold that there is unhappiness behind the screen of privacy point to an event that recurs once or twice a month. There draws up at the door an old car battered in body and spirit, with the air of a pregnant woman whose child has been smothered to death in her womb : a mother who gives birth to death, where others produce new life. Out of the car steps a huge-bodied attendant, in charge of a tall thin man with a sallow face, a shifty glance, and hair in wild disorder. He is always slily on the look-out for the moment when he can regain his freedom, and fly off in pursuit of an enemy who has destroyed his spirit, his consciousness and his reasoning powers, and left him a flair for using language as disgusting as a piece of chewed sugar-cane which has been spat out — words that he masticates with relish as his peculiar form of self-expression. The trouble is that he does not know who that enemy is. He grips hold of the car-door, then of the front door of the house; the attendant hauls him away, and with the palms of his hands,

(1) Long, loose, shirt-like garment, worn by a man.

(2) On these occasions, the hero's parents organize a *Zar* or ceremony of exorcism.

sets the man's face looking forwards so that he shall not twist his neck, and so that passers-by might be protected from the looks which he shoots at them like bullets and the foul language which would disgrace the most disreputable brothel.

When this outcry starts up, all the windows in the house slam shut at one and the same instant, as though they did so automatically and without anyone touching them. An hour or two later, the attendant emerges, still chewing the remains of a meal, wiping his moustache with one hand, his other hand held tight by the gentle, tender clasp of a tall emaciated child with a gentle soft look, who takes his seat in the car, and gives a quiet little gasp, as though he has just come back from a long ride on a lame horse and has found his own familiar bed waiting for him.

Those who maintain that the family has a secret grief assert with a discoverer's exultation and with the triumph of a gambler who has won a bet, that this is the man of distinction whom the family has produced, a man whose great fortune alone prevents them from praying earnestly for his death, since our religious law does not allow a killer to inherit the wealth of his victim, even if he kills him out of mercy for him.

It often happens that after the car moves off, the bottle-washer comes out of the café carrying a pail brimfull of slops out of the hubble-bubbles. He stands on the pavement and empties his pail in one powerful sweep, and the earth feels a delightful tingle, as the water splatters down upon its skin while the aroma of the dottle spreads out like an opiate soothing the nerves of all creatures who are passing by — men, horses, mules, and donkeys alike.

* * *

The truth is simpler than any of the surmises which have been made. The veil of secrecy had been draw, not to hide any happiness or grief, but for another purpose, which has never been uncovered in spite of all the ingenious guess-work, and because it is more plausible, and truer to human nature — for deception plays with illusions and not with the truth, and makes fancied things shine brightly so as to dim realities. The family have chosen the only observance which requires a screen to be drawn round it if its rites are not to be disturbed and their effects nullified. They have broken with the world of men. To them it is a hornets' nest which you must keep clear of, a landmine which does you no harm so long as you merely walk around it, but which you must never touch, a sealed wineskin with the promise of a deliciously intoxicating bouquet,which when you break it open,transforms itself,and your mind with it, into floating vapours of lightheadedness. For them, life is not a vertical progress in which the new builds itself up upon the old and from which you can view an ever-widening horizon as you climb upwards. Neither is it the circling orbit of a planet, rising, climbing to its zenith, sinking, and then setting. . It is, instead, a faint horizontal line, made up of a myriad of identical dark spots, soldered together so thoroughly that you can no longer make out any colour in them. Even their food is chewed for them in advance by mincing-machines and pestles : they eat meat and vegetables all pounded into one soggy mash; what they relish is the way that every ingredient loses its distinctive flavour. Opting out of life was their way of escape from direct confrontation with the most powerful and unconditional form of a grace, to which they would otherwise have had to bow down their heads as low as the earth and never raise their foreheads. This would have been a wearisome posture, and weariness is the broadest of the gates through which faithlessness finds its way in. In their rejection of a professed blessing, they acknowledge its value more so than others; they are far more conscious of an obligation which should be owed in return.

They had disengaged themselves because of a fear of receiving, as a recompense, something in whose aridity they might drown, or in whose floodwaters they might be sucked dry. They were trying to ensure in this way that they would be free from mental distress, safe from regrets at the monstrous faithlessness of others, or from grief at the baseness which they would discover in their own personalities if they ever stood in abject fear of the lassitude which lay in wait for them, and which would pin them down in terror as a snake does a sparrow. For you may stake your life upon your always remaining a stingy cowardly creature, but you dare not venture so much as a farthing upon your remaining — always and in all circumstances — courageous and generous. Having withdrawn from others, they no longer distinguish one day from another by name : they tell the passing of the days by the way in which the shadows, cast by familiar objects, gradually circle round in an arc, by identifying the calls of migrant birds : for those who cut themselves off from the world of men draw closer to nature. As the days have become confused, so have their ages; the husband calls his wife "Mother" : she calls him "Father"; both of them call their only son "My friend", while he calls his mother "Darling". He has no word at all for his father, since he stopped addressing him when he was five years old; he never speaks *to* him, never speaks *of* him in his presence, and if he is not there, he uses the plain personal pronoun, the mere monosyllable "Him".

Often, if they both turned their backs upon each other, while one of them was leaving the room, the father would look behind him and find that the son was staring back at him. The son would feel that his father was giving him a piercing look which foreboded something. The father would feel that his son's glance was the look of a person with a gleaming scalpel hidden in his hand. Then the interchanged looks would turn into the embarrassed, apologetic smiles of men whose ruses have been detected; then the smiles, in their turn would change into two looks of understanding, love and esteem : the whole incident would take only a brief moment — and revealed that the family was close-knit, and shared a distinctive feature : every one of them was tender, soft, hypersensitive, as a result of having disengaged himself from others.

* * *

Life without a programme. No wonder the parents showed no surprise, no objection, no regret, when the son broke off his studies at the Faculty of Commerce, after spending a year there which had started out for him with no anxieties or fixed dislikes, but left him with a burning hatred of money and of book-keeping : whenever he swore now, he spat out a figure. They did not react any more strongly when he broke off his study of literature after devoting another year to that : he found that the standards of his mind and his language had been depraved, and that he was taking to a fatuous prattle. He followed this with a year spent idling at home : this fundamentally altered his life, for when it was over, he had altered his attitude. He found himself entering the Faculty of Law, and applied himself to his studies there, passing his examinations every year, though he was placed every time at the bottom of the list. His mind found rest in his studies there : he settled into them, and came within a year of graduation. He liked the way that the Law cut itself off so totally from the ordinances of nature, with their confusion, their contradictions, their claim that injustice was sometimes true justice in disguise, their lack of any final settlement — or, at the most, their postponing of it until the whole world lay in ruins. The Law has invented for itself a self-supporting logic which looks beautiful on paper, distinguished by ingenious subdivisions and sequences, and swift to take effect; as though it has demolished the structure of life, and has turned the rubble into numbered and catalogued matrixes with which it has built its own stronghold. A judge does not pronounce judgment by drawing upon his knowledge of truth — he relies upon paper — for Paper is clearer than Truth. A judge will reject any truth, as easily as a lie, unless it is supported by juridically-admissible evidence which has not been shown to be spurious. He gives vice clearly-defined limits; while virtue becomes a vague notion which is not taken into account at all : the judge imposes his penalty upon the adulterous husband, but does not grant a reward to a husband who remains faithful to his wife after their honeymoon is over.

With all this, the virtue of the law is that it relieves mankind by converting the world of the spirit into logical argumentation where there is no distinction between knowledge and ignorance, between freewill and the determined : it has dropped the word *fate* from the vocabulary of man, and in so doing it has at the same time dropped the word *pity*. No matter, for such is the logical sequence of arguments which the law follows; and however many injustices it may involve, a logical sequence of arguments is to be preferred to a just law which has no discernible logical structure. Forensic logic is so different from the logic of nature's ordinances, that little by little, the young man lost the sense of there being any distinction between virtue and vice. A beggar, who always receives and never gives, withdraws from the bustle of life, lies down on the pavement in front of a mosque, and lays his chest bare; he gives it up both to sunlight and to swarms of lice : and when the two streams that flow over his breast blend together, he finds a delight which makes him at one and the same time whimper with pain and quiver with pleasure.

* * *

During the period that the young man spent idling at home between his year as a student of literature and the beginning of his law-studies, it was natural that one occupation should present itself as a cure for his torpor — an occupation which, of all others, is the simplest to enter upon, the easiest to continue in, the worthiest, the truest and most sensible — and that is the occupation of a husband. He was a virgin, but was determined that the woman he married should be one who was sexually experienced. He decided to make his choice without any intervention from his parents, to pick for himself the workshop that was going to yield up its products for him. He did not run through the list of his relations and neighbours and acquaintances, but seated in his own home, like a priest anointing an emperor, he stretched out his arm upon the head of a penniless girl, and he uttered the one brief phrase, "This one !" like a child in a toyshop. It filled him with boundless joy to think that he had returned to nature and her ways, and had trampled underfoot all the conventions which men had thought up for the winning of a wife : the pursuit, the cornering of the quarry, the carrying off of the prize, the deed of purchase, the hero's proving his prowess in battle, the courtship, the sleepless pillow and the sighings. Sometimes he smiled to himself because he had surmised by sheer mother-wit, without any direct knowledge of the matter, that the unrealized cause of the misery of modern woman is that she has inherited traits from every one of her ancestresses, and wishes her husband to win her by combining all these devices together and bringing them into play, although she falsely claims that because she is a civilized person, courting is the only method it is necessary to use. Why should he bother himself with all this palaver ?

The penniless girl, together with her mother, used to come on visits with her father, who was a tenant on the land owned by the young man's family. They came to town whenever the half-yearly instalments of their rent were due. For a dress, she still wore the old-fashioned *malas* of crinkly dyed silk; on her feet, instead of shoes, she wore slippers. She only revealed the tiniest portion of her face; in the grip of a crushing shyness, she would have buried herself in the ground if she could whenever anyone addressed her. He mentally added up her pink ankles and those parts of her face that he had managed to catch a glimpse of, and decided that it was she who would suit him. A simple, raw girl. Downcast eyes that dared not glance at you. A forehead free of any thought. A body in which the finer points of every part had been distributed in common throughout the whole. Matted hair which you could see would be bewitching once it was washed, and once it had been plaited so that it would hang upon her forehead and cheeks : he would rinse it for her with his own hands, and his tongue would find that the taste of soap could intoxicate as well as wine.

He knew that she had already been married to a relation of hers in their home village. The husband had had a rival who had a feud with him. Maliciously vindictive, he would not let him enjoy his newlywed bride in peace, but lay in wait for him when he was on his way home from the fields, and emptied bullets into him from a home-made rifle that he had bored for himself. A mangled corpse was carried home to the bride : she wiped the wounds with her handkerchief and in this way it became bloodstained for the second time in one week.[1] To the young man, then, she was all that he could have hoped for : an easy path to take, already opened up and smoothed out for him by someone else. In the same way if he had bought an earthenware pot,

(1) A reference to the old-fashioned wedding-night custom by which the blood from the torn hymen is made to soak into a handkerchief, which can then be offered as proof that the bride had been a virgin.

turned and fired for use, he would have left it for someone else to dirty his fingers and scratch them in lining its inside with oil, so that he could use it for cooking. The girl was a better proposition than such a pot, because she was ready moistened — moist with blood, even if the outer layer of it came from the wounds of her murdered husband.

In order to complete his fancy, the young man set out to furnish the bridal-chamber which he had set aside for himself in his family home, in the style of a peasant of his wife's own class : a rush-mat at the edge of which slippers and wooden clogs were to be taken off and lined up; an iron bedstead with wooden planks stretched across it, and a mosquito-net of pink silk; a wooden chest to store clothes in, painted red and green, a basin and jug for washing. But when the bridal equipment was ready, he was taken by surprise to see her lips draw up and whisper in her mother's ear, after which she turned her face to the wall out of excess of shyness, keeping hold of her mother's hand and tugging at it, to make sure that she did not start saying anything while she was still in the room.

As soon as the young man was alone with his mother-in-law, she told him that what her daughter had whispered to her was, "As I'm marrying a Cairo man, and such a high-class man at that, I'd like to have at least a spring mattress on my bed instead of those planks of wood."

On that spring mattress the young man received the deepest shock of his life; it shook his being, and brought his illusions tottering down; it left him naked in their ruins, nursing the wounds of his bewilderment.

On the wedding-night itself, the raw simple girl turned into a fierce wild beast, the downcast eyes gleamed like the eyes of a pouncing hawk, sending into the darkness of the night a glimmer like the flash of a sword or the sudden flaring-up of a smouldering fire; enough to set a brand ablaze, it was a thing that not the waters of all the sacred rivers flowing together could have quenched; it was a look that rasped his body like a file. The forehead that never gleamed with a single idea now had drawn upon it, in place of the smooth blankness of resignation, the execution order of a Court of Summary Justice that allowed no deferment and no appeal. The delicate, ever-closed lips opened and closed in audible smacks, and never kept the one shape for a single moment : at one instant, it was the circular brink of a volcano; the next, it was the inside of a funnelshaped vortex; next, a long slit like a dagger-wound; spasm succeeded spasm as though her gullet contained a grapnel which was being handled by a merciless grip. The open mouth revealed a set of teeth which gleamed with hunger, and dispelled the surrounding shadows by sending them scattering in alarm. The parts of her body which had pleaded that they had lost their individual attractions by having shared them out in common amongst them all, each retrieved its rights and in addition seized and used as its own the enticements that are proper to a body as one single whole. Even her big toe reared itself up and tried to overreach itself. Her voracity was intensified by an underlying contradiction : the palms of her hands lay flat, resigned, passive, bestowing themselves, her arms were limp, the saliva of her mouth was cool and sweet as honey, and her breathing came like that of an innocent babe.

What was he to do ? He came from a family which had never given anything of itself : he wanted a goblet of wine that he could swallow down in one gulp, not one that glued itself to his lips like a leech. He had sought his own pleasure, but before he could take it, he was caught in the grip of a liability. He could only accept a liability that he had undertaken of his own free will; he hated any obligation that was imposed upon him, like a poll-tax or a tribute — it was an invasion of the privacy behind which his self-respect preened itself. His self-respect, which was genuine enough, and true to itself, was a thing he was well satisfied with — so long as it remained insulated; he would allow no one else to scrutinize it; it was mortifying to be put in the balance, even if the opposite dish on the pair of scales contained no more than a mustard seed. If any uninvited hand claimed the right to weigh him, to test him, to assess him, then that hand ought to be lopped off.

In spite of his holding this view, he was too astonished to reach any decision. It was the raw simple girl who did so before he did. She bore with him for a second night; on the third, she gave him a kick and said, "We women from Upper Egypt were made for Upper Egyptian men. I piss on your money and your elegance and your fine words."

And she added, as though a prophetic voice spoke through her, "Find yourself a mummy all daubed with white and black and red : there's thousands of them in this town of yours."

She got up and gathered her few pieces of clothing together. In spite of his astonishment, the young man noticed for the first time the fine bridge of her nose, her long, slender neck, and a pair of firm haunches that the noblest Arab mare would have envied.

In the morning it was she who dragged her mother away by the hand, and glided out gingerly as though she were escaping from a captor who had fallen asleep and who might wake up at any moment; her crinkly *malas* of black silk hung forward, making her look as though she were preparing to run for it the moment she had got past the door. And so her second marriage, also, lasted less than a week. When her mother caught a glistening in her eyes of what she took to be the vestiges of tears, she said to her, "Don't you grieve over him : God will send you better than that. This was your lot, and you had to go through with it."

And the daughter replied to herself, "You're so kind, mother, and such a fool ! If I were to cry, it would be for my first husband all over again."

* * *

After that, the young man could only satisfy his urges and heal his wound by visits to women who traded in passions; none of them had any rights over him. and he had no liabilities towards any; he was happy to deal in cash purchases and not barter — a primitive method which time and progress have overlaid and buried. He made no distinction at first between any one of these women and another. But, after some time, he began to spruce himself up, and to search out the ones who attracted purchasers to their wares with the same draw that a lump of sugar has for a swarm of flies. The larger the swarm, and the more completely he was swallowed up in it, the more it pleased him :

it made him feel that his face had become a mask. But he did not find the absolute pleasure he had hoped for : even with the ones in briskest demand, he thought he detected some turn of the head, some curl of the lip, some thrust of the arm, which upset his assurance. What he wished for now was a woman whose face would remain frozen in perfect stillness, even if it had to be made of wax, with lips rigid as wood, or fashioned in a mould, a woman who could not move her arms, even if that meant that she would be as cold as ice..and where should he find one like that ?

* * *

No one can tell what would have become of him if he had not had a strange illness which kept him in bed for some time. The doctors said that it was a minor infection, a harmless microbe which is present even in the bodies of the fit, where the red corpuscles easily destroy it without artificial aid. His body, however, was unable to resist it, not because of any organic deficiency, but because he had lost his will to resist. Every medicine they gave him was so much lost effort : his physical frame became a field tussled over by the sweetness of life and the putrescence of decay.

It seemed animated by mere clockwork. He was like a breathing creature under whose skin every morsel of flesh had been eaten away by a gangrene, leaving nothing but the look that gleamed out of his eye-socket. The doctors recommended his father to consult a psychologist.

This piece of advice stung the young man to the quick. As soon as the doctors were out of the house, he got up, and went to the bathroom to draw the evil out of himself, and put the past behind him : he washed himself, purified himself, reaffirmed his faith. Freshened-up, his face, when he emerged, wore a look of content, of gentleness. His movements and gestures fell into a harmonious order, and grew unusually calm. As a result of this, in the days that immediately followed, some people looked upon him as dull-witted, although he thought of his mannerisms as the height of elegance, and now paid great attention to his fingernails and necktie, and saw to it that his clothes matched one another.

He took to moving with a demureness which suggested a woman's coquettishness, to speaking in a low, nasal tone; there was languor in his eyes; although his tall body now stooped slightly, this did not impair his good looks, but added a touch of deference, and, by setting off his head, even gave him, in some people's eyes, a deceptive air of acumen. In fact, to some, his stoop made him seem cunning and inquisitive — though God knows he was innocent of this.

And so that phase of his life came to a close. He entered the Faculty of Law, where his elegance and his sober bearing drew the notice of his fellow-students. They would hover around him, not knowing quite what attracted them to him : could it be his nails, his lithe fingers, the honey that flowed out of his eyes, or the curious quality in his voice ? And yet not one of them advanced his acquaintance with him far enough to become a true friend, to be joined to him in an attachment which would separate them off from the crowd they were in. He did not feel lonely, but was quite at ease : to the honey of his looks he added a sweet-natured smile, which made him into a model of kindness and high-mindedness, in the eyes of the other students : "That", they would say to one another, "is how a really high-born young man behaves."

* * *

It was within a year of his final examinations. He lay on his bed one morning, and glanced out of his window. It was autumn. The Nile had fallen out of its summer stir and back into repose. It had been the liquor of zizyphus fruit coursing down from distant mountains : now it was a muddy browness as scaly as a fish's skin. Exhausted with its work of fecundating the earth, it withdrew into its burrow to hibernate; losing its prowess, it now suggested, more strongly than anything else could, the ague, the darkness of the lower depths, an enormous heaviness. The fields had put well behind them the days when they had been dry and naked, with a cracked skin; now they wore a mantle of blossoms, and offered its nectar to the bees and the grazing herds. A fresh breeze from a blue sky annihilated all malignancy. Lying on his bed, he could see the sky and watch a train of maiden clouds, brightly decked out and freshly combed, making fun of earth-dwellers by mimicking some of the things which can be seen in their lives. An unseen hand had poured out over the world a flood of happiness. A bird flew into view with a broad span of black wings, crying out as it bathed in the sunlight. It was a plover : the cry of that bird, according to his mother, presaged the arrival of a traveller. The bird's call only lasted a brief time, but in those moments were expelled from man all his chains and fetters, his captivity and fears, his uncertainties, delusions, and pollutions, and he became a pure and innocent being, who enjoyed a freedom that had no bounds, fit only for an angel or a fiend. This freedom floated down into the heart of the young man with a tremor. It vexed him that it should be so vigorous, and that it should not make itself fully plain to the limited vision of one who was a cross between angel and fiend. Well, then, he had no need of it. He turned his face to the wall. An appalling weariness seeped into him, and took over the whole of his being : it tinged his gullet with the bitterness of wormwood, it ran in his veins where his blood had run before; his body now sweated it out, his eyelashes were now spun out of it, and the dirt between his toes was now made of it.

* * *

He did not go out that day until later than his usual time. As he stepped out of his doorway, his eyes fell upon the small shop which stood opposite. It had lain empty for many months. Now, he saw that it had been opened up : a man upon a ladder was hanging up a board which read "Undertaker for Whole of Imamein District". His heart sank. Was it a mere chance that one and the same morning had brought him this world-weariness, and had seen the arrival of this servant of death ? Could one of the two be the traveller whose arrival the plover had heralded ? Or were events contrived according to some set plan, working out a pre-arranged purpose ?

He saw the undertaker's apprentice — for that is what he took him to be — urging the workman on the ladder to hurry, with the result that the man misjudged the centre of the rope as he was attaching it to its nail. As soon as the workman had come down off the ladder, the apprentice brought out a coffin and hung it up on one flap of the door. He felt that there was someone looking at him, and he looked up : the two glances met, and the appearance of the apprentice registered itself in the young man's mind in a clear-cut image, standing out from the rest of things, as though he were shining a spotlight onto him through some gaping hole in his own body. He saw a youngish man, with a body bulging like cotton in a hooped bale; stunted in height, with stumpy arms and bulky hands, a low forehead and narrow-slit eyes; his piercing look had the tinselly gleam of sequins, the whites of his eyes setting off a flame-coloured glitter which spoke of cunning and rancour, of a disturbed and malicious spirit and the hunger of an animal : a creature determined to kill a rival with a glance would wear a look like this one. The young man was sure that he had seen this figure before.. But where? He could not tell. Until he remembered that it had been in a book he had read about the theories of Darwin. His look, too; that was the look in his own father's eyes when the time had come for a sniff of cocaine or a shot of opium.

As he turned away, he saw that the apprentice was smiling at him, and raising his had to his forehead in a friendly greeting. He walked away, knowing for certain that he would be coming back to him.

* * *

The friendship between them grew. The young man now took up the habit of spending his evenings sitting in front of the shop with the undertaker's apprentice. At first he used to come to him fully dressed in his suit and shoes; but after some time he gave this up, and saw no reason why he should not come out in slippers, and in the *gallabiyya* which he wore indoors. The apprentice's conversation was all about his work, its seasonal fluctuations, the glories it had known in the past, its pleasures and pains, its ritual and artistry, and the little tricks of his trade. One day he said to the young man :

"You're so interested in everything I say about it — you ask so many questions — you want to know so much; why don't you come with me next time we're sent for ? I can say you're one of our boys. No one will be any the wiser."

In his great boredom, he accepted the offer, and went indoors.

* * *

He had never seen a dead body before. They turned into a narrow, muddy alleyway, towards a house that stood shrouded in silence. When the people in the house noticed them, the building burst out in shrieks, wailings, the striking of cheeks in lamentation, and the pounding of feet upon the flat housetop; the house was behaving like a sick woman at an exorcism, when she hears the drumming of the exorcists starting up. At first, he was dumbfounded, and almost forgot himself so far as to clap his hands over his ears. Then he found himself threading his way through a crowd of small boys who were celebrating the obsequies with jollification : the discrepancy between the sounds and the boys' faces calmed him down. They clambered up a narrow staircase which the apprentice measured with his eyes, to estimate whether it was broad enough for the coffin. When they were inside the flat, the screaming anf wailing, and the striking of cheeks, flared up once again, but in the middle of the uproar, his ears were able to distinguish the hiss of a primus stove, and he realized that they had not forgotten to put some water on the boil for the laying-out. Surrounded by tearful women in black headveils, he nevertheless had the impression that they were receiving him as they would receive a first-aid man. In fact, one old voman patted him on the back and said :

''Come on, sonny; you'll be wanting to get down to your work — and may God send you down His blessings."

He understood now how men of this profession could take a pride in their work and be contented with themselves. The apprentice drew him by the hand into a room where a corpse lay upon a mattress on the ground. He asked him to help carry the body to the bathroom, where the laying-out table, with a can of water upon the primus stove, had been placed, complete with jug and bowl, a loofah, and a piece of soap in readiness. But some of the members of the family were unwilling to allow a strange hand to touch the body until this was absolutely unavoidable, and so it was they themselves who carried it in on to the table : the apprentice then turned them out of the bathroom, allowing only one of them, an old man, to remain there, reciting verses from the Koranic *Sura* of *Yassin* — for a laying-out is not canonical unless a witness is present.

With the deft hand of a pastry cook tossing a pancake, the undertaker's apprentice flung the white sheet off the corpse, so that it seemed to the young man like the wing of some legendary bird flapping above and around him, trying to touch him. Now that the cover had been removed, he stood for the first time face to face with a dead person.

Something that lies outside the division of things into three kingdoms, and forces on to you a new classification into two kingdoms that know no third : into corpses and non-corpses. A solid thing, and yet made of soft flesh, in the shape of a human being, and yet not human — and not animal either, or 'mineral'. What affected him most was that when he looked at it, he could not tell whether he was confronted by a resignation which had reached the point of torment, or a torment carried so far that it passed into resignation. Was this dead body an arrested shriek, or was it the echo of a paean of praise ? Was it a cry of jubilation which meant "I am your servant, o my beloved !"? Or was it a stifling of a moan which tried to say, "Enough, o Lord of mine !" ? Neither. It was simply nothing. And this thing which was no thing was in the form of a human being, but this was not a face that could be averted, this was not a mouth that would screw up in disdain, these were not arms that would push one away.

The young man's fear dissolved, and he fell to washing the corpse, gently, with a pitifulness that made the undertaker's apprentice lose his patience.

"Come on," he cried, "Hurry up — before they hide the counterpane from us."[1]

* * *

It now became his habit to come down to the shop every day in *gallabiyya* and slippers; he insisted on accompanying the apprentice

(1) As in the preceding story, Hakki alludes to the fact that undertaker's men regard the dead man's quilt as a perquisite of theirs.

whenever he was sent for — in fact he would hurry to the address before the other did. A day that passed without a body seemed dull and colourless. He worked with the ardour of a passionate craftman. His hands were eager to finger the merchandise all over. At first sight, all corpses may look much the same, but to the contemplative lover every one is different : Does it have open palms or clenched fists ? Are the legs outstretched ? Or are the knees bent, so that the legs are raised up stiffly towards the breast, like those of a newborn child, and the undertaker's apprentice has to press down upon them with all his weight in order to get the body into the coffin, and he sometimes wishes he had a hammer or a saw with him ? A dwarf as heavy as lead. A giant as light as a feather. A corpse which is nothing more than rotting flesh upon decaying bones. Another which is a filled-out balloon. A face convulsed in fear. A face in repose, as though it were enjoying the calmest of rests.

The undertaker's apprentice realized that the young man could no longer leave him : he saw his smile becoming sweeter and gentler, and his eyes more langorous, while his body grew more softly pliable. When he sat with the young man now, he would sidle up right next to him, put his arm round his shoulders and then let it drop round his waist. Whenever he spoke to him it would be in a whisper during which he held his mouth to the young man's ear. When he thought that his dish was cooked, he whispered one day :

"If you don't know what to do with yourself, just put yourself in my hands. Come on. Don't be standoffish. Don't be afraid. It's quite dark on the inside of the shop. And there's a big coffin there that'll take the two of us."

The young man brushed off these assaults, but he never complained or showed any anger : his thoughts were wandering in the dream kingdom of the grave.

* * *

The undertaker's apprentice resorted to a ruse which he had picked up from others of his kind. When the young man joined him on the day when he put it into operation, he made a point of keeping his distance, as though he had given up hope, or had come to his senses. He gave him no particular attention, but fell to making general reflexions, cursing the times and regretting the old days. When he felt that the young man had been lulled into lowering his guard, he broke off his chatter and exclaimed that he had suddenly remembered a piece of news of prime importance.

"Have you heard ? That woman who's our opposite number in the trade tells us that this blessed morning she's had the biggest day's takings that she's ever made in the trade and that she's ever likely to make in it to the end of her life. She was sent for to lay out a bride. Comes of a rich lot and was to have got married the next day. Her white dress was hanging up ready for her. The wedding attendant turned up and went into the bathroom with her to get her spruced up. She's hardly scrubbed her down, and she's just got up from beside the washstand to spray a bottle of scent over her, when she holds her hand to her heart and gives one sigh — and she's gone. They had music at the funeral, and they've strewn the ground over her grave with henna. And what's more, they insisted that she should have her wedding dress on, and her head wreathed with jasmine."

A bride in her first youth, bathed twice over and lying in her wedding-gown with flowers strewn over her. And tonight a new moon.

"Fair or dark ?" the young man asked with a catch in his throat.

"Dark. They say she may have come from Upper Egypt."

When he heard that, he jumped up and seized the undertaker's apprentice by the collar.

"Show me the way to her grave," he pleaded hoarsely.

And the man whispered back :

"On condition that you won't refuse, this time. On condition that you'll let me."

Two shadowy figures hurried off in the dark — a ravenous animal which would have swallowed gravel, and a broken, putrescent spirit from whom God had withdrawn His mercy.

* * *

One morning a message comes to the family from the hospital : their man of mark can no longer cut any figure in this world. His bed is empty, and waiting for a new occupant.

Translated by Mahmoud Manzalaoui; revised by Leonard Knight and Lewis Hall.

NANNY KARIMA AND THE HAMMAM

Saheir el Kalamawi

SAHEIR EL KALAMAWI, (b. 1911) a member of our editorial committee, belongs to the first generation of Egyptian women to enter the field of university teaching. She was until recently Professor of Modern Arabic Literature and Chairman of the Department of Arabic at the Faculty of Arts of Cairo University; she is now Director of the Egyptian General Organism for Information, Publication, Distribution and Printing. Her schooling was at an English school in Cairo; this was followed by studies at the American University in the same town. She then studied in Paris, and was one of the first modern Arab scholars to give serious critical attention to the *Arabian Nights*; her Arabic study of this collection was published in Cairo in 1939. Saheir el Kalamawi's stories have appeared regularly of recent years in the monthly *Al Hilal*.The present story,which is from the collection *Ash-shayāṭīun talhū* (*The Devils Sport*), carries on the vein of family reminiscences which is found in her first collection *Aḥādithu-jaddatī* (*Tales of My Grandmother*), 1936.

I still remember the small room which belonged to 'Nanny' Karima, my grandfather's black freedwoman.[1] It was furnished with the utmost simplicity, isolated on the roof of my grandfather's house behind a rough wooden door.

As children, curious to see what she was doing, we often wandered into her room. Sometimes we would go there in her absence, tempted by the possibilities of mischief.

The dominant colour was spotless white. On her head Karima always wore a white head-veil and the bed-sheets too were dazzlingly white. Nothing was hung on the walls, leaving their pristine whiteness undisturbed. There were two windows in the room; a west window

(1) After the manumission of slaves, in the last quarter of the nineteenth century, many stayed on with their former masters as free domestic servants.

which caught the soft rays of the setting sun, and an east window which for a few moments caught the early morning light. So the sun was never seen there for very long. Our particular goal was usually the window facing east, because it looked down onto he lower roof, over the *hammam* of my grandfather's great house. This roof was inset with upturned bowls of red, green, yellow and blue glass; each bowl being topped by a small, thick, round knob. The sun's rays, striking the glass, were filtered down to the room below as a gentle coloured light that danced on the white marble paving of the large *hammam* on the ground floor.

This *hammam* was no longer in use because modern bathrooms had been installed in each of the flats into which some wings of my grandfather's house had been divided. Ever since we had become aware of our surroundings the old *hammam* had held the aspect of a haunted room, a place of unholy terror, deserted by human beings, but frequented by ghosts and demons. We loved going up to Nanny Karima's to pelt the attractively coloured glass with marbles and pebbles; and when the smashed glass tinkled down to the floor we would shiver with delight. Then, jumping out of the window, clutching an outstretched hand or leaning on the shoulders of the one of us who had gone before, we would peer down through the broken glass to learn the secret of that strange room. What met out eyes was unforgettable, a unique sight. Below us lay a wide marble hall. Against the walls there were thick marble basins; whose rims bore richly veined carvings. The walls also were of marble and where the basins touched them they too were decorated with carvings with the same veining. The coloured lights played everywhere with a delightfully irridescent effect.

All this abandoned splendour was coated with a thin film of dust and cobwebs, which gave it an air of age and decay and brought out the magnificence of the tinted marble.

Sometimes we would catch a glimpse of the feathers of a dead sparrow that the hall had held captive until it died amidst such confined beauty, its heart consumed by a yearning for space and freedom.

We felt no aversion for the dust; for twice a day our mother would send us out of her own flat to play in the courtyard of the big house, and there we spent our mornings and afternoons, entirely covered with dust. We felt almost a comradeship with all that dust, and we would wipe it off the glass bowls to make the colours shine more brightly, using the handkerchiefs which were intended for our hands and eyes.

If we were ever surprised by Nanny Karima during these escapades on the *hammam* roof she would scream at us and threaten to report us to our mother or grandfather. Then, smothering her with hugs and kisses, we would cajole her with entreaties until, at last relenting, she would dissolve in laughter, showing her white teeth, which looked whiter still against her dark skin. Then we knew that she had taken pity on us : there would be no report, no spanking, no scolding. She would wash our hands and faces. When, in gratitude, we offered her the sweets that usually happened to be in our pockets she would refuse laughingly and bless us saying : "God preserve you, little ladies, and little masters !". If we insisted, she would answer more firmly : "God be praised, I have everything I need."

This little episode would take place again and again, every week-end holiday, and it must have been one of the principal reasons for our drawing closer to Nanny Karima. Our playing on the roof of the *hammam* had become a tremendous shared secret which drew us together with her into a hidden order. Karima had no real friends in the household and I can see now that she was afraid we might suddenly stop coming to see her, for our visits were very welcome, even though they could have led to unpleasant results. Had we been wiser we would have known that she would never have reported us. We might have spared ourselves the cautious stealth and dissimulation of our manoeuvres. It was more than likely that she would have turned a blind eye to our activities.

Karima was, by nature very quarrelsome and a day never passed without at least one violent argument between her and the staff of the big house. In her eyes they were nothing but servants, but she was in the position of a daughter to the Master of the House himself. She called them lazy and filthy — while she was active, clean and hard-working. We had no conception of the vital part she played in the household. We would simply see her at work in the ironing-room, standing in front of a pile of dazzlingly white washing. She used a long pair of tongs for putting hot charcoal into the heavy iron which she wielded with rapid and energetic movements. It never occurred to us to ask why this work was without end, and we always heard her cursing vehemently when linen had to be starched. The time and effort were more than she could spare, over and above the ironing of table-cloths, bedspreads, blouses and other clothes. Besides all this, she was even obliged to iron the men's suits, as well as my mother's complicated and heavily pleated dresses.

Her love for the children of the household was deeply sincere. Certainly she used to beat us, but I cannot recollect her ever doing so unless it were for that greatest sin of all, dirtiness. How many times she would call out to us, "Children, cleanliness is next to Godliness : are you not true Believers ?"

Late one afternoon, there was a slight drizzle and we crept stealthily away to play among the puddles on the roof. Fortunately for us, Karima was not in her room. As usual she was in the laundry-room, engrossed in her ironing, and the hiss of the stove prevented her from hearing our footsteps. We climbed out of her window, down to the roof of the *hammam*, and lifted some of the glass bowls out of their sockets in order to let the rain water drip into the room. We hoped it would wash the floor and make it shine, allowing the coloured light free play upon the marble surface. We broke a lot of glass that day, some by accident and some by design. We fought among ourselves to peer through the several peepholes. Our faces became covered with mud as we pressed them against the holes in order to see better, the rain-drenched light being too weak. Suddenly we felt Nanny Karima's black face looking down upon us from her window. This time she threatened, in a voice carrying the utmost conviction, to take the matter up with our mother, "Because", as she said, "it is raining." So we rushed to her and went through the same rigmarole which ended as usual at the door of our own flat as if nothing had happened.

That evening, when my mother was combing my hair before putting me to bed, she suddenly noticed that one of my ear-rings was missing. I was terrified and felt the blood throbbing in my temples as I struggled to find an answer to her questions. My mother scolded me. It was at least the twentieth time that I had lost a piece of jewellery. How many ear-rings, bracelets and rings had been mislaid ! My mother had punished me by forbidding me to wear any kind of jewellery for a whole month. Then I had been forgiven and she had offered me a pair of precious ear-rings. Now I was left staring at the one that remained, tempting and costly — my mother had drawn it off my ear crying : "What a waste of good jewellery ! If there were such a thing as tin ear-rings, that's what you'd deserve !" I gazed at the solitary ear-ring, bidding it, and all its kind, a silent farewell, but my eyes, as usual, were dry. This always irritated my mother all the more; she supposed that my lack of tears was due to my insensibility : in fact, I became obstinate and defiant in the face of her vehement reproaches.

My mother began to question me about my movements during the day. I was able to recall everything except the episode on the *hammam* roof. The servants searched everywhere and my sister helped them, trying, as usual, to shield me. Karima appeared and rushed up to my mother asking with a touch of haughtiness for the cause of the upheaval. When told, she muttered angrily, complaining about my mother's treatment of me and assuring her that one of the slovenly maids from the Big House must have filched the ear-ring. As she said : ". . Why blame my own little mistress when you allow such dreadful women in the house ?" Nanny Karima's anger turned against my grandfather's laxity in allowing such riff-raff to serve in the household. At the end of the harangue, her anger broadened to embrace present-day morals. Whenever Nanny Karima digressed about the age she lived in, it became impossible to stop her or even to follow her — so violent and rapid was her torrent of words. "What changes since the good old day ! At one time there were only decent black servant girls in the house and the whole house was clean and tidy. There was no thieving in those days, and no negligence !" But times had changed; Amna had married, and Zaafarana and Mabrouka had followed her example. She was left alone to undergo the humiliation of living in the age of decadence into which the Big House had fallen, especially in so far as servants were concerned. Only that execrable foreign woman remained, and only the black *man* servants, without whom all hope of better days would have been irretrievably lost .. These local girls were the source of all the trouble. For Karima they were strange creatures,a blend of dirtiness and sloth and moral depravity — naturally they were capable of any treachery or theft. It was more than likely that they had stolen the ear-ring, given that their dissolute ways were enough for a regiment of thieves. That any servant dare laugh in front of her was to Karima a sign of tremendous impudence, unless, of course, she had first encouraged it — or at least given her permission : in that case, she would give her blessing by flashing her teeth in a gleaming white smile.

As soon as Nanny Karima had left the room and her voice could only be heard in the distance, my mother beat me, for she was afraid to lift a finger in front of Nanny Karima. I was ordered to bed. It was still raining and the faint monotonous sound of the rain falling in the street weighed down my eyelids, but I was so frightened that I could not take my eyes off the street lights which I could see through the gaps in the shutters, flickering in the wind.

I cried for a whole hour. In the meantime, my sister tried to console me. She promised to lend me her own ear-rings and bracelets for school the next day, but nothing could stop my tears. Suddenly, in a flash, I remembered the *hammam* roof and the thrilling games we had played on it that day. Perhaps the ear-ring had fallen off then ? But my sister protested, "We can't look for it now, it's too late." "*We* can't go", I replied, "but Nanny Karima can." But how were we to reach her ?

I sat up in bed and thought hard. Once my plan was made I slipped out of the bedroom but my mother called after me. I answered that I was only going to the bathroom. Instead, I went to see Baheyya, the little maid whom Karima hated so much. I begged her to give a message to Karima, in spite of the bad feeling that lay between them. I returned to my room hastily and found my sister holding her breah in expectation and fear.

Time passed slowly. After an hour or so, we heard the doors being flung open and noticed that the lights had been turned on. Nanny Karima, deeply incensed, stormed into my mother's bedroom. She wore a triumphant expression on her face for she had — she claimed — found the ear-ring on the steps of the big house. No doubt some thieving girl, whose identity God alone knew, had dropped it there. There had been no reason to upset her little mistress or even to have punished her. My mother, furious, scolded Karima for her folly in disturbing the entire household at such a late hour! This, on account of an ear-ring ! Karima retorted by saying that in that case there was no point in severe punishment for the sake of an ear-ring and no point in getting rid of servants who were nothing but treacherous thieves. And if you accepted dishonesty in small matters you would have to accept it in large ones. There was very much more in the same vein of which I understood little. However, although the ear-ring had been found, in my mother's view there was no reason to mitigate the punishment. The mere fact that it had fallen from my ear at all was a sign of negligence, and it might well have been lost for ever. This was her argument for continuing my punishment.

The next day, on returning home from school, we found that events of great moment had taken place. Baheyya told us some of the news in a whisper. We hurried off to Nanny Karima's cosy little room to hear the rest of the story. Baheyya had climbed down from Karima's window with a lantern, but she had not found the ear-ring on the *hammam* roof. Karima had been forced to go into the *hammam* itself. She had managed to open the stiff old door, but with such a loud creak that many of the servants were woken by the noise. Carrying the lantern high, she went inside and discovered the object of everyone's persistent search on the marble floor. Then she left the room, neither closing the door behind her nor returning the lantern to its place. Some of the servants heard her and they seized this opportunity to spread rumours which finally led to a prolonged enquiry. The fact which had lain secret for so many years at last came to light : the fact that we idled away our time playing with the coloured glass on the *hammam* roof. Karima was blamed for not telling our mother of this secret game. She became very cross and retired sulkily to her room. It would not have mattered much if the affair had rested there. But a mason was sent for and hired to come the next day, fill in the gaping holes in the roof and take away all the glass. Looking out of Nanny Karima's window we were met with the sight of black holes, staring at us like the eye sockets of a skull — a sort of *memento mori*. We cried and cried and Karima cried with us. Amidst her tears she comforted us by saying that she would buy glass bowls just like the ones that had gone and that she would hide them in her room, letting us play with them whenever we liked. But how could these joys compare with those of the large *hammam* and the pretty coloured lights playing on its floor and walls ? Could she buy us a new *hammam* ?

The following day, on returning from school, we found the roof white with plaster, and there were other signs too of that most hateful business. Saddest of all was Nanny Karima .. The same day she went out to buy medicinal herbs, at least that is what she told them in the house. She said that she intended to retire to her room for a month, a practice she adopted every year at some stage, in order to collect her thoughts and pray. When my mother chided her, saying a twelve-month had not yet passed since the last retreat, she muttered that, if she had had another home, she would have gone to it. Her old master would never have tolerated such a degrading insult to her dignity, she complained. She continued this strain for some time, so much so that everybody was reduced to silence.

That night we crept stealthily to Nanny Karima's room and discovered, wonder of wonders, a large box heaped up with coloured glass bowls. We played with them and held them up against the light, but our spirit was dampened. We looked towards the window, but did not have the courage to lean out and look at the wide roof stretched out below. The magic had fled, for the roof had ceased to be a playground for our boisterous games. Gone too was our enjoyment of the lights and colours that had played their beautiful symphony on the resplendent marble. Alas, we were never again to see the *hammam* with its dust, lights, cobwebs and marble. But Nanny Karima's gleaming black face was transfigured by tenderness and her triumphant smile flashed consolation. And so we accepted her comforting — what other choice was there before us ? We flung ourselves at Nanny Karima and covered her with kisses. But this time our little ceremony remained unfinished. Karima did not wash our hands, dust our clothes and tidy our rebellious hair, in order to shield us : we stood before her, clean and tidy, with lumps in our throats. Our hearts were filled with a cold resignation and an obscure nostalgia for the beauty that had been. When we left her, we had calmed down : we were untroubled by anxiety or fear — we had also lost our previous exhilaration. We felt that something had come between us and Nanny Karima, for we no longer had our fascinating secret for her to share with us.

In the night, we were haunted by dreams. And the fleeting years have glided by, yet to this day the memory of Nanny Karima's face and the *hammam* is imprinted on our minds.

Translated by Magdi Wahba; revised by Ronald Ewart.

THE MOSQUE IN THE NARROW LANE

Naguib Mahfouz

NAGUIB MAHFOUZ is the outstanding novelist of the Arab world. Born in 1911, he graduated in philosophy from Cairo University in 1934. His first publication had already appeared in 1932, and he has since produced some twenty volumes of fiction. After a start in the historical novel,he turned to realistic descriptions of Cairo life, usually setting his work a generation or so before the date of writing, and often, especially in his trilogy (*Bayn ul-qaṣrayn, Qaṣr-ush-shawq, As-sukkariyya,* — the titles are names of districts of Cairo) showing an awareness and a skillful portrayal of the gradual changes brought into Egyptian life in the twentieth century by the passing of time. In his third and most recent phase, to which both these short stories belong, but which is best illustrated in the novel, he has turned to more subjective themes, dealing in particular with individual heroes in search for an identity. In the novels of this phase, symbolism, allegory, and a Faulknerian blend of past and present, internal and external, play a significant part. Mahfouz is at present Director of the Cinema Organization of the UAR Ministry of Culture. His novels have been adapted to the screen, television, radio and the stage, with very varying degrees of success and sensibility, by a variety of adaptors: among the successful adaptations may be mentioned the film of *Bidāya wa nihāya* (*A Beginning and an End*), in which Omar Sherif starred.

Although primarily a novelist, with the novelist's need for a spacious canvas and for leisurely development of themes, Mahfouz attempted the short story at the start of his career (his first collection dates from 1938) and returned to it in 1960, having freed himself from the melodrama and surprise endings which had revealed the hold over him of such models as Maupassant. Both the stories by which he is represented here are from the collection *Dunya-llāh* (*The World God Created*), published in 1964. The stories touch upon the two questions which run through Mahfouz's later work: the problem of true identity, and the difficulty of coming to terms with one's environment—or, more basically,of being clear to one's own satisfaction what the true relationship is between self and environment. There is a very full bibliography of works by and concerning Mahfouz on pp. 346-54 of Shukri Ghaly's critical study of this writer, entitled *Al-muntamī* (*The Insider*), Cairo 1964. Mahfouz states that he has read and been influenced by many European writers, ranging from Dostoevski to Mann.

It was time for the afternoon address and, as usual, only one outsider was present. Ever since the arrival of Sheikh Abdu Rabbuh as Imam of the Mosque, only *Am*[1] Hassanein, the vendor of sugar-cane juice, had come to hear him at that time of day. Out of respect for the idea of a sermon and deference to the Imam, the muezzin and the mosque servant made a habit of coming too. One might have expected Sheikh Abdu Rabbuh to be vexed by this, but with time, the Sheikh had resigned himself. Perhaps, too, he had expected a worse plight when he was first appointed to this mosque on the outskirts of the red light district. He had resented the transfer and had tried to have it rescinded, or changed to an appointment elsewhere, but, in the end, very much against his wish, he had been obliged to accept the post, and submit, as a concomitant, to the derision of his rivals, and the banter of his friends.

And who would come to the sermon ? The mosque stood at the crossroads of two lanes : one was an alley noted for the debauchery that occurred there, and the other housed procurors, pimps, and narcotics dealers. It seemed that the only pious man in the whole quarter, or even the only normally decent man, was Am Hassanein, the fruit-juice man. For a long time, the Sheikh had shuddered every time he chanced to look up the alleys, as if he feared the contact with lewdness and crime would contaminate his soul if he were to breathe too deeply. In spite of all this he delivered his sermons with a regularity which was paired by Am Hassanein's regularity in attendance. He once said to the juice vendor : "You'll soon become an Imam yourself, and people will be quoting you as an example and an authority." The old man smiled timidly, "Oh ! I have still so much to learn.."

The homily that evening was on purity of conscience, considered as the basis of sincerity and integrity in a man's dealings with himself

(1) 'Uncle'.

and with others, and with the act of contrition as a commendable practice for starting the day. Am Hassanein listened intently as usual. But he rarely asked questions, except for an occasional enquiry about the meaning of a verse in the Koran, or the practice of the ordinances.

From the southern window of the mosque, looking in the direction of prayer, one had a full view of the lane where the brothels were situated. It was a long and narrow lane, crooked in parts, with doors of dilapidated houses and cafés on both sides. It had a strangely stirring effect on the senses. At this time of day the district seemed to wake up and stretch as if after a long sleep, and to prepare for the evening. People spattered the ground with water from pails, doors were opened furtively in answer to knockings which were in fact pre-arranged signals; chairs were set in order in cafés; women appeared at the windows, smartening themselves up between snatches of conversation; brazen laughter echoed in the air; incense burned in hallways. A woman could be heard crying, with the voice of the *madame* urging her to pull herself together, in order that they might not lose more money : it was enough that her pimp had lost his life in a brawl. Another woman laughed hysterically because she was unable to forget her friend who had been killed as she sat next to her. A gruff voice was heard to say indignantly :

"Even a European ! Who would have expected it ! How could a European have ditched Fardos ! Fleeced her of a hundred pounds and then disappeared."

Voices rehearsed an obscene song, which was to be performed later. At the end of the lane a fight was taking place; it began with a simple exchange of words and ended with chairs being thrown. Libliba slipped out and sat in the doorway of the nearest house. A street lamp had already been lit. One could feel the lane coming to life.

One day, Sheikh Abdu Rabbuh was summoned by telephone to the office of the Inspector General in charge of Religious Affairs. He was informed that there was to be a general meeting of all imams. Although this was not very unusual, particularly in the circumstances which preceded the summons, the Sheikh wondered anxiously what lay behind it. The Inspector General was a formidable figure who derived his importance from a close family connexion with a certain high official whose name was anathema to everyone. He appointed and dismissed ministers at will and abused the institutions which were venerated by the common people. In his presence, the imams were helpless and would no doubt incur his anger for the slightest thing. The Sheikh murmured a brief prayer of invocation, and prepared himself for the meeting as best he could. He put on a black and almost new *kaftan*, wound his turban round his head, and set off, trusting in God.

He found the corridor in front of the Inspector's room as crowded as if (to use his own expression) it had been the Day of Resurrection. The imams chatted together and asked each other what it was all about. Finally the large door opened and they were allowed to enter the spacious office, filling it to overflowing. The Inspector received them in a dignified and formal manner and listened to the flood of prepared panegyric with a constrained air, trying to suppress an enigmatic smile. When the recitation of complaints ended there was a moment of heavy silence. The mood of expectancy grew more intense : he shifted his glance from face to face. At last, he replied : he responded tersely to their greetings and expressed his confidence that they would live up to the good opinion he had of them. Then, pointing to the photograph above his head, he said :

"It is because of the duties we owe him and the Royal family that we are holding this meeting."

Many of those present felt uneasy, but they did not lose their composure. The Inspector General went on :

"The firm bond that unites you to him is something that can hardly be expressed in words. It is a mutual loyalty, rooted firmly in our history."

The listeners' faces radiated approval, in order to conceal their inner distress, and the official continued :

".. and now, in the face of this storm which is sweeping the country, he is calling upon your loyalty.."

The inward agitation increased.

".. to enlighten the people. You must expose all impostors and agitators in order that the rightful ruler may be firmly established in power."

He continued relentlessly, elaborating upon this theme, then, scrutinizing the faces before him, asked if there were any questions or comments. There was a silence, until one imam, bolder than the rest, pointed out that the inspector had indeed admirably expressed their own inner feelings. If it had not been for their fear of acting without instructions they would already have hastened, of their own accord, to carry out the duties which they were now being called upon to perform. As soon as the inspector began to speak, Sheikh Abdu Rabbuh realized to his relief that they had not been brought here to give an account of their own actions, or to have their attitudes investigated, but rather that the authorities were appealing to them for help. Perhaps even some genuine move to raise their salaries and pensions might result. But his feeling of uneasiness soon returned, just as a wave that beats upon a clear sandy shore inevitably falls back seawards in a thin line of foam. He realized with perfect clarity what he would undoubtedly be forced to say in the Friday sermon things which went against his conscience and were hated by the people. He felt certain that many of the others shared his feelings and were passing through the same crisis — but what could they do ? He went back to the mosque brooding over this new anxiety.

Shaldam, the pimp, a well-known figure in the district, was at that moment holding forth to a gathering of his assistants in the Welcome Bar which stood only a few steps away from the mosque. He seemed to be in a towering rage which augmented with every glass of red wine.

"Nabawiyya — the crazy fool — is in love" he roared, "with that blasted little twerp Hassan. I'm sure of it !"

"Perhaps she just thinks of him as a client, no more than a client.." said one of his cronies, trying to pacify him.

Shaldam struck the table with an iron fist which scattered the lupin seeds and salted peanuts that were being offered as refreshment.

"No !" he said savagely, "he lays her for free. I'm sure of it : as sure as I am that my dagger never misses. He doesn't pay a single millieme and she gives him all kinds of presents."

The faces mirrored a feeling of loathing and the drunken eyes expressed a readiness to co-operate.

"The bloody swine usually comes in when the bitch is doing her turn." He added. "Wait for him to arrive then start a row — leave the rest to me."

They emptied their wine glasses, their eyes reflecting an ominous determination to act.

After the evening prayer, Sheikh Abdu Rabbuh received a visit from two of his college friends, the Imam Khalid and the Imam Mubarak; they informed him gloomily that some of the imams had been dismissed from their posts for refusing to take part in the campaign.

"Places of worship indeed," murmured Khalid angrily, "They were not built for political controversy and not, in any case, to uphold tyranny."

Abdu Rabbuh felt a fresh pang and he retorted with the conventional phrase :

"Do you want us to be reduced to starvation ? Do you ?"

A heavy silence fell. Sheikh Abdu Rabbuh refused to admit defeat and in order to save his face in front of his friends he pretended to be convinced :

"What you consider a controversial point may be the actual truth.."

Khalid, quite amazed at the Sheikh's reversal of attitude, withdrew from the discussion; Mubarak burst out in his usual rash way :

"In that case we shall be doing away with the Islamic precept which tells us to teach what is commendable and to condemn what is evil."

Abdu Rabbuh realized that he was going against his own conscience and this made him all the more angry with Mubarak : "No," he said, "We shall be reviving the Islamic precept that calls for obedience to God and His prophet *and* to the secular authorities."

Mubarak retorted with tremendous indignation :

"And would you call these people *authorities* ?"

"Tell me" said Abdu Rabbuh defiantly, "Are you really going to refuse to deliver the sermon ?"

Mubarak rose and walked away angrily, followed soon after by Khalid. The Sheikh cursed them as he cursed his own conscience.

Around midnight the courtyard of the seventh house on the right-hand side filled up with drunks. They sat on wooden chairs round a sanded area lit by a pressure-lamp; inside the circle, Nabawiyya was dancing. She wore a pink nightgown, holding in her right hand a quarterstaff wound with a ribbon studded with flowers. Hands clapped rythmically and brutish cries of rapture rose from drunken mouths. The pimps sneaked into the yard, and placed themselves in various corners, waiting. Shaldam crouched at the foot of the stairs, his eyes fixed on the entrance.

Hassan made his appearance; his hair was smoothed down and he wore a radiant smile on his face. Shaldam darted vicious glances at him. The newcomer stood watching Nabawiyya. As soon as she saw him, she acknowledged his presence with a large smile, a specially enticing wiggle of her belly, and a wink. Hassan put on a proprietorial air, looked for an empty seat and sat down. Shaldam's blood boiled. His fingers twitched. He gave a light whistle. At once, two of his gang began a sham fight. The others intervened and the fight spread, growing more and more violent. The drunkards, taken by surprise, rose drowsily and made quickly for the door. A chair flew at the pressure-lamp, shattering it : darkness fell heavily on the place. Screams blended with curses and the stamping and shuffling of feet. In the middle of the fray, out of the darkness, a woman's shriek pierced the tumult, followed by a man's agonized cry. The yard was soon empty, except for two bodies which lay in the silent darkness under a cloud of dust.

The following day was Friday. When the time for noon prayers arrived, the mosque was crowded with worshippers. On Fridays, in contrast to weekdays, people came to the mosque from distant parts of Cairo such as El Khazindar and El Ataba. After the recital of the

Koran, Sheikh Abdu Rabbuh stood up to deliver the sermon. The congregation were more astonished than ever he could have predicted, at the political bent of this sermon. They listened and received the rhymed phrases about obedience and the duty of allegiance with both disbelief and irritation. And when the speaker began to condemn the revolutionaries saying that in inciting the people to revolt they were only fostering their own interests, a general murmur filled the mosque; voices rose in indignant protest, and some cursed the imam. Upon this, the police informers who had sneaked in among the worshippers fell upon the most vociferous dissidents and led them away amidst scenes of angry protest. Many people walked out of the mosque; the imam led the rest of the congregation in prayer. It was a sad and gloomy prayer.

Meanwhile, in the second house on the left-hand side of the lane, Samara was entertaining a new customer in her room. She sat on the edge of the bed, half undressed, and reached for a wedge of cucumber from a glass which was half full of water and crunched it between her teeth. On a chair near the bed, sat the client, with his coat off, drinking brandy out of a bottle. His gaze wandered absentmindedly over the bare room and settled on Samara. He put the bottle to her lips, let her take a mouthful, then drew it away. The recitation of the Koran coming from the mosque reached his ear. A ghost of a smile appeared on his face. He lowered his eyes and muttered irritably :

"Why did they have to build a mosque here ? Was there nowhere else ?"

"This place is as good as any other," retorted Samara, nibbling at her cucumber.

He swallowed about two tots of brandy, and screwing up his eyes scrutinized her face :

"Have you no fear of God, woman ?" he asked.

"May God forgive us all.." she replied, rather piqued.

He laughed thinly and reaching for a wedge of cucumber, thrust it whole into his mouth.

Abdu Rabbuh was now delivering his sermon. Samara's customer followed the words, nodding his head as he did so, and then began to smile sarcastically :

"Old hypocrite !" he said, "listen to what he's saying !"

His gaze wandered over the room once more and settled on an old, faded picture of Saad Zaghloul.[1] He pointed to the picture and asked, "Do you know who that is ?"

"Of course I do ! Who doesn't ?"

He emptied the bottle down his throat and said heavily :

"So Samara's a patriot, and the sheikh's a two-faced hypocrite."

"I do envy him !" she sighed. "He makes a fortune just by saying a few words. But the likes of us can only earn a few piastres and that by the sweat of our bodies !"

"They're nothing but a bunch of self-important men" he said sarcastically, "the kind they call 'respectable'. Not really different from you — but who's got the courage to say it ?"

"Everybody knows who killed Nabawiyya, but who's got the courage to name him ?"

He shook his head in sorrow :

"Poor Nabawiyya !" he said. "Who did do it ?"

"Shaldam, God rot his soul."

"Good God ! Anyone who gives *him* away is asking for martyrdom ! Thank God we're not the only sinners in the country !"

"You're wasting a lot of time talking !" she said, very annoyed by now.

Sheikh Abdu Rabbuh decided to exploit the situation at the mosque for his own advantage. He wrote a letter to the Ministry saying that he had been exposed to great danger because of his 'patriotic' sermon. He also managed to get his story into the press in a heavily exaggerated form, emphasizing that police intervention had been needed to protect him and to arrest his assailants. He nourished vast hopes of promotion. However, when it was time for the afternoon homily, there was not a single listener present. He looked across the lane into the fruit-juice shop and caught a glimpse of the owner at work. Thinking that

(1) Egyptian nationalist leader of the nineteen-twenties.

Hassanein had forgotten about the lesson, he took a few steps outside the mosque and called out cheerfully :

"The lesson, Am Hassanein.."

When he heard his name called out, the man automatically looked up, but he then turned his head away with determination, in a gesture of rejection. Abdu Rabbuh was ashamed, and was sorry he had called him. He went inside, heaping curses upon the man.

At daybreak, the *muezzin* climbed the minaret. It was still dark and cool and the full moon shone down in perfect stillness. No sooner had he begun his chant with the words "God is Great" than the air-raid siren burst out in a terrifying, broken howl. The muezzin's heart beat violently; he murmured a silent prayer and prepared himself for a renewal of the call to prayer as soon as the siren should stop. Ever since Italy had declared war on the Allies, the alert had become a common occurence by night, but never developed into anything serious. Putting his heart into it the muezzin chanted "There is no God but God," intoning the call in a fine voice. Suddenly there was an earth-shaking explosion and his voice died away. He stood chilled to the bone, his limbs trembling, staring blankly into the distance, to where a red flame loomed. He took a few heavy steps towards the door, and went down the stairs with shaking knees. He reached the interior of the mosque in pitch darkness and directed his footsteps towards the imam and the mosque attendant, guiding himself by their whispers.

"It looks quite serious, my friend," he said in a quavering voice, "What are we going to do ?"

"The public shelter's too far off," said the imam; his voice slightly hoarse, "and by now it must be filled with the rabble. The mosque is very solid. It'll make an excellent shelter."

They sat down in a corner and began to recite the Koran. From the outside quick footsteps reached them, shouts, agitated cries of advice, the creak of doors opening and closing. More explosions were heard, leaving nerves shattered and hearts beating in silence. The mosque servant suddenly cried out :

"My family is at home, Your Reverence, and the house is rather rickety."

"Put your trust in God.. Don't move from your place," said the imam in a strangled voice.

A group of people rushed into the mosque. Some were heard to say:

"This is the safest place.."

"It's rather serious tonight.." a rough, hoarse voice said.

The imam shuddered at the sound of the voice.. the brute.. surely his presence here was a portent of doom. Another group came in, larger than the first; and women's voices not unknown to the sheikh, were heard.

"The effect of the wine has quite worn off.."

The imam lost his temper. He jumped up and shouted in agitation:

"Off with you to the public shelter. You must have some respect for the house of God. Off with you, all of you..". A man's voice answered :

"Your Reverence — shut up !"

A mocking peal of laughter burst out, to be drowned in a fresh explosion which deafened the ears and left them ringing. The mosque was filled with screams : the imam was terrorized. He yelled savagely as if he were addressing the bombs themselves :

"Away with you.. don't defile the house of God !"

"You ought to be ashamed of yourself !" said a woman's voice.

"Go away!"screamed the imam,"The curse of God fall upon you.."

"This is the house of God, not your own house," answered the woman sharply.

Once again the man called out in coarse tones :

"Do shut your mouth, Your Reverence, or I'll throttle you." An outpour of sharp comments and biting remarks fell on the imam, and the muezzin whispered in his ear :

"Don't answer, I beg of you."

Abdu Rabbuh said with great difficulty :

"Do you think it right that the mosque should shelter the likes of these ?"

"They have no choice." pleaded the muezzin, "Don't you know that this is a district of old houses. They can come tumbling down at a mere knock, let alone a rain of bombs ?"

The imam struck his palm with his fist.

"I wish I could put up with all these vicious rogues," he said. "God must have a special reason for bringing them together here."

A bomb exploded. It seemed to their over-wrought senses that the explosion was in Midan el Khazindar. A flash of light lit up the courtyard of the mosque to disclose terrified figures almost immediately swallowed up in the blinding darkness.

Savage howls rent the air. The women shrieked. Even Sheikh Abdu Rabbuh screamed, unaware to himself. He lost his head and rushed blindly towards the entrance. The mosque attendant ran after him and tried to stop him, but Abdu Rabbuh pushed him away violently and shouted :

"Follow me, both of you, before you perish."

He darted out, shrieking in a tremulous tone :

"God undoubtedly has a design in bringing all these people together.." And he plunged into the thick darkness.

The air-raid lasted for another ten minutes, during which four more bombs were dropped. The city remained wrapped in silence for about another quarter of an hour, and then the All Clear sounded.

Faintly, with the dawn, the darkness dispelled; the morning light was an assurance of safety.

But the body of Sheikh Abdu Rabbuh was not discovered until after sunrise.

Translated by Nadia Farag, revised by Josephine Wahba.

HANZAL AND THE POLICEMAN

Naguib Mahfouz

The sound of heavy footsteps reverberated ominously within his breast, and the 'humph' that accompanied it, was a forewarning of pain and trouble. It was the police-constable approaching in the dark. He longed to run away, but could not. With great difficulty he managed to lift himself up and to throw his weight against the wall at the corner of the lane. He staggered. At any moment now he might collapse. With difficulty he opened his eyes and focused them in the direction of his oncoming doom. Several times, he tried to move in the dark but could not, and his thoughts and recollections were all scattered. His face, colourless, dusty and rugged, looked numb by the light of the street-lamp. He wore nothing but the remains of a torn *gallabeyya* and his frenzied entrails burnt with a craving for the forbidden shot.

"Hanzal, come here .."

That fateful call, that was followed by blows and kicks. In a desperate, sickly voice he pleaded.

"Constable, have mercy on me, for God's sake."

He stood facing him, blocking the light of the street lamp, with his gun hanging from his shoulder. Hanzal pressed himself harder against the wall of Shanafiry Lane. In his fear, he tried to resist the faintness that threatened to overcome him; he whined miserably. But what was the matter ? Why did the policeman not shout and scold and strike ?

"Have you had the shot ?"

"No, I swear I haven't."

"But you're in a stupor, or you seem to be."

"That's because I haven't taken it."

"Come with me, the officer wants you."

There came a sigh from his maddened, famished breast.

"I beg you .." he cried.

But the hand that was laid on his shoulder was not an iron grip, nor was it a policeman's clutch; it was a human hand. Surprised, Hanzal could not utter a word, so the policeman said:

"Come on, don't be afraid."

"I've done nothing wrong!"

He led him along gently and whispered soothingly:

"You'll find that everything's all right. Don't be afraid."

He stood in the superintendant's room, about a yard away from the door, which was closed behind him. He could neither step forward nor raise his eyes and meet the glance that would be directed towards him from a stern face. The bright light shone on his mud-bespattered and almost naked body. Here, between the smooth white walls and the imposing furniture, he appeared like something that time had forgotten. A thunderbolt was what Hanzal expected, but to his surprise the commissioner's tone was a human one. Everything was surprising that night.

"Good evening, Hanzal. Sit down."

God in heaven! What on earth was happening?

"Heaven forbid, sir. I am your unworthy servant."

But the officer cast a reproving look at him and pointed a peremptory finger at a leather armchair. He hesitated for a long while, but seeing that there was nothing for it he gave in and perched himself on the edge of the chair with eyes fixed on his dusty feet. They looked so huge, like the feet of a statue, under their layers of grime. Hanzal could still not really believe these signs of courtesy and in an obsequious voice he said:

"Captain, sir, I'm a poor man with a lot that can be held against me, but my misery is far greater than my wrongdoings .. and in God's eyes mercy is a higher thing than justice."

The officer retorted in a voice that was both gentle and earnest:

"Don't worry, Hanzal. I know your ill doings are very many, but your sufferings are greater. You know your wrongdoings best .. The constable is not to be blamed for his cruelty to you, for the law is the law. But new conditions call for a change of treatment .. a change in everything. As for us, it is true we are policemen, but we are also human."

Full of bewilderment he kept on gazing in wonder at the office while trying very hard to overcome his feeling of faintness. The man cast a pitying glance at him. "Trust in me, Hanzal," he said. "You must believe everything you hear and everything you see. You cannot concentrate because you have not had your shot. All your money is gone, and you have not had your shot. The poison-peddlar has no mercy and wants his price in advance. But you will be cured of all this .."

"I'm a wretch," Hanzal replied, whimpering. "All my life has been sheer bad luck. I used to be strong and now I'm weak. I was a trader and now I'm bankrupt, I've loved and suffered, I've become an addict and a beggar."

"You'll leave the sanatorium a better man and then we shall meet again."

In the yard of the police station he was surrounded by a group of policemen. Instinctively, from habit, he cowered as though to avoid a blow. Their thick lips broke into smiles under wayward moustaches !

"You !"

"Yes, Hanzal. Everything has changed."

"Get well soon, Hanzal."

"Let bygones be bygones."

He was carried away half-asleep and soon gave in altogether, in the carriage that lulled him to infinity. He opened his eyes in a strange room; it was dazzling white and brilliantly lit. He saw a strange face bending over him and he felt weak and sick, afraid and utterly lonely.

"The shot, the shot, Uncle Matbouli !" he humbly begged.

A soft laugh tickled his ear and a pungent smell penetrated his nose. He suffered a devastating hunger in his head and senses; the sides of his head were splitting, then he lost consciousness.

Hanzal left the sanatorium a new man, just as the police officer had promised. His features glowed for the first time and he swaggered along in a voluminous white *gallabeyya*. He had shaved his beard and his moustache looked healthy and strong once more. He wore bright yellow slippers, while the lion tattooed on his wrist was visible again, as well as the bird on his temple under the ornate turban. A policeman walked along with him, like a friend. Everything was friendly. His clear, dark skin gleamed in the sun. He had to laugh; surely, he said to himself, he must have lost weight with all this cleaning. He was wide awake, he could see, he could hear; he loved the police constable and he no longer felt that gnawing pain inside him. He was so full of selfconfidence that he felt he could fly. He had faith in everything around him and was not surprised when police constables came towards him and congratulated him. There, in the yard of the police station, they all crowded round him and cordially shook him by the hand. He was not over-surprised either when he saw the police officer standing up to greet him. He was deeply moved and humbly he stooped forward in order to kiss the officer's hand. But he was received with open arms and embraced with kindness. He broke down with bashfulness and gratitude and his eyes overflowed with tears. The man seated him in the armchair and then went back to his own seat behind the desk. He gave a gentle, clear laugh:

"Congratulations on your recovery," he said.

Hanzal's eyes swam with unshed tears.

"Now you can start afresh," the officer went on.

His tears flowed freely:

"Thanks be to God and to you," he answered.

"Do not exaggerate. Thanks are due to God alone."

The officer then opened a book in front of him and with a pen he wrote something at the top of the white sheet; quietly, with a look in his eyes, as deep as moonlight, he said, "State your wishes, Hanzal." Hanzal was confused and could not reply. His lips moved and with them his uncouth moustache, but he remained tongue-tied. The officer urged him on, "State your wishes, Hanzal. That is an order," he was saying.

"But .."

"No buts — state your wishes."

He hesitated a while, then said, "All I want is God's protection."

"Make yourself clear. State your wishes. That is an order."

Hanzal remembered a mother's prayer, tales at night, tunes on the fiddle; then he chuckled, "I used to go around the streets with a fruit cart," he said.

The officer said :

"A fruit shop in the Hussainia" said the officer, writing in his book, "double shelves, electric light for better display .."

In a daze, Hanzal enquired, "And the money ?"

"Do not trouble yourself, that is our responsibility and a matter for the public concern. Speak up and state your wishes. That is an order."

Hanzal found new courage which he drew from his new personality and from the fruit shop.

"Saneyya Bayoumi, who sells liver." he said in a shaking voice. "The truth .."

The officer interrupted while his hand continued to write :

"No need to explain, everything is known, known to the policeman at the station and by all the other police. Known also to the watchman in the market place. Saneyya is a bold and a pretty girl, and she is not yet married in spite of all that has taken place. There was a time when she was more harm to you than the heroin you were taking. And the crueller she became, the worse your condition grew. She has deserted you, but she will come back to you. Let it be a fruit and liver shop. There will be nothing else like it in the Hussainia. Just like a very exclusive grocer's. Anything else ?"

Greatly moved, he bent his head and, as in a dream, he saw green pastures in which red, purple-fringed flowers grew; and in his ears a tune sounded, repeating the refrain *Tell me my heart's desire.* But then, he saw a dark blur, like a cloud of flies, and his whole body winced.

"I fear, sir," he said, pitifully, "this friendliness of the police may not last; because not the least of my miseries, in the past, was the way the police behaved. They were always after me and my cart, with reason or without; they'd confiscate my stock and beat me up. As for that business over Saneyya, it was Constable Hassouna who first began to turn her head."

The pleasant, clear laugh rose again.

"You will not find one enemy among the police," the officer retorted, in a tone that left no room for doubt. "From now on, and for good, they will be your faithful friends. State your wishes, Hanzal. That is an order."

Hanzal felt an intoxicating courage that had never been his, even in the days of his youthful exploits. A courage that was backed by a fruit and liver shop, by the love of Saneyya and the friendship of the police.

"There's many poor like me," he said, "and you, sir, you probably don't know them."

"I know everything," the officer broke in, though his hand never stopped writing, "Tell us who they are and every one of them will have his shop, his woman and the friendship of the police. All this will come true, and so state your wishes. That is an order."

Hanzal laughed very loud and pressed his hands hard together. "This is too much like a dream," he said.

"Reality is a kind of dream; dreams are a kind of reality. State your wishes. That is an order."

He took a deep, full, confident breath.

"How many prisoners really deserve to be in prison ?" he said, musingly.

The officer answered while his hand still continued to run over the paper :

"Everyone who does not really deserve prison will be let out, even if it leaves the prisons empty."

Full of exaltation Hanzal cried out :

"Long live justice ! Long live the Superintendent !"

The courtyard of Hanzal's house in Shanafiry Lane then witnessed a party of a unique kind, at which the Superintendent and the constables, the poor and the one-time jail-birds were there. Saneyya wore an orange dress with a green shawl round her shoulders so that no part of her plump body was visible, except a wrist adorned with a golden bracelet and an ankle encircled by a silver bangle with dangling crescents. She herself served the drinks, tamarind and *karkadeh* while, in a corner, a band with touch of Mohammed Ali Street blared out its welcome. They all enjoyed their freedom; even the policemen danced and sang under the eyes of their superior officer. Then a Koran-reciter rose amidst his followers and started a chant in praise of the Prophet:

With his advent came the light of truth.

The poor, the ex-convicts and the policemen, all sighed with satisfaction and Saneyya's joyous trilling-cry[1] sounded like the descant of a reed pipe. Then finally, at the close of the festivities, the police officer stood up and addressed them all, and said, "It never rains but it pours .. and these are only the first drops. Goodnight to you all."

Once more, Saneyya uttered her trilling-cry and the guests began to leave. The day was just breaking, the roosters glorified God and the silence glorified Him too.

Hanzal stretched himself on a couch to rest, and Saneyya sat down by his head and toyed with the forelock of his hair. He was happy, peaceful and contented, and wished that things would remain as they were for ever.

"You're the source of all things good," he said gently.

Her fingers went down to his temple as though she wished to feed the bird that was tattooed there. He went on to say :

"I don't think of all that's happened as miraculous. The real miracle is that your heart should have softened after being .."

Her hand slipped down to his cheek, then to his chin and finally rested at this throat. He surrendered himself to her caresses and in the depths of his heart he longed for this moment never to end. But,

(1) Uttered by women as a sign of happiness and festivities.

suddenly, he became aware of a strange feeling, a kind of pressure on his throat, a pressure too great for any kind of fondling. He wanted to ask her not to press so hard, but his voice would not come out and still the pressure increased. He stretched out his hand to remove hers from his neck but he felt as though a nightmare or incubus were pressing him down; he felt as though a heavy weight, a sandbag or part of a wall, had fallen on his head. He wanted to cry out, to stand up, to move, but could not. He turned his head brusquely to get rid of this torture and scraped it against the couch, or rather against something that felt like the ground — dust and mud. A strange feeling overwhelmed him, new in its nature, its flavour, the depth of its sadness. He heard a well-known, mocking, voice shouting at him.

"And so now you go to sleep in the middle of the road !"

How very like the police constable's voice this sounded. The old police constable with his rough voice that was always a forewarning of trouble. He felt suffocated. Saneyya's hand knew no mercy. Suddenly the wall was lifted from his chest and he sat up moaning in the dark. He seemed to make out the shadow of a giant blocking the light of the street lamp and towering up towards the stars. The cocks of dawn were crowing and a rifle appeared behind the shoulder of this spectre. The pain upon his chest gave way when the heavy boot was lifted from it.

"Constable," he called out, "What of the police superintendent's promises ?"

The policeman kicked Hanzal savagely.

"The Superintendent's promise !" he cried, "You crazy dope-fiend.. Come along to the station."

Hanzal looked around in terror and bewilderment; and all he found was a slumbering street, an enveloping darkness, a silence .. no party, no trace of a party .. no Saneyya .. nothing.

Translated by Azza Kararah; revised by David Kirkhaus.

JUST A PUPPET

Rashad Rushdi

RASHAD RUSHDI (b.1915) is Professor of English Language and Literature atCairoUniversity. He has studied at the Universities of Exeter and Leeds, and combines his academic work with imaginative writing in the fields of the short story and the play. He has also translated English works into Arabic, seeing it as one of his main tasks in the interpreting of western culture and literature to the Arab reader. His interest in the theatre goes back to the late thirties, when he collaborated with a group of young actors called the *Vanguard Group,* who performed in Egypt and other Arab countries: for them he provided translations of Marlowe's *Faustus* and Gogol's *Inspector General.* He has produced his own plays on the UAR broadcasting service, and has written Arabic scripts for the BBC, giving his impressions of English life. He has lectured in American universities as visiting professor and has published three books in English on Egyptian themes in English Literature, besides producing literary criticism in Arabic including *Fannul qiṣṣatil-qaṣīra* (*The Art of the Short Story*) and *Ma huwal-adab?* (*What is Literature?*). He has edited a general cultural magazine as well as one devoted to drama. A one-act play of his, *Odysseus,* has been performed at Yale University. Since 1959, a succession of his plays have been very successfully produced on the Cairo stage.

The present short story is entitled, in the original, *'Adhabuj-jismi wa 'adhabur-rūh* (*Torment of Body and Torment of Soul*) and is from the collection *'Arabatul-ḥarīm* (*Ladies' Compartment*). It is written entirely in Egyptian colloquial Arabic.

Yes, it's cool in here. The shop faces due north, you see, Why don't you sit down and have a soft drink or a cup of coffee ? You'll be wondering where I'll get the coffee from. I prepare it myself. I've everything in there : coffee and pot and all. How else could I stay up until one or two in the morning night after night ? Come right in.

Do you like the coffee ? I'm so glad. It's a pleasure to have you here, Mister Salah, a great pleasure. I was wondering where you'd got to. I thought you might be ill, or have moved away from here. You haven't been getting your cigarettes from here for over a week; and I haven't so much as caught a glimpse of you. Oh, I see, you were out of town. Welcome back.

Yes, I always take the night-shift. I've got a partner, but he looks after the shop by day, and I take over at night. Until two months ago we used to take the night shift in turns. But he's got married now, and I think it's a shame to make him relieve me and leave his wife all alone at home.

Oh, no, thank you very much, I'm not married. I've been a single man for over seven years now. I've been married twice. My first wife was a relation of mine. I lived with her for a year, then I divorced her. The second was a city girl from right here in Cairo. That only lasted three months, but, God help me, every day of those three months was like a year !

Why ? I'll tell you why, *Ustaz*[1] Salah — it was torment, one long, endless torment. Do you think I could stay in the shop of a night having a quiet chat with you like this while she was alone at home ? Not on your life ! I was never quite sure what she was up to — whether she was in or out, dressed or undressed, who she was talking to, or who might be flirting with her. She was fair-skinned and young — and so pretty. She was just turned twenty at the very most. The men down our way are just like wolves, and the Devil's a sly one. Here I was tied down to the shop for maybe seven hours at a stretch, and there she was alone at home. I couldn't stop my imagination running riot, whenever I was away from her, during the night — and the day as well. I'd have gone stark staring mad if I — God help me — hadn't thought things over, and divorced her.

I don't know — I didn't actually *see* anything and no one told me anything I could hold against her — but there was one of these dandified barbers living in the same building. Name of Mahmoud. Well, he seemed to be gone on her. He paid her all sorts of attentions — and

(1) "Mister".

him always dressed ready to kill, he was — and used to send his sister to keep her company, for hours on end.

One night as I was standing here ın the shop at about ten o'clock, I began to smell something fishy. Perhaps she was with Mahmoud just then ? Barbers shut up shop at eight. They'd probably been together for two hours already. But what was I to do ? I almost went out of my mind — feeling tied down to the shop like this. Why not slip back home and have a look ? But who could I leave in charge ? I was worrying this over when, luckily, the newspaper boy — you know, that bleareyed lad — happened to pass by. I called him over and gave him five piastres — asked him to look after the shop for half an hour or so while I was gone. So I hopped on to a tram, half out of my mind — I'd made my mind up to kill my wife and kill her lover — but I suddenly remembered that I'd nothing to kill them with. Then I thought, "Why kill them ? Why not divorce her and make an end of the torture I'm in ?" I rushed into the house and opened the door. The lights were out and there was no sound. "She must be asleep," I thought. I dashed into the bedroom and switched the light on. The bedclothes were crumpled, but she wasn't there. I heard her singing in the bathroom.

"Come out !" I cried.

"What's the matter, Ismail ?" she asked coolly. "I'm drying myself. I'll be right out."

"Come out," I yelled again and threw the bathroom door open like a madman.

There she stood, fairskinned and her body slim and pliable like a wand — really beautiful ! I looked at her for a minute or two, then the blood rushed to my head. To think that Mahmoud the barber should enjoy all this, the filthy swine ! I fell upon her, grabbed her hair and dragged her stark naked out of the bathroom.

"How dare you have a bath at ten o'clock at night, you brazen bitch. Who ever knew a filthier slut than you are ?" And I fell to slapping her on her face and her thighs and her breasts and all over her body, while she screamed and she whimpered :

"What have I done, Ismail ? What have I done ?"

"Taking a bath at ten o'clock, you bitch !"

"What's wrong with that ?"

"What about the bed ? Why is the bed all in a mess ?"

"I had a rest after I'd finished cooking. Oh, Ismail, you should be ashamed of yourself."

"It's you that ought to be ashamed of yourself, you dirty sow."

The next day I divorced her and moved away and swore I'd never get married again. I'm much better off like this.

My first wife ? Women are all alike, Mr. Salah. She was a calamity too, and the year I spent with her was miserable from start to finish. No, she wasn't as beautiful as the second one, but she was . . how shall I put it ? Engaging, seductive. She never stopped giggling for one instant whether there was any reason for it or not. "Stop giggling, woman !" "Oh, *Si*[1] Ismail, where's the harm ? Hee, hee, hee !" Well, a woman like that will laugh with the first man she comes across, and you know how it is. It usually starts with a joke, then a chat, and soon turns into friendship — and then, I'd be a goner. She was a dark woman, tall and full of life — and so jolly. As I say, she loved to laugh and joke and have fun.

"There was a tall husky chap who ran his own carpenter's shop down our street. His name was Saad. He was one of those layabouts who think they're clever; always cracking jokes and fooling around. Very amusing, she found him, and she'd laugh out loud at whatever he said, no matter how silly it was. I'd asked him to make us a little round kitchen board to chop the vegetables on. One day, as I came back from work I found the board at home.

"Whoever brought this here, Halima ?"

"Saad dropped in and brought it. Said we could pay later."

"Did he now ? Are we living on his charity or something ? How dare he come in here when I'm out ?"

Oh *Si* Ismail, where's the harm ?"

A bugbear began to haunt me. From that day on, I'd be standing

(1) Shortened form of *Sidi*, *my lord*, used in the sense *Mister*.

behind the counter and I'd tell myself, "Who knows ? Maybe Saad is with her in the house now, or maybe she's gone to see him in his workshop."

Tall and well-built he was, just right for her, because she was nice and plump herself. When I went home at night she was always flat out and zizzing away. Of course, why not ? wasn't she free to do as she liked all day long. . no one to pry at her, and no one to put a stop to things ? At night, I used to stretch myself out next to her, unable to sleep a wink for the black thoughts that gnawed away at me. Whenever I looked at her plump, shapely, body, there'd come into my mind the manly figure of Saad the carpenter, with his tight blue jeans and his rubber belt. I'd nudge her and pinch her arms and her thighs. She'd turn heavily in her sleep ages afterwards, thinking she'd be dreaming. One night I'd been giving her a good beating, and when I went to sleep, I dreamt that she'd turned into a she-devil and was chasing me upstairs and downstairs all around the house, and trying to push me off the roof ! By the end I'd grown to hate her and hate myself, and whenever I was at the shop I imagined her and Saad together in the house. No sooner had she gone to the village for her father's funeral than I sent her the divorce paper and got rid of her, and saved myself from the agony. Ah, I had some peace and quiet after that !

What ? you think I did her wrong ? Oh no, *Ustaz*[1] Salah, there's nothing I hate more than injustice, but you will agree that women are like that — one long harrowing torment. Do you honestly believe that there's a woman alive who's satisfied with one man ? Even when her husband lies in wait all day long and keeps a sharp eye on her, she still finds a way to cuckold him and waggle her tail around — even more so when her husband's a working man like me, and has to be away for seven or eight hours a day ? Do you think a woman is going to sit and wait for him all those hours ? Not on your life ! Why should she ? There's many another man around.

(1) 'Mister'.

Loyalty and honour and that sort of thing ? Oh Mister Salah, women don't have any such noble sentiments. They're just like animals, they follow their instincts : whenever there's food in front of it, an animal will wolf it down. And a woman, if there's no one around to hold her back, will just gorge herself, sir, stuff herself to satisfy the hunger of her body.

I'm not exaggerating, not in the least. All women are like that. The main thing is to keep one's eyes open and not to judge by appearances. You want an example ? The world is full of examples, Salah Effendi. Why go far — only last month there was an incident in that building over there. You may have heard of it. A lovely woman, fair skinned, with green eyes and blond hair, and elegant at that. Her cheapest dress costs ten or fifteen pounds. And not young, mind you, she couldn't have been under thirty, thirty-two. Well, her husband was an important civil servant who made eighty, ninety pounds a month, ran a car and lived in a fifteen-pound-a-month flat and was madly in love with her. They say he'd ditched his first wife and his children for her sake, and made a love match. He wasn't much older than she was — about forty, forty-two — a real gentleman from a good family. And do you know what happened ? They'd been married for just three months — three months, mind you ! He went away on business, and came back one night — opened the door and found her in the servant's arms ! Damn every woman in the world, I say ! And what has she gained from her doings ? Her husband's in jail, her servant boy was killed, and she got away with a few days in hospital to recover from a bullet in her leg. Women, Mister Salah, ought to be shot ! Didn't you hear about it ? The papers were full of it, though. Anyone could have told you about it. And what about that European woman on the seventh floor ? That one can't keep her fingers off any man. There's not a man in the district who isn't one of her boyfriends : the laundry man and the grocer and even that bleareyed newspaper boy.. Me ? Oh no ! I've got nothing to do with her.

How do I know about it ? It's crystal clear. If you keep your eyes peeled you see women as they really are. Men are such fools, honestly —

I'll tell you a story that shows it. Three years ago I used to work in a cigarette shop just like this one, but at Giza. I got to know the customers pretty well. There was this very nice man, a doctor — specialized in women's ailments, he was twenty-eight, twenty-nine years old at the most and his wife was a young woman of his own age who was also working. They used to stop at my shop every morning on their way to work, to get their cigarettes. He smoked Players and she smoked American blend. They made such a nice, loving, happy couple. They had a Citroën, and drove to work together. One night as I was standing behind the counter, I saw her in a huge Buick with a strange man. Two days later I saw her standing at the tram-stop, the one that goes to the Pyramids, dressed to kill. I smelt a rat ! I called a young lad who worked at a pastry-shop nearby and asked him to look after the shop for a while, and followed her. She saw me and walked away. I walked after her. Then do you know what ? The big Buick suddenly appeared, with the stranger at the wheel ! They each gave the other a look. He took the hint and drove off, but very slowly. She kept on walking and looking behind her, and whenever she caught a glimpse of me following after she'd walk faster until she got tired. She stopped and waited for a tram. When she got on I followed her, but unfortunately I made no discovery, for I'd left my wallet behind in the shop, and when the conductor asked for my fare I had to jump off the tram, though I was determined to catch her red-handed on some other occasion.

No, I didn't. Of course she was on her guard, and I never saw her except in the morning when she stopped with her husband to get her cigarettes — and she joking with him and being nice to him, the fool!

Figments of my imagination, are they ? That's what you think, *Ustaz* Salah. You don't know women, you've not been tormented by women as I've been tormented now for many a long year.

Of course I'm not married now. I'm through with women, washed my hands clean of my wives long ago. And yet will women give me any peace? There seems to be no escaping from 'em. They're still plaguing me !

That's just it ! They're after me wherever I go, no matter how often I move house. I haven't a friend left in the whole wide world, and do you know why ? Because of women ! My relatives aren't on speaking terms with me : not one of 'em will pay me a visit unless it's a matter of life or death. You see, they disapprove of my refusing to get married again, they think it's shameful to be a single man at my age. And my friends — they've all deserted me. Why ? Because of their wives, that's why! Ah ! they never gave me a moment's peace. Now that I live on my own, do you think I have a friend I can sit with at a café, or open my heart to ? I haven't been able to live in the same house for more than a couple of months, and to get to know the neighbours, without having to pack up and move to another part of town. I'll tell you why. Only last month I had a nice room on a rooftop near the shop and I was very happy with it. My next-door neighbour, right opposite me in a little flat on the rooftop, was a Syrian grocer. We soon became very good friends. He brought me as much oil and sugar as I wanted and we used to sit together in the café, smoking a hubble-bubble and passing the time of day. Now, how long do you think this lasted ? Just one month ! After that his wife started meddling and made a mess of everything. And who would have thought it ? Why, she said her prayers regularly, and looked a real, decent lady.

One afternoon I was lying down after lunch when there was a knock on my door. When I opened it, I found her standing there, holding the kitchen board she'd borrowed the day before to chop the herbs on.

"Sorry, *Si* Ismail, did I wake you up ?"

"I wasn't asleep — just lying down."

"Oh well, cheerio for now."

"Good afternoon, madam." And back I went to my bed.

Not fifteen minutes later she strutted in, in a short red nightgown that showed her arms and her bare legs and half way down her breasts, carrying a coffee-tray.

'I thought we'd have our afternoon coffee together. No, you're not to get up. Don't bother to move.. we don't stand on ceremony, do we ?"

She set the tray on a small table by the window and sat down on the bed beside me. I was stung to the quick. I sprang up, ready to get out of bed.

"I'll have my coffee sitting up.. if you don't mind !"

"Oh, please don't get up — just you lie down quietly."

And she rested her hand on my knee and looked me in the eye.

"Shame on you, woman — why, you say your prayers regularly."

I leaped up, went out of the room, and stood outside on the open roof until I saw her leave my room carrying her coffee-tray about half an hour later. The next day we weren't on speaking terms. Her husband too : he looked down his nose and slammed the door in my face whenever he sawme. What could I do ? I packed and left the house. And I'd thought I was cosily set up there for a couple of years or so. I wouldn't have thought that a pious woman like that would behave like the rest of them — but can you talk of a woman being *pious* ?"

It's always the same — one of these she-devils bobs up wherever I am. The house I'm in now. I've been there under a month and the problems have already started. My landlady's a widow — been one for years — she's about thirty-five or forty. She's a midwife and has a grown-up daughter, sixteen, seventeen years old, dark, tall — lovely. You should see the way her curves bulge out of the tight blue dress she wears ! She's in and out of my room all day long. Now it's some sugar she's after, now some coffee, another time a pinch of salt. This goes on every day. Two or three times a day. Knocks on my door and then asks for whatever it is she needs. And looks at me with her lovely big eyes — like doves' eyes they are. And peals with laughter — and then she's off. The night before last, it was my day off and I was coming back about nine o'clock at night, when I saw her in the doorway, looking agitated, and trying to chase away a huge bat that was flitting round high up near the ceiling.

"The bat, Mister Ismail ! Please help me get rid of it. Ooh ! It's heading straight at me ! Ooh ! It'll dig its claws into my face." And she flung herself in my arms burying her face against mine. When

I felt her body clinging to mine, do you know, I was set all on fire inside of me. Really aflame I was, not just glowing or smouldering. I pushed her away and scurried up the stairs. Ever since, I haven't had a moment's peace at home. The cooking mortar's pounded at all hours of the day or night — thump-thump ! The water's cut off for hours on end. "Lady — isn't that enough pounding ?" "Well, now, we're making meat balls, *Si* Ismail, and they need a lot of pounding. And isn't every one of us free to do as she likes in her own house ?" What am I to do ? Oh, my life's one long torment, nowhere to go, no one I know any more, and all because of women !

Give in ? Not on your life ! When I was married I used to look at my wife lying next to me, fair, blooming, lovely — I couldn't get to sleep after that, and I'd spend the rest of the night tossing and turning in dreadful agony.

No, no ! I'll just steer clear of women. You're right there, that's just as harrowing, but at least as long as I keep away from women, I keep my self-respect — I'm as good as any other man. The moment I'm with a woman, even if she's only a twelve-year-old girl, as long as she's reached the age when they fill out, I feel I'm just a puppet on a string, absolutely worthless, and that any man — just any man — is better than I am.

Translated by Nadia Farag; *revised by Lewis Hall.*

THE MASTER-MILKMAN

Youssef el Sebai

YOUSSEF EL SEBAI combines humour with a knowledge of, and affection for, the life of the popular quarters of Cairo. He was born in 1917; his father, Mohamed el Sebai, was himself a man of letters. Youssef el Sebai passed out of the Staff College as a cavalry officer in 1937, and later taught military history. Between 1933 and the present day, he has published over thirty-three volumes, consisting of novels, short stories, and plays. He has also written film scenarios. He is Secretary General of three organizations : the UAR Higher Council for Arts and Letters, the Afro-Asian Peoples' Solidary Movement and the Afro-Asian Writers' Solidarity Movement. In the original, the present story is called *Abu Sri'*, after its hero; it appears in the volume *Bain Abu-r-rīsh wa Gunainat-Nāmīsh* (*From Abu-r-rish to Gunainat Namish*) a collection of short stories set in different quarters of Cairo.

It is four o'clock in the morning. From time to time a cock's crow rises here and there. Abu Sarie rubs his eyes and turns over in bed stretching and yawning. From the farthest corner of the room a shrill, piercing voice calls continuously, persistently, like frogs croaking.

"Abu Sarie ! Abu Sarie !"

Abu Sarie goes on stretching and yawning and the voice goes on calling insistently :

"Abu Sarie ! Abu Sarie !"

Abu Sarie growls, but the voice evidently does not regard the growl as a sufficient answer, for it goes on with its plea :

"Get up, son .. Get up, dear .. Do be reasonable ! Abu Sarie ! Abu Sarie !"

Losing patience Abu Sarie suddenly shouts angrily :

"Oh, alright, alright ! I'm awake now, so stop your racket — or are you possessed by a devil called *Abu Sarie* ?"

"It's for your own good. I don't want you to lose your job and go back to idling from café to café !"

"Cheerful, aren't you for this time of day ?"

This conversation between Abu Sarie and his mother went on every morning at the crack of down, almost word for word — like a tape being replayed — in the rooftop room that they shared in Sharia Mumtaz in El Baghala, — the Muleteers' Quarter.

Abu Sarie had just started on his new job as a tram conductor. His mother had felt when she saw him for the first time in his khaki uniform that her greatest dream had come true, and that there was only one thing more she wished for to complete her happiness before she died, and that was to see him safely married to a decent girl.

She was not overdoing it to feel such joy at seeing him settle down as a public functionary, in his jacket, his trousers and his *tarboush* — in other words, as an *effendi*. It was really worth rejoicing at, in the first place because he was the first *effendi* in that fine family, and in the second place because Abu Sarie was the last person you would imagine could settle down to any job.

It was truly a gift from heaven ! A most unexpected climax to a life of roguery and mischief. Who could have believed it possible that this light-headed, irresponsible, vagabond who never had a care in the world, or worried about the future, or did a stroke of work — who would have believed that this hooligan for whom fun and games were every thing in the world, would ever settle down to a job and abide by rules and regulations, restrictions and timetables ?

As his mother put it, he had always been a bit of a fighting cock ever since he had come into the world, full of play, reckless, undependable, and utterly irresponsible. He only went to the *kuttab*[1] because he was encouraged by a daily beating from the paternal cane first thing in the morning. He often played truant and was renowned for the pranks he played on the good *sheikhs*. His mother still relates how when Sheikh Shahtout tried to put him in the school punishment room at the age of seven he jumped out of the window, not just to get away but to creep up to Sheikh Shahtout's own room and lock him in while

(1) Primary school of the more old-fashioned type.

he was at his prayers, so that he remained a prisoner until the caretaker set him free next morning. His mother still remembers how he used to save the water-melon rind to take to school: "I'm saving it for a rainy day", he would say: in fact he had innumerable uses for it, the most noteworthy being to pelt the boys on the nape of the neck during lessons, and make Sheikh Bondok slip on his way in and out of class.

He finally ran away from the *kuttab* altogether and from every other *kuttab* in which his father tried to enroll him. He did not do much better when he went on to elementary school. His father despaired of ever giving him any book-learning and of himself becoming the proud and envied father of a well-educated 'official' whom he could show off to his envious relations and neighbours. He decided to use his son in the dairy he ran and do without one of his milk-boys, hoping he could eventually let Abu Sarie take over the business after his death.

Abu Sarie became a milk boy in Sharia[1] Mumtaz. He was supposed to deliver the milk to the customers in El Baghala in the morning, measuring it out in his cans, and to carry the wooden yoghourt tray round in the evening. And in between he had to wash out the cans, collect the empty bowls, light the stove, and clean up the shop. This was what an ordinary, well-conducted milk boy was supposed to do. But Abu Sarie was by no means an ordinary person. And if the world were full of people like Abu Sarie what a chaotic world it would be. Abu Sarie, as I have said, had shrugged off all responsibility; Abu Sarie held it as his opinion that he ought never to be saddled with any responsibility; Abu Sarie behaved pretty much as he liked; as long as he was happy, let the world take care of itself. Whenever he was reprimanded for his mischief, he would answer, "I'm happy that way !" The world was his oyster, though as his mother kept saying, "There's no eating your cake if you don't bother to bake it."

This being so, it would be foolish to imagine that Abu Sarie carried out a milk boy's duties obediently.

The first time he went out balancing the yoghourt tray on his head, he was delighted with the novelty of the situation ! He roamed the

(1) Street.

streets crying : "Lovely yoghourt ! Creamy yoghourt !"

Then it occurred to him to go to Sharia El Touloul where he used to meet his playmates for a game of street football, to see what was up and to show them how important he had become : master of a trade, and keeper of a tray.

As he appeared at the head of the lane the boys saw him and stopped the game and asked, "What have you got there ?" "Yoghourt" he announced proudly, "Anybody feel like some ?"

One of the boys kicked the ball. Abu Sarie felt his foot itching to join the game. He fought against the temptation, but when the ball rolled towards him, it was too much. He stood at the ready, and drew his foot backward to give a tremendous kick which landed the ball at the end of the alley and Abu Sarie on his back with the yoghourt bowls on top of him. He emerged from beneath the yoghourt in a daze, with his friends piled over him; they busily set themselves to the task of licking the yoghourt off his clothes and helped him pick up the pieces. Abu Sarie went back carrying the broken bowls and what was left of the yoghourt, and announced to his father quite simply that he had slipped on a piece of melon peel !

His father in desperation, kicked up a great row and swore to send the boy to a reformatory. His mother intervened and reminded him that this was the boy's first round.

On the second round, he headed straight to Sharia el Touloul, rested the tray on a window sill, and started to play with his friends. The ball rose in the air, landed in the middle of the tray and upset the bowls. Abu Sarie calmly informed his father that this time, it had been a piece of watermelon peel.

His father raged and stormed and threatened to break his neck. The mother intervened, to remind her husband that this was only his second round, and begged him to give the boy a third chance.

On the third round, it looked as if he had not let his mother down. He returned late in the evening with an empty tray and announced to his proud parents that the customers would pay at the end of the month.

Abu Sarie went out every afternoon with the bowls full of yoghourt and returned to his contented parents with the empty bowls. He was as contented as they were, for all he did was head straight to Sharia el Touloul, and instead of resting the tray on a window still where it might tumble down, he simply gathered the boys and handed the yoghourt round. When the bowls were all cleaned up they piled them on top of each other, placed them in a pit in the ground and covered them with the tray. After a strenuous game Abu Sarie carried his empty bowls home.

At the end of the month Abu Sarie was found out, and his father swore that if his son did not leave the house at once, then he would himself. His mother wept and wailed and said, "It's this blasted football that's at the bottom of every thing !"

But his absence from home did not last for more than a day. Fate intervened, and decided that it was the father who was to leave the house forever, and Abu Sarie came home to become the Master of the house after his father had been placed in his last abode in the cemetery of Bab el Wazir.

The mother had hoped that Abu Sarie might settle down, adjust to the situation and take charge of the shop, but once more she was disappointed. The first thing he did after his father's death was to buy a pair of football boots, a striped shirt and some coloured socks, and to announce to his mother that he had become the skipper of the "Roaring Lions" team. The poor woman took charge of the dairy in order to feed herself, her son and the "Roaring Lions" — a pack of tramps and beggars who had become addicted to yoghourt and expected it every evening after the game.

The team moved from their ground on Sharia el Touloul to a field in El Tibi so dusty that the players sank in to the knees. Abu Sarie and his team spent half their time buried in the dust and what remained of the other half in Abul Fadl's café at the corner of Sharia el Sad.

Abu Sarie soon gained fame as the Captain of the "Roaring Lions", who won every match, for they insisted that the game should take place on their own field where no other team could compete. The dust rose and formed a thick cloud which hid the players from one another;

everything disappeared from view including the ball, which always emerged, by some miraculous intervention, in the opponents' goal. And so the *Roaring Lions* XI, skipper and manager Abu Sarie, never lost a game, having made themselves experts at playing behind a curtain of dust.

The resigned mother put everything in the hands of God and gave up expecting anything better. Pressed by her son, she even went a few times to watch these dust storms which he and his team stirred up in the El Tibi field. Until one day without the slightest warning Abu Sarie announced to his mother that he was going to take a job !

She gaped in amazement and refused to believe him at first. He repeated emphatically that he was going to take a respectable job as a tram conductor. The poor woman thought that he was joking, for it was unthinkable that Abu Sarie should ever lead a normal life.

Abu Sarie a conductor ? Impossible ! Abu Sarie in a khaki uniform and *tarboush* instead of the striped shirt and football boots ? Impossible ! Abu Sarie carrying a satchel and a ticket book and collecting money from the passengers ? Never !

And yet a few days later he appeared at the head of the alley, the conductor's whistle announcing his arrival, and sauntered in, in full costume!

The woman uttered her first trilling-cry ever and rushed to kiss and hug her son, her eyes bathed in tears, thanking God for guiding her son along the straight path and so fulfilling her first wish ! She prayed fervently for her second wish, that her happiness might be completed by seeing him safely married to a suitable girl.

The incredulous neighbours wondered by what miracle Abu Sarie, the good-for-nothing loafer, had been transformed overnight into a respectable official, a responsible, reasonable human being ! Indeed nothing less than a miracle could have made Abu Sarie, of his own accord, abandon the field of El Tibi and Abul Fadl's café for the running board of the tram with its discipline and hard work.

Yes, it was a miracle, but not one from heaven. It was an earthly miracle, one wrapped round in a *melaya*,[1] with protruding breasts and

(1) Woman's black cloak, worn swathed around the body.

swinging buttocks ! It was a miracle who chewed gum, snapping and cracking it behind her *borko*[1] with the golden ornament set on her delicate nose, between two bewitching black eyes !

The miracle was Nagaf. Nagaf and no one else was behind it all.

Abu Sarie first saw her as he sat at the café; she was in a No. 5 tram which plied between Ghamra and the Slaughter-house. He saw her for the second time, also in a No. 5 tram, and the third time, and the fourth and the fifth .. In fact he never saw her anywhere else. She was either going to the Slaughter-house or coming from the Slaughter-house.

Abu Sarie fell head over heels in love — and became a martyr to love on tram No. 5 — the more so as Nagaf, who was well versed in the art of coyness, always sat in the women's compartment where he could not get at her.

The days went by with Abu Sarie pining away, sleepless, without a chance of success or a hope of a rendez-vous. Deliverance finally came when his friend Hanafy, the tram driver, suggested to him that he should work as a conductor in the tram company, which would welcome him, especially as he was a football player who would strengthen the company's team, and promised to use his influence to get him on to the No. 5 line so that he could see Nagaf every day and talk to her.

This is how the miracle happened and how Abu Sarie became an official. The passengers in tram No. 5 began to witness the most extraordinary performance in Abu Sarie's tram. His whistle became well known for its cadenzas of burning desire, of which he became a masterly player. He often stopped the tram and began to delight the audience with his *Nagaf Song*, which went

It's Nagaf, o Nagaf my Nagaf,
My beautiful, beautiful Nagaf.

and

When I see you tightly wrapped in your melaya.

---

(1) Veil covering lower half of woman's face.

I'm rapt up away from my folk.
Oh for the day when that wrap gets worn away.
And your hips and my eyes win their freedom.

Or, he would run after the juice vendor to get Nagaf a glass of liquorice-juice or scurry off behind a peddlar to get her a couple of carrots or a fresh lettuce or some cucumbers.

In spite of all these amorous gestures, Nagaf was still playing hard to get and Abu Sarie was still patiently hoping, until one day the disaster fell and he and his friend Hanafy were transferred to another line as a result of a "slanderous" report that one of the inspectors had written.

One morning Abu Sarie left his house and walked dejectedly to the terminus, where he and his friend Hanafy took tram No. 7 which plied between Ghamra and Rod-el-Farag. The tram started off in gloom, and when it got to Nagaf's stop, she looked at the number, then in amazement to Abu Sarie.

"Climb on", said Abu Sarie.

"No, I'm going to the Slaughter-house".

"So are we !"

"But this is a No. 7. It's going to Rod-el-Farag."

"We'll take it to the Slaughter-house for the sake of your lovely eyes. By the Prophet, it's going nowhere else but to the Slaughter-house !"

Nagaf had an inward urge to go with Abu Sarie even if he were to take her to hell. She had become so used to taking the tram with him. that she could not do without him. Was it love ? Nagaf got on and Abu Sarie's whistle began to dance and wriggle with joy and sigh with desire and he began to clap his hands and bellow

It's Nagaf, o Nagaf my Nagaf.

At the points,Abu Sarie shouted to Hanafy before he blew his whistle, "Straight on, Hanafy! We're going to the Slaughter-house for the sake of Nagaf's eyes !"

He rushed to the switch-man and changed the course of the tram for the Slaughter-house, and for the first time ever, tram No. 7 and its bewildered passengers were taken to the Slaughter-house instead of Rod-el-Farag. The passengers shouted and protested but Abu Sarie coolly informed them that he was "quite happy that way" and that if anyone did not like it he could get off.

Abu Sarie went home that day dancing all along the lane, wiggling his hips in joy, and asked his mother for her blessing, for he was going to get married: Nagaf had accepted him, having admitted that she loved him. For the second time the woman uttered her trilling-cry, for had not both her dreams come true ? She cried with tears in her eyes:

"Praise be to God, son, for He has granted me the two things that I have always wanted !"

"Two things ?"

"Yes, a job and a bride for you !"

Abu Sarie hung his head for a moment then said sorrowfully, "Listen, mum, God's taken away one of them."

"What ?"

"Yes, the job. I was fired today, because I took Tram No. 7 to the Slaughter-house for the sake of Nagaf."

The woman struck her breast and cried out in dismay. But her dismay did not last very long, for marriage reformed him. Abu Sarie took charge of the dairy and became 'Master Abu Sarie' the milkman, famous in El Baghala and in fourteen provinces.

Translated by Nadia Fadrag; revised by David Kirkhan and Ronald Ewart.

A BOY'S BEST FRIEND

Ehsan Abdel Kuddus

EHSAN ABDEL KUDDUS (b. 1920) is the most popular writer of fiction in the Arab world, and his work has been adapted for the cinema, television and radio. He is the son of Mme Fatma (Rose) el Youssef, a well-known journalist and magazine owner of the thirties, of Lebanese origin, who had earlier had a distinguished career on the stage. Ehsan Abdel Kuddus began to write after graduating in law. His output of romantic novels and short stories is very large, covering some twenty volumes.

This story is quieter in tone that the typical story by Abdel Kuddus : it is from the volume *Bint us-sulṭān* (*The Sultan's Daughter*), published some four years ago. The original title is *An-nās yadribūna 'Antar* (*People Beat Antar*). It has been adapted for television.

My full name is Awad Ahmed Hassanein el Nahlawy, and I work as a copyist in the Ministry of Justice. I am fifty-two, though I look much older than that, for my face is full of wrinkles. My eyes are always a little bloodshot, and appear slightly bleary from behind my silver-rimmed spectacles. Very likely, people think I am unhealthy because I am lean and inclined to slouch a little, but I am perfectly fit really, and have never complained of any ailments. I may have acquired this worn appearance from the long hours I spend bending over the bits and pieces of those watches I am always pulling apart. You see, I have a passion for repairing watches. It is my great hobby.

Watches have always had a strange fascination for me. Ever since I was a child and lived in my native village of Kafr Elewa, I was attracted by watches, any kind of watch. I remember how I used to crouch in front of the *omda*'s[1] gate waiting for him to appear in the huge courtyard in front of his house, so that I could feast my eyes on the watch he wore in his breast pocket. I would hold my breath and

(1) Omda : village headman or mayor.

stare, spellbound, at the heavy silver chain hanging across his chest, and shining against the cloth of his *gallabiyya* until he raised his hand and pulled out the bulbous watch that was attached to the end. My greatest joy then would have been to touch this fascinating object, to feel the magic of that enchanting treasure the eminent man carried against his heart. Once, when the irrigation superintendent came on a visit to the village, I patiently dogged his steps a whole day, drawn irresistibly by the handsome watch that shone on his wrist. I even ran after his carriage until I caught up with him where he stood on the embankment surrounded by a crowd of villagers. Slowly I crept up until I came close to him, then timidly stretched out a trembling hand and laid it on the gleaming surface. He wheeled round sharply, and thinking I was trying to steal his watch, brought his hand down and struck me full in the face. I can still feel that blow, even now, and I remember how I was saved from being turned over to the authorities only by the intervention of the villagers who knew me. But that did not cure me. I never could overcome my fascination for watches.

Later I went to live in Cairo. I had failed my primary certificate, so my father, through the recommendation of the *omda,* who had high connexions, got me this job as copyist in the Ministry of Justice, at a monthly salary of exactly five pounds twenty three piastres. Out of that, I hoped to save enough to buy myself a watch, which was then my greatest ambition. Until I could do that, I contented myself with admiring them in shopwindows where they were on display. For hours, I would stand gazing at them, studying their shapes and designs. I came to recognize their different makes and learned their names. I knew them all by heart, every one of them : Movado, Rolex, Génie, Omega, Arcadia . . there wasn't one I did not know. Now I may have a weak memory for names sometimes,and I may easily forget a man's name, but never that of a watch.

Finally, one day, I counted what I had saved over the year, and found it was enough to buy me a watch — the first I ever owned, and I felt as if I owned the entire world -- it was as if I had got married to it, or as if I had been reborn. Looking at it every day, compact and neat, ticking away quietly through the day and into the night, it intrigued me, and I felt a strong compulsion to open it and probe its inner mysteries. Tentatively, at first, I began to pull it apart and examine every tiny component; then I would put it carefully together again as though I had been performing surgery on my sweetheart. It drew me like a magnet. Every day, after I finished my work at the Ministry, I would hurry home in order to look into its intricate mechanism once more, and play with its little heart. Then with its tiny parts spread out before me, I would be so completely lost in them that nothing else mattered; I cared for nothing but those tiny little bits of metal which alone had any meaning for me. Screwing, and unscrewing, taking them apart delicately, and putting them together again delicately, time after time, I completely forgot myself, and others, and the whole world. And so began my passion for repairing watches. I only really started living when I sat down in the evenings and took them apart: this was my world. I had no friends or companions. I even forgot about getting married. Actually, I did get married just in time, when I was thirty-nine, and then only because my mother — who died two years later — insisted so much.

Nothing changed with my marriage except that I moved to a two-room flat on the outskirts of Giza. I continued to cultivate my hobby, completely submerged in its delights, leaving my wife (who was a girl from our village) to a world of her own, far removed from mine. All I cared for was repairing watches — my colleagues in the Ministry all gave me theirs when they were out of order; I was happy only with a gutted watch in my hands, its cold entrails scattered around me, fascinating as ever.

Actually, come to think of it, there were one or two other things I enjoyed as well. I had a second hobby and that was repairing shoes. I repaired my own, and occasionally did not mind doing those of my acquaintances too. I knew how to patch a hole, to make a half-sole and a full one. I still keep all the shoes I have ever bought since I came to live in Cairo, and they are still quite fit for wear. Cooking too, is something I am very fond of. I swear I can prepare a rice stew with sheep's trotters far better than the famous Rakeeb. But after I married I had to give that up a little, as I could feel it offended my wife, who considered it trespassing, although she never really complained.

Two years after I married, my son was born and I called him Abdel Fattah, after my father. I was very happy to have a son, but that did not mean I was going to change my habits, and I left the child entirely to his mother. Only his wailing came to me from time to time as I was at my watch-repairing or my cobbling, to remind me of his presence. When he grew a little older all I wanted from him was that he should not intrude into my private world, and that he should keep his little hands off my watches and the delicate instruments I used on them.

When Abdel Fattah was six years old, my wife died. Of course, I grieved over her, I grieved very deeply, but that, again, changed nothing except that I could once again indulge in cooking, and that, from now on, I would have to look after Abdel Fattah myself. But that was no trouble. He was a quiet amenable boy, rather frail, but quite healthy on the whole.

We got on quite well together, Abdel Fattah and I, although we did not talk much. I spent most of my time sitting in my room with my watches and my shoes, while he sat in his, minding his own business. Sometimes I would notice he was reading, or scrawling on the walls, or playing one of his odd games that I never could understand. Anyhow, like me, he rarely left his room, and, like me, he spent hours on end all alone. I never worried about him. I was happy enough with him, and assumed he was happy to be with me. It never occurred to me that he should want anything more. He was now eleven, and in Middle School.

One day, he came to my room, and sat quietly watching me as I thinkered with my instruments, the lens, through which I peered at my wonderful little ticking universe, tightly screwed to my right eye.

"Dad," he said suddenly. His voice seemed to come from far away. I looked up and saw him through my lens, a big blurred shadow.

"Dad," he repeated, "where can I find a friend ?"

I heard the question distinctly, but I did not understand what he meant. I took the lens away from my eye and looked at him, puzzled.

"What did you say, Abduh ?"

"I said, I'd like to find a friend." he repeated in a hesitant tone, with his face turned away from me.

I grew more puzzled. A friend ? What did he want a friend for ? In fact, why should anybody want a friend ? After all, I wondered, what is a friend ? I knew a lot of people : there was Hag[1] Abduh the grocer and Master Eleish, the butcher from whom I bought my meat, there was Mr. Mohamed Nofal, who sold watches, and there were my colleagues at the Ministry — but could they be considered my friends ? I knew nothing about them if it came to that, or about their worries. We never visited one another, or spent the time in a café together, and I never felt a need for them, except that which was imposed by everyday requirements. Could they count as friends ?

"Surely, you can find a lot of friends among the boys at school," I said coldly to Abdel Fattah.

"I've got no friends there," he answered sadly.

"You can make some." I tried to smile this time.

"But how ?" he asked quite bewildered. "How ?"

I hesitated for a while. I did not know how people made friends, I had never wanted any, and had never tried to make them.

"Well," I ventured, "if you begin by talking to them, you may get to be friends."

"What shall I say ?" he asked eagerly.

"Oh, anything .. anything at all," I put in, not very helpfully.

"Suppose I say something silly, they'll only laugh at me."

"What makes you think you'd say anything silly ?" I gave him a look of sympathy. "Just try. They might like what you say. Besides, if one of them doesn't like it, another one might."

He seemed to ponder over that for a while, but said nothing. I thought I heard him sigh. Then he got up to go, dragging his feet. At the door, he paused and opened his mouth as if to say something,

(1) Egyptian colloquial form of *hajj*, title or mode of address for anyone who has made the pilgrimage to Mecca.

but changed his mind and went quietly out with his head hung down.

I screwed the lens back to my right eye, looked into the works of the watch I was examining, and tried to get on with my work. But I could not see what I had in front of me. There was only Abdel Fattah's downcast little face, sad and worried. I had always believed he was enjoying himself sitting on his own in his room playing those funny games I didn't understand, just as I was thoroughly happy in mine toying with my watches and my pairs of shoes. Yet here was the boy, obviously unhappy, tormented by something I could not fathom. I tried to dismiss the matter as a childish whim, but I could not dismiss Abdel Fattah's hurt expression from my mind. His bewildered look was always before me. Everywhere, I felt his eyes upon me, so that I could no longer settle down to repair a watch or a shoe. His problem was the only thing I could concentrate upon, and I found myself as unhappy as he was. Our relationship was slightly strained, and there was a distinct feeling of embarrassment between us, neither of us caring to look the other in the eye. When we spoke to each other, it was only briefly, and we were more cut off from each other than ever before. Now, as we continued with each keeping to himself, there was more to it than sheer habit.

Two weeks later, I plucked up enough courage to ask Abdel Fattah nervously, "Well, have you made a friend ?"

"No," he said curtly, with a cruelly reproachful look, and walked off into his room, his lips drawn into a sulky pout. I looked at him in despair as I felt the full weight of his disappointment fall on me. Now I realized the extent of my responsibility and of my failure. Because the boy had grown up beside me, quietly, unobtrusively, making no demands, I had never paid heed to any but to his material wants. Now, I saw myself as a father who had failed, inadequate, weak, worthless.

Growing daily more aware of this, more ashamed, I could hardly look my colleagues in the face. I imagined them all to be accusing me of having failed my son. I lost interest in everything, even in my watches, those watches that had stood between me and my son. Surely there must be a way to help Abdel Fattah, and I had to find it.

I thought, and thought, and finally hit on something: Hag Ali the decorators' contractor, who was a neighbour of mine, had a son of about Abdel Fattah's age. He was a cheerful, ebullient sort of man, and he always greeted me volubly if we met at the top of the lane, although I never encouraged his friendly advances, but cut them short in my hurry to get home or reach my work. It occurred to me now-perhaps if I made myself a little more pleasant, he would surely not withhold his friendship, or his son's? Yes, Hag Ali, that was an excellent idea.

I kept a look-out for him until I met him in the street one day. I summoned up my courage — it needed all I had — and instead of greeting him at a distance as I would normally have done, I went right up to him. He stretched his arm out and shook hands with me, looking quite astonished at this unusual show of friendliness. It was a very vehement handshake, all the same, while boisterous salutations poured from his mouth like a torrent, so that I could hardly catch up with them, let alone reply, but had merely surrendered my hand to his clutch, while my mind was busy preparing the words I ought to speak. Finally the Hag felt he had greeted me for long enough, and he released my crushed fingers with a concluding phrase :

"This is a very happy encounter, Hassanein Effendi."

"It has been a long time," I replied clumsily.

"Indeed, it has," he said, with a beam as broad as his belly.

"I .. I — how pleasant it would be if we visited each other. I wish you would come and visit me one day," I mumbled meekly. "I live alone — with my son — as you know."

"Of course ! Of course, Hassanein Effendi ! Any time. Just name the day," he bellowed.

"Tomorrow, perhaps ?" I suggested almost choking with embarrassment.

"That will be an honour. Tomorrow, then, just before the sunset prayers, God willing."

"And perhaps it would be possible for you to bring your dear son ?" I added timidly,after some hesitation."So that he can make the acquaintance of Abdel Fattah.

My son ? which one do you mean ? Hag Ali's astonishment showed once again. He looked at me as though he was questioning my sanity.

"Oh, the one who's eleven years old. Or thereabouts." I put the winsomeness into my voice again. "I've often seen him around with you."

"You mean Khamis ? That nogood little brat ?" He laughed. "But tell me," he added, "is it a special occasion ? Are you having a celebration, or something ?"

"Oh, no, nothing like that," I stammered, forcing myself to smile as I added, "It's just my boy .. Abdel Fattah .. he'd so much like to have a friend."

Hag Ali looked doubtfully at me, but what he said was, "I understand perfectly, Ustaz Hassanein. We shall be honoured."

He had certainly understood nothing, but I stretched my hand out again to him, and repeated, "Tomorrow, then, a little before sunset."

He once again shook my hand vehemently, pouring forth more torrents of salutation as he departed.

I cannot describe my anguish as I prepared for Hag Ali's impending visit. Except for a few of my relatives who came from our village from time to time, no one had ever visited me before, so that I had no idea how to set about things: in particular I could not imagine what one ought to talk about with one's caller. I had a sleepless night, working out arrangements, but, the next day, all I could think of was to buy half a kilo of little cakes, and a half kilo of sweets, on the way back from the Ministry. I laid them out carefully on plates, and set them on the table in the middle of the hall. I had not told Abdel Fattah what I had prepared for him. I waited until he came home from school.

"Well, now," I said cheerfully, "get ready quickly; there's a friend coming to see you."

He looked at me with his large doleful eyes, as though he had not taken my words in, and said nothing.

"It's Khamis, the son of Hag Ali from down the road." I went on. "His father's coming to see us, and bringing him with him. He's about your age and you can make friends with him."

Abdel Fattah remained silent and unmoved, his doleful eyes fastened on me. It seemed to me as if he were ridiculing my efforts — and my whole outlook. But that should make no difference, I told myself. Now, I wondered, how was I to receive my guest ? Should I wear my suit, or would it be alright to remain in my *gallabeyya* ? I pondered over that for a while, then opted for the suit, and told Abdel Fattah also to wear the shirt and trousers he wore for school. He obeyed as usual, keeping his eyes averted.

Presently, the visitors arrived, and immediately Hag Ali's breezy salutations filled the house. The walls shook. There had never been so much noise in the house before. I could have believed that I had been whirled out into the din of the street and was standing out there. We all sat down, Hag Ali, still talking, facing me, and Khamis facing Abdel Fattah. After a while, I passed the cakes round. They each took one and started to eat; Hag Ali talking between mouthfuls while I smiled on and nodded helplessly, quite overpowered by the torrent he was letting forth. I stole a glance at the boys and found they were silent, surreptitiously eyeing each other. That won't do, I thought, I must get them to talk. When Khamis had swallowed his last bite of cake, I got up and offered him another one.

"What's the name of your school, Khamis ?" I asked, hoping this would help them start a conversation. But Khamis made no reply, letting his father answer for him. His second piece of cake soon vanished, and he was stretching to pick up a third without waiting for me to offer it. When that also disappeared, he simply got up and went and posted himself near the table where he could get at the cakes and sweetmeats more rapidly. He wolfed them down at an incredible rate: Abdel Fattah and I watched him in fascination, as though we were watching a conjuror. Meanwhile, Hag Ali was thundering on, stopping only to refill his mouth alternately with cakes and sweetmeats. Time was passing. I forced a smile and made a last attempt.

"Why don't you go and play in your room with Khamis ?" I said to Abdel Fattah. A most ridiculous suggestion, I gathered, from the look Abdel Fattah gave me.

"I don't want to play," declared Khamis, who was now resolutely attacking the sweets.

"Let them be," bellowed Hag Ali, "it won't hurt them to sit down quietly for a while."

After which, I resigned myself to Hag Ali who continued to fill the house with noise, while his son filled himself with food.

And so the visit came to an end, with Abdel Fattah and myself looking on in a daze. Hag Ali got up to take his leave, crushing my fingers in his big paw again. Without so much as a look at Abdel Fattah — whom he had hardly noticed — he blustered his way out, his voice receding with his great bulk. In my exasperation, I stopped Khamis, and collecting what was left of the sweets, stuffed them spitefully in his pocket.

"Many thanks for your generosity," called back his father loudly, "too good for the little beast."

I quite agreed, but smiled without saying anything, as I watched them making their way off, leaving me to renewed despair. I could not look Abdel Fattah in the eyes.

During the week that followed every moment that Abdel Fattah spent alone in his room was a moment of frustration and torment for myself. What could I do to people his lonely world ? He should have a crowd of friends to play with, to chat with, and to laugh with. I blamed myself for my neglect. But it had only been because I had not known, I tried to tell myself. I had been ignorant of his suffering. I tried to find comfort in this thought.

"Have you seen Khamis lately ?" I asked one day as we sat to lunch. He curled up his lip.

"No."

"Well, why don't you go and call on him ?"

"Children don't pay calls on each other." he replied scornfully.

"Then meet him somewhere," I insisted.

"What for?"

"Why, to play with him."

"I don't want to play with him," he declared with finality.

There was nothing more to be said. A few days later, I had a new idea. Why not make friends with Abdel Fattah myself? After all, I thought, friendships ought to start in the home, between father and son. It was not right that we should live in this manner. Far from having been a friend to him, I had been less than a father, no more than a stranger to him. We were two strangers under one roof. I had to make a fresh start.

"Shall we go for a walk?" I suggested one afternoon.

"Why?" he asked with his usual pout.

"Oh, nothing, just for a breath of air. I get bored sometimes just sitting at home like this." His face brightened at that. He could hardly believe I could feel like him sometimes. I had never seen him smile as he did then.

"Shall I change into my shirt and trousers?" he asked eagerly.

"No, no," I said casually, in a bored and indifferent voice. "It doesn't matter, just put your shoes on."

We started out and made for the open road that led out of Giza. I looked down at the little clouds of dust which the flapping of our *gallabeyyas* stirred up as we shuffled along. I was feeling self-conscious, hardly knowing what to say to him, what to talk about. But Abdel Fattah seemed unusually gay. He began to ask questions about my father, and my home village, and about watches, and I found myself telling him all about them. I discovered that he knew very little about me, about our relatives, about my hobbies. I discovered there was so much I wanted to tell him; I felt I could go on forever, as if I were making up for all those years when I had so rarely talked to him. We returned after sunset, elated and relaxed, and sat down to a hearty meal. I had never known him eat with such an appetite. We both slept contented that night.

From that day on, we made a habit of going out every afternoon, and taking a walk in the open country. On our way, we used to pass by a vacant lot where the boys of the neighbourhood gathered to play ball, and we used to stop and watch them sometimes. Something gripped at my heart every time I stood there. Some sort of secret envy, perhaps; a muffled longing for Abdel Fattah to be one of them. I knew it was not enough for him to have made friends with me: this was the life for him; running, shouting, and playing with other children. But while this wild desire grew on me daily, Abdel Fattah remained perfectly indifferent. He never showed the slightest interest in the boys or their game, nor did he care in the least that he was not included.

"Why don't you play with them ?" I asked as we stood watching one day — for I had made a point of pausing whenever we passed the boys, although he merely paused because I did, without sharing my feelings in the least.

"I don't know them."

"That can be arranged."

"I don't want to play. I wouldn't know how, anyway."

"You can easily learn."

"How ?"

I had no idea. But I wanted my boy to play ball just the same, and to have friends; moreover, I wanted to go back to my watches, and my shoes, and pottering about in the kitchen.

I continued to loiter deliberately every time we passed the playground. I tried to smile to any of the boys who came near us, in the hope that he would smile back.

One day, a bad shot sent the ball volleying in our direction, and one of the boys ran towards us to fetch it back. I smiled at him and asked him his name. The boy simply gave me a sharp scornful look, picked the ball up, and ran back. Abdel Fattah blushed with embarrassment, but he said nothing. I must confess that we had exchanged very few words in the last day or two. We seemed to have said all we had to say to each other. Once again, we were each going his own way, as though we had met only to turn away from each other again.

I was still determined that Abdel Fattah should join the boys' game. Some days later, as we were standing there, the ball again came rolling towards us. This time, before the boy who was hastening after it could reach it, I picked it up and held it out to Abdel Fattah as though I was offering him a rare prize.

"Go on," I said with an encouraging smile. "Shoot."

He turned scarlet and shook his head vigorously.

"No, no, please, father, no." he pleaded.

One of the boys came up after the ball.

"Give us the ball, mister," he shouted roughly.

"Just a moment, just one moment," I said gently, and I turned again to Abdel Fattah, "Go on, shoot !" I shouted at him.

"Please, father, no," he repeated, almost in tears, as though I were making an immoral proposal.

"Give us the ball, mister," repeated the boy who had come after it. My entire life seemed to centre on that ball now.

"I said wait !" I retorted sharply, and again pleaded with Abdel Fattah, and again he refused.

Meanwhile the boys had all gathered round us. The eldest stepped up to me.

"You let go of that ball," he said threateningly.

I was not going to let go. Abdel Fattah must kick that ball. I clutched at it more firmly and turned again desperately to Abdel Fattah. He was shaking, his face was the colour of a carrot, and his eyes were full of tears. The big boy was moving closer now, and stretched his hand out to take the ball, but I was not going to let go. Abdel Fattah must kick it first, he's got to..

I cannot remember what happened next. I know I got shoved around. I found myself rolling on the ground. Someone kicked me in the ribs. I could hear Abdel Fattah crying, "Dad ! Dad !" Then he was rolled down on to the ground beside me, a thin trickle of blood streaming from his nose. The boys had taken their ball back now, and were crying in a savage sort of chant.

The bullock's fallen —
Fetch the knife !

Abdel Fattah was sobbing bitterly. I straightened my spectacles, taggered up, and smoothed down Abdel Fattah's *gallabeyya* and my own.

I mopped the blood from his face, and wiped away his tears. Then, without a word, and not daring to look at each other, we began to walk home.

A little black dog, skinny and with running eyes, trotted along behind us all the way, wagging his tail, and rubbing himself against my son's legs. The boy watched him through his tears and bent down and patted him. We let him in the house with us, and because he was black, we called him Antar[1].

Antar and Abdel Fattah have been great friends ever since. They are very fond of each other .. as fond as I am of repairing watches, and mending shoes, and cooking .. it's just that I have a little problem. It's people .. you see, whenever they see Antar, they beat him, and throw stones at him, because they call him .. an unclean animal.

Translated by Wadida Wassef; revised by Lewis Hall.

---

(1) Shortened form of the name of 'Antara ibn Shaddad, Pre-Islamic poet, and hero of a popular romance. 'Antara was dark-skinned, as his mother was an Abyssinian slave : in the romance, those who meet him for the first time show scorn for him, until he shows his prowess.

MASTER LOAF THE CROSS-GRAINED OAF

Abdel Kader el Samihi

ABDEL KADER EL SAMIHI is a Moroccan writer who is equally at home in Arabic and in French. His output, which includes poetry and radio plays, shows a great variety: for example, the radio play included (pp. 219 ff.) in Mohamed Sadik Afifi's *Al-qiṣṣatul-maghribiyyatul-ḥadītha* (*The Modern Moroccan Story*), Casablanca 1961, is set in a sophisticated Parisian background, and is a total contrast to the monologue of the earthy tourist-guide which constitutes the story we have chosen. The story appeared in the Cairo *Al Magalla* for April 1965.

I don't claim that I'm right every time in my judgements. Still, I'll venture to say — and I'm sure you will agree — that the weird and vulgar hotchpotch that makes up my name is quite devoid of the least trace of beauty. It's as rough as a hedgehog's back. When I was a boy, it led me into a dozen or so street-fights with some of those young down-and-outs ruffians who are always roaming our streets. I was K.O.'d in three of them, and I gained some indelible marks of ruffianism upon my face and both my hands. There's this unsightly swelling over my right eyebrow, which looks rather like a marble, with a black rim below the eye to set it off. And there was then the loss of one of the toe-nails off my right foot. On the other hand, I scored nine victories. My principal achievement was to bequeath a life-long deformity to the face of Khnifar el Tamkhoukh, the son of Haja Taw, the baker-woman.

The fact is, when I was young, each time someone called me Rayyes[2] Khobza — Master Loaf — (I ask you!) — I had an almighty urge to set on him like a thunderbolt and wring his filthy neck as you might wring your laundry. If I were passing in front of the Café Central

(1) Feminine of *haj* (*j*).

(2) Skipper, captain.

or the Café de España in the Inner Market and one of the boys, another tourist guide like me, called me by the name of Rayyes Khobza, I would feel my uncontrollable Spanish blood racing up to my brain and it was all I could do to stop myself from acting like the hero of a western and making the fellow feel his feet leave the ground with a swift butt of my head — and I've quite a beetling forehead — or a silent punch in the belly in the well-known Chicago style of Al Capone, or, alternately, from lifting him up by the scruff of the neck and then hurling him over the café tables, and following him after with all the chairs, bottles and glasses that were within reach.

Sometimes, I was in a real dilemma. I might be on my way to the docks, near the big mosque, and I'd hear a sailor friend, calling me; I'd see his head, wrapped round in a blue scarf, jutting out between the pale-green iron bars of a café window, and I'd see him holding the reed mouthpiece of a hubble-bubble in one hand. He'd be calling out :

"Rayyes Khobza ! Master Loaf !"

If I walked on, pretending not to have noticed him, he'd cry still louder and louder :

"Rayyes Khobza ! Hey, man, what's the matter with you ? Since when have you grown to be too high and mighty for the likes of me ?"

And if I looked at him, he'd say at once, "The parcel is with Haj Kdour Lheisha", the *parcel* being a delivery of hashish. If it were a delivery of smuggled American cigarettes that he had in mind, he'd say, "The American steamer's expected today. Get in touch with Rayyes Mrabet." Merely to hear me being called in this familiar manner and in the crude lingo of sailors was enough to arouse the curiosity of passes-by and make them look at me inquisitively to see what this creature, Rayyes Khobza, was like.

Again, if I chanced to be at a wedding party and one of those villains in my profession saw me sitting snugly on a soft cushion in a corner of the hall and picking up the silver sprayer to sprinkle my neck, face and head with essence of orange-blossom, he'd look at me with wide-open eyes and say :

"Well, well, well, Rayyes Khobza ! Fancy your being here without my noticing it ! I *am* sure glad to see you ! But why are you skulking in a corner like a rabbit ?"

In a minute, he'd be whispering something or other to the host, who usually stands just within the hall-door to receive his guests. Presently, the host would come up to me, a sudden feeling of friendliness lighting up his face, and say, "Your presence with us, sir, is an honour which we greatly appreciate." Then, getting a shade more confidential, he'd add, "Master Azzouz Lafyouni" — that is, my colleague 'Poppyjuice' — "has just mentioned to me that you're a first-class expert in tea-making. Surely, you understand that this little party of ours here can't be a complete success unless we can offer our guests some *really* well-made tea. Really *strong* tea, as you might say, ha, ha !"

Imagine what an off-putting effect the name *Rayyes Khobza* would have upon the smart crowd which filled the large hall and all the adjacent rooms. Imagine how I'd feel as I tried to rise from my unobtrusive corner, assisted by the host who'd give me a hand up, and then cut across the hall, watched by scores of inquisitive eyes, to sit on the small mattress set aside for the tea-maker. In a situation like that, I would feel the blood rushing to my brain and wish to lift up the large silver tea-urn from which there'd be clouds of steam issuing — making it look like the kettle of the great Sidi[1] Badani, who fed on poisonous snakes, and drank his water on the boil — and pour it all over the head of that louse, Rayyes Azzouz Lafyouni, who had disturbed my quiet. Yet the merry-making going on, and the lovely Andalusian music, the scent of orange-blossom essence, the fumes of burning sticks of incense, the luxurious china plates laden with confectionary and sweetmeats such as *kaab* and *mulawwaza*, the crystal glasses and coloured bowls passed round on silver trays — all this would prevent me from giving vent to my inward rebellion and letting it burst out in some dangerously violent action. I'd try to take matters calmly, to oblige my host and, having rolled my sleeves way up over the elbows, I'd begin by looking critically at the caddy of green tea, the sugar bowl, and the peppermint.

---

(1) Saint (literally 'my lord').

Didn't someone say that troubles never come in ones ? Well, once upon a time, I had an acceptable, a quite respectable name, Hamidou. But this was filched from me in broad daylight on His Majesty the Sultan's highroad. The name *Khobza,* meaning *a loaf,* was given me instead in shameful exchange. And then take the name *El Mghandeef,* which means *the Cross-grained,* a base appellation that has clung to the skirts of my family's honour as shadows cling to solid bodies, and settled upon the head of every one of us like pots of wet clay. I haven't been able to tell where it comes from. No one else in my family, either, knows how it ever came to plague us like an endemic disease. Even my grandmother, old Dame Zhour, who was both an encyclopaedia and a *Who's Who* of the history of our city,who knew all the names and street names in it and could recall all the events which had occurred in it, such as the arrival of that cargo of enormous cannons which the Sultan had had made by special order in England and how the cannons were set up in front of the keeps of the city walls and of each of its coastal fortresses such as Bourj el Kasba, Sidi Bou Knadil and Dar el Baroud, and how the Sultan's Viceroy, when he had decided the moment had come to test the new weapons, commanded all the inhabitants of the town to take a stroll up the big mountain or at least to ramble for a few hours in the outlying suburbs in case the cannon fire scared them dead or brought their houses tumbling down or something, and how, when the good-for-nothing artillerymen had begun trying a gigantic cannon which was shaped like a square tower made up of several storeys and embodying corridors, stairways, wrought-iron paraphernalia, and whatnot, a sound was produced from the mouth of the gun, when they released the catch, which resembled very closely the sound that's made when the wick of an oil-lamp snuffs itself out, while the cannon itself split neatly in two, like an earthenware pot — and who would also tell amazing stories about the so-called *Year of the Kilogram*[1] as well as knowing the lay-out of the town like the back of her hand,

---

(1) The time of the change-over in Morocco, under the Protectorate, from traditoinal weights and measures, to the metric system.

being able to declare solemnly that where the rows of modern blocks of flats and cafés now stand in the Inner Market, there used to be nothing in the old days except booths of sackcloth within which bedouin greengrocers, bakers and coalmerchants sat, surrounded by piles of the dung of camels, donkeys and mules — even this omniscient grandmother, I say, could not tell what the origin of our family name was. One thing I am sure of is that it is *not* derived from the name of a town, such as, you might say, *Maghandafa*, nor from the name of a tribe, such as, you might say, *Beni Maghandafin:* as you know, it's a habit among some people to name themselves after the towns they come from, so that you get names like Kdour Lzilashi — from Zilash —, Sidi Larabi el Fasi — from Fez —, Hamidou el Tanjawi — from Tangier —, and so on.

It was my grandmother, old Dame Zhour, who had chosen the name of Hamidou for me. But this name has vanished out of my life and I've acquired, instead, the name of Loaf — Khobza. Now I'll tell you how this happened. It was when I was still very young. I went to borrow a loaf of bread from our neighbour, Hajja Rahma. For, as always happened when our own bread was late in arriving from the baker's, my mother, said, "Child, go to Hajja Rahma and borrow a loaf of bread from her." The Hajja peeped down at me from a high garret-window, poking out her mass of henna'd hair, and, as she was mightily deaf, I had to shout at the top of my voice, "Ma sends you her kindest regards and says she'll pray to God to preserve you for your children's sake, if you would lend us a loaf of bread, *just — one — loaf*. As ill-luck would have it, my voice came out on the word *loaf* in a highly-nasal twang. And, suddenly, the gang of children in our lane, who had gathered at our usual meeting-place on the doorsteps of the cadi's house, exploded with mirth, their laughter all but ripping up the walls of the houses, and that devil Majido fell on his back in a convulsion of merriment and jeered at me, saying, "Look, boys, even his face is like a round puffed-out loaf !" Then he fell to mimicking me, and yelled out the word "*Loaf* !" through his nose.

When I called him names back in return, I hoped that this would make people laugh at him instead. But nobody laughed. They just stood there, silently and derisively, as severe a punishment and show of contempt as could ever befall anyone. Then they expressed their mockery by producing comic sounds :

"*Feess, feess, feess*, ! *Teer, teer, teer*! *Breem, breem, breem* !"

When I looked up, I saw the neighbours' daughters, with their mothers, tittering behind the lattice-work of their windows. I couldn't restrain myself, so I lifted up the hem of my *gallabeyya* and held it in my teeth, in readiness for a fight. Then, thinking better of it, I stripped it off completely, and then flung off my waistcoat, kicked off my slippers, and ran at them, baring my teeth like a mad dog, and served them a fair round of punches, buttings, and kicks, spitting at them in true Spanish peasant fashion. The fight resulted in three wounded, and severe damage inflicted upon the clothes of all combatants concerned. The thing is, you see, I couldn't put up with the boys' unexpected insults, specially as they were hurled at me in front of the virgins of our street when I had been so careful to appear neat before them and had often assumed the part of a Romeo and performed gestures which in those days were recognized as the classical demonstrations of love, such as putting the first finger of the right-hand on the nose, or winking, or biting the lower lip while beating the breast with the right hand and sighing "Lord o Lord ! O my gazelle, my very own !"

On beautiful Ramadan nights, we used to take out a collection of rugs and sheep-skins and spread them out in a corner of the lane and hold a gathering which, if all went well, would extend far into the night. Each one of us performed curious acts to attract the attention of the young ladies who, day and night, watched our every movement from behind the interstices in the lattice-work of their windows. Sometimes, I'd act a leading part in an imaginary adventure and, once or twice, when I was singing, "*Yaleil, Yaleil, Yaein, Yaleil*[1] !" while my pals chirped in with the chorus, "Allah ! Allah !" or joined in the words of the song, I had no sooner finished singing "whenever I see you, you set

---

(1) Tradition a refrain, literally 'O night, O my eyes'.

me on fire", than I heard a cry of admiration issuing from behind a window, so I repeated the song all over again — rather more passionately, you bet — as an offering for the unseen golden-voiced damsel whom I thought I recognized.

A few days before I was born, a dispute had arisen between my father and mother concerning the name which I should have. My mother was in favour of calling me 'Omar', hoping for good fortune from the name of the Prophet's Companion, Omar ibn el Khattab, for she had often heard her own father narrating the lives of the Companions and depicting the exceptional heroism which they had shown in their wars and, as a result, she had developed a great veneration for this particular Companion. My father, on the other hand, wanted to call me 'Tarik' after the illustrious Arab army leader, Tarik Ibn Ziyad, for my father, through working in his youth on the ferry-boat between Tangier and Algeciras, had time and again crossed the same waters which Tarik had crossed on the expedition in which he conquered Spain and, in this way, my father had heard numerous vivid accounts of that hero's deeds. Whenever anyone started talking about Andalusia, father would sigh and shake his head sorrowfully over the loss of that paradise and mutter, "There's no success or power without God's will. If Moslems had held to their faith properly, the Infidels would never have been able to drive them out of their homes."

When the fighting between my father and mother had grown highly involved, my mother had thrown in a magical word which abruptly put out the fires of their dissension. "Let's wait till we see if it is a boy," she had said. "You're right," my father had answered, and he held his peace. Now when I was born, the feud, naturally, started up again — on the very day of my birth.

Each of my parents stuck fanatically to his own choice. Although my mother was still lying in childbed and had not recovered yet from the pains of childbirth, while a number of rags soaked with blood lay around the bed, she lifted up her head with an effort and yelled at my father :

"Now which of them is better, do you think : my blessed Lord

Omar or that army oaf of yours ? If you can't make your mind up, go and ask your learned father or ask his learned spouse, Hajja Amina, for they are both equally wise as far as I am concerned."

Then, overtaxed by this ill-timed excess of activity, she sank back on her bed, her bosom kept heaving up and down in a violent manner.

When my grandmother arrived upon the scene, coming from her orange grove on the mountain-side, and had taken in the whole situation, she looked at my mother calmly and said in a gentle voice, "This boy is my own son and I'm naming him Ahmed." Then she kissed her hand and placed it solemnly upon her head as a sign of the deepest veneration and as a sign of faith in an auspicious future — for had not the name Ahmed also belonged to the Prophet Mohamed ? and, while she admitted that the name Omar was a blessed one enough, she declared that the name Ahmed was the most blessed of all. Suddenly, she set up a prolonged, winged, silver-sounding trilling-cry which reverberated through the entire house and out in the street as well, a pure, resonant *zaghrouda* such as you might hear only from a girl of twenty-five. More *zaghroudas* were heard, presently, from the womenfolk who chanced to be in the house at the time and who were mostly neighbours and relatives. In the middle of all this rejoicing, my father emerged out of the room, carefully freeing the curtain from his very tall head-wrapping which resembled a green pepper, a look of profuse self-satisfaction illuminating his face. He went to the Outer Market to pick up a fat ram, with horns winding like those of a gazelle and with a black patch on its forehead, exactly following out the recommendations of Grandmother Amina, who had announced that this would ensure me good luck throughout my life. My father did his duty and bought and slaughtered the ram, and yet, as I am well aware, good luck has passed me by several times in my life, and sorrow after sorrow have found their way into my heart.

Finally, when I could no longer bear the annoyance that the names (Khobza) and (Mghandeef) caused me in Tangier, I decided to move to Tetuan. Arriving there, I chose a fine name for myself, as film and stage directors are known to do frequently. For an actor or actress might have a vile and disgusting name like Si Hamou Lkaakooi or Zarouk Lzaatouti or Tamo Bou Khnafer or Aisha Qandisha, and then the producer comes along and selects for them bright and beautiful names such as Camellia or Moon-Flower or Fuad Jamal. So I called myself Kamal el Din and was known by that name among my new friends.

My life continued as peacefully as anything for about three months during which I forgot the worries of the past and the doldrums into which Master Azouz Poppyjuice had often thrown me.

Then, one day, as I was sitting in a café which was full of tourist-guides like myself — I was wearing my clean white outfit, which I had preserved for use on Fridays only, and was deeply engaged in a game of cards — I suddenly saw Rayyes Azouz Lafyouni standing in front of me. He looked extremely surprised and cried, "Hey, it's Haj Khobza el Mghandeef ! Here's where you're hiding ! And we have been wondering for months where you'd got to !"

I felt the ground give way beneath my feet. Sweat poured down my forehead. My eyes were blurred and the cards we were using in our poker-game went fuzzy. My head spun round and round. I saw the kings, queens and knaves floating all about me.

My new friends noticed how stunned I was. Sarcastic smiles appeared on their faces. They didn't just keep quiet. My embarrassment was nothing to them. One of them exclaimed, "Good God, man ! How many names have you got ?"

I stepped out of the ring of players, stumbling over the cards which were arranged on a rush mat on the floor, and kicking over the ashtray. I took the bastard Poppyjuice by the hand and led him out. When we had entered the passage known as Little Jug Lane, I took him by surprise and gave him a hard butt with my head which made him sprawl and cry out with pain and beg for my forgiveness. "I beg a thousand pardons of you, brother," he cried," In the name of your valour, in the name of our gracious Saint, Sidi Bou Arkia, I beg you to lay off me ! I won't call you Rayyes Khobza ever, ever again ! I won't call you El Mghandeef, either !"

I left him writhing on the floor, bleeding at the mouth and nose, and walked home. That night, I decided to go back to my beloved home-town, Tangier, I was sure that the ghost of Khobza would appear again in Tetuan, whether it be in El Faddan Square or in Little Jug Lane, and arouse as much curiosity and cruel smiling as it had done in the Inner Market and Harbour Gate Streets in my native city.

I told myself that, since suffer I must from my names anywhere and everywhere, it was better to endure it in my beautiful town and enjoy the air of Sidi Ammar and the summer nights out on the pavement in front of El Hafa Café than to hear these coarse names pronounced again in El Faddan Square in Tetuan.

Translated by Sami el Kalyoubi; revised by Lewis Hall.

THE SCORPION HUNTER

Abdel Rahman el Sharkawi

ABDEL RAHMAN EL SHARKAWI (b. 1920) is a socially-committed author, deeply attached to the rural life of Lower Egypt, especially in his native Menoufia. His is best known for his novel *Al-Ard* (*The Earth*) which has been translated into English by Desmond Stewart. There is a notice of it in French by Naguib Baladi in the Cairo Dominican publication *MIDEO* (No. 2, 1955: pp. 307-10). Sharkawi has written a second novel, *Ash-shawari'-ul-khalfiyya* (*Back Streets*); he is also known as a poet, and has written two verse plays, *Ma'sāh Jamīla* (*The Tragedy of Jamila*: on the Algerian national heroine Djamila Bouhaired) and *Al-Fatā Mahrān*. Sharkawi graduated in law in 1943, has worked as a lawyer, a civil servant, and a journalist, and is now in charge of the scenario-writing department of a film corporation.

The present short story was written in the immediate post-war years, and gives a dual picture, of Cairo as a leave-city for Allied troops during the Second World War and of the difficulties of life in a Lower Egyptian village during those days. The original title is *Al-'aqrab* (*The Scorpion*): it is found in the author's collection *Aḥlāmun saghīra* (*Slight Dreams*), as well as being anthologized in the two collections *Alwānun min al-qiṣṣat-il-miṣriyya* and *khamsatu-'ashri qiṣṣatan miṣriyya*, given in the Arabic reading list at the back of this volume.

And now it has become difficult to find a bite to eat, Hassan, even though you own a house of your own in your home village. And you're better off than many others, Hassan. Ever since the day His Reverence the Sheikh kicked you out of the mosque, you've been shifting aimlessly from one job to the other. You even went to Cairo to work on the gharry[1] that your relative runs, lived through the air raids, got beaten up by the English soldiery, and broke a few ribs, only to come back

(1) The Anglo-Indian name for the hoosled horse-drawn carriage, or *fiacre*.

just the way you'd gone. You beg and plead with His Reverence to hire you again as the attendant in the mosque, but he won't. You try to get yourself drafted into the army, but you're turned down. And the only way left for you to get a bite to eat is by catching scorpions.

Catching scorpions ? Just one sting from a scorpion is enough to get rid of you once and for all. You're in a fix, Hassan. But a scorpion sells for a piastre—ten for the price of a measure of corn. Ten scorpions, man, will buy you enough bread to fill a sack. And a single man in the depths of Upper Egypt can fill a can to the brim with scorpions and nothing ever happens to him. The boys in Boulak said the men in Upper Egypt were never afraid of scorpions, hunted them easily and made great piles of piastres.

But this has never been heard of here in the village before.

* * *

Hassan raised his head from between his palms and sighed. He scratched his back against the wall of the guest house against which he had been lolling since late morning. His bare toes played in the hot dust. He stared across the sun-drenched village street at the mosque on the other side. Only his head was shaded by the wall of the guest house in the suffocating heat of the afternoon.

The sheikh passed by, looked towards Hassan and spat on the ground.

"Why look at me like that ?" Hassan asked. "You could at least say good morning. Isn't it enough that you sacked me from the mosque ?"

The sheikh stopped at the mosque door, took off his slippers, reciting some verses of the Koran as he did so, then tucked his slippers under his arm. He cleared his throat, spat again on to the roadway, and said, "You just stay there. Just stay slumped there in front of the mosque in the heat of the sun. Go on, punish yourself if you want to, Hassan, son of Zeinab . ."

"You leave Zeinab out of this, God rest her soul," Hassan murmured, "If it weren't for her I'd have been in the army today with something to eat. But when I was first called up they said I was supporting her, and when she conked out they said I wasn't fit."

The sheikh halted, his white beard shaking in sudden anger. "What are you muttering about, boy ?" he shouted, "Isn't it enough that the wrath of God should bring you down to scorpion-catching ? God have mercy on this village. It is God's mighty anger that blew this scorpion-laden wind against it. God damn you, you unbeliever : all you do is just lie sprawling there in front of the mosque; you don't even bother to make your ablutions though I'm about to call the noon prayer."

Hassan's reply came with a vigour that did not hide his fear. "By God, I'll never set foot in the mosque again. What did I ever get out of it ? Only getting kicked out, having to tramp here and there, knocked about in Cairo with its air raids and drunken soldiers. And after all that to end up scorpion-catching just to find something to eat. And Heaven alone knows what I'm in for next."

A quiet, solemn voice rose from inside the mosque. "Let us bless the Prophet, Your Reverence; it is noon and you had better call for the prayers."

The *imam* swirled round, scrambled into the mosque, and made for the clean mat next to the pulpit where a fat, pale man sat, wearing a *tarboush* and a white linen *gallabeyya*. "Right away," said the sheikh, "right away, sir."

He shifted his gaze from the man in front to the scattering of people behind him on worn-out old rush mats. He muttered "Greetings and God's blessings on you, sir; how have you been, sir ?"

The man, who was the owner of the nearby estate, returned his gold watch to his pocket, and said, "What they are saying is that the government needs all the scorpion poison it can extract, to use it in place of the stuff they can't import because of the war."

He turned around to look at the men who were seated on the decayed rush mats; they were looking at him intently and listening in wonder to what he was saying. Then he added, laughing and letting his amber prayer-beads fall one by one through his thick, reddish fingers: "The war has made scorpions valuable." He shifted his gaze forward again, towards the cracks in the mosque walls. A low, hoarse, anxious voice rose from behind: "'And made men worth nothing."

When the *effendi* turned round to reply, Hassan grabbed at his hand and bent low over it. The man withdrew his hand and said with a smile, "Why, so it's you, Hassan. So you've come into mosque after all ?"

He was silent for a moment while Hassan went to sit behind him, well clear of the clean mat. Then he added, "And why has the war made man worth nothing, Hassan ? It's provided work for layabouts like you, hasn't it ? Can't you ever say 'Thank God' ? Was there ever any scorpion-catching around these parts before ? Why don't you get to work ?"

Hassan was at a loss for a reply. He laughed in bewilderment. The *sheikh's* voice rose from the rooftop of the mosque, calling to prayer. Hassan said: "How many scorpions do you think there are in the whole village ? How much can each of us make ? If His Reverence were not so greedy, would he have done this to me ? Call this Islam ? He gets two pounds a month from the mosque funds. The *omda* gives them to him every month, before my very eyes. Out of which he gives me a measly five-piastre piece every month. I spend all day long carrying water to the mosque, shuttling back and forth from the river to fill the water-tank, come rain or summer blaze, never tiring or grumbling. A bull calf in a farmyard, or a government mule, would have collapsed. All this for a five-piastre piece a month. *And* I'm contented, *and* I thank God for what He gives. Then when the price of corn shoots up, and the measure costs ten piastres, and I come begging His Reverence to raise my pay a bit, he picks a fight with me. And when I ask the *omda* to put in a word for me, he grows furious and kicks me out. And swears by God's holy Book never to allow me near the water tank again. So that's why I'm scraping about like this."

His Reverence was slowly descending the stairs from the roof after having called for prayer. He entered the mosque and headed towards the clean rush mat near the pulpit mumbling, "Now is the time to pray. Now is the time to pray."

Hassan hissed, "I hope to God it won't be long before we pray for your soul."

One of his neighbours shook him by the shoulder and whispered, "Drop it, Hassan. Why don't you just forget it and praise Almighty God ?"

"Just take the skewer that the government man gave you and do as he told you," said another. "You'll make more than ten piastres a day. The mosque by itself should be good for more than a hundred scorpions. Then there's the guest-house, and the waste land behind it. You can make twice as much as His Reverence makes every month. How much do you think we make working all day in the fields ? Stop your grumbling. You'll be making as much as a government employee."

As soon as the prayers ended, and the congregation had shaken hands with each other, the *sheikh* started complaining to the landowner about Hassan, and asked him to talk to the district authorities, and have Hassan sent to El Tor prison. He said that a man like Hassan, without a steady job, unworthy of the charity shown to him, would pollute every one around him — and although His Reverence had always helped him out, Hassan once accused him of robbing him of his dues from the mosque funds. And when the *sheikh* had booted him out, he had failed in all the other jobs he had tried. He had been to Cairo, only to come back after he got into trouble with English soldiers. And ever since his return, he had been complaining about the *sheikh* to one and all, slandering him and his womenfolk.

The owner of the small estate smiled and told Hassan not to slander the *sheikh's* womenfolk.

Hassan burst out, as he hurried towards the entrance of the mosque behind the landowner, "May I be struck down by a scorpion's bite before I get to use any of their money if . ."

"May God bring this to pass !" interrupted His Reverence.

"Yes, may God bring it to pass," Hassan continued, panting, "*if* His Reverence is telling the truth. His womenfolk ? After I strain my heart lugging water about for Granny Om-el-Izz, ever since the day I returned from Cairo, without seeing the colour of her money, only on the promise she'll get His Reverence to take me back in the mosque for that five-piastre piece .. after all this, Your Reverence, you come and tell me I don't know what about your womenfolk ? Why don't you let the Master ask Om-el-Izz herself ?"

The sheikh was very ashamed when Hassan blurted out his wife's name before the landowner and all the men who were standing around. He charged towards Hassan and slapped him, trembling and shouting, "God punish you, you vile creature."

He turned towards the landowner ans said in obvious embarrassment, "I am sorry, sir. It was out of place to hit him in front of you. I'm sorry."

"Never mind," replied the landowner, bending down to pick up his shoes. "But that's enough". The *sheikh* came to his assistance by helping him to keep his balance while he put on his shoes.

Hassan walked out of the mosque and stood by the wall of the guest-house, looking at the *sheikh* and at the men gathered around talking to him; one of the men was holding the silver-studded reins of the land-owner's donkey, with its velvet saddle protected by white cloth.

Hassan gazed reflectively at the silver studs on the reins. Every one of them would be worth the price of his risking death ten times over with the scorpions.

The landowner got through the round of salutations, and then announced in a loud voice to one of the men standing near him that he still had a large number of bags of fertilizer which he could no longer sell because he needed them. The man told him, imploringly, that he was ready to pay any price for ten sacks. Placing his foot in the stirrup, the landowner said, "Alright, Sheikh Younes. I'll let you have seven sacks to save your cotton. You'll buy them at the price Sheikh Abdel Aziz paid. You all know that the fertilizer I have is a rare quality and from now on it won't be available any more. There'll be no more of it imported until the war's over — you mark my word."

"But that's a hundred and fifty piastres more than its official price," murmured Sheikh Younes submissively. "Anyway, I agree, *effendi*, I'll get the money ready, and call on you tomorrow when the afternoon prayers are over."

The donkey moved forward with the landowner settled astride it, and one of his men scurrying behind. "Daylight robbery !" Sheikh Younes grumbled, "Call this buying and selling ? Doesn't he make enough ? What about those who can't pay his price — what are they to do ? That's what we get from this damn war . ."

A voice interrupted him, "You're only buying fertilizer, Sheikh Younes. What am I to do, sir ? I have to buy my *corn* from him ?"

The donkey carrying the landowner was moving away; the grumbling increased, telling of his deals with the commandant and the police authorities. Hassan stood in his place gazing after the donkey and listening to what was being said about the landowner's greed and the prices he asked. He moved a little as though to follow the donkey, but he halted and turned around towards the crowd. As soon as he saw the *sheikh* leave, he rushed towards the men and said, pointing in the direction that the landowner had taken, "By God, his greed is enough to frighten you away from ever talking to him again. And I wanted to beg him to put in a word for me ? May he drop dead. May he go straight to hell."

There was laughter all round. A voice asked, "Damn you, Hassan — what did you want him to put in a word for you about, man?" Hassan went on, not hearing the interruption, still gazing at the donkey which was disappearing into a cloud of dust far away, "Who do you think you are compared to those who are really making money out of the war in Cairo ? You can't get anywhere near them. Believe me, men, the things I saw and heard in the short time I was in Cairo ! You've seen nothing. You know who the wealthiest people in Cairo are these days ? Belly dancers, tarts, a cabaret owner. Any one of them could buy and sell this Master here who imagines he's so smart in dealing with us. You know, men, one of these dancers just has to shake her belly for the English soldiers, and you know how much she gets for it a night ? A hundred pounds. A hundred ! In four nights she's got the price of a full acre of land. So, you see, if she wiggles away with her hips for two months she can buy those thirty acres of our smart Master over there."

The crowd began to disperse, laughing, and filled with a strange feeling of satisfaction.

* * *

In Hassan's mind, memories whirled around in rapid succession.

From the day that the sheikh refused to raise his pay to ten piastres a month, and hired someone else for the job, everything had gone against him. He could not get work in the fields anywhere. There was none there for him, nor for twenty others like him in the village. He worked in the *omda's* house for his meals but the *omda*'s wife threw him out because he ate more than enough for two men. One of his relatives took him to Cairo and dumped him in Boulak. His relative taught him how to get the gharry ready for him every day before he started his rounds. He often dreamt of riding on the gharry, and of seeing the streets of Cairo. But his relative never agreed. Still, he was happy in Cairo. He ate wheat bread, *halawa*[1] and *falafel*[2] and all the good things he had never tasted back in the village. But when the sirens wailed and he experienced an air raid for the first time in his life, his blood froze in his veins. He was seized by a fit of trembling when he heard the explosions and the screams and saw the skies bright with fire, while the earth was shaking under him. There was panic everywhere around him. He was certain it was doomsday. He swore if he got through that night safely he would head straight back for the village. When the raid was over he saw pale frightened faces everywhere. He told his relative he was going back to the village to die of hunger there, rather than perish in a fire, away from it, in one of these raids. He was almost in tears. His relative started to calm him down, trying to convince him that one has to put up with things in order to make a living, promising that he could ride next to him on the gharry, promising even to teach him how to drive it.

In the morning there he was on the gharry next to his cousin, staring in amazement and delight at the streets of Cairo. At night the

---

(1) The sweetmeat known in the west as *halva*, and made of sesame-seed meal.

(2) Bean rissoles: also known as *ta'mia*.

carriage pulled up in front of a night club. He would never forget that night. The streets were not all lit up as he had imagined. The lamps were painted blue. The city was cold, shivering, sad, deserted except for swaying English soldiers, women laughing and women shriecking.

Three soldiers came out of the night club with a tall woman; fair-skinned, with bare shoulders. They got into the carriage in silence. The woman said, swaying as she sat in the carriage, "Drive us around Zamalek, cabby, for an hour or two."

This made his relative happy. He cracked his whip and whispered to Hassan, "We're in luck tonight. These are American soldiers and they have heaps of money. And you know the lady with them ? She comes from a very good family. Father's a big man around here; so is her husband. She only goes out with Americans. I know her. She's taken my carriage several times. She loves gharries. You know, gharries are for those who are out to enjoy themselves. Taxis aren't a patch on them."

There was laughter from behind and Hassan heard strange noises. He turned around. When he saw what was going on, he stuck his head inside the carriage, gaping with astonishment. He was taken by surprise when the woman inside slapped his face and started to swear at him. Hassan withdrew his head and cursed back at her. Then pandemonium broke loose. In a minute he was flat on the ground while fists and boots pounded him. His relative was screaming, shouting for help, and cursing Hassan, while at the same time trying to shield himself from the blows.

The woman was walking away with the soldiers. His relative clambered back on to his driver's seat, cursing himself for bringing along such a catastrophe that had ruined his work. Hassan swore back at him, upbraiding him for renting his carriage for such a purpose.

As Hassan stood feeling his ribs before getting on the carriage again the sirens wailed and once more he saw the skies afire with high explosive. For a while he was afraid they were going to come tumbling down on his head.

Next morning he was back at the village. He could not obtain work in the fields, nor a decent word word from the *sheikh*. Om-el-Izz tricked him into working for her, and when he asked for a sack of corn for two months' work, she chased him out. Now there was no help ! Was there anything left but scorpion-catching ?

* * *

Hassan felt he had to talk to somebody. He looked around but found near the wall of the guest house only his own shadow. He went home, still uncertain what to do.

When he opened the door of his dark little home he was met by a gust of cool air. He walked into the room; a single beam of sunlight crept in through a gap in the roof. He rummaged in the basket and slowly began to munch the only loaf of bread he found there. Then he stretched himself out behind the door, enjoying the cool of the room.

When he woke up dusk was drenching the road with its yellow light. This was the hour when scorpions crept out of their holes. He picked up his tin can and the iron skewer, reviewing in his mind the instructions the official had given him about hunting the scorpion.

He left quickly, feeling a tremor of disgust run through his body. The man from the *markaz*[1] would be coming in the morning with plenty of piastres, to buy all the scorpions collected by the men in the village. A piastre for every scorpion. But the truth was, Hassan dreaded the sight of one. He wished he had talked to the landowner, and had asked for his help in getting drafted into the army. He was sorry he had not. He had failed his medical test. They said he had ringworm and his body was riddled with diseases: he was pronounced unfit. And yet he was tall and broadshouldered and could pick up two petrol-tins full of water and carry them twenty times round the village.

He reached the guest-house. There he found three others who, like him, could not find work in the fields. Each of them was armed with the tin can and the iron skewer which had been issued to them. They sat in the guest-house waiting for the scorpions.

The village was dappled with afternoon shadows. Hassan learned

(1) Centre of administrative district.

that each of the others had already bagged three piastres' worth of scorpions from the waste-land behind the guest-house. They were bragging about it and claiming that there was more money to make where they were than on the waste land. Hassan was rather surprised at what they said, but gradually became engrossed in his own need to fill his tin can with game.

One of the men spotted a scorpion crawling towards them, followed by another. "Come along now. Now, to be quite fair, and so as to have no quarrelling amongst us," the man said in a sober tone, "this one is Hassan's. Come on, Hassan, get up and take your chance."

Hassan was nonplussed. His heart was pounding furiously and his body was cold all over. He gave a start, as his eyes fixed upon the scorpion in mingled alarm and hope. He shut his eyes for a moment, then opened them wide. Firmly, he clutched the iron skewer in one hand, the tin can in the other, and took one step towards the creature which was creeping along very slowly.

"What kind of a deal is this ?" shouted one of the young men. "Hassan has the whole of the mosque to catch as much as he likes in it .."

Hassan, in secret relief, hung back, but a firm hand pushed him forward and he heard a voice saying, "Get on with it, Hassan. Go on, man. There are two of them. By God, three .. and — oh, lovely — here's a fourth. Four piastres, boys. A piastre for each and no need to fight."

The lad who had spoken plunged his iron skewer into the back of a scorpion and quickly dumped it in his container, with a gleeful shout. He tried to spear another, but one of his companions pushed him away saying, "Don't be greedy. Aren't you the one who's pretending to be fair ? Come on, Hassan. It's your turn."

Hassan came forward and threw his whole weight behind the iron skewer; he impaled the scorpion. His face was contorted in disgust and he avoided looking at the creature. He hastily drew it off the skewer against the inner side of the tin can, and moved away, carrying his prize, and breathing in relief — contented and hopeful. "That was the first piastre. Steady now."

The boys squatted on the ground once more, waiting for more scorpions. The deep blue colours of the evening were driving out of the village the straggling glimmers of the late afternoon.

They waited for some time, their eyes searching the cracks in the walls around them. Then they slowly got up and spread themselves out, poking at the gaps and scrutinizing the ground. "There's nothing here," said one of them with annoyance. "That contractor imagines that it's the same here as in Upper Egypt. Truth is, he ought to pay us two piastres for each."

Another said in a faint and shaking voice that he had almost got stung by one of the creatures. They all fell silent. Then they heard the voice of the *sheikh* calling for the evening prayer. After the prayers a few men walked out of the mosque. The boys remained in the guest-house, silent, their eyes searching the emptiness around them, their hearts pounding. "Why don't we go and look in the mosque?" Hassan said feebly. "Yes," replied one of the boys, with more enthusiasm, "it's teeming with them in the wash-place[1] there. Last night there was one that crawled towards the *sheikh* while he was at his ablutions."

Hassan went ahead of the others. He picked up the lantern from the inside of the mosque and placed it in the open space around which the ablution stands were laid out. He held the skewer and the tin and began to search around the bottom of the walls, the three other boys following behind. Suddenly, he lifted his bare foot, and gave a yell; the three others rushed to him. One of them bent down, then straightened up saying, "Just a piece of dried mud. You're a bit of a coward, damn you."

They resumed their search. Then one of them gave a shout. "Come on, boys. There must be a dollar's[2] worth here. At them, men, at them."

---

(1) Provided in mosque for ritual ablutions.

(2) The term *dollar* (riyāl, from the Spanish *real*) is used in Egypt for twenty piastres.

They dived quickly at the scorpions, driving the skewers into their backs as they came towards them one after another. The young men were shouting. Hassan asked them to give him a chance to catch three for himself, to make up for what he had missed on the wasteland. No one took any notice. Time and again, each stood up straight for a moment to inspect the ground cautiously around his bare feet, plunged with his skewer, then happily slipped the game off the skewer against the rim of his container.

"Here we are" said Hassan, laughing and stabbing away, "Here's a whole measure of corn. Now for the price of some clothes. Or perhaps a pound of butter. Here, how much do you think a *gallabeyya* would cost, boys ? I could use a good shirt too. Or maybe I should get a really fancy *gallabeyya*."

"Why don't you buy yourself a length of cashmere ?" one of the boys answered, as he busily stabbed at the ground, "or a fancy *caftan* ? Or a *tarboush* maybe ?"

Everyone laughed. They were all bending forward, working their skewers at the ground. "By God," gasped one of them, "this is a treasure-trove. What a Night of Miracles, boys .. There's just nothing like it .. it's a Night of Bounty !"

He cut himself short. "Watch out, Hassan," he shouted in alarm. "Watch out ! Under your feet !"

The laughter ceased abruptly. An ominous silence held them motionless. Hassan fell heavily to the ground. "Oh, no !" he moaned, "You're done for, Hassan. No time to enjoy anything, Hassan,"

The voice died away. The boys did not look up. The iron skewers in their hands picked up the crawling scorpions and their tears fell on to the dust, where Hassan lay stretched out.

Translated by David Bishai; revised by Ronald Ewart.

THREE MEN AND A DOG
Abdel Rahman Fahmy

ABDEL RAHMAN FAHMY read Arabic at Cairo University. He has worked as a schoolmaster, later entering the Ministry of Education, and is at present in the Translation Office of the UAR Ministry of Higher Education. Most of his short stories appeared first in the periodical press, but a selection of them has been collected in two volumes: *Suzie wadh-dhikrayāt* (*Suzie and Memories*) and *Almulku lak* (*Thine be the Kingdom*). Abdel Rahman Fahmy says that he is half Ethiopian and half Turkish by blood, but, as Shukry Ayyad has written of him (in the daily *Al - Missa* for July 2, 1967), he has a thoroughly Egyptian outlook.

This story is from the anthology *Qisas min Misr,* listed in the bibliography at the end of this volume.

The hero of this story follows a folk custom in composing brief poems—always couplets in the original—to express the mood of the occasion as it arises. The custom has been transmitted to the Spanish, and it is said that the Spanish Copls, with an emphatic repetition of the second line, form the original of the authentic blues form of New Orleans.

A cold wind howled outside and the ring of three men drew closer to the flames of the fire they had made out of the bits of wood left behind by the builders. The huge dog crouching amongst them barked. Abdel Megid looked at the shadows of his two companions that were dancing with the flames on the bare unplastered walls, and his coarse voice sang the praises of broad-leafed lettuce:

''O food of princes, the lovely moisture of a virgin's soft lips, as sweet as musk."

He stopped his singing to take a sip of the tea they had boiled in a tin jug. The huge dog barked and wagged its tail. Abdel Megid patted its back and resumed his singing:

So fresh the greenness they sowed at sunrise
And sold at market before the dusk :
O lettuce tasty. .

Asham interrupted him with a laugh :

"You're in a very good mood tonight, Abdel Megid. Is it because of the *gallabeyya* the proprietor gave you ?

Abdel Megid sang in answer :

A king you are tonight Abdel Megid.
Kneel down you scum — I'm passing on my steed.

Asham laughed sarcastically. The dog barked so loud that Hassib gave him a kick, shouting :

"Why don't you shut up? You've given us all headaches, damn you!"

The dog's bark turned into a pained yelp, and it rubbed its head against the thigh of Abdel Megid who began to sing again, stroking the dog's head :

You can bear for a while
A yokefellow who's vile,
When you know that the yoke
Will that summer be broke.

He ended his song with a long sigh that was abruptly stifled by a slap from Hassib.

* * *

The men had spent two days practically without seeing the sun, that had been blotted out by thick clouds which endlessly poured down rain sometimes mingled with hail. A cold, cruel north wind blew with devastating force and there were no doors or windows to protect them against it. In the room where they gathered, the doors and windows were merely gaping openings without shutters or panes of glass. Its walls were bare and unplastered. Its floor was dust mixed with bits of cement that had dropped from the builders as they carried it in. The building was still under construction. They themselves were a desperate lot. Two of them were linked together by having the same hometown and the same work — Asham and Hassib. They had 'emigrated' from Upper Egypt to Cairo and became part of what people call the 'labour force'. Their life consisted mainly of using their muscles to carry bricks and cement from the bottom of the building to the highest point the masons had reached. At night they became watchmen and guarded the contractor's building equipment against thieves. Asham was small, his eye-sockets deep and his looks malicious. He had a sad voice. Hassib was a giant, his neck as thick as a mule's and his thick lips always viciously parted. His large eyes cast fatuous looks at you, and his only means of expression were a kick or a slap: he would give you one of them long before his tongue had a chance to utter a word.

Abdel Megid, their companion, was an entirely different type. He had nothing to do with construction and builders. He was a street vendor who roamed the Cairo streets peddling his lettuce. He had not fared well. The owner of the building had taken pity on him when he had seen him, and had appointed him the caretaker of it and of the piles of ironmongery, wood, and building material littered in front of it. That is how he came to join the other two. Naturally, they considered him an intruder and they persecuted him. He suffered the vileness of Asham and the brute force of Hassib and he looked back with regret at the days when he had sold lettuce. He spent his nights reciting the songs he had sung when he had sold lettuce in the streets. He even continued to wear the clothes he had worn as a costermonger : a torn *gallabeyya* that was black in colour, or that had been black, an old shawl wound around his waist, and a skull-cap around which he wrapped a length of green cloth which, he claimed, was a turban that gave him the cachet of a holy one, and so helped him obtain a free dinner on saints' days and at festivals in honour of the Prophet.

The fourth of the group was a stray dog whose size and viciousness made it impossible to tame it. It roamed the roads by day scavenging for food in the piles of garbage strewn up narrow lanes. At nightfall, it sought shelter in the unfinished building, against the cold and the wind. The three men had got used to it and the dog had taken to them. They never attempted to chase it off. They allowed it to squeeze between them as they huddled round the fire each night, and when they stretched themselves out to sleep, at different spots on the floor, the dog looked for a corner of the building in which it too went to sleep.

* * *

Outside the wind was roaring and it penetrated their shelter around the fire. The dog howled and nestled its head against Abdel Megid's chest. The fire trembled under the lashing of the wind. Asham said : "It's a freezing cold night, men. What are you going to do about this cold, Abdel Megid ?"

There was a malicious tone in his voice to which Abdel Megid did not pay any attention. He answered, as usual, singing :

Others may freeze : Abdel Megid feels warm
For God will keep His poor and meek from harm.

* * *

The group had been suffering the biting cold for the past two days. Asham and Hassib each slept on an empty sack, covered themselves with two other sacks and used a block of wood as a pillow. But such a cover could not ward off the lashing of the terrible cold. Abdel Megid was worse off. He was not a watchman hired by the contractor like them and therefore did not have the right to use the contractor's sacks. On his first night with them he tried to use one of the empty sacks strewn around the rooms on the first floor but the two men objected, and threatened to beat him up if he so much as touched anything that belonged to the contractor. He tried to squeeze next to Hassib under his cover but Hassib growled and kicked him away. He turned to where Asham slept, but Asham gave him a shove in the chest and said :

"Let those who hired you provide you with a cover."

He had had to spend the night next to the dying fire, seeking an illusory warmth from its nearness. The succeeding nights were the same. Yet there was nothing really wrong with spending nights like this : it was no worse than spending the night in the fields back at the village, or sleeping out in the streets of Cairo. But the cold of the last two days was beyond his endurance. It was beyond the endurance of even Asham and Hassib. When he got up that morning Abdel Megid felt as though a thousand hammers were beating against his back and ribs. He was hardly able to drag his frozen legs around. As soon as he saw the proprietor he ran towards him complaining of the bitter cold. The man asked him:

"Haven't you got something to cover yourself up with ?"

"How, sir ? I am a poor man. Even the sacks lying around here, they wouldn't let me use. They have no fear of God, these men."

Asham had planned to ask the contractor for a little advance money with which he could buy a blanket. But he was surprised to find Hassib telling him:

"I'm going to the second-hand market to buy myself a blanket."

Asham asked:

"Do you have any money ?"

"No. I'll take some from the boss."

Asham, nasty-minded, could tell that the contractor would refuse him the advance if Hassib also asked for one. Or, at most, he would give them just enough to buy one blanket which they could both use. He hurried to the contractor and whispered:

"That lad Hassib is planning to ask you for money to go to the café tonight and gamble. Watch him."

The contractor nodded his head silently. A few moments later the workers heard his voice cursing Hassib and threatening to sack him. Hassib returned, shaking with anger and told Asham:

"You did it, you rotten . ."

Asham smiled innocently and said:

"See here, mate, aren't you ashamed of yourself ? Can you really believe that I'd turn the boss against you ?"

Hassib left it at that, but was not fooled by Asham's smile. He kept his opinion to himself. Asham waited until the contractor had cooled down and asked him for the loan. The contractor exploded in his face :

"So you too want to diddle me ? You call yourselves men ? — Leaving your work and going off to gamble ? Why tell tales about Hassib ?"

Asham hurried away before Hassib could overhear the contractor and find out the whole story.

When the builders left that evening, Abdel Megid was surprised to find the proprietor drive up in his car and call him. He handed him a parcel and said :

"Take this and cover yourself with it at night. You're a good man."

Abdel Megid stabbed the wrapping with his finger and felt the wool of a thick blanket. He ran after the owner's car shouting his thanks and praying for his continued wealth and prosperity, and for God to shield his house from scandal, until the car was out of sight. Then he returned, clutching the parcel to his chest as though it were a precious treasure.

Abdel Megid was overjoyed with the blanket. It not only meant warmth, deep sleep and an end to the hammering that broke his back every morning, but it also carried a more significant meaning to him. He now had more prestige than Hassib and Asham. The proprietor who had hired him gave him a better coverlet than that provided by the contractor for whom they worked. He was going to taunt the vile Asham and that idiot Hassib with his blanket. He was going to leave them to their ragged sacks that let the cold in to gnaw at their bodies. He alone was going to revel in the warmth of a blanket. Abdel Megid imagined their being woken in the middle of the night by the cold, and saw himself snug under his blanket. He imagined the surprise that would make their eyes pop wide open, and the envy that would stab at their hearts. He was roused with a start by Asham's malicious voice asking:

"What have you got there Abdel Megid ?"

— Abdel Megid was confused, and held the parcel more tightly. "Er .. Nothing. Just an old *gallabeyya* the proprietor has given me."

He hurried off with his parcel, his confusion making him stumble. He hid the blanket in a room at the far end of the building and covered it over with a couple of planks of wood.

* * *

The rain was again pouring down. The wind outside grew more savage and a cold gust penetrated into their shelter, making the flames twist and swirl. The three men raised their tin cups to drink their third round of black tea. The wind brought to their ears a noise which came from the wooden boards piled in front of the building. Hassib and Asham knew from experience that it was the sound of the wind blowing through the piles of wooden boards. But Abdel Megid raised his head, listened, then asked in a husky voice:

"What can it be, men ?"

Hassib looked blandly at him, as though he had not heard. Asham smiled cunningly and said:

"Why don't you go and find out ?"

Abdel Megid looked at him carefully out of the corner of his eyes and said:

"You want me to go out in that cold ? You really expect me to ?"

"It may be a thief."

"A thief ?" said Abdel Megid, spreading his hands out close to the fire, and turning them round to warm them. "On a night like this ? He'd have to be mad."

"Thieves aren't afraid of the cold. Isn't that so, Hassib ?"

Hassib turned towards him as though awakened from deep slumber:

"What's that ?"

"Thieves."

"What about them ?"

Abdel Megid took no notice and concentrated on the last sip of tea from his tin cup. Their conversation did not bother him. He knew they were making fun of him, particularly that mean little creature Asham who wanted to trick him into going out in the cold so he might fall ill and die.

The wind was becoming fiercer. Thunder raged above. Lightning flashed and filled the room with its brightness, lighting up the three faces. Abdel Megid's face wore a happy smile. Asham's face was cunning and cringing as he told Hassib amusing stories to try to make him laugh and forget the affair of the contractor. The room soon sank back into the faint, stifled half-light of the dying fire. The noise made by the wind blowing through the piles of wooden boards and iron struts came to their ears again. Abdel Megid raised his head attentively. Asham nudged Hassib with his feet.

"The thief, Abdel Megid," he said.

"What thief ?" asked Abdel Megid, straining his ears.

This time his voice was full of doubt. Asham realized he was beginning to believe him.

"Don't you believe it's a thief ?" he went on. "Honestly ! Go and have a look at the things outside."

"Eh ? Why don't you go yourself ? Aren't you a watchman just like me ?"

"The proprietor didn't give me a *gallabeyya*."

That was true, Abdel Megid .. The man was generous to you and gave you a blanket, not a *gallabeyya* as this idiot thinks. It's your duty to look after his property. But the cold, Abdel Megid ! And the rain, Abdel Megid !

Asham urged him on, smiling maliciously:

"Go on. Take a look at the things outside. Are you afraid of a bit of cold ?"

Hassib looked at Asham vaguely and said, "You should give him the sacks to cover himself with tonight."

Asham turned towards him in surprise.

"And what about me ?" he shouted in alarm.

Hassib did not reply. Asham looked searchingly at him with worried eyes. Was that Hassib's way of getting his own back ? Forcing him to give his sacks up, to Abdel Megid ? Asham's face contorted with hatred and gloom but Hassib was busy poking at the fire, his face showing nothing of the sort. Asham quietened down somewhat. Hassib was not smart enough for that : he might take his revenge by punching and kicking, maybe by cursing and swearing, but by deep plotting ? Never !

Hassib took him by surprise by saying to Abdel Megid:

"Tonight you take Asham's sacks and cover yourself up against the cold."

Abdel Megid laughed sarcastically and started to sing in his hoarse voice :

Leave the man without a sack
To moan about his naked back,
But don't expect a broken hack
To call a rest and slip its pack.

Hassib's face turned purple. He swung his leg back in order to give Abdel Megid a kick, but he kicked the dog by mistake. The dog yelped with pain and Abdel Megid sprang to his feet and fled from Hassib, and went to perform his duty towards the landlord who had given him the blanket.

Abdel Megid stood at the entrance, sheltering from the cold. His eyes tried to penetrate the darkness to where the piles of iron and wood lay, but he could not see further than a few steps. It was pitch black outside, and the darkness was solid as coal. He could almost touch it with his hand. The wind was sharp and whistled like a steam train. The rain had settled into a drizzle and he felt the cold piercing his flesh. He shrunk into himself and turned to go back but the wind brought to his ears once more the sound that had made him get up and leave the warm fire in the first place. He stared into the darkness, in vain. Then he shouted :

"Who's there ?"

No answer : he only heard Asham laughing sarcastically and saying:

"Expect the thief to answer you ?"

He grumbled to himself, resenting this sarcasm. Did Asham take him for a fool ? He knew the thief wasn't going to reply. He only shouted to scare him, that was all. He shouted again:

"I can see you over there. I know who you are."

But all he could hear was Asham's laughter. Hassib called out:

"Come back and get some sleep. Don't be a fool."

Sleep ? He was not such a scrubby creature as to go to sleep and let the thieves rob an employer who had been generous to him. He was determined to go out and inspect the piles of wood and iron in spite of the cold and the wind. As he started to walk out he felt the dog rubbing its head against his leg. That gave him a little courage and he started to trudge through the dark towards the timber with the dog at his heels. He went around the piles, searched them, but found no one hiding there. He felt at ease again and said in a loud voice :

"See what a fool Asham is ?"

The dog barked.

"Didn't I say a thief would never venture out on a cold night like this ?"

The dog barked again.

"Or is he trying to make a fool of us ?"

The dog barked yet again.

Suddenly thunder and lightning broke loose. The rain started pouring down heavily. Abdel Megid screamed in alarm, unwound his old shawl, which he was wearing as a band round his waist, and spread it over his head and shoulders to protect his *gallabeyya* from the rain. If his *gallabeyya* got wet, then that would really be a catastrophe beyond redemption, no matter what comfort he was given by the blanket or by its donor.

He felt the dog sidling close up to him as though to seek shelter from the rain, and he murmured:

"You're just as miserable as Abdel Megid. Come.. come in here under the shawl.. come on."

He placed one end of the shawl over the dog's head and back, and the two returned to the room and to the fire which had almost died out. He saw Hassib stretching and Asham yawning. As soon he was back with them, Asham said, mockingly:

"Did you catch the thief, big man ?"

Abdel Megid threw himself down by the fire and started poking at it to put some life into the ashes. Then he started to sing:

One of them asks me, "Have you caught the thief ?"
The other questions me, "Who was it ? who ?"
My answer isn't very far to seek :
The only thief in sight's one of those two.

Hassib shouted at him angrily:

"Cut out that braying and let's get some sleep."

Abdel Megid was instantly quiet. He had learned not to disobey Hassib, as far as possible. But he kept murmuring in an inaudible voice.

"So, why don't you go to sleep ? Who's stopping you ? Drop off to sleep, the pair of you, so's a man can fetch his blanket !"

Abdel Megid's plan was to wait until the others were asleep, then bring out his blanket and go to sleep rolled up in it. In the morning, the two would get the surprise of their lives.

"Why don't you go to sleep, Abdel Megid ?" asked Asham.

He replied in a sarcastic whisper:

"Why don't *you* go to sleep yourself ? And mind your own business. Anyway, I'm not sleepy."

Asham stood up:

"Alright then, don't go to sleep."

He went over to his sacks and spread them out, then got under them. Hassib followed suit. A few minutes went by; then their snoring started up. Abdel Megid waited a while longer then sneaked out on tiptoe and hurried towards the far-off room where he had hidden the blanket.

* * *

The room was as black as the night itself and you couldn't see your hand in front of your face. Abdel Megid carefully felt his way by shuffling his feet so as to avoid the planks of wood strewn all over the floor. He stretched his hand in front of him until his fingers touched the wall. Then he turned right, and followed the wall: he had hidden the blanket in the corner under a pile of wood. His foot stumbled against a block of wood and he went down on his knees and began to feel the ground with his hands. He grabbed a few pieces of wood and pushed them aside. The blanket was under them. He put out his hand to grab the parcel but it hit against a plank, with a nail in it that nearly pierced his hand. He pulled his hand away then again started feeling for the parcel. He took the risk of striking a match and looked around. Then he burst out:

"You thieves!"

He dashed back towards his sleeping companions. He stumbled against a piece of timber and fell on his face. But he jumped up again unmindful of the pain, and continued running in the darkness shouting:

"You pack of gypsies ! You scum ! Where is my blanket ? You won't give anything yourselves, and you can't bear to see your God giving anyone else anything either !"

He reached the room where Asham and Hassib lay stretched out. By the faint light of the drying fire he saw Asham quickly hide his head under the sack and he thought he saw the tail-end of a smile on his face. He rushed at him shouting:

"I know .. There's no one took it but you, you son of a .. you thief .. you —"

Asham stuck his head out from under the sack, took hold of a piece of wood which lay nearby and raised it at Abdel Megid without uttering a word. Abdel Megid withdrew in fear, and fell over Hassib. He threw himself at him shouting:

"Where is the blanket ? God, if you don't give it back to me I'll —"

Hassib kicked him squarely and powerfully in the stomach and set Abdel Megid hurtling backward and down on his face. He went quite wild, slapping his own cheeks, and moaning, while his companions went back to their snoring.

An hour went by. Only the whining of the wind could be heard, mixed with Abdel Megid's sobbing and the snoring of Asham and Hassib. Then Abdel Megid, tired out, stopped weeping, and fell asleep.

* * *

By the faint light of the dying fire Asham quietly stood up and, in his turn, sneaked out on tiptoe to the staircase where he raised some pieces of wood and picked up a paper parcel which he had hidden there. He hugged it eagerly. It contained Abdel Megid's blanket which he had stolen. He climbed stealthily up to the second storey. He went into a room where he had prepared some sacks and laid them out as bedding, folded some into a cushion, then stretched himself out on them, sighing comfortably when he felt the softness of his bed. He had prepared himself to enjoy the blanket to the utmost. He picked up the parcel and undid it. He took out its contents and threw them over his body. Then he sprang up in surprise. He struck a match to look at this odd blanket that did not reach down beyond his waist and he found only one of the old sacks which were strewn about in the building.

He sat staring at the darkness in disbelief. His pulse raced and he gasped for breath. It must have been Hassib. He must have seen him while he was hiding it and have stolen it to get his own back for the incident with the contractor, which had prevented him from getting the price of a blanket out of him. But . . what now ? He had left him sleeping under his sacks. So what had become of the blanket ? Had Hassib done the same thing as he had ? Hidden it somewhere to sneak up to it in the middle of the night ? In that case all he had to do was wait and watch, until Hassib started out for the blanket, then to wake up Abdel Megid, and sit and look on and watch the fight between them. Hassib was not going to enjoy having the blanket !

He sneaked back to his sleeping-place, and got under the sacks, pretending he was asleep.

* * *

A long time passed, with Asham stealthily watching Hassib, his head hidden beneath a sack. The first light of dawn began to filter into the room and Asham began to feel sleepy. But he fought against the desire to fall asleep. Finally, Hassib got up and looked around. Abdel Megid was slumped on his face, fast asleep. Asham was hiding his head under his sack. Hassib tiptoed across the room and had just reached the doorway when he heard a voice which made him freeze on the spot. It was a painful sobbing moan from Abdel Megid, who turned over without waking up, and continued his sleep. Hassib pulled himself together and made his way towards the bathroom. Behind him sneaked the shadow of Asham, hugging the walls.

Hassib entered the bathroom, went down on his knees and felt for the blanket. He took hold of it and tried to draw it towards him but it wouldn't come. He heard a growl. He struck a match and looked. The huge dog was crouching on the blanket staring menacingly at Hassib. The man lost his temper, jumped to his feet, and gave the dog a kick. The match burned his fingers and went out. The dog barked furiously and clamped his jaws into Hassib's leg.

* * *

The dog's barking, and Hassib's yell, woke Abdel Megid from his sleep. He dashed towards the noise until he stumbled against Hassib's body slumped in the doorway of the bathroom. There was a flash of lightning at that moment : he saw Hassib nursing his bleeding leg, and Asham with his back to the wall, his eyes wide with terror. He saw the dog crouching on his blanket in the bathroom. He shouted in joy:

"'Got you at last, you thief. You filthy brute. I knew God would show me His mercy. I knew He hadn't forgotten poor Abdel Megid."

He dashed into the bathroom to retrieve his blanket but the dog started to growl, his eyes gleaming in anger. Abdel Megid stopped in his tracks, too astonished to move. Did the dog want to enjoy the blanket without him .. when it was his very own blanket ?

He stretched his hand out to pick up the blanket, and the dog barked at him. He quickly withdrew his hand. He tried again and the dog barked at him again, more menacingly this time. He knelt down beside it and started to plead:

'You ought to be ashamed of yourself .. You know we're both o us wretched. You know I'm your friend. Go on ! Give me my blanket. I'm your friend. I *love* you. Don't you see how cold it is ? Haven't I looked after you well ? I'm your friend, honestly ! Give me the blanket to cover myself. I'm an old man."

The dog stopped its barking and growling. It moved over and made a place for Abdel Megid next to it.

Translated by David Bishaï; revised by Lewis Hall.

IN THE SURGERY

Shukry Ayyad

SHUKRY MOHAMED AYYAD (b.1921) is Associate Professor of Modern Arabic Literature in the Faculty of Arts of Cairo University. He was born in a Delta village, Kafr Shanawan, in Menoufia, and has combined the academic life with translations of European (mainly Russian) fiction. He has been schoolmaster, journalist, and diplomat, has worked in the secretariat of the Arab Language Academy, and has studied in the United States. His most recent publications include an edition of the mediaeval Arabic translation of Aristotle's *Poetics* (1967), a collection of essays (*Tajārub fil-adabi wan-naqd — Experiments in Literature and Criticism,* 1967) on modern Arabic literature, and a study of the indebtedness of the Arabic short story to the indigenous tradition (*Al - quiṣṣatul-qaṣīra fī Miṣr — The short story in Egypt,* 1968) He is an assistant-editor of *Al Magalla,* the leading cultural magazine of Cairo, and member of the editorial board of this present collection. Alone among the authors, he has himself chosen and translated his story. It is from his collection *Mīlādun jadīd* (*A New Birth*), which was published in 1957, but had first appeared in the daily *Al Misri* in 1953. A second collection of his short stories, *Ṭarīq uj-jāmi'a* (*The University Road*) appeared in 1961.

As he sat there, he looked intently at the doctor's assistant, black and huge, shifting smoothly around, and wondered how that big mass could move so lightly. His mind started analysing the causes of this bulkiness. First: the ten and the five piastre pieces the patients slipped connivingly into his hand so that he would not keep them waiting. Secondly, the ten and the five piastre pieces he took condescendingly from them after thrusting his syringe into their bodies. Then the absolute contentment enveloping his fleshy face. *Of course he is married — very much so — and has a lot of children. He sleeps well at night and sleeps again in the afternoon. He eats a great deal and never complains of liver trouble. He lives in one room with his wife and their offspring, and his lawful earnings exceed his needs by far.* Absorbed, glued in his chair, barely living himself, it was delightful to live, just for one moment, the life of that huge assistant. Delectable oblivion, heavenly dullness. Then suddenly he pressed his right side with a mixture of pain and gladness.

He was glad because the abominable pain had reappeared just at the right time. It was really disappointing that his right side had given him no pain at all for the last two days. He became superstitiously afraid that his ailing body, which had tortured him for months, was now playing tricks on him, feigning to be completely sound, to deceive the doctor's eye. Then the two pounds fee, paid in advance to the black giant, would be thrown away. The pain in his side was a small matter, compared to the certainty that the two pounds were not wasted.

The room became like a surrealist mobile. *The three light-bulbs gyrated frantically, meeting and then separating, soaring and shooting like meteors, and then standing still and gazing at him sardonically. The chairs started stamping their feet on the linoleum, and danced to their own frenetic music. The walls soon caught the gay tune and swung their breasts and their buttocks, then linked their hands in an uproarious roundel,* while the relentless pain wrung his intestines and twisted his body.

The room grew tired of dancing, and his intestines had a rest. As things settled down before his eyes, his sight was fixed on a strange object.

There was a big white spittoon in one corner of the room, and around it roamed a small dark creature, a cockroach.

It began to climb up the smooth white slope of the spittoon till it reached the brim, and then stood still twitching its whiskers as if it were relishing its victory. The young man was astonished at there being a cockroach in the surgery of a famous physician; he even wanted to draw the attention of the assistant to the fact, but soon dismissed the idea: why should he ? he was not a regular patient; he had no right to interfere, to rebuke the assistant, *this* assistant..

He reached for the small heap of printed matter which lay on a big round table and began to dip into it to pass the time. It was a motley collection of medical journals and trade papers and old issues of *Time* and *Newsweek*. These appealed to him because of their crumpled pages and torn covers. For he loved torn scraps. He was always fascinated by the scraps of reading-matter in which shopkeepers wrapped his cheap food: he spread them before him carefully and gobbled their contents before he became aware of the quality of the food, and was never put off by the grease which made the paper transparent, one side of it becoming, as it were, a background for the other. It was much more pleasant reading than a brand-new magazine or a handsomely-bound volume: it took in all the cultures and all the languages he knew and gave wonderful glimpses into the most varied mentalities. There were art reviews and books by literary pundits and essays, notebooks, ledgers and legal documents and a thousand other things.

That was why he picked the oldest number amongst those magazines to browse in. However, it could have been the very latest. It is wonderful how little the political scene has changed. Only a few names. It carried the account of the lynching of a negro boy. *Raped a sixty-year old white woman, it was alleged, in a public thoroughfare. Mob set upon him. Woman crushed to death in crowd. A prison, a break-in, a tree and a fire and no trial at all.* Irritated, he threw the magazine back. Then suddenly he remembered the cockroach's adventure.

He looked at the spittoon and had to wait for a moment till the creature emerged from the further slope and poised itself at the summit of the concave crater in a wild attempt to know what was in it. The poor thing, he thought to himself, was simply going to its death : there was a lake of poison lying in wait where it expected food. Most probably it was a cockroach with a low I.Q., for it should have smelt the noxious chemicals and inferred with perfect cockroach logic that this was no place for it, and that it ought to withdraw with all caution. Hadn't nature endowed it with that much intelligence ? But then, who knows, it might be an outstandingly adventurous type of cockroach ?

A door opened and three villagers came out, two of them holding the arms of a sick woman, whose deadly pale face looked still paler against her black clothing: her whole body was covered except for her hands which looked like an X-ray picture of hands. Her eyes were rolling in dumb expectation and the young man had to lower his gaze so as not to meet hers. When the shaking feet in the awkward new black townee shoes had passed he discovered himself watching the cockroach for a third time.

It was still struggling, still determined. This time it was looking down into the very heart of the spittoon, into the mouth of the volcano. Nothing seemed to scare it away; it was going to see the adventure through to the end.

A voice awakened the young man; it was the black giant. "Your turn," — and he looked at him, from high up, with only a small fraction of his eyes, as a god might.

The young man stood up apprehensively, and went in by a different door from the one the woman had emerged from.

A bulky man of about fifty blocked the kneehole of the desk at the farthest end of the room. His thin hair was neatly brushed flat upon the crown of his head and his whole appearance was heavily, stockily brisk. He motioned the new patient to sit down and asked what the trouble was. The young man started to describe the pain in his side, but soon realised that he was exaggerating. Would the doctor think him a weakling, a coward ? Would he think that he was soliciting the greatest possible attention for his two pounds ? If he made this last guess, he was not far from the truth. At last the doctor said, "Let's see," and proceeded to another room; the patient followed him.

The young man was seized by a childish fear when he saw the small, white, metal bed. He lay down, bared the part that was giving him pain and gave himself up to what was to follow. The doctor's pudgy index finger was cold where it touched his skin, but it gave him burning pain inside. The finger was on the spot where it hurt most, circling around it. Then something gave a sound like a sigh, and the whole thing seemed an elaborate and painful conjuring trick. The stethoscope came into play. It was a relief when the doctor told him to dress, although the pain had now spread all over his stomach.

Back at the desk, the doctor asked him further questions. He answered without thinking. At last the doctor said, "You've got appendicitis. You should have the operation as soon as possible."

The matter-of-fact, everyday tone of this statement made him all the more conscious of its significance. He asked apprehensively: "Soon ? .. How soon do you mean ?"

"It had better be done within a week."

He felt as if his heart was slipping from its place. The pain in his side became so localised and hard and stone-heavy that he could not stand up straight. He felt sorry for himself. Would the doctor feel sorry for him ? Should he ask the doctor about the 'conditions' with regard to the operation ? Could he tell him he did not even possess a single pound ? The doctor's face was as impassive as a statue's, feeling nothing but his own enviable health, conscious of the knowledge that he made two pounds off every patient, and quite determined not to feel anything else.

Coldly, the doctor said:

"In the meantime I'm prescribing a painkiller and an ointment."

The young man walked out with his head down. The electric lights seemed to him very weak. He rolled his eyes in dumb expectation, but the big empty chairs in the waiting room were doggedly still.

He did a strange thing before he left: he looked at the spittoon, to see what had become of the cockroach. But, his tired eyes saw, not one, but many black cockroaches.

Translated by the author; revised by Leonard Knight.

DEARLY BELOVED BRETHREN !

Haseeb El Kayyali

HASEEB EL KAYYALI is a Syrian. His story may be found in the Cairo anthology *Khamsatu-'ashri qiṣṣatan sūriyya — Fifteen Syrian Short Stories* (second collection), published in April 1958. Kayyali is considered an iconoclast and rebel, but the satirical portrait he gives us here of an *imam* of the traditional type in fact shows a gentle affection towards his foibles.

The few people praying in the village mosque that Friday knew what Ibrahim el Shaar had to expect when the imam, Sheikh Sherif el Akrai, began. Ibrahim himself knew better than anyone else what this Friday's sermon would be about. Informers had told the Imam that they had seen Ibrahim come out of the house of Om Moazziz . . The imam — a shrivelled old man of seventy or so, seemingly kind, with a radiant face, obvious benevolence, a slightly humped back and a drowsy absent look — did not believe in sermons which tended to generalize. He was imam in the mosque of a village; and had known all of the villagers and the parents of a great many of them as well, ever since they had been born.

He took it as his duty, therefore, to limit his sermons to their own affairs, both spiritual and mundane. Those who wanted deeper theology could either check the wireless programmes or make their way to Damascus where the devil had laid traps for them at every step.

This Friday, the Sheikh was sitting crosslegged in the pulpit, listening to Darweesh el Batous — the one-eyed, fifty-year-old muezzin with a yellow scarf — summon the faithful to prayer with the piercing voice of a rooster.

The pulpit was low, built of rotting, worm-ridden wood and whitewashed on the outer surface with lime. The stairs leading to the preacher's seat were covered with a tattered carpet.

A small window, left of the pulpit, brought light into the aisles. Dangling between the doorway and the outer court was a rough curtain behind which the womenfolk prayed. No one bothered to draw it properly for two reasons: first, the ladies were only hags; secondly, the praying men within the mosque always had their backs toward the doorway and only the imam, when he addressed them, could see it.

When the muezzin had finished his task, the Sheikh stood up. "Praised be God," he started. "Praised be the Almighty Who has guided us to the true faith, and without Whose guidance we would—".

For a while, he was silent. Then he resumed:

"Every week I have to repeat this formula. Isn't it time that you learnt it yourselves ? Blindness take you ! I shall not recite it to the end, so there. I'll move on to my subject directly. Praised be Allah and praised be Allah again. Praised be Allah Who has guided us to the true faith and without Whose guidance we would have gone astray. Praised be Allah Who has sanctioned procreation, forbidden manslaughter, provided you with wives of your own flesh that you might cling to them, and Who has diffused amity and compassion among you. Now, brethren, I am an old man. For fifty years I have been preaching to you in this mosque and instructing you in virtuous behaviour, but you do not respond at all, as though I were beating water or kneading the air.

"Dearly beloved brethren, your personal conduct displeases me. That's the pith of the matter. Let us take for example your brother, Ibrahim el Shaar. Where is Ibrahim el Shaar, brethren ? He hasn't come to prayers today. Why not ? You ask him. He's afraid of me, brethren. Afraid that I should tell history in public and draw a moral out of it. The reason, you know better than I do. El Shaar is now definitely exposed and beyond redemption — God protect us ! They saw you yesterday, Ibrahim, coming out of Om Moazzez's house. Now, I have told you a thousand times that going to that woman's house is a mortal sin. If this world were an honest world, Ibrahim would be laid out this moment before me to receive a scourging at my hands — eighty strokes at the very least. But, alas, it's the current fashion for young men of today not to marry. You have learnt, brethren —

God protect us ! — to gad about, and to travel to Damascus with or without reason. Marriage, dear brethren, keeps you from fornication and other sins. We say this to the younger generation but instead of listening to us they cough and mumble and invent fancy excuses. Imagine it, brethren, your brother Zoheir Hemesh said to me, 'There's a gaping gulf between men and women and each side lives in a world of its own, so that we cannot marry !' What kind of foolish talk is this, brothers ? It is all very well for master Zoheir to mouth such bookish words, since he studied in the secondary schools of Damascus. Heaven preserve us from the secondary schools of Damascus! I tell you with absolute frankness that sending boys to such schools is throwing them into a bed of corruption. It's a sin to send boys to schools of that sort. 'A gaping gulf' he calls it." (The Sheikh pronounced the phrase in a drawl in imitation of Zoheir Hemesh). "I don't know what gulf he is talking about. For my own part, when I married Om Safeya, I discovered between her character and mine not a gulf, but a sea of darkness, a swamp. She was so ugly, oh — God forgive me, brethren — so repulsive. Yet what did I do ? I stanched my wound with salt and accepted my lot. Who was I, anyway, to defy the decision of Providence ? It was my mother who had chosen her for me, you see, and would I disobey my mother, brethren ? Never ! It says in the Koran that 'Paradise lies at the feet of mothers.' Well, I traded in this world's hell, for the next world's heaven. Fair exchange, that's what it seemed to me."

Here, a bunch of little heads peeps in through the window overlooking the lane. Their mouths cry in juvenile tradition,

Left and right and sharp on your feet,
Sugar soldierman, keep to the beat !
Stirrup jumper, donkey thief,
In your own big jaw there's a donkey's teeth.

The preacher, in a fury, comes two steps down the pulpit stairs, and leaning forward so that the children could see him, snarls at them:

"See here now. May God blind every one of your hearts. See here now. What do you see me doing ? Playing, or — the devil take you — preaching ? Off with you all, and play somewhere else. May they be damned who bred you !"

The children vanish and the Sheikh continues.

"God confound the archfiend !" he says, and then, turning to the muezzin who sits at the bottom of the pulpit steps, asks, "Where were we, my son Darweesh ?"

"We were in favour in the eyes of Almighty God."

"You ass. That is a proverbial saying. I am asking you about the subject."

"The subject ?"

"Yes, the subject."

"But we never touched the subject, Your Reverence. We never even came near it."

Here, a member of the congregation interposes. "We were discussing marriage, Your Reverence," he says. The Sheikh, recollecting, brightens up. "Exactly," he says, "Mercy be upon your father. I was telling you, brethren, (and may God preserve us) of the young men of today. What reason do they have for not marrying ? Expenses ? That's all nonsense ! Take, for example, your brother Ibrahim el Shaar — God's will be done. We always return to this distasteful name. Well, I myself said to this man, 'It's time you got married, Ibrahim,' and he said, 'I am broke, Your Reverence'. Said I, 'Come, O beloved of His Reverence and marry my daughter, Safeya. There won't be any expenses. The Seven Basic Needs and a few pennies over are enough to furnish your love-nest.' Do you know, brethren, God help us, how that hopeless sinner replied ? He curled his lips up, and said in disdain, 'I'm not that crazy yet'. Why does he say this ? Because Safeya is so plain-looking ? Granted — but what does this depraved man, the enemy of the Faith, mean by refusing her so ? Am I to have her as a burden on my back forever ? Is she to become an old maid ? Is she to nestle in the beards of my forefathers till they wake up on doomsday ? This is unfair, brethren. Downright unfair. I tell you frankly that if a man marries a woman for her looks, God will smite his looks and hers — or for her money, God will sweep away his money and hers. Marriage, brethren, should be considered, first and foremost, with a view to piety and virtue. Do you understand, you sons of — ? May God forgive me. Besides, Safeya is not all that repulsive ! Forget about her slight limp and she'll be as fine as the silver of Roubas. And then, she says her prayers regularly, brethren. But what does it matter ? — we have wandered away from our subject." (To the muezzin who was sitting motionless, with his chin between his hands) "Do you understand now, you donkey there, what the meaning of the word *subject* is ? The *subject* means the *topic* of consideration."

The muezzin barely raises his head, looking grave and deep-thinking. The Sheikh continues: "If you had served a governor for twenty-five years, you'd have been reponsible today for, say, a hundred executions. But, bad as the people's conduct is, here, I've never held this arm of mine in sway over anyone. I'm just unlucky, that's all." Then, raising his voice, "Go, my son Darweesh, tell the woman there behind the curtain to cover her hair. It is contrary to the faith that a woman's hair should be seen. It is a very private part of her body."

"As you wish, Your Reverence."

For a while, the Sheikh is silent, his face clouded over and thoughtful. Then he addresses the congregation in a mildly chiding tone.

"So, here we are. I want to get down to brass tacks with you. God blind evil thoughts. My purpose is to complete the sermon. Listen to me, will you ? God confound you, Satan, now and forever more." (A flash of perspicacity passed over his face.) "Actually, brethren, I have no more news for you today. Except for your brother Mohamed el Hussein" (waving his arm deprecatingly) "And master Mohamed, as you certainly know, has begun to read Modern Sciences, begging your pardon, in the secondary schools of Damascus, and he no longer calls his mother 'Mother' as all Moslems do, but calls her *Maman.* I wish this were all, brethren, but master Mohamed el Hussein, brethren, now sings in French. And what does he sing, brethren ? God damn the devil. What does he sing ? Our Prophet's Mohamed's name be blessed ! He sings 'Marie-Lou, Marie-Lou !' Brethren, to let one word of French after another roll off your tongue, to wriggle about and act effeminately and to yell, 'Marie-Lou, Marie-Lou !' — all this is deeply sinful. Sinful, I tell you. May God damn him that lies, and may those who have heard me tell those who have not. Singing 'Marie-Lou, Marie-Lou !' is nothing but emulation of the non-believing foreigner, and know you all that he who emulates any party will be cast down with them on the Day of Judgement into the same place — and may God have mercy upon us all. Now, are you trying your best, Master Mohamed el Hussein, to be pierced through your very heart and be cast down — you who have been born to good Moslem parents — cast down with the Peters and Pauls and Georges and Michaels and with the very Raiser of Fire ? Tell us, tell us, so that we might know on what sort of pillow it is we lay our heads on if we should chance to lay them next to yours.

"It is reported that our Blessed Prophet said on a certain occasion, 'I love Arabs for three reasons. First, because I am an Arab myself. Secondly, because the Koran is in their language. And thirdly, because, in the life to come, everyone in Paradise will speak in Arabic.' And now, as he said on another occasion, 'I have spoken, and I ask God to forgive me.' "

Having said this, he sits in the position taken up by a preacher between the two addresses of a Friday service. The muezzin stands up and calls, "Amen, Amen. Praised be the Lord of Mankind !"

A multiple humming reverberates through the hall, praising God and asking for His forgiveness. This is interrupted by the Sheikh standing up in readiness for the second sermon in which he habitually sums up the major items of the first.

"We thank God," he began. "We thank God, the Lord of all Mankind, and blessings be upon Mohamed the last of the Prophets and seal of their line. O God, we do beseech Thee to bless Thy servant, Thy prophet and Thy beloved, our intercessor, Mohamed, the blessed, on whom be peace."

All the praying congregation reply in unison, "Amen."

"O God, in the noble name of our prophet Mohamed and his family and his Companions who preached the faith, we beseech thee to guide Ibrahim el Shaar."

"Amen."

"We pray that Thou wilt make him forget Om Muazzez."

"Amen."

"And inspire him with chastity and with love for matrimony."

"Amen."

"And make him choose his wife from among us in this our village."

"Amen."

"And, Lord, guide Thy servant Mohamed el Hussein to address his lady mother as 'Mother'."

"Amen."

"And not '*Maman*'."

"Amen."

"And to stop singing, 'Marie-Lou, Marie-Lou' !"

"Amen."

"Oh, God, if Thou hast inscribed on Thy everlasting tablet that this man must sing, mercifully grant that at least he shall sing, '*Away, lad, my patience ca-an no-o more endure*'."

"Amen."

"*And the fai-air one fo-orsakes me whose smi-ile was my cure.*"

"Amen."

Translated by Sami Kalyoubi; revised by Lewis Hall.

BY THE WATER'S EDGE

Edward El Kharrat

EDWARD EL KHARRAT comes of an Upper Egyptian family, but was born in Alexandria, in 1926. He read law at the university in the same city, graduating in 1946. He had already by then begun to write short stories, but gave this up until 1955, when he returned to the genre. He has worked as a store-keeper, a bank-clerk and an insurance clerk, and is at present a professional translator. Among the fifteen or so translations he has produced of the world's classics is an Arabic version of Tolstoy's *War and Peace.* The present story was written in April 1955. It is found in the author's privately-printed collection *Ḥiṭānun 'āliya* (*High Walls*) which appeared in 1959.

It was quite hopeless. Each time he reached the old wooden doorway and stepped into the house, coming down the narrow winding lanes from the direction of the sea, he was struck in the face by the overpowering smell of the dark and narrow staircase. It was a composite smell, a smell of life itself, made up of people's cooking and their sleep, of their children and of the dirt which had accumulated around their lives over the years; a smell that never vanished, but hovered in the air in clouds, clung to the wooden banisters which had acquired a dark polish from the constant touch of greasy hands; a smell that lingered close to the stone wall which had lost its plaster and had gained instead countless children's drawings, and ribald inscriptions which, fortunately, could hardly be deciphered in the dimness of the staircase. As he went up the stairs slowly, he could hear the wheezing of primus stoves from behind doors and the voices of exhausted housewives scolding their constantly noisy children, screaming and striking, and heaping curses upon evil days.

These were full, crowded lives. What part did he have in it all ? He was going up to a solitary room on the roof, a room with silent walls that hemmed in his days and, staring down at his loneliness, marked out the emptiness which was his life. He had neither wife nor mother. Each evening he had to prepare his meal himself, and he was sick and tired of it all. Now it was time to leave all this behind. Tomorrow he would move. But what was the use ! It would only be to move to another solitary room on another roof in another town. He was to carry out immediately the orders transferring him; and tomorrow he would start looking for a room in Damanhour. He would move the shoddy piece of furniture which he called his desk, and his old bed, the table he used for cooking, a few utensils and his chairs. These were all the objects that made up his life. Tomorrow he would once more start correcting exercise books, filled with sums by yet more pupils. He would explain the multiplication tables, long division and how to convert ardebs into kilos and feddans into square metres. But what of Noussa, his puppy ?

How the problem troubled him ! What was he to do with her ? He could not take her with him, that much was clear: it was unthinkable. Tomorrow he would start a new life, and form new relationships. He could not live all his life in this manner, alone with this dog. He would start a new page tomorrow. He would teach his new pupils how to respect him. He would not lose control: he would know how to maintain discipline in the class. And from tomorrow he would study advanced mathematics. He had always wanted to do this, and now there would be nothing to stop him; he was quite determined. He would also do daily exercises, every morning, five minutes at first, then ten, then fifteen minutes, very regularly. Every day, for something would have to be done about his personal appearance. It was a disgrace. How could he have allowed himself to go to seed in this way ? And he was going to look for a wife .. And why not ? His heart leaped at the thought. Yes, indeed, he would. He would go about all this with care, and prudence — and with tact, of course. When he had been some time in the new town, and without great fuss, he would commission a matchmaker to look for a dependable bride, kind and obedient. She would not have to be a great beauty — not at all. In fact, he would rather she were not particularly good-looking. She would not have to be rich either. Heavens, no ! — just as long as she was a reliable girl who came from a good, decent family. Never mind looks — but above all she would have to be quiet, and devoted to him and to his home.

He reached the door to the roof slightly out of breath. Noussa was yapping behind the door, leaping with joy, scratching away at the door and yelping with suppressed pleasure and anticipation. How rough she was ! How full of vitality ! She broke into short husky barks, burying herself between his legs, smoothing her body against his legs, longingly, submissively, as if she were presenting him unreservedly with her fidelity and homage.

He bent down and stroked her soft white hair, feeling her animal body under his hand, warm, and writhing with excitement at his return. In his palms he felt her frank unmistakeable warmth. Yapping and grunting a welcome, she raised her moist and shiny eyes and jumped into his arms as though she wanted to annihilate herself in them, to lose her separate identity. He could smell the sea in his nostrils : from a distance the moist breath of the Mediterranean rose to the roof, throwing up its abundance of buoyant energy. He fondled his puppy, punching her playfully on the jaws; on his lips a mischievous smile fixed itself, while a strange look crept into his eyes.

Noussa sensed her master's elation, and could not contain her wild delight. Barking, growling, skipping around, she scampered off in jerky little steps, rushing back to throw herself headlong upon him, and gave him little bites, the saliva running lightly off her teeth, then rubbed the side of her face between his palms with a low yelp of entreaty.

And yet he would have to get rid of her.

The blows he was giving her grew more brutal and determined; the puppy responded to this violence by showing an ever-increasing delight.

He stood up straight and walked away to the low balustrade of the roof. He had neither appetite nor energy to prepare a meal tonight.

In the darkness he looked down at the narrow street. The sky was bright and speckled with stars. Forgotten in one corner, a half-moon shone down on the roofs of the close-huddled houses which stretched out on every side to the rages of the horizon, seemed to hang down and touch them. In the distance, neon signs shone persistently, like an unquenchable desire.

He called the dog after him, and went downstairs into the lane. Noussa ran behind, skipping impetuously in and out between his steps, past the doors of the old dilapidated houses round which stood the accumulated dirt of years, the smell of fish and the clamminess of sweaty hands. Her lithe, agile body rejoiced in its little life beneath the skies: she scampered around, sniffing, exploring the byways, running back to him with a whimper in brief flashes of fright when she came across street boys, but fearlessly thrusting her muzzle at the occasional woman numb and weary-jointed who sat sprawling in a doorway, her flimsy worn-out skirt drawn up off her weary legs which lay stretched out in the dust of the roadway.

Suddenly, he found that he had emerged from the labyrinth of close-standing houses, out on to the Corniche, where the Anfoushy tram was rattling past as if it were carrying a luminous message to the people at the other end of town. The lapping of the sea-water reached him on the salty air, soothing, comforting. At the sight of this sudden expanse the puppy was overwhelmed; they might have reached the boundaries of the world. It seemed that nothing but the clean metalled street separated her from this wilderness. She drew near to his feet seeking protection, looking up at him in questioning bewilderment, yelping in fear and perplexity.

He crossed the street and called her. The cars skimmed by, swiftly, unconcerned, coming from one world and going to another — worlds he and she knew nothing of. He jumped over the low stone parapet onto the narrow strip of beach with its soft damp sand. Overcome with lassitude he collapsed, and lay on the beach. The wavelets splashed over the sand before him in mocking serenity. Small fishing boats, drawn up on the sands, lay scattered here and there around him —

meaningless wrecks, swathed in their treacherous nets.

The din of the world behind the stone parapet had died away. A lone cricket chirped away in the quietness of the night, faint yet clear, poignantly clear, against the stillness of the sea. Its tiny tone, tremulous yet persistent, would not be stilled — it acquired an unflagging persistence in the face of the broad stretches of dark sky.

Tomorrow he would start anew. Tomorrow he would find the meaning of life that had so far escaped him. The exercise books would make sense both to him and to his pupils. After all, arithmetic was rational, *was* method, was the measure of logical truth. Arithmetic was the way to reality. Yes, as from tomorrow he would teach his pupils how to go to the heart of the matter, how to solve a problem calmly, methodically, rationally. And he himself, he would start searching, would know how to start searching, for a meaning to this life that was slipping through his fingers. He would go about all this with care, and prudence, and with tact, of course, and without great fuss, calmly, methodically, rationally. The meaning — no question about it — had been awaiting him ever since the start. It had stood within sight, but he had lost it, had lost his way to it.

A beautiful girl ? Heavens, no ! She would not have to be a great beauty — just sweet, understanding and kind.

He woke up to the fact that Noussa was leaping at his shoulders, licking his face gently, as though to bring him out of his reverie and attract his attention to herself. Her whole body was dancing at his side as she drew her wet pointed nose up to his cheek, her belly tightly wedged between his arm and side as she tried to bury herself beneath his shoulders, her friendly tongue darting short, childlike licks at him, her eyes flowing with a love and submission which she bestowed freely, unreservedly, unconditionally.

He pushed her away with sudden roughness. She fell on to the sand only to spring up quickly, yapping delightedly, thinking that he was playing with her and that the real fun had just begun. She flung herself on to the sand, rolled in it on her back, leaped up again, running and skipping. It dawned upon him with perfect clarity that he had to get rid of her — right away, for tomorrow he was going to start living. Now was the time to put an end to his loneliness.

He stood upright, seized hold of her, and clasped her in his arms, his mind working at full speed: how to get rid of her ? She lay snug and confident, perfectly at ease, still glancing hither and thither with little, gentle growls. He felt her small body peaceful and submissive. But there was no going back now.

Yet how ? Was he to hold her head under the water with his bare hands until she choked and died ? She would try to free herself with every ounce of strength ! She would fight and squirm with every muscle, in a fierce desire to live, an obstinate, intense love of life ! Should he strangle her under the water ? His fingers would press about her little neck in brutish determination ! He would watch the rest of her body twitching under the water, trying desperately to slither away from his grasp till she gave one last sudden sigh; broken, motionless, her pulse now still, she would stare at him sightlessly with terrified, reproachful eyes, disowning him ? No, he would never have the courage or the determination..

He had reached the edge of the water. He stood watching it with an unnatural look in his eyes. He leaned against the stern of a fishing boat which cut him off from the city and stifled its noise; there he could become one with the sea. The boat towered up behind him, screening the rest of the world, one last rampart where all life came to an end. The water was sucked into the sand under his feet, and the forgotten moon was almost hidden behind the towers of a distant fortress out in the sea. Over there lay the museum of marine biology. He had intended to take his pupils on a visit there, but had never been able to, for some reason or other. It stood there now like an ancient citadel on some legendary island he would never reach.

The water suddenly rose over his head, rose until it reached the sky. He lay on the sand at the bottom of the sea, about him, all around him, huge waves rose quietly, moved over him weightlessly, in their huge watery masses. He felt no stranger to the sea — rather that he was in his element. His eyes and lips were closed, yet he could see the transparent blue waters that lay over him, limpid blue flowing round him, warm and familiar. Lying on his back on the sand, not daring to open his mouth or his eyes, he could still see the distant stars shining down from the surface of the waves above him, as if the sky and the sea had merged.

Noussa had disappeared. He did not think about her. She had never been a part of his life; he had never known her, the thought of Noussa never so much as crossed his mind; she was far, far away, a perfect stranger to him. Yet, this was a crucial moment for him, crucial in a quiet way — a sadness that was inevitable. Every moment was decisive, not a minute that passed would be recovered. His young sister who had died in the prime of youth, years ago, was standing in the water by his head, speaking to him through the shimmering atmosphere of water, urging him not to open his lips yet, not to open his eyes (and yet he could see her) telling him that all was almost over. She was speaking to him through the limpid waves, and he could see her smooth dark oval face through his closed eyes, and she spoke to him as if she were speaking from above the sea, from above the sky, from the great expanse where the lungs expand to breathe in the purer air. She was whispering in his ears gently, "Wait a little longer. You must wait too," as she pulled him towards the beach without effort on her part or resistance on his. Lying on his back on the sand, he waited quietly and patiently, for the moment when he would be allowed to open his eyes and his mouth; waited as moments that were decisive and minutes that were irrecoverable slipped by. He was calm in his crucial hour, calm in this sadness that was inevitable, calm amidst the waters which flowed round him and over him, filling his sight as far as the skyline .. And still his sister pulled him over the sand as if he were weightless, without body; pulled him slowly, immeasurably slow, as moments passed that were vital. She was whispering in his ear gently, lovingly, in low tones that had been familiar long ago. The crisis heightened, yet he felt no anguish, nor oppression, nor grief — as if he actually did not want to breathe at all — in spite of the weight on his chest. And still he did not open his eyes. In a few moments it would be over, if he remained as he was, in a very few moments indeed, if he did not go out to the shore, under the dry light of the sky where the world was vast and clear and full of air.

The situation was irrevocable now, it was beyond thinking. So he lay there stretched out at the bottom of the sea, near — very near — the shore and yet unable to move, and his dead sister whispered in his ears, "Not now — not yet — in a few moments," as she pulled him without effort to the moonlit shore, to a shore lit by the moon which lay drowned in the sky, to the dry sand under the night sky, the open spaces, far away, high above.

Translated by Nadia Farag; revised by Josephine Wahba.

THE CHEAPEST NIGHT'S ENTERTAINMENT

Youssef Idris

YOUSSEF IDRIS, b. 1927, is one of the most outstanding writers of plays and short stories in Egypt today. He is a graduate in medicine, and practiced as a doctor and worked as a health inspector until he decided to devote himself exclusively to journalism and literature. Idris graduated in 1951, but he had already written his first short story in the previous year. It can be seen from the theme of the first of the two stories printed here, that it is his medical studies which led him to an interest in social problems here, the problem of overpopulation. Indeed, this story, of which the original title is *Arkhaṣ Layālī* (*The Cheapest of Nights*), was the first of his publications to gain general attention, and it is under its title that his first collection was published in Cairo in August 1954. Both stories we have chosen deal with the country life which Idris knows well having been born in an Egyptian village.

Youssef Idris turned to dramatic writing after he made his name as a short story writer, but, contrary to the usual current notion of his later career, he has practiced the two arts almost concurrently, for his first play was written in 1954, only four years after his first short story. The latest of his seven collections of stories is *Lughat ul-Ay-āy* (*The Language of* '*Ah*! *ah*!') published in 1967. Idris states that he did very little serious reading until he had already established himself as a writer, and that his initial impulse was neither foreign nor literary, but indigenous and actual.

After the evening prayer a torrent of abuse gushed out of Abdel Karim's mouth, falling upon the fathers and mothers of the village and sweeping before it Tantawi and his ancestors.

Barely getting through the four prostrations, which he speedily dispatched, he stole out of the mosque and turned into a narrow alley. With his hands behind his back, irritably and angrily pressed together, and his body bent forward, he was fuming within; his shoulders looked as though they would give way under the weight of the heavy shawl which he himself had woven from the wool of his own ewe. But this was not all. He twisted his neck about cussedly, and sniffed around him with his long nose, hooked and black-pitted. As he growled, clenching his teeth, the skin of his brass-yellow face wrinkled, and the tips of his moustache ran parallel to the tops of his eyebrows where a few drops of water still hung, left over from his ablutions.

His physical discomfort was due to the fact that no sooner had he entered the alley than he had lost the feel of his thick bloated legs under him, and he no longer knew where he was placing his two big flat feet whose soles were so cracked that they might well have swallowed up a nail, head and all. In spite of the severe constraint he put upon himself, he was agitated because the alley was swarming with children dotted around like breadcrumbs, playing and screaming, and running back and forth between his legs. One headed towards him from a distance and butted into him, another tugged at his shawl from behind, and a third mischievously aimed an old tin at his protruding big toe.

In the face of this, all he could do was lash his tongue at them, calling upon God to bring their homes tumbling down upon the heads of their fathers — and their forefathers as well — and cursing the midwife who had hauled them into the world, and the unholy seed that had conceived them.

He shook with rage as he swore and spluttered and spat in disgust upon a miserable country that surged with children wherever one turned. And he, Abdel Kerim, marvelled, as his shawl swayed, at an incubator that hatched children more multitudinous than the hairs on his head. But he suppressed his fury, consoling himself with the thought that the morrow would attend to them. Starvation would, no doubt, put an end to it all, and the cholera would soon spread and claim at least half their number.

He heaved a sigh of relief, and a genuine sense of peace now fell upon Abdel Kerim as he left the swarming brats behind in the alley, and approached the waste ground which surrounded the pond in the middle of the village.

Thick darkness spread before him where the low grey mud huts huddled together, and the heaps of manure lay before them like long-neglected graves. The only signs of the crowded life under the roofs were the lamps scattered in the dark wide circle. These looked like the eyes of crouching water-sprites spitting fire : their deep red looning up from the distance, to sink into the blackness of the pool.

His vision lost its bearings in the empty darkness. As he turned his head here and there, the stench of the mire spiralled up the curve of his nostrils. Overcome by a feeling of suffocation, he clenched his fist, bent his body still lower, and almost flung his shawl down at the edge of the pond. What irritated him to bursting point, as it increased with the growing darkness, was the loud snoring of the human rabbits in their village warren. And what fanned the flame of his fury even more at that particular moment was the thought of Tantawi, the night watchman, and the glass of tea he had offered him just at sunset. If it had not been for his weakness and greed, if his mouth had not watered so at the sight of the tea, he, Abdel Kerim, would never have touched it.

Padding through the waste ground, he could detect neither sound nor movement, not even the clucking of a hen. He felt as though he were in the midst of a cemetery, rather than the heart of a village teeming with God's creatures. When he reached the middle of the waste he stopped, and with good reason. Had he obeyed the summons of his legs and gone on walking, he would have reached home in a few paces. Once there, he would have had to turn in for the night as soon as he closed the door behind him. But at this moment he could not for the life of him have slept a wink. His head was as clear as pump-water and as unclouded as pure golden honey, and he was quite prepared to stay up until and see in the next month of Ramadan.

It was all because of his weakness and greed and that glass of black tea, all because of Tantawi's craftiness and deceptive smile, that Abdel Kerim had never thought of refusing. And now there was no sleep for him. *Ah, well* !

The village louts, all sound asleep long ago, had left the night to the wretched youngsters. What could he do ? How could he spend the night ? How indeed ? Play hide-and-seek with the boys ? Or have the girls form up in a procession around him, singing "Father Feather, live and prosper" ? Yes, indeed, where could Abdel Kerim go when he was stone broke ? He did not have a single piastre, or he would have found his way to Abul Isaad's den, and drunk a cup of coffee, on its little brass stand, followed by a hookah. On the strength of such an order he would have sat as long as he liked, watching the lawyer's young clerks at their expert card-playing, listening to talk he could not understand on the wireless, laughing to his heart's content with Sebai, and nudging Abu Khalil sharply with his elbow as he guffawed. He would then have moved on to the company of Master Ammar and the cattle dealers, and might even have joined in the conversation about the slump in their market.

But not a piastre did he have. *May God forgive you, Tantawi* !

Nor could he dash off to see Sheikh Abdel Megid who, at this moment, would be sitting cross-legged in front of the fire with the brass coffee-pot gently simmering before him, and El Shihi seated next to him. There, the Sheikh would be relating in his vibrant voice what had happened on the nights that had turned his hair grey, and talking of events long gone by which had brought an end to the livelihood he had been able to extort from the simple-minded soft-hearted people of the past. He would be narrating the story of the wily members of the present generation, and of his repentance at their hands, of his former swindles and robberies and his arsoning of other people's crops.

But Abdel Kerim could not knock at Abdel Megid's door and announce his presence with a discreet little cough, because only the day before yesterday he had had a disagreement with the Sheikh over the price of repairing the water-wheel, and had pushed him over the edge and down the well-shaft, making him the laughing stock of the villagers who had been standing around or passing by. Since then they had not spoken to one another.

That had been an instant when Satan had indeed been wily. But Tantawi, with his invitation, had proved even more insidious. *A blight on your house, Tantawi* !

He thought of collecting his staff, the one made of apricot wood with the iron ferrule, and calling on Samaan. From there, they could go off to the Balabsa farm were there was entertainment galore that night — a wedding, dancing, lute-playing, jollification of every sort.

But where would he get the money ? What is more, night had set in, the road was pitch dark and treacherous, and maybe even Samaan had gone to make it up with his wife, at her uncle's.

Dear God ! Why was he the only wretched creature still wide awake ! Tantawi, on his beat, had, no doubt, chosen a nice clean bench to lie down on, and was now fast asleep. *May the thickest wall crumble down upon him and lay him flat, the wretch* !

Why not go back home like all decent people ? He would wake his wife up with a nudge, get her to polish the lamp-glass and light the lamp, stoke up the oven, toast him a loaf of bread, and serve him the heads of green pepper left over from lunchtime, or better still a piece of the pie which her mother had treated her to in the morning. And how delicious if she were to prepare him a mugful of *helba*[1] while he sat, in his element, like the greatest sultan of his time, patching the three baskets which had worn through at the bottom, and making new handles to replace the old ones which had frayed with use.

What would happen, pray, if he were to go home ? Sooner ask if the railway station would budge an inch, the *omda* give a free dinner, or the sky collapse over the threshing-floor. Never ! none of this would happen. He knew his wife only too well. He knew, better than the devil himself, how she slept like a sack of grain with her six offspring strewn around her in a huddle like pups. She would never wake up even if the angel of doomsday were to sound his trumpet. And should a miracle get his wife out of bed, what then ? Was he trying to delude himself ? He could hardly throw dust in his own eyes.

The lamp, to put it bluntly, was only half full of oil, and the woman needed the whole lot for her all-night kneading and baking on the morrow, that is — let him not tempt Providence — if any of them all

(1) Fenugreek, trigonella foenum-graecum; here used for the drink or tonic prepared from the grains of this plant.

were still alive the next day. Then, the children would, no doubt, have been hungry at sunset, and eaten the green peppers with the last loaf in the basket. And was it at all likely that this morning's pie was still there waiting for him ? He had better reconcile himself to the fact that there was neither *helba*, nor sugar, nor anything at all at home — praise be to God all the same !

Never again, till his dying day, would he have the good fortune of an invitation to such a glass of tea as he had drunk to the dregs at Tantawi's. May you roast in hell-fire, Tantawi, son of Zebeida.

* * *

If anyone had come out on to the waste ground to satisfy the call of nature, and had seen Abdel Kerim rooted to the earth like a scarecrow by the dark pool, he would immediately have thought the man was touched, or possessed by some evil spirit.

But Abdel Kerim was not to blame, for his perplexity was much greater than he could resolve for himself. The fact is that he was a simple-minded fellow who could neither read nor write of an evening; it was winter, his pocket was empty, and his head was burning with the effect of the strong black tea he had drunk, while all those unused to late nights, like himself, had long since fallen fast asleep.

He stood for a long time in this state of bewilderment. Finally he settled the matter.

He walked the remaining distance across the waste ground, resigned to his fate. He had now decided to spend the night as he had been in the habit of spending all his earlier chilly nights.

He went home and bolted the door behind him. Then, stepping over his progeny as he crawled in the dark along the top of the oven where they lay scattered, he tut-tutted in disgust at the sleepers and the dark, and sotto voce reproached Him who had bestowed upon him six stomachs capable of wolfing down solid bricks. He knew his way. This the cold nights had taught him well. Presently, he was where his wife lay. He did not nudge her, but started cracking her fingers by pulling them about with his own, and rubbing and roughly tickling her feet, which were smothered in a pile of dust, until with a tremble of her body she began to wake up. She was wide awake as he uttered his last curse upon Tantawi that night. Yawning, she asked him, without much interest, what crime the man had committed to be cursed thus in the middle of the night.

As he undressed in preparation for what was to be, he answered, "Huh. May God send ruin upon the home of him.. for he has been the cause.."

* * *

Not very long afterwards, as usual, the women were congratulating him on the birth of another boy, while he was condoling with himself upon the addition of yet a seventh child. There would not be enough bricks to fill this one's stomach either.

Months after, years after, he was still stumbling over the antlike army of brats who lay in his way as he went back and forth. And every night, with his hands behind his back and his nose sniffing around him, Abdel Kerim still marvelled at the breach in heaven or earth out of which they tumbled.

Translated by Nur Sherif; revised by Phillip Ward-Green.

PEACE WITH HONOUR

Youssef Idris

This second story by Youssef Idris is, in the original, entitled *Ḥadithat-sharaf* (*An Incident touching upon Honour*). It is the title-story of a collection published in Beirut.

We have followed it here with stories by other hands which also deal with the reluctance of a present-day conscience to accept the traditional duties associated with family honour and revenge.

I think that they still refer to love over there as The Shame, and no doubt they still find it somewhat embarrassing to mention it without meaningful winks, but it is there none the less and can be detected in wandering, confused glances, and in the girls' faces when they hang their eyelids down over cheeks which are either blushing with embarrassment or green with fear.

The *ezba*[1] — like any farmstead — is not very large: a few dozen houses built with their backs to the outside, and giving on to a large inner courtyard, one part of which is a level space where weddings take place and where sick calves are slaughtered and hung up, the passable meat being sold by the *oke*, the rest being sold in bits and pieces. Little ever happens on the *ezba* and the little that does happen is predictable. The day begins before dawn and ends soon after sunset. The favourite spot is the doorway, the coolest place for an afternoon nap or for a game of pebble-draughts[2]. You can be sure that the little child playing hopscotch will grow up in a few years, her muddy complexion will clear, her body will be moulded into female shape by the immortal turner of clay, and she will marry one of these lads who go naked but for a torn *gallabeyya*, and who swim in the canal, diving off the bridge one after the other like chained monkeys.

---

(1) Agricultural estate, with the houses upon it.

(2) Siga: a game in which pebbles are used for pieces, and the 'board' consists of squares scooped out in the sand.

A simple present — and a predictible future: that is life in the village. Occasionally, however, things do happen that you can neither expect nor predict. Like that day when the cries rose up in the fields. Strangled cries would occasionally burst out in the emptiness of the countryside, echoing in an alarming manner, calling for help. Even though you may not know at first where the cries come from, you realize that something dreadful has taken place and you find yourself running if not for help, at least to find out what has happened.

But on this occasion, there was no need to help. What is more, the men returning from the fields found it rather embarrassing to explain what had happened, when the women asked them. Indeed, what could they say ? Were they to say that Fatma had been caught in the maize-field with Gharib ?

What could they say, since Fatma was no stranger, and neither was Gharib ? Fatma was Farag's sister and Gharib was Abdoun's son. The matter was plain to everybody; the *ezba* was small and the people one family. Not only did every one know every one else well, but every one knew everything about every one else down to the minutest detail. If one of them had a little money that he was hoarding away this would be known to all: they would know exactly how much money he had and where he kept it, and also how it could be stolen. Not that anybody would dream of robbing anybody else. If they stole at all it would be from the crops of the *ezba*, and even then, it would be no more than hiding some stolen cotton under a *gallabeyya* or filling a lap with stolen maize; they might also wade into the drainage canal of a rice field, and catch the fish in it, when the watchman was not looking, and keep it all instead of sharing it with the overseer as was the custom.

Fatma was well known. Everything about her was known and she did not have a bad reputation. She was not loose — but she *was* pretty, or to be more precise, she was the prettiest girl in the *ezba*. And there was even more to it than that, for while beauty in the countryside is usually measured by fairness, Fatma was dark-skinned. There was some indefinable quality about Fatma which made her different from all the other girls in the *ezba*. You would have thought from the healthy glow on her face that she had honey for breakfast and chicken and pigeon for dinner, and yet in fact the glow came from nothing more than platefuls of whey and pickled green peppers, onions and radishes and tiny fish baked black in the oven. Her eyes were jet-coloured, radiant and luminous and full of life. They were eyes which you could not fix your gaze upon; you could not endure their look upon yours for more than a moment. If we were to grant that her hair was soft and black and that her loose gown did not succeed in concealing the roundness of her breasts, her slender waist, and the fullness of her legs, we would still not do Fatma justice, for her physical beauty was the least important thing about her. The most important thing about her was her essential femininity, a femininity which was alive, pulsating and fast-flowing. You could not tell precisely what was the secret of her attractiveness. Her smile was feminine, her gestures were feminine, so were the way she turned her head to look behind her, the way she tapped her girl friends on the shoulder, the way she bowed her head when a passer-by was helping her to lift the water jar onto her head, the way she had of nibbling at her food, the way she held a loaf of bread, or a jug, the way she half-parted her lips and let the water dribble in between them.. The angle at which she crowned her head with the disk-shaped clout on which she balanced her water pot .. her cabbage-green head-cloth — the only one she had — when she tied it on her head slanting slightly to the right to disclose some of her lank black hair .. her dimples when they appeared suddenly only to vanish as suddenly, setting off the most beautiful smile in the world, her laughter bursting out and gradually fading away, her voice as purely feminine as her body, so that even a word, even one syllable would have enough of this femininity to slake the thirst of dozens of men ..

Fatma stirred men, or rather she stirred men's virility. She seemed to have been born to this purpose; she even awakened the virility latent in small boys. Whenever they saw her approaching from the distance, they had a powerful urge to uncover themselves in her presence: sometimes they actually lifted their *gallabeyyas* way above their knees, and no amount of scolding and spanking would stop them from doing so, although they did not know why they exposed themselves whenever they saw her.

Because of all this Fatma was a great worry to her brother Farag. Farag had no brothers and was a poor peasant who owned nothing but a cow. The overseer allotted him only three feddans to farm. His efforts each year to increase his holding by even half a feddan were useless. Farag was a man in his prime. He could eat three loaves of bread at every meal if he could get them; he could drain a whole jug of water without catching his breath. The calf of his leg was as thick as a thigh of mutton.

Farag was uneasy about Fatma. She lived with him and his wife — a kind soul with a snub-nose and sallow complexion, but whose kind heart did not prevent her from drawing Farag's attention to his sister's breasts which, she claimed, she deliberately shook in walking, or to the kohl which never left her eyes, or to the chewing gum which she asked every one who went to market to buy her. Farag did not need to be reminded of these things, for he could see and he could hear and his blood rose every time he saw and heard. Yet, Fatma was above reproach. She wore the same clothes as the other girls did, she applied kohl to her eyes in the same way as the other girls, and chewed gum as they did. She was never seen in dubious situations and was never caught doing anything unseemly. When her sister-in-law accused her of colouring her cheeks with the dye of the red cartons in which loose tobacco was sold, he took her to task and unwrapping and wetting his turban he rubbed her cheeks with it until they almost bled. Nothing came off on to the cloth however and he had to be content with glaring at her suspiciously and scolding her. Fatma could not understand why she was being treated in this manner. She certainly knew the meaning of 'Shame', for Farag had often warned her against it in vehement terms. She had never committed this Shame nor had any intention of doing so. She would rather have died. But she could see that everyone made much of her and so she behaved as would anyone who had received a lot of affection: with freedom and simplicity. Whenever she felt like smiling or laughing, she did so with all her heart. She knew that people admired her beauty and she was careful to appear attractive all the time. She never left her house without washing her face and tidying her hair. When she worked in the fields, she borrowed socks from Um George[1] the wife of the overseer and used them as gloves to protect her slender hands from branches and thorny twigs. She took equal pains with her speech and never used any vulgar or offensive expressions. Everybody was her friend. Everybody loved her and she loved everybody. Everybody spoiled her and she accepted it. People wanted her to be happy and so she was happy; they wanted her to laugh and she laughed, hoping only to make them happy in return. Why then was she being treated so harshly by her brother ? What was the meaning of his vicious looks ?

Farag himself could not answer this question. He was responsible for his beautiful sister and men's eyes following her seemed to pierce his own flesh. His only hope was to marry her off, and let someone else worry about her, preferably far from the *ezba*. Yet Fatma, for all her beauty, had had hardly any suitors: who would be rash enough to take on this bundle of sex ? And if such a man were to be found, what could he do with her ? People in this part of the country did not marry in order to enjoy beauty and put up walls to protect it, for in truth they did not live in order to enjoy life — their only ambition was to survive somehow, to marry in order that their wives might help them and bring forth sons to help them. And so Fatma remained unmarried and without suitors.

The farm was full of men and youths, and Fatma, who like all the other girls worked in the fields exactly as the men did from dawn until the call to evening prayer, stirred up a commotion wherever she went — unlike the other women and girls — and filled her brother with anxiety.

Farag, however, worked out his anxiety in a curious manner. Boisterous and good tempered, he filled the farm with life and hearty laughter. He often bounced playfully after the other men, forcing them

(1) A polite form of address in Egyptian rural custom in the *paedonymic*, i.e. a name derived from the name of a person's son. This coptic woman has a son called George: she is therefore addressed as *Um George*, i. e. *Mother of George*.

out of the spurious dignity they put on, making them join in his horseplay. He challenged the youths to swimming races. He snatched the baskets from the women's heads and even the most straight-laced of them did not mind as he ran away laughing. He wore his white *gallabeyya* to weddings, tied on his raw-silk turban, had his beard and scalp shaved close, and he danced for the bridegroom, and distributed largesse to the entertainers in honour of the bride and the overseer and the farm-steward and the peasants from the proceeds of cotton stolen from the storeroom or of a sackful of produce pilfered on its way to the lorry.

He spent money lavishly and filled the *ezba* with hubbub. He was loved and respected by all, and it worked wonders ! Though his seductive sister could melt rocks and though the men were bursting with desire for her, Farag won them to his wishes with his kindness and friendliness and his laughter. Whenever Fatma passed by, they would avert their glances, and if one of the men found it unendurable and sighed voluptuously there was always someone around to give him a sharp dig in the ribs.

And thus Fatma remained like a luscious forbidden fruit. No one came near her and no one allowed any one else to come near her. Men's hearts repined — even those of the elderly — and their nerves were shattered with desire whenever she passed, but Farag was always around. The echo of his hearty laugh invariably came to your ear from a distance, reminding you of his existence and of the fact that you were slipping towards The Shame. You regained enough composure to realize that you were just in time for the afternoon prayer or for a glass of tea at the village shop.

But today she had been caught in the maize field with Gharib. This was not the first time, however, that people had said Fatma had been caught with a man in the maize fields or behind the stables or under the thresher. These had occasioned only provisional suspicions, and had always proved to be mere rumours, which were bound to arise around Fatma just as the longing sighs of men did. The people on the farm were not malicious, in fact they were quite kind and considerate and loved their neighbours as themselves.

Even their geese were good-natured. They started out in the morning, a few from each house, cackling and quacking, and assembled near the threshing floor, then wobbled in a formidable procession to the canal where they spent the day dabbling in the water and teaching the young ones how to swim. At sunset, the flock made its way homewards. Hundreds of geese went through the gateway of the farmstead and each group found its way to its own home. If a greenhorn among the geese went by mistake to the wrong house, before you had even realized that the bird was missing, you would find your neighbour knocking at your door with the stray.

Fatma was the object of general adulation. At a wedding feast she received more attention than the bride herself. And this may have been the reason for their anxiety about her, for they feared that she might sin. It was as if they found it inconceivable that a girl as attractive as Fatma could possibly remain pure. Such was their conviction that they had even designated the very man with whom Fatma was going to fall. They had fixed upon Gharib.

Gharib was the son of Abdoun, who in spite of his advanced age was never addressed as Uncle Abdoun. He was an ill tempered and quarrelsome old man addicted to chewing tobacco, and to slurping plain black coffee. He would fly into a rage at the least word. Even the overseer feared his short temper and avoided him. Abdoun never had a good word for any one : on the contrary, his only contribution whenever any misfortune befell the farm was to stand by the canal lifting up the back hem of his *gallabeyya* and looking like a crow of ill-omen, heaping abuse and accusations on the peasants as he spat out his chewing tobacco, as though they deserved the most thorough contempt. No one paid any attention to his offensive behaviour, however, for they knew that he was not really vicious, only bad tempered.

As for his son Gharib, neither the men nor the womenfolk had confidence in him. He was bold and impudent with women. He had a forelock which he left hanging down below his white woollen skull-cap. The reason why he was so unpopular with the men was that not only had he an eye for the women but he was generally successful with them. He could make any woman succumb to him and would not stop at the wife of a neighbour or of an uncle.

He was dusky, but not too dark in complexion, and unlike his father was quite good-looking. He said little, but had a pleasant way of speech, with a voice that sounded husky, innocent and cheerful, as though it had just broken. He did not have the stolid appearance of most village youths, but looked self-confident, quick-witted, and full of energy. He always wore a clean *gallabeyya*. He could sing folk-songs, had his own tea equipment and would insist on making you a glass of tea. When night fell, he usually jibbed at the thought of sleeping at home and preferred to lie down on the village straw heap. He buried himself in the straw and told his companions all about his conquests with women — a matter about which they knew very little — rubbing his chest and his thighs as he spoke. He was bold and insatiable. The first thing he examined in a woman was her legs and his unabashed interest made her feel uncomfortable. There was an expression of settled scorn in his look, or of faint amusement: this was unconscious, but somehow a woman imagined, whenever he looked at her in this manner, that he could read her secret thoughts. And if her secret thoughts were shameful — and more often than not they were — she became embarrassed and felt as though he had undressed her. She tried to cover herself up, only becoming still more embarrassed and in her confusion she would fall an easy prey. Every new conquest added to his sense of pride and intensified the look of boldness and contempt in his eye — and so increased the number of his victims.

There must have been something quite unusual about Gharib which singled him out from the other men. It may have been excessive virility — and it could have been something else. No woman could catch a glimpse of the nape of his neck or of the cord of his knickerbockers as he was at work in the fields, without feeling faint, as though she had seen a man stark naked. Gharib was not very particular about what tactics he used with women. At wedding parties he forced himself in among the crowds of women and mesmerized them. At the mill, he offered to carry their baskets for them, and to turn the wheel of the hopper. He did not spare even a sick woman and had it not been for his fear of the overseer's rifle he would have attempted to pay Um George a visit by night. Whenever people complained about Gharib to his father, he would retort gruffly and with a mean expression:

"There he is. Do what you like with him. He's no son of mine.." Generally there was nothing they could do, for Gharib, in spite of his short stature, was as strong as a bull and could lift the iron wheel of the *sakia*[1] with one hand while he was choking a man with the other, without losing the habitual gleam of faint amusement in his eyes.

Of all the men, he was the most virile, and of all the women Fatma was the most feminine. Therefore it was most natural that rumour should have linked them together. It was most natural, but most untrue. Fatma avoided Gharib whom she knew by reputation to be bold and shameless, and Gharib was afraid of her. He was up to the mark with the overseer's little maid or with Shafia, the widow with several children, but Fatma .. Fatma was not one of them. Fatma was different — she was in a class apart. He often bragged to the youths who spent the night buried in the straw heap with him that she loved him and sent him messages, but he was always the first to be disgusted with himself afterwards at his empty boasts. He worked in the fields like a horse, seduced women with the virility of his glances so that young girls and older wives alike abandoned themselves to him at wedding feasts and on market days: but with Fatma he felt quite impotent.

And she, for her part, was terrified of him. When he wished her a good day with his heart palpitating wildly, her answer came out weak and constrained. Her fear of him was a fear of The Shame, while his fear of her was a fear of failure. However, the people of the farm kept associating them together in their minds and Farag kept up his loud laughter and hid his true feelings by throwing dust in their eyes, by cultivating everybody's friendship, especially that of Gharib, around whom hung the main clouds of his anxiety. All these complicated tactics went on underground: outwardly, appearances were calm;

(1) Water-wheel.

the farm was small, and people formed one big family, and Abdoun's house was the third to the right of Farag's house. Even the incidents of stray geese were minimal. Yet, there was a general expectancy that something would happen. Something must happen. People would undoubtedly be awakened in the middle of the night by the sound of a bullet or they would hear a loud cry from the fields announcing that Fatma had been caught in the maize fields with Gharib.

And today it had actually happened. The news was received without either surprise or condemnation. It was taken for granted and had been anticipated. Even the children — and children on a farm have their own small world and their own notions and gossip about grown-ups — even they felt certain that Fatma had finally committed that forbidden thing against which their fathers and mothers had often warned them, that Fatma had committed The Shame.

When they saw Farag returning from the fields, turban off and head bare for the first time, his waistcoat unbuttoned and his knickerbockers stained with mud, when they saw his face pale, his moustache trembling and his eyes bloodshot — the children crawled nearer to the stable wall, having realized intuitively the magnitude of the disaster that had befallen him. When he tore through the *ezba* gateway they followed him in silence and at a safe distance until he went into his house where they saw him scream at his young son who was beating on an old rusty tin, and heard him ask his wife in a voice, terrible yet hardly audible, to prepare his hookah, which he proceeded to puff at, inhaling deeply, and blowing out clouds of tobacco-smoke as thick as the smoke off a wet log fire. When some of the men sneaked into the house, the children, though still afraid, became bolder and stood at the doorway observing what went on. But nothing frightening was happening in the house. Farag sat, pale and silent, smoking away and piling thick flakes of tobacco on the burning charcoal of the hookah, while the men sat around him not knowing what to say. Whenever one of them fidgeted and thought of saying something that would soften the blow, Farag would hand him the mouthpiece of the hookah in order to make him smoke and keep him silent. What was there to say ? The moment had come that Farag had dreaded for so long, and which had made his blood course violently through his veins with fear. Whenever he had noticed his sister's body undulating beneath her loose, shabby black dress or caught a glimpse of her skin through a tear, whenever he had seen her laughing as she spoke or even ate, he had felt a sudden pang and had directed suspicious glances at her like red hot nails, or else he had burst out into the wild laughter of an anxious man.

He had often asked himself: What was he to do if — God forbid — it should happen ? Whenever he thought this his hair would stand on end, and he would look murderously at his sister. Today it had happened. He was now expected to act like a man and a brother. Now he was expected to kill both of them — Fatma and Gharib. To kill Fatma, his sister whom he used to carry across the canal in his arms as a child, and whom his dying mother had entrusted to him. And to kill Gharib, the dirty beast, to whom he had opened his heart and his house, all the while expecting to be betrayed. And today he *had* been betrayed. Indeed what was there to say ? There was no need for words — only for blood. The only thing now was to make sure that it had actually happened for he did not want to have their blood on his conscience without being certain of their guilt. Since he was going to kill them both and ruin himself and his wife and his children, he had to be sure first. Let him smoke in silence and pause before taking up his knife. His verdict would be cold and merciless. Farag lived on a farmstead, and farmstead folks were often accused of being less strict about morals than village folk, but he would show that the farmstead too had its principles and that evil was rooted out there as vigorously as anywhere else.

A black swirling mass appeared in the distance throwing up a low cloud of dust. As it approached the farm the children ran to meet it. Women with old black dresses and shabby veils, waving their arms, tramping steadily through the dust — this was the threatening darkness. And in the middle was Fatma.

For the first time the glow of her dark complexion was replaced by an ashen paleness. All her attractiveness was gone. She had tied her black shawl over her head like a mourner and her features were as wooden as those of a dying woman.

As they approached the farm, the young women began to argue with one another in the sharp strident tones which the menfolk of the *ezba* usually use in their arguments; they were arguing about the most suitable place to take Fatma. Some suggested that she should be taken to the farm-steward's house, others thought that her proper place in the circumstances was the house of her brother. After a tussle, Fatma was finally conducted to the steward's house which stood at one corner of the *ezba*. The children remained in wait outside.

Gharib, it was rumoured, had run away — he was hiding in the fields — he might never come back. No one knew exactly what was going to happen. So many confused ideas were bandied about that no one could offer clear-cut advice. The men kept their silence and the women went on heaping maledictions on Gharib. Some merely cried, "Curse the creature !" while the more violent besought God to afflict him with every kind of incurable disease. But even these noble sentiments could not clear the air or break the apprehensive silence which weighed upon everything in the *ezba* and left even the dogs mute.

The circle of women closed in on Fatma and began to cross-examine her, quite determined not to believe anything she said. She told them that she had been carrying her brother's breakfast into the fields and that when she crossed the runnel in the maize field Gharib had suddenly appeared before her and had tried to hold her hand and draw her towards him. She had resisted and screamed. At this point in her disjointed story, Fatma stopped. When the women urged her to go on, she simply added that her screaming had gathered a crowd, and Gharib had run away. The women would not believe her; they pressed her to say more. There was no more, she replied again and again. The women shook their heads and tried to interpret this act of hand-seizing by bringing all the wildness of their imagination into play. A merciless obsession to know exactly what had happened by now possessed every one of these women. The more Fatma persisted in her silence. the paler and more haggard she looked, the more intense became this passion to find out the truth. Even the men sitting around

Farag, far away from Fatma and the circle of women, seemed to have been possessed by the same fever, though they did not show it. It expressed itself in a hopeful word spoken by one good man:

"Patience, my friends! By God Almighty, maybe nothing has taken place."

* * *

Gradually the thing every one had been trying so hard to suppress came to the surface. It must have happened, surely, as everyone had been expecting it to happen: if any man were to be alone with Fatma, the inevitable would take place, let alone if this man were Gharib! It never crossed anybody's mind that Fatma might feel differently and offer any kind of resistance. Were she to be alone with Gharib, all would be over. It only remained to prove that all was actually over. Even Farag, as he guessed at people's secret thoughts, wanted to know the result, not for its own sake, but in order to make sure that Fatma had ceased to be his sister, that he was at liberty to do what he pleased with her.

Women — surprisingly enough — are much bolder in these matters than men. They whispered it among themselves and to Farag's wife — who had left her home and had gone out weeping and wailing over her sister-in-law — and to Fatma's aunt. When they told Fatma what they intended to do, she grew angry and very pale, her nostrils flared, she shed a few tears — fewer than the contents of a green lemon when you squeeze it — and she screamed at them that this would never happen and that, by the Glorious Koran, no one was going to touch her. To this they retorted, "If you are so afraid of the examination, something must have happened." All of a sudden the blood rushed to her cheeks and she could say nothing — she who had been so often told by people that she did not know the meaning of shyness that she had believed it herself.

If this had happened in a village, the family would have undoubtedly tried to cover up for their daughter. But this was a farmstead where everything was known about everyone and where there was no need for covering up. It became the sole concern of all, young and old alike, to find out if what had seemed bound to happen to Fatma had actually taken place. Fatma felt faint. They sprinkled water over her face and neld out an onion for her to smell. Her head reeled at the enormity of the problem, at being accused of the greatest of transgressions, at having the most intimate of her private affairs discussed by the whole population of the farm. She, the beautiful queen, was being discussed openly before her brother and her family by all those people who had once loved her and made much of her, and whom she in her turn had cherished and upon whom she had relied.

She asked the women to leave her alone. They stood silently watching her with tired eyes, now no longer suspicious but full of conviction, a conviction tired and sad like their eyes.

Fatma's face was set stone-firm. The gush of blood which only a moment ago had flushed her cheeks had now ebbed away. She said, "I am ready."

Farag's head was by now spinning with having smoked away at his hookah too fiercely on an empty stomach. His head hung down and with his hand on his forehead, one might have thought he was a widow weeping and wailing, rather than a man.

There was no one on the *ezba* who knew anything about these matters except Sabra the *mashtah*[1] who was not a professional, but owned an old manual sewing-machine on which she made clothes for men and women alike. She looked younger than she really was, had a fair complexion and a kindly, motherly face. But when she spoke, her voice gave her away and you could feel that she was a vicious woman, experienced in the ways of the world, and never to be trusted.

When Fatma announced her readiness to be examined, they could have sent for Sabra, but they hesitated. They really wanted to know the truth; and although Sabra was sure to find out everything she could not be trusted to tell the truth for she was held in disrepute by the men and the women alike, and even by the children. Although

---

(1) Woman's hairdresser, who, in particular, helps deck a bride on her wedding dav.

she was the only dressmaker on the farmstead and sewed everybody's clothes, the very fact of being found in her house, even if you were only seen trying on a *gallabeyya*, was a matter about which there was a certain uneasiness. You see, it was known that Sabra did not mind herself and her house being used as a blind — her home was a place where a man and a woman could meet with a perfectly valid pretext for either of them being there. No one had actually seen anything with his own eyes and this might be true or might be a mere rumour, but the fact was that Sabra was not to be trusted. She could find out the truth about Fatma and withhold it, and she might deliberately say something contrary to the facts.

Farag's wife then suggested they should call upon Um George, and the suggestion was accepted at once. Um George was the only 'lady' on the *ezba*. She was educated and could read and write; furthermore, she came from the city and city folk undoubtedly knew things that farm-dwellers, peasants and villagers did not know.

The children crowded around the group of women and followed the procession from the house of the farm-steward to the house of Um George. The procession, now eager, now dejected, stumbled along the lanes of the farm which were littered with heaps of earth and rice straw. It was still light, but the sun lay low by now. Fatma walked blindly in their midst, her face still lifeless, her heart sinking to her feet, feeling, at every step, that she was treading on her own heart, treading on her innocence, on the sweetness of her childhood, on the memory of those days when she had grown up and had sung at wedding feasts while she dreamed of her own wedding night, with its procession, its hustle and bustle, its ritual of dyeing the hands in henna — a night when everyone would be watching her coming out like a queen. And today they were all watching her coming out, hundreds of eyes looking at her, staring at her, not hundreds, thousands, the whole world was nothing but eyes, glaring and bright like torches, not looking *at* her but *through* her at her innermost depths, immodestly, savagely, burning into her body, raping her. Her blood flowed and dribbled on the stones with every new step she took as she stumbled along, mercilessly, barefooted, naked, defiled.

Her friend Hikmat tried to pull Fatma's veil over her face and cover her up, but Fatma pushed it back. What was the use of covering her face when her whole body was naked ?

The eager yet dejected procession advanced, dark, with flashes of lighter arms and faces, followed by a trail of children and hungry dogs. A cloud of dust rose round it, the caravans of white geese scattered; the sparrows and the pigeons sought refuge. The judicial procession moved towards the *nazir's* house.

* * *

At this time of day, Am Durgham, the watchman, was having one of his fits of bawling, and as usual, no one was paying any attention to him, for every one had got used to his ways. He was the only Upper-Egyptian on the farmstead and ever since he had landed up there he had been watching over the threshing floor. He was now over seventy and was still watching over the threshing floor. He had a huge swarthy head with coarse disagreeable features, a long white moustache as thick as a dog's whiskers, and crinkly hair. His face was always running with sweat and his black skin looked shiny, as if he sweated oil. He spoke in a grunt which sounded like a dog barking, and he barked whenever anyone came near the threshing floor, even when they were well-intentioned. He had lived on the *ezba* for thirty years, but still felt a stranger there — every one knew his name, but he knew no names and never concerned himself with any one provided they remained away from the barn. But if any one approached he barked him away.

Am Durgham barked away without stop, for he was barking at Gharib. Gharib had crept back and had hidden himself among the piles of maize in order to watch closely what was going on in the *ezba* as a result of his doings. His face seemed darker and he had pulled his skullcap over his head, concealing his once-prized forelock. He was genuinely sorry and apprehensive. It was as if he had suddenly wakened from a long sleep. The full monstrosity of his behaviour with women had dawned upon him. He caught sight of Fatma and her procession on their way to the *nazir*'s house, and his face grew still darker. He buried himself deeper in the heap of maize stalks and looked elsewhere.

He had been so afraid of Fatma and she had been so unattainable in his eyes, that his longing for her had grown intolerable. The greater his passion, the more distant and inaccessible she had become to him. He had had no wish to hurt her, nor in any way force himself upon her; all he had wished was that she would return his greetings — not too impersonally. He had desperately wanted to feel that she was addressing him, Gharib; she had never done so, and he had consoled himself by enticing still more women, while all the time he had longed to receive only some slight attention from Fatma: a word, or a gesture, or even a side-glance from behind her shoulder or under the weight of her basket.

It had not been the first time that Gharib had waited for her as she picked her way to her brother's strip, carrying his breakfast in a basket, sauntering along in her black dress, wearing her basket like a hat. The fields, the trees, the greenness and the canal all at once had taken on the grace that she gave out. This had not been the first time that he had waited for her on the open road, watching her, unobserved. On the other occasions, he had been afraid of her catching sight of him, but now for the first time, he had wanted her to see him, as in a chance encounter. Now, for the first time, he had wanted that unspeakable thing to take place between them which had tormented him on sleepless nights on the pile of straw. And what had he wanted ? To ask a girl who was neither your mother nor your sister, "How are you getting on, Fatma ?" and for her to return the greeting shyly, unlike your mother or your sister. This was the forbidden shame for which he had yearned.

No sooner had she seen him coming out of the maize field than she had stood nailed to the ground, as if she had seen him naked, as if she had seen the image of The Shame itself emerging before her, that shame against which Farag had warned her with looks of fire. Suddenly her basket had fallen from her head and she had begun to scream at the top of her voice. The world had burst into turmoil and he had fled.

After that, he had wandered aimlessly in the fields.

* * *

Contrary to the general expectation, Um George crossed herself, expressed an excessive regret and a willingness to do her utmost to uncover the truth of the matter, swearing by the living Christ that she would get her husband to put Gharib in jail and set the officer in charge to tie him to the tail of a horse and then hang him on a telegraph post.

Um George was renowned for her kindness, piety and courtesy. No one would have thought of being so familiar as to address her by her given name; no one even knew what it was. She used to force her husband to accompany her to the town church every Sunday morning in spite of his reluctance, for he usually spent his Saturday nights drinking *arak* in the nearby village at Panayotti's the Greek grocer's, who had turned his shop into a haunt for drinkers.

She was a short, very fair, plump woman with grey hair and three tattoo marks on her chin. She knew Fatma personally and was quite fond of her and often sent for her to come and help make the biscuits that Abu George[1] insisted on having for breakfat. Sometimes she would have a chat with her in order to learn all the gossip of the farmstead, for her position did not allow her to mix with the other women. Had it not been for the difference in age they would have been close friends.

It was with an agonizing sense of shame that Fatma approached the house of the *nazir*[2], not sent for, not welcome, but with her honour at stake, to be examined by Um George, the very person who only yesterday had kissed her affectionately on the lips, and had said to her that if it had not been for the difference in religion she would have married her off to her own brother who worked as a cashier in the province of Beheira. She stood nailed to the ground at the threshold, but the women pushed her in roughly so that her veil fell from her head. Um George got rid of Abu George and closed the main door and the door of the inner room as well as the shutters and the windows. Fatma's

(1) *Father of George*: see note on p. 238.

(2) Overseer.

resistance was that of a strong instinctive shyness. The women overpowered her and forced her on to the bed, and one of them tied her hands while two others got hold of her legs. Many hands stretched forward: dry, knotted hands — even the remains of *mulukhiyya*[1] on their fingers were dry. Dozens of eyes bulged, intent on their search for honour, in their concern that honour be safe. They peered and pierced and scrutinized even when they did not know what they were looking for. Um George had become terribly agitated as if she were the examinee and not the examiner. She despaired of either keeping the women quiet or of comforting Fatma. The pushing and pulling and stifled cries continued, muted into a terrifying whisper. A silence of expectancy now hung over the room and spread to the whole house and from there to the outside, to the farmstead, to the whole world it seemed. Everything fell silent. The men sitting around Farag fell silent. Those who were hanging around the houses or near the irrigation-pump or in the fields, they too fell silent. All were following closely what went on inside the *nazir*'s house, even without witnessing it.

Everything fell silent except Am Durgham's bawling which seemed to be carried out for the benefit of Abdoun, Gharib's father, who, the hem of his *gallabeyya* lifted up, had made his way to the threshing floor in the hope of talking to Am Durgham in order to vent his anger and to curse Fatma and his son and all the people of the farm to any human being, even if it were only Am Durgham.

Suddenly a long-drawn trilling resounded from the inner soom, echoed by many other trillings in the house while the news went round:

"She is safe, thank God ! Honour is safe !"

Only then did Farag raise his head. He had regained his former colour. "Bring her to me!" were his first words.

A few moments later, and although Am Durgham had ceased his racket, there arose the most formidable commotion that the *ezba* had ever witnessed. On the edge of the deep shaft which fed the old water-

---

(1) The herb *Jew's mallow* (corchorus olitorius), which is chopped up to make a thick green soup.

wheel — it was deeper than the height of three men standing feet on shoulders — there stood Abdoun, holding his son Gharib by the scruff of the neck, trying with all his decrepit strength to throw him down the shaft, while dozens of men joined in the scuffle, and tried to act as peace-makers. Abdoun's rage increased with every new failure to thrust his son over the edge and he poured forth abuse like a volcano in full eruption.

Someone seeing this curious performance might naturally conclude that Abdoun was seriously trying to drown his son. Yet, there was something in his manner, in the tone of his voice, in the choice of insults perhaps .. something which suggested somehow that in his heart of hearts Abdoun was not really ashamed of his son. One might go a step further and say that he was almost proud of the virility of his son and of his being charged with rape.

While this was going on, a regular massacre was taking place in Farag's house. Farag was hitting his sister with the coffee grinder, and she was screaming. Farag's wife was screaming for fear that he might kill Fatma and get into trouble. And the neighbours' wives joined in the screaming while a crowd of men, both inside the house and outside it, tried in vain to stop him. Farag seemed like a wild beast determined to do away with her.

And yet, from a certain restraint in the blows which he gave Fatma, or possibly from the glitter in his eyes, which was neither a glitter of pure anger nor of pure relief, one could catch a glimpse of a hidden meaning: it was perfectly true that Fatma was innocent, but he had to do something quite spectacular to answer the thousands of suspicions that must have crossed people's minds, to silence the rumours that had been started.

And of course Abdoun never drowned his son and Farag never killed his sister. The sun went down as usual as the cowherds brought the cattle home, carrying their fodder on donkey-back. Smoke began to rise from the roofs and cracks of the mud houses; the smell of frying food filled the air and made one's mouth water. The men went to evening prayers and the women made the final trip to the roof where fuel was stored. The chickens were settled for the night; the cattle were fed. And when the night call to prayer resounded, a great and uninterrupted peace reigned once more over the farm. Everything connected with the affair had been discussed over and over again until there was no more to say. Heads drooped; the wicks of the lamps flickered and were snuffed out and sleep crept in with the darkness; people stretched their bodies out, exhausted, motionless.

When all had gone to sleep, leaving her awake and shattered, Fatma began to cry. She did not want to cry, but the tears flowed in spite of herself, forming two shining streams which fell down from her eyes on to the flat top of the earthen oven, where Farag had made her sleep without mat or cover. She began to sob convulsively, until her whole body shook. The chicken coop which was beside her began to shake in time to her sobs and her cries filled the night, almost waking the sleeping peasants. It was the crying of a creature with a pain which cannot be relieved, a deep wound whose pain increases as the night closes around.

* * *

Well-meaning people tried to persuade Farag after some time to accept Gharib as a husband for his sister but he refused so categorically that they gave up any further mediation. As for Gharib, he had ceased to talk about Fatma or any other woman for that matter. He shaved his forelock and began to observe the prayers. But he was sometimes seen, hovering on the outskirts of the farmstead, stopping by the open window in Farag's house.

Fatma was locked into the house by her brother and forbidden to go to work in spite of his need for the money she earned. That did not disturb her in the least for she seemed to have renounced the world and had no desire to go out. Her former liveliness which had made her eyes sparkle and had animated her face seemed to have dried up. She had turned into a languid creature, like a lamb for the slaughter. She never smiled, and rarely moved, and when she spoke it was in a submissive tone, without any pride or sweetness or femininity.

But this state of affairs did not last for very long. Fatma did not remain a prisoner at home for ever; Gharib's praying practices did not continue, and Farag could not deprive himself of his gambolling and laughter. After many market days, the affair had been blotted out: the farmstead stored the matter away in the dark, under the lock and key of oblivion. Thanks to the efforts of mutual friends Farag's estrangement from Abdoun and his son Gharib came to an end and they met at work and in play as before. Gharib grew his forelock once more and resumed his conversations about women on the stack of straw. But his conversation was not without bitterness, for Fatma had taken to going out again, and, as beautiful as ever, her headcloth tied at an angle, the hem of her dress lifted up, she strutted along provocatively, greeting everybody, except him, not giving him the cold shoulder deliberately, but as if she did not see him, as if he no longer existed.

Fatma went back to her ways of looking and talking and smiling and driving the men out of their minds. She might appear quite unchanged .. and yet people found that she had acquired something new which she did not have before, or perhaps had lost something genuine which she used to have: the thing that had made her seem to belong to them all, to love them all and to be loved by them all, which had given her a kind of transparency and purity, making one feel that her smile was genuine and her anger real. She had lost her innocence and was now capable of pretence. She could now look at something without seeming to do so, and laugh when she had no desire to. Now, she could desire a thing and conceal her desire for it.

Not only that. Sometimes Farag caught her emerging from Sabra's house, and, taking her home and closing the door behind him, he would hold her firmly by her plaits and ask her what business she had at Sabra's .. Whenever this happened, she was now capable of saying, "I was trying a dress on. Leave me alone." And she would free herself from his grip with a strange violence and would stand in the corner of the room rearranging her hair, and facing him with, beautiful and defiant eyes, unflinching and unabashed.

Translated by Nadia Farag; revised by Ronald Ewart.

TRIAL BY ORDEAL

Ghaleb Halassa

GHALEB HALASSA is a young Jordanian writer who studied at Cairo University. He is a critic as well as a short-story writer, and has contributed to Lebanese reviews. The present story appeared in the Kuweiti magazine, *Ar-rā'id ul-'arabī*, in November 1964. The original title *Al-bish'a* is used by Halassa in the sense *the branding*, but the word carries the overtone of the cognate *al-bashi'a*, *the violent crime*, a word which is spelt in exactly the same way in Arabic, and is more familiar to most readers than the dialectal *al-bish'a*.

The light was fading slowly inside the house. Evening shadows gathered among the granaries and fodder-stores, and stretched into the house, spreading idly on the ceiling like a lazy cloud of smoke above the hubbub of the men's voices, with their short, weighty phrases.

One last strand of light, in which a million specks of dust were dancing, dangled down through a small opening high up in the west wall of the room, and fell, as a blotch of quivering brightness, upon the back of one of the men gathered inside. Beyond the hills, the sun was sinking fast. Now one small bright sliver was poised there. Then that too slipped down, and the sky was drained of its blue flush; the rose-coloured clouds lent greater breadth to the horizon. Creeping out of the desert to the east came the night. Quite suddenly the house was in darkness. The man who was talking stopped, as though nightfall had smothered his words. A hush followed. Only the hissing of the primus stove, and the muffled thud of dough being kneaded could be heard above the familiar but indistinguishable sounds drifting in from outside. Then the master of the house broke the silence. He cried out, as though calling for help: "Lights ! Light the lamp !" Immediately there was an agitated movement, outside the ring of assembled men, as the women hurried to perform the rites of eventide, their urgent whispers rising as they looked for matches, quickly filling the lamp with oil. When the first feeble gleams began to flicker, the men's voices surged up again, now in reverent murmurs, piously invoking God's grace and mercy. Then the air became tense with expectation as one of the men coughed and made to speak. He looked fierce, with tousled hair, a large nose, and lustreless eyes, sunk in a dark furrowed face. The others looked towards him. He gave a hollow laugh.

"As the saying goes, my brethren," he began, "one swallows the sour from fear of what is bitter." His laugh again, thick and guttural "We have always been brethren, your family and ours, there never was between us anything to anger God or man. We have been together through weal and woe, and always shall be as long as good endures on earth. Now evil talk will harm us as much as it will harm you. The truth, however, ought to offend no one."

Outside the circle of men huddled around the pots of bitter coffee, sat an old woman leaning with her back against the wall. Faces turned to stare at her as her voice rose above those of the men.

"Do you dislike frankness ? And will the truth offend you if it were told ?" she asked.

"Give us the truth," they all said together, "it is the truth we are after." She was staring vacantly before her, with the sightless look of the blind, in spite of the gimlet eyes that bored through her stony features.

"Do you think my son would shun the soft, clean bed of a full-bodied woman, whose white skin would make any man lust for her body, to go after a dried-up tawny faggot of twigs like your daughter ? Were his eyes so purblind that they could see only your daughter ? I am old and on the brink of the grave, and all I care for is to see the truth acknowledged, even if it be against me. The matter is clear as the light of the day, so that even an old woman like me can see it — let alone men such as you."

"As God is our witness," the dishevelled man interrupted, "we are accusing no man. Who said we are accusing anyone ? I swear by Almighty God, that were I to see our daughter in your son's arms with my own eyes, I still would not believe it, for he is a brother, and a brother will not defile his sister. "But people are talking, and we must stop them. Or would you have us hang our heads in shame when we pass before a gathering of men ? What we ask is fair enough. Let him stand the ordeal. His tongue shall be touched with the brand. If he be guilty, it will burn, and that will be fair punishment; if he is innocent, then will the fire be cool and harmless to him, as it was of old to the prophet Abraham."[1]

"People always talk," the mother replied, "who can stop them? They talk from envy, and they talk from idleness. Women especially. Woman is a topsy-turvy jade, with her brain hanging downward. Unless you lay a firm foot on her trailing skirts, she's off a-wandering. Little does a woman care if men's hearts grow filled with evil, or of they rise one against the other." The tea-kettle beside her boiled over, and doused out the stove. The mother shrieked, "You miserable wretches," and the women replied with nervous shouts; soft abuse slipped out from one of them, and a child received a slap on the face. Then the stove began to hiss again, and all was calm.

The mother burst out suddenly: "The curses of God — !" and then fell silent. The silence lasted for some moments. Then it was the eldest son's turn to speak up. He spoke quietly, although there was a hint of anger in his voice.

"I will not have you leave my house offended, even though your quarry be my kin. Yet I will ask you one question: how should we feel — both you and me — if my brother's tongue burns, and he remains mute for the rest of his life (even if he should live) and then it is discovered that he was innocent of your daughter's dishonour ? As innocent as Joseph was of Potiphar's wife ? Will it be fair to my brother if I agree with you ?

One of the younger men, red in the face, brandished his stick.

"And are we effeminate cravens to let an insult go unchallenged ?" he cried heatedly, "by God, we will avenge it though blood flow in

(1) When his polytheistic kinsmen tried to burn him alive for having destroyed their idols (*Koran*, sura 21).

streams." The unkempt man cut in coldly. "Get up and feed our mounts," he ordered. The youth hung his head, "The women will do that," he muttered between his teeth.

Then the man addressed the eldest brother. "Saïd is as much our brother as he is yours, but the wound has cut to the quick. Let me tell you the story of Dirdah who called in a physician to heal his broken leg. When the bandage was removed he found that it was as bent as a bow, so he reached for a hammer and struck it so that the bone was cracked again. 'Would you have me go amongst men with such a leg?' he told the physician. 'Now make it set properly.' Place yourself in our position and we will accept your judgement. If not, listen: shall we put your son Ali in your lap, and will you swear on the head of your child that your brother is innocent ?"

"Do you doubt me as well ?" asked the eldest brother.

"Who doubts you ?"

"How can I swear by my own flesh and blood to what I have not seen ?"

"Ask her husband," cried the mother, "ask him and he will tell you."

"Her husband," groaned the elder ruefully, "poor man .."

* * *

The old woman remained alone in the deserted house. After the men had gone, it seemed suddenly to broaden as though the walls, unseen in the dark, had stretched outward, beyond the benches and the empty corners, upwards to the giant beams of the loft. The solitary lamp stood wan and desolate, encompassed by endless reaches of darkness, and the mother, big and awesome a while ago, was now a poor frail thing lost in the immensity of the gloom, like a cast-off garment. Fear stalked out from the walls, and coiled around her heart, drawing her into a terrifying vision. There was a long caravan in which mingled the faces of the living and the dead, journeying to their doom. And a dirge rose from the ground where shrouded corpses lay.It mourned for a presence that once had filled the house, and told of waiting without hope .. of a young man complaining to the passing caravans of the rugged road and the gloom .. told of a mother who waited in vain.

"So shall I be in my grave," the old woman thought without fear, "alone .. all alone."

The sad song of death enveloped everything, undulating with the beating of the heart, and with the motions of breathing, with the tread of the cattle, the chirping of the crickets, and with the quiet rustlings of the village at night.

And at the heart of the song was the sad loneliness of life, that loneliness which cries out wordlessly to be destroyed: hands and lips burning to embrace; clothes hanging in the wardrobe inviting the husband to take them and put them on in sumptuous ease; the threshold of the house awaiting the tall body of its guardian; the ear anticipating the voice which had continued to ring in it .. Everything was a question awaiting an answer and the melody embraced it all, overflowing and dispersing into the air.

The mother became aware that the melody was coming from outside. She trembled with anger and muttered, "He's not dead yet, not dead." As she stood in the centre of the house, leaning on her stick and breathing heavily, the nightmare movements of her vision ceased abruptly, came to a halt, yet did not depart, as an expression of surprise is captured on a stone face.

She glanced around and the gloom retreated into the corners of the room. The lamp shone as brightly as the sun and inside her, sadness changed into harshness. She made her way up the slippery flight of steps with difficulty, supporting herself with one hand on the shaky wooden banisters and with the other on her stick. The door of the upper room opened and a flash of light pierced the dark. The woman's silhouette filled the door, then she went inside shielding her eyes from the strong light of the lantern with her broad calloused hand.

"Where's his lordship ?" she demanded. Out of a corner hidden from the light by a large brass bedstead came the voice of Saïd: "Please come in, Haja".

"'Please come in, Haja' repeated the mother, 'Please come in.' The Haja has already pleased to come in."

Before her stood Warda. Her body was sturdy, her large pretty face devoid of any expression, its features drawn downwards as though pulled tight by invisible threads. She plodded heavily across the room to draw a pallet from the corner and set it upon the ground: she had the splay-legged gait of a pregnant woman.

"Sit down and rest, Haja," she said in her soft voice which never seemed to address anyone directly.

"In my grave," sneered the Haja, "there only will I rest from you all, and from the troubles of this world."

"God forbid, Haja. Won't you tell him to eat something ? He has had nothing since yesterday. Tell him, Haja."

"Hold your tongue," snapped the old woman. "Saïd, get up and follow me."

She turned to go out. Saïd stood up and followed her, walking softly.

Warda's sobbing rose from inside the room. The mother looked back across the threshold, her face convulsed with anger: "Quiet, you fool ! I don't want to hear a sound, do you hear ? Just shut up !"

The banisters shook violently under the weight of her hand. Saïd tried to help her as she went down but she snatched away her hand.

"Take your hands off me, you lecherous son of a lecher," she hissed. "Your father, before you, was as shameless as you are. If he so much as caught sight of a woman's skirt a day's journey away, he'd drop everything and follow her. You whoring son of a whoring father."

"Haja, pray for me," implored her son.

"May your miserable carcass burn in the fires of hell like your father .. the swinish whoremonger !" Suddenly she halted. "Are you crying ?" she exclaimed with contempt, "true, your father was debauched — but he never wept. He died a man, roaring like the he-camel he was — and kept his brows knitted firm. I never once heard him moan or complain."

They made their way in silence across the broad courtyard with its muted sounds : the ruminating of the camels, the goats frisking, the miaowing of cats whose luminous eyes from time to time flashed in the dark, as they carried on their nightly conversation with familiar spirits.

From a nearby house came a whining howl. When they reached the door of her room, the mother pushed it open and the son followed her in. The small room was crammed with bedding and rugs, among which stood locked wooden chests whose paint had faded. One small lamp gave a pallid light.

She poked her finger between the folds of the bedclothes, and pulled out a small yellow box wrapped in several layers of blackened rags. Opening it with the slow deliberate movements of one who is short-sighted, she took out a bundle of banknotes. She stared down at it, "My whole life's savings, son," she mumbled, as though speaking to herself. "They were to buy a goat to be offered up over my grave," she added absently, as she turned them over in her hands.

"May your days be long on earth," said Saïd, and his voice faltered.

"Take it," said his mother, "take it and go, for there's no life for you here any more. Marry her and go south where the men are still men; there only will they protect you. Come back in two or three years. You will not find me; I shall be dead by then, and my flesh will have rotted in my grave. Go now, I have had the mare harnessed for you, and there is food ready in the saddle-bags: you'll find them by the gate."

"It's no use, she has refused."

"Refused ? You let her refuse ?"

"She did agree at first, but then the cripple began to whine and threatened to kill himself."

"Let him. It would be better for him."

"He kept on hobbling madly around the house, on his bent legs, whining and wailing, and he seized her feet and kissed them. And he said, 'If you go away, there'll be no one to look after me. I'll starve to death'."

"Wait. I shall speak to her myself."

"It's no use now. There are armed men standing at every entrance to their quarter and on the rooftops of the houses."

The mother was still holding out the bundle of notes in her hand, her eyes staring vacantly. Swiftly regaining her self-control, she replaced the money in the box, and hid it again among the bedclothes.

"Everything will be alright." she assured him. "Don't be afraid. Wait here. I shall be back soon."

* * *

She was back after a while, followed by Zeina, her long gown rustling faintly as it trailed behind her on the ground. They found Saïd sitting on a cushion on the floor, his elbows resting on his knees and his hands covering his face. But the mother was studying Zeina closely and took no notice of him: she looked carefully at the tall figure, gaunt and angular beneath the loose gown. She noted the small pointed breasts, the long thin neck, and the dark face with the high cheekbones. Her slightly protruding upper lip gave her face a strange expression compounded of mature motherhood and heedless childishness "I marvel .." said the old woman at last, "I marvel at what my son sees in you, dark as you are, and scrawny, and as dry as a dead twig .. and to think I chose for him a plump woman with white skin." But Zeina was staring at the figure on the floor, and made no reply. "If I were a man," the old woman continued, "I would not even have looked at you. What spell have you cast on him to hold him like this ?" Then Zeina began to speak, pulling herself up proudly, towering above them both.

"Night after night, through summer and winter, when the snow fell through the night until it covered everything, or when the rains came, and turned the spouts into cataacts .. for long, long, nights — I cannot even count them — your son pursued me . I felt his eyes on me from behind the cracks in my house door until I almost believed that the door was haunted. But I kept him off. Night after night, his eyes were on me. I saw them in my dreams, like an incubus. In the daytime, he stared down at me from his room above .. Night and day I would come up against his eyes, so that I began to be afraid of my own body. I never once tried to entice him. I am only a poor orphan, and I know there can be nothing but trouble from being pursued by the likes of him. Then one night he took me by force, while I was asleep .. I was asleep .. do you hear ? I was asleep, and I woke up, and the cripple was moaning, and begging him to go .." Her voice trailed off weakly, and she added absently, "Then things took their course .. as they were ordained."

"I did not bring you here to offend you, my child," said the mother, "everything will be alright. I shall leave you now, the two of you together. You need not be afraid. I shall sit outside and keep watch." And she closed the door on them.

She sat down, and leant her back against the wall.

Threads of light came from the room through long vertical cracks in the door, and spread themselves over the ground before her. One solitary beam shone down through the whole length of the door, and not only played upon the ground but traced a pattern over the body of the old woman — a shapeless heap of black. From the houses nearby, gay voices of women would, from time to time, throw out laughing cries which would go unanswered and would be swallowed up in the silence so that it seemed to the old woman that she had imagined them.

But she was straining her senses to recapture the sad chant which rose from the whole village — the lament of a bereaved mother mourning a son who will never return.

The streaks of light in the courtyard were blotted out as a body moved between the lamp and the door; then they again spread over the ground and nothing but silence came from the room.

Somewhere beyond, a dog gave a long-drawn howl and its echo was repeated from all around, clear and sharp, as happens in dreams. The howling mingled with the tones of the elegy that hummed in her ears. The mother heard the voice of a woman scolding the dog and the thud of a stick on its body. The dog now set up a whine and the shriek of the woman rose from beyond the wall: "You filthy scabby cur."

"The creature is roused by the scent of hiding men," reflected the mother, and the thought chilled her heart. A weariness came upon her, a longing to sleep, and to have an end to it all.

"Haja, can't you hear me ?" came a woman's cry, pleading. She turned questioningly but did not answer. The other continued: "What is happening, this evil night ? Has not this village had its fill of misfortune ? Do you hear me, Haja ? I ask you, what is astir, this ill-fated night ? Meteors are falling everywhere like dead birds. Ever since nightfall, they have been dropping behind the hill. Did you see the star that rent the sky a moment ago ? .. it was blazing like a sun .." She was interrupted by the dog which set up its pitiful howling again. "Shut up, you strumpet." The mother turned her head to the wall and cried out, "Aren't there any men to cool the fever in your belly, and cut short your chatter ?"

"Did you see the meteor ?" repeated the other, unheeding, "it tore the sky apart, I tell you, and, ever since, the dog has not stopped howling."

Another woman's voice rose from the darkness.

"Can't you stop the dog howling, woman ? He woke me from my sleep, and my whole body is trembling."

"The meteor ! Did you see the meteor ? It split open the sky a short while ago ! Look ! There goes another one ! Oh God, have mercy on us. A while ago, a star passed over from the south, from the direction of the Holy Kaaba, and rent the sky in two, and it left behind a long bright tail from one end of the sky to the other."

"I was awakened by the sound of weeping and wailing," said the other woman, "and I am drenched in a cold sweat and shuddering all over."

"You shameless strumpets !" swore the old woman sourly. "Your tongues should be cut out." There was a sudden lull as the two women stopped, intimidated and pained by the rebuke. She could hear their apologetic muttering. Then all the sounds of the night broke out again, as though they had only been quelled momentarily by the women. From a distant spot in the hills a song arose, a lament at being far from a loved one, complaining of the sadness and loneliness of the night.

The streaks of light were blotted out, as Zeina came softly out. To the mother, that instant, she seemed a titanic presence overflowing with power and vitality and femininity — a violent emotion almost like desire overwhelmed the old woman as she watched Zeina come forward gracefully, in her rustling gown.

"Did you cry out ?"

Zeina did not answer.

"Have you finished so soon ? How is he ?"

"Lying down in there, soaked in his sweat," said Zeina in a submissive whisper, "he cannot stop trembling."

"Is he frightened ?" asked the mother in disgust.

"He says he is not, but he is bathed in sweat and his clothes are soaked through as if he had just climbed out of a well, and he can't stop trembling."

"Why did you not comfort him ? That was why I called you."

"I was afraid."

"Of him ? Is that why you called out ?"

Zeina remained silent.

"Is that why you screamed ?" repeated the mother. Then Zeina began to speak hurriedly, with the words following quickly upon one another.

"We were not alone. Others were there watching us. I felt that from the very moment I left my house, but it was just a feeling. And your son's body kept pouring with sweat, and I was watching his tongue parched and rough like a piece of old worn leather. I took him in my arms, and I tried to comfort him, but he closed his eyes and lay still against me .. so still, that I thought he had fallen asleep. I asked him, 'Are you afraid ?' 'No,' he said, 'I swear to you .. I swear,' he added with a strain, then I looked up, and *he* was there .. he had been there all the time, his broad face filling the window ..".

The mother shuddered slightly, then pulled herself together and said. "Whose face ? .. But that is impossible .."

".. And his eyes were so large .. so large, and glowing like lanterns .. and so full of pain, and reproach .. — how can I describe it ? Then he was gone."

"It's nothing, child. Only your fear working on your imagination. Since I closed the door on you, I have seen nobody pass."

"But the window faces south, and you cannot see it from here."

"I would have heard. I was listening, and not a whisper escaped me; it's your imagination, I tell you. Go to him now, and comfort him."

"I cannot go back. It's impossible."

"You are afraid, aren't you ?"

"How can I go back to him, when he is lying there, helpless as a child, and stricken dumb with fear. Spare me, I beg you, I cannot .."

"Come," said the mother, a note of tenderness softening her voice, "sit here by my side." Zeina sat down and the mother took the girl's head in her lap gently, and began to stroke her hair softly.

"Such is a woman's fate, my child," she brooded slowly, "One measure of joy, and no end of suffering. She must endure pregnancy and childbirth, and suffer degradation and beating, with no right to protest. When I look back on my life, I see nothing but humiliation and pain .. Do you know how much humiliation a woman goes through when her bed is usurped by another ? Four times I have endured it, and each time it gutted me through afresh .. Go in to him now, my child, and comfort him."

Zeina lifted her head: "I cannot. I've told you that is impossible. How is it possible to be with a man who is afraid ? Oh God, what have I done to suffer so ? A man is going to die because of me, and I know that I shall be tortured with the thought until the day I die. Isn't that enough for me ?"

For a long time the two women were silent. When at last the mother spoke, her voice came from a distance.

"Do not blame yourself, my child. This was ordained. If it were not you, it would have been another. I have known that this was to be, ever since he was a child. Every time I saw that piercing look in his eye, my heart stood still, for I knew .. That look, which makes a woman come crawling on her knees .. I used to fool myself sometimes, thinking I had him married to a beautiful woman, fairskinned and plump .. but he was never satisfied. In the middle of the night, the head Sheikh's wife used to meet him in the cave. And she would weep to me and say 'I cannot help it, Haja,' .. and there were others and others.. and all the time I knew .. I knew that one day, they would hunt him down like a rabbit."

Zeina got suddenly to her feet. "I'll go back to him," she said. She opened the door, and paused a moment on the threshold. Then she let out a piercing scream and rushed inside.

That same instant, a falling star dropped behind the hill.

Translated by Wadida Wassef and Derek Hopwood; revised by Ronald Ewart.

SNOW AT NIGHT

Zakaria Tamer

ZAKARIA TAMER, who is still under thirty, is a largely self-educated Syrian, who has worked as an apprentice to a craftsman. He has worked in television and journalism, and has published several collections of short stories, which have appeared in Beirut and Damascus. The original title of this story is *Thaljun ākhiral-layl, A Snow fall towards the End of the Night*: it is from his collection *Rabī'un fir-ramād* (*Spring in the Ashes*), published in Damascus in 1963.

Youssef glued his forehead to the pane of the window overlooking the street. The night outside was a cold black rose; a little snow floated slowly down through the faintly glowing void.

Youssef's mother put a tea-kettle on the stove, while his father sat in silence, lines of sadness etched into his wrinkled face. His eyes flickered in secret disgust, while his hands lay listlessly on his knees like two tired old friends.

It irritated Youssef to have the cat rub itself up against his legs; he kicked it in exasperation. The cat cringed away in pain and crouched near the stove, closed its eyes in defeat and began to dream — of a high-walled garden, carpeted with a layer of wingless birds, from which it would select a nice fat one, to be stared at, greedily, till the bird shrunk away in terror crying brokenly :

"I'm a poor little bird."

"I'm hungry."

"I'll sing for you."

"I'm hungry."

And it would spring ferociously at the bird, getting its sharp little teeth into its tender throat, tearing at it till the blood ran crimson and warm.

Youssef pressed his forehead to the damp glass as he brought to mind his runaway sister's face.. a quiet girl, always smiling.. and thought, "I'll kill her when I find her. I'll slash her head off !"

"Aren't you tired of standing ?" his father asked.

Youssef remained still, and gave no answer; his mother broke in hastily to say, "I forgot to tell you what I saw last night: I saw her !"

Youssef whirled round in surprise and as his eyes lit on his mother's face, realized immediately that she had seen, once again, the viper that lived hidden in the earthen walls of the old house. In his mind's eye, he saw the viper: black, smooth, slithery, writhing its way silently across the courtyard in the light of last night's moon.

"How lovely she was. Like a queen," said his mother, and Youssef felt that the viper was indeed a magnificent queen whose slaves had all died, leaving her to reign alone in a waste land.

An old anger rose in his breast as he turned to his father and said, "She'll harm us. We ought to get rid of her."

A secret pleasure shone briefly in his father's eyes as he answered, "She'll only hurt those who hurt her .. She's lived in the house since before I was born, and never harmed anyone".

Youssef was certain that the viper knew of his hate, and was only waiting for an opportunity to slither towards him and destroy him. He had often asked his father to move to a new house, one that was built of cement and steel and stone; a vision of white walls, pure as poems and suffused with eternal sunlight would come before him, but his father would refuse, obstinately: "I was born here, and I'll die here".

He watched his father's face in exasperation. The old man coughed, and went on to say, ironically, "Find her if you can, and kill her," and Youssef thought to himself, "I'll find her .. she won't get away from me," as he stared angrily at the empty seat near the window. His sister used to sit there of an evening, laughing, chatting; playing with her cat .. where was she now ?

He felt like smoking. The cigarettes were in his pocket, but as he dared not smoke in his father's presence, he turned to the door. His father forestalled him by asking, "Where are you going ?"

"I'm tired. I'm off to bed."

"Poor chap, how you must exhaust yourself. Do you break stones all day ? How can you be tired if you do nothing ? Does it tire you to yawn ? Tell me, can't you find a job ?"

"He's ill," protested his mother, "Look at him. See how pale and sickly he is."

Youssef felt that the moment he feared had come.

"You're the one I blame," his father cried out irascibly, "You're the one who's spoiled the children.. the boy just eats and sleeps, and the girl runs away from home, and my wife gossips with the neighbours, while I, I work like a donkey."

"Don't shout so. The neighbours will hear you," pleaded his wife.

"I'll shout as I please." And his head drooped as he wondered sadly, "Oh God, what have I done to be shamed at the end of my days ?"

"Didn't I tell you to tell the police that she's disappeared ?" said his wife.

"You shouldn't have left her alone. If you hadn't left the house and gone to the neighbours', she couldn't have get away. Why didn't you take her with you ?"

"Well, poor thing, she was so tired after having cleaned out the house .."

"Poor thing ! The poor thing deserves to have her throat slit. What are we going to say to her kith and kin when they call and don't find her in the house ? Do you want us to say her mother was at the neighbours' so the girl packed her things and cleared out and we don't know where she's gone ?"

He turned to Youssef. "I want you to look for her," he said in a peremptory tone, "Find her at all costs and slit the bitch's throat".

There came into Youssef's mind the image of sheep being slaughtered on the butcher's doorstep on feast days when he was a child, and he remembered the sheep's terrified bleating as it squirmed unavailingly under the butcher's weight; and the butcher's big-bladed knife, slicing into the sheep's throat, and the blood welling out of the deep red gash.

His mother burst out sobbing, "She's my daughter, mine." she cried. "You've neither of you given much care for her or me."

Youssef opened the door and sidled out. When he had closed the door to his own room he felt a strange security and hurried to light his cigarette. He inhaled deeply, and then began to pace up and down the room, with short agitated steps, listening to his footfalls on the tiles. After a while, he stopped before a wooden table which he contemplated sadly, for on it had stood his small wireless set, which his father had obliged him to sell. The radio had been a faithful friend to Youssef, and here he was now, a young man without music. He began to feel the cold growing round him, so, taking off his clothes, he switched off the light and scrambled into bed, pulling the counterpane right up over his head, and sinking his head into the pillow.

Youssef was convinced that the viper must be hiding somewhere in the house, or quietly slithering through the rooms. He closed his eyes, and his longing for music grew like a cloud gathering . . the cloud burst, and rain poured down on a ground thick with gritty dust. He listened then to a secret music, the lament of an obscure trembling creature crouched deep within him. He felt he was going to cry desperately . . He was the rain, he was himself that dry gritty dust . . He seemed to be on the threshold of an unknown world, from which only a pane of glass separated him. "I'm ill, ill," he thought.

Youssef leapt up and floated through the barrier of glass into the gentle embrace of a vast unknown world whose lord was the dense night itself. The ruins of whole cities took shape before him, their buildings shattered, and he cried out mutely, "My life is being wasted; give me another one, without a father." He was overcome by the sadness pent up within him. "The trees are green stars," he thought. "My heart is beating against a closed door. My tears are the children of an ancient sorrow. For whom does the sun grow pale ? The night is a pillow to welcome weary folk. My blood is flowing out of me, drained by the absence of a woman longed-for, and her breast rests on a blue coverlet, and it dreams of a city of men."

Youssef shivered under the covers and felt certain he was ill as he lay there, star-gazing, and thinking, "Let the open wound be still, and cease its call to the sun of Anger." He called to Death, disguised in sailor's clothes, "Ferry me across, Death, in your boat," and the far bank was a green voice calling tenderly to Youssef. But Death gave no answer, and cast off, and Youssef waved to travellers whose faces were indistinct. And the music-lovers appeared, carrying drums and trumpets, and strolled in deserted gardens. The night was a woman's hair. "No, no, the night is a viper, writhing its way into the heart of the world !" One of the musicians groaned and raised his trumpet to his mouth; the metal glittered brassily for an instant, and then gave out a long, choked, shameless blare, that was like the cry of crushed humanity, existing miserably on the hard crust of the earth.

Youssef had become a sword now, a cloak flowing in the breeze, a stallion galloping over desert sands as he hard a woman's call for succour .. "My sister .. she's calling me."

He wished now for the viper, not for its poisoned death, but for the feel of its cool body, coiling round his neck and choking him till all movement should cease, and taking him away from father, mother, sister, and the bloodthirsty knife.

Youssef licked his dry lips, resisting sleep, for he knew that if he slept he would dream of seven lean cows, lowing sadly, as they grazed in an arid field, under a low, dense sky of flies and locusts.

But he would not despair. He would look for his sister all winter, walking in rain and snow, indifferent to wind and cold, not finding her; with his fingers ever round the handle of the knife hidden in his pocket, as he sadly contemplated the barren, impoverished shapes of the trees.

He recalled the day his sister had asked his father's permission to go to the cinema with her girl cousins, and been cruelly slapped. He would never forget her look of misery and her stiffled sobs.

And when spring came, and the skies cleared, and the sun shone warmly, and the trees were covered in green, he would go to the vegetable market, walking slowly and listening to the hawkers' cries. Suddenly he would see a girl carrying a cloth bag, busy haggling with a hawker, and he would hesitate, disturbed, for it would be his sister.

He would finger his knife as he watched his sister, a small woman, rather tired, poor yet happy, and he would remember a day when, lying on his back, ill and groaning in pain, he had opened his eyes to find her beside him, crying silently.

She would walk along carrying her bag, filled now with vegetables, and be accosted by a carrier offering his services, which she would refuse, and he would think to himself, "Thrifty little housewife."

Youssef would follow her till she reached a dismal alley, when he would catch up with her, and their shoulders would touch and she would turn, startled to see her brother, and stand rooted to the spot, her bag slipping from her fingers. She would look at him with eyes filled with weariness and sorrow and tenderness, and would extend her hand; and he would feel that she was not his sister, but rather a friend who had come a long way and now wished to take his hand in greeting. Youssef, bemused, would extend his own hand, and they would stand together without words, and a youth would walk by and glance at them slyly as if to say, "A pair of lovers," and Youssef would bend down to pick up the bag of vegetables and ask her gruffly, "How do you live ?"

"I married a poor young man."

Youssef would be at a loss for words and would understand how it had happened; a young man, decent, poor, and a girl who wanted to live her life.. and a father who would refuse to give his daughter to a pauper.

They would walk together till his sister would stop at a doorway and say, "Here we are," and Youssef would know that she lived in a basement, and he would put the bag down as his siser opened the door, then pick it up again to go into the house, to be met immediately by the smell of two beings who shared a bed, laughed and made each other laugh, and slept without sorrow.

Youssef would throw himself into a chair, which would be, oh, so comfortable, and his fingers would again touch the knife .. And he would get up again and clutch the sharp-bladed knife, and grasp his sister's hair,and throw her to the floor and cut her throat as she whined in quiet terror, "Brother, brother !".

He would remember how, when they were small, she had come to him, crying (for he was a few years older than the was), to tell him that the neighbour's boy had beaten her, and how he had hurried out into the lane and given him a thrashing.

So, "Die, keep away from blood," he would say to his knife, and his sister would take off her coat, and stand before him; what a lovely dress she would be wearing, a lovely housewife's dress, and she would ask, "How is Mother ?" and Youssef would watch her in silence, and suddenly she would burst into tears, and stammer, "It's all Father's fault .. I'll never forgive him. He tortured us too long, tortured us, tortured us." Youssef's hand would retreat from the knife and reach out to his sister's chin to raise her tear-stained face; he would dry her tears with his handkerchief, and say kindly, tenderly, "Don't cry." And she would jump up suddenly to kiss his cheeks, sending the blood coursing through his veins in a powerful song of joy, and he would say, "There, there .. Let's have a smile now."

On his return to the house then, he would find the viper lying in the court, cold and dead, and he would look with triumph at his sad-eyed father.

His being overflowed with tenderness as he lay there on his bed: he felt the urge to get up, turn on the light, and look at himself in the mirror.

The musicians came again, this time without their drums and trumpets, but their singing voices were like an endless green plain. Youssef fell into a deep sleep and, in the courtyard, a cat mewed sadly as if calling for someone to come back, while the snow went on falling outside the room, covering houses and streets and people in a white sheet.

Translated by Medhat Shaheen; revised by Leonard Knight and Jack Debney.

THE NIGHT TRAIN HOME

Mahmoud el Saadani

MAHMOUD EL SAADANI (b. 1927) is a playwright, novelist and short-story writer. He started his career in 1946 as a journalist. Largely self-taught, his early life is the subject of his autobiographical *Mudhakkirātul-waladi-sh-shaqiy* (*The Reminiscences of a Mischievous Boy*), which appeared in serial form in the weekly *Sabah el Khair* in 1964.

Saadani's most recent volume (February 1968) is *Aṣ-ṣa'lūki fī bilādil 'Ifrīkī* (*An Idler in the lands of the African*), an account of his travels, written in his own blend of literary and colloquial Arabic.

The original title of this story is *Ilā Ṭimā* (*To Tima*). It is found in the author's collection entitled *As-sāma' us-sawdā'* (*The Black Sky*) — which appeared in 1955. A short study of the element of humour in this collection can be found in a chapter (pp.161-9) of Dr. Abdel Kader el Kut's work, *Fil-adabil-miṣriyyil-mu'āṣir* (*On Contemporary Egyptian Literature*), Cairo, 1955.

This story is typical of Saadani's work, in which the hard life is depicted in a sympathetic but ironical manner. Saadani's heroes belong to the lower or lower middle classes and in speaking for themselves — as he makes them do — they reveal the gap in comprehension which separates them from the environment in which they find themselves.

At last the train was coming in. Haridi Abdel Aal stood up on the platform, where he had been sitting, and lifted the sack which contained all the presents he had bought for his family, there far away in a little-frequented corner of Upper Egypt. He dumped the sack in the train, caught up the end of his *gallabeyya* between his teeth, took a firm grip of the window-sill and began to run alongside the still-moving train. One of his tattered shoes fell on the rails under the train, and he had a fleeting notion of letting go of the train and dashing after his shoe. But the thought was gone when he found himself somehow inside the train, still holding tight to his huge sack, trying to find a place for himself and his bundle among the crowd. Hundreds like himself were there on the floor of the dark coach. They all talked and talked and scratched themselves, paying no attention to the others who were stepping over them in their scramble.

At last Haridi found somewhere to sit in the middle of the crowd. There he sorted his few things out slowly to make sure that all the presents were intact. But he felt a wave of uncontrollable anger when he discovered that in the scuffle the melon had received a gash in its side, the conical paper packet of castor sugar had worked loose, and the medicine bottle had got uncorked so that everything else had been stained, by its contents. When the train began to move on its way to Upper Egypt, Haridi tied his bundle up again and leant his arm against it. It was more than ten hours to Tema; then he would take the bus to the village of Mit el Hallagi and from there he would complete his journey on foot. So he thought of trying to snatch some sleep, but the loud chatter of the crowd, and the distraction of their scratchings, the calls of vendors selling soft drinks, water-melon pips, eggs and semolina bread, and the thought of the presents in the sack and the twenty pounds in his pocket drove away sleep. He sat there looking at the telegraph posts as they ran hastily in the opposite direction like frightened children scampering for shelter.

Presently Haridi's mind had wandered away from his surroundings. He remembered the day he had come to Cairo — exactly a year ago. He had never been there before.

The time twelve o'clock, and the place Cairo. The crowd was suffocatingly dense. There were more cars there than all the buses that passed through Mit el Hallagi in a whole year, and they were running in all directions. The clanging of the trams rent his ears. There were hawkers selling melons, water-melons and newspapers and there were so many people, more people than there were in the whole of Upper Egypt. But an unpleasant smell hung over everything. The people all had a tired look, and were pale. Everyone coughed. Yet they were all well-dressed, in clean tidy clothes and sometimes they had good-looking fairskinned women with them. Haridi had looked down at his bare swollen feet, and his tattered *gallabeyya* and remembered Sabha, his wife; he had longed for a pair of clean shoes, a new *gallabeyya* and a beautiful woman for himself like all these people around him. He had lifted his sack on to his shoulder, and walked on, his fingers tight on a folded piece of paper, and he had walked ahead.

Before long he had stopped a gentleman, who was also crossing the square, and showed him the folded note. The *effendi* had looked at it and then instructed him to go straight ahead, then turn right, then left, then..directions so complicated that Haridi was unable to understand a word of them. Then suddenly the *effendi* ran as quickly as he could to catch a huge bus which was lumbering past and in next to no time he was inside it, still holding the slip of paper; the bus was away in the distance, and Haridi had lost the address. Thus it took him four long days to find out the whereabouts of Sheikh Ahmed Marwan, the contractor for builders' gangs. Of these four days, three were spent at the Mousky police-station — why, he could not tell. Neither did he know why they had eventually released him. All he knew was that when they hauled him in, the first things they questioned him about were his name, where he lived and what he did. Haridi answered truthfully. All he knew and told them was that he was physically as strong as a bull and that he could easily knock down a wall, or haul a bus along, or kill any one of these pale-faced city men.

Suddenly the train shook so vehemently that Haridi emerged out of his daydreaming with a jerk. A lot of people stood up and looked out of the windows to see what was going on, and some of them shouted, "Repairs..repairs on the line."

"When you're in a hurry, there's sure to be a delay," exclaimed others.

Then everything was quiet again. The train stopped for a while and then resumed its journey and Haridi was back to his memories of a year ago. He remembered how he was out of work for weeks until Master Marwan found him work on a building site. It was all such easy work. All he had to do was to carry a load of fifty bricks on his shoulders, clambering up the scaffolding like an acrobat up to the fifth floor and then back again to repeat the act till the end of the day. In the evening he was paid a whole twenty piastres, no less. On his first day he spent it all down to the last penny; but as soon as he began to save a bit on his second day and the remaining days of the week, work on the building stopped, and the masons didn't need him to carry bricks up to them any more. For weeks he was out of work again. Sometimes he had to go without food but he was always sure of finding a lodging in the yard which Master Marwan owned at the foot of the hill at El Darrassa. So Haridi came to know the city districts of El Darrassa and El Azhar and of Abbassieh, where that first building site had been. He also came to know many men from his native district. They all used to frequent a particular café in the evenings: they would smoke tobacco in hookahs, sip their sweet black tea, and play backgammon. Sometimes they would eat wheat-bread with a dish of beans. Every now and then Haridi would have a spell of work at a building site and then move to another. Every day the ground would split open and give birth to a huge building, followed by another no less huge building, whether beside the first one, or far off in another part of the city. Haridi would always carry up the bricks on his shoulders singing as he swung up the scaffolding. At lunch time, he would drink several cups of sweet, black tea. At night he would sleep on the sand enjoying its delicious cool softness in the hot nights more than he ever enjoyed the hard hot soil he used to lie on at night back home in Upper Egypt.

Remembering those nights of the past, Haridi let out a deep sigh; and he trembled all over when he remembered how one evening in particular, sitting there on the sand, he had thought of deserting his wife and family, to unyoke himself from that bond which made him always turn wearily round and round like a big tethered bullock. The thought of it took hold of him and he was disturbed. One night, sitting there on the sandy spot, his fingers playfully exploring the cool inside of the heap of sand, he made up his mind not to go back to Upper Egypt at all. What a dreary life people led there! Darkness everywhere—and the women who were no different from the crows of the air. Even the bread was as hard as bricks. And now here he was in Cairo, the flower of all cities, where there are boiled beans in plenty and the bread is soft and toothsome. Here the streets are clean, and money is easy to make. People here are different from the people of Bahada, his own village, or Mit el Hallagi or even Tema. Here they are cleaner and certainly more cheerful, their voices are softer and their purses are deep. Yet he could not help wondering that night why people in Cairo were a lot more stupid than the people of Upper Egypt. They spend their time doing things that were quite pointless. They make their way to open spaces, pass their time at what they called "places of entertainment," or walk along the river-side. He could see no pleasure in this. If they were really sensible people, wouldn't they spend all their spare time eating ? Food is plentiful in Cairo but people do not appreciate it. If all these huge quantities of *foul*[1] and *falafel* and pickled egg-plants were to be found in Upper Egypt, the people there would have wolfed them all down in an instant. In Cairo, Haridi had seen shopkeepers throwing the remainder of these precious things on to the streets.

Again the train suddenly shuddered and then came to a halt. Some of the passengers stood up; some tumbled over; and some ran to the window, exclaiming, "Minia !" Passengers getting off the train, and passengers getting on, all trod upon the poor creatures squatting on the floor. A man who sat very near Haridi fidgeted impatiently when a dirty shoe was shoved into his mouth.

"Be patient with one another, you people," shouted an old man who lay on his back under a bench, "It's only for a few hours. The whole of life is not much more than a few days."

Thereupon some of those around sucked their lips in appreciation, and one of them cried, "May God bring it to a safe end."

At last the train began to move on its way to Assiut, and Haridi fell back to his reminiscing, and back to that strange fancy which had him in its grip for a while; the need to desert his wife, his family and the whole of Upper Egypt. Now he remembered all that happened

(1) Beans.

afterwards. He had squandered all the money he had saved; what was the point in saving ? But one incessant thought kept beating upon the cells of his brain regularly, persistently and forcefully nagging him on: the raging hunger for a woman ate into him and burnt him up like a flame.

That night he whispered his confidence to Bilal, the Upper Egyptian negro who had come to Cairo five years before he had. He told him about this fierce desire which he had never felt before, in Upper Egypt; perhaps because his wife looked like a crow and was as scrawny as a faggot of firewood. Perhaps it was the delicious food he was eating in Cairo that awakened this fearsome monster in him.

In the morning Bilal led him to a hill near the Morgue, where there were some fat women, with painted faces which bore all the shame in existence and were covered in curious pimples; their clothes gave off a peculiar odour. Yet for all that, they were far more beautiful than the woman who was waiting for him at Bahada with half a dozen children at her side. Haridi would never forget what happened there that day. Some men beat him up so badly that he almost died, and they robbed him of the twenty piastres he had brought with him. Although he was as strong as a bull and they were as weak as flies, they moved with an extraordinary agility and beat him on the head and in the face with great skill as if they were fighting according to a pre-arranged plan. He dearly wanted to catch hold of any one of them but he could not; and they left him there lying half-dead, unable even to open his eyes. When he did so at last, he was in the centre of a circle of soldiers all as black as Bilal, carrying whips in their hands.

Suddenly the train rocked. Some passengers stood up and some tumbled over. Haridi raised his hand and ran his fingers over his nape and his back. True, the pain had gone but he was scarred by the severe whipping he had received; it was as if it had all happened only yesterday.

A most malicious smile showed on Haridi's face. A long time was to pass before the train resumed its journey. Haridi asked his neighbour the time. His neighbour asked another man, and that man in turn asked his neighbour. At last they got an answer, from a man who sat at the far end of the carriage.

It was two o'clock in the morning. It was suffocatingly hot and the smell of men mingled with that of melons, of water-melons and of the bottle of medicine. Haridi began to scratch his neck and back again. In his head, waves of thoughts and memories piled one upon the other and scenes followed one another as quickly in his mind's eye as the telegraph posts were skeltering in the opposite direction, now unseen to him because of the dark. Haridi remembered how after the beating he spent ten long days lying in the yard unable to move; and how he managed then and there to kill the thought of deserting his wife, his family and even Upper Egypt. Back at work, he moved on from one building site to another, until one day his employer handed him on to another employer who passed him on to a man who looked quite unlike the employers he had previously known. He was smart and clean-looking and it was said he was an engineer. Haridi was told that from that time on, his job was not to carry bricks or climb up scaffolding, but to dig in the sand. Lost labour in itself, he knew, but they would pay good wages — thirty piastres a day — and he would work non-stop.

There in the desert, beyond the Pyramids, Haridi worked hard at the ground with his hoe. It was an easy steady job, and those fools paid him well. The absurd work held no meaning for him — dig-dig-digging in the sand ! Perhaps luck had come his way as it had to other people before him. There were people in the city who did nothing at all and were paid big salaries. After all, that gentleman who did nothing but sit all day under an awning on a chair behind a big desk — he did no work: he neither dug the ground nor carried bricks, and yet it was clear that he was paid a high salary, for he bought his cigarettes by the boxful[1], and drank tea and coffee and sometimes paid generous tips to those who were digging. Even Sheikh Marwan, the navvies'

(1) One can also buy cheaper brands singly, which was the habit Haridi was familiar with.

contractor did nothing but sit all day at a café and play backgammon and enjoy his hookah. Yet he was paid so well that he had been able to build himself a block of flats in Cairo, buy ten feddans in Tema, and afford four wives. It must be his turn to be lucky now. There was indeed no other explanation for all this luxury he was enjoying, of being paid thirty piastres for digging in the sand for only five hours every day — and there seemed to be no fear of stoppages here as there had been in house-building, because the vast desert stretched endlessly on every side, and digging it up would indeed take the whole of created Time.

Haridi now remembered how month after month had passed gently and easily, until a week ago, when a strange thing happened all of a sudden. Haridi was by himself working at a slow rate. He was bored stiff and there was nobody watching. The *effendi* had gone home, the foreman was at the café, and the vast desert would not sift away if work were delayed or slowed down. Haridi went on digging in the sand slowly — then he began to work more energetically, heaving his hoe up with a swing and bringing it down into the earth viciously, for no reason that was apparent to him. Perhaps he might have remembered his wife — and his mother whom he had left dying in Upper Egypt. Suddenly he stopped; for the hoe went deep into the sand and would not come out, until some of the men helped to pull it out. It left in the sand a huge dark aperture as black as Master Marwan's heart. Haridi looked stupidly inside and then jumped up in terror. It looked like a room, and there were a lot of dead bodies lying there as if they were only asleep. There were also cooking utensils and all sorts of other things — among them were some loaves of bread which seemed very much like the bread they ate in Upper Egypt. Haridi went pale as he thought of it all. This must be a huge cemetery and these were people dead long ages since. There he remembered the words that Sheikh Dessouki, the village preacher repeated in his sermon every Friday at the mosque — that in the ground were hidden the corpses of the millions who had died, going back to the days of Gog and Magog. Haridi was not of course sure when Gog and Magog could have lived, but it must have been an immemorial time ago, far away in the depths of past history. Haridi's face went pale when he thought that these were perhaps the people whom God had transmogrified because they denied Him. Again he remembered Sheikh El Dessouki's words that God turned the wicked into lower forms, and that soon He was going to do this to everything and everyone in this world. This then must be the sort of thing he meant when he said the things of the world would be transformed into lower forms. Or these might have been some of the relatives of the engineer gentleman: perhaps he was digging all over the desert just to find their graves. For all his confusion, Haridi at last, without realizing what he was doing, called out to the men who were digging around him: "Come here, men ! Over here !" Work suddenly stopped and everyone clustered around the pit. Haridi let himself down into it and looked around. In spite of the putrid stink, the persons lay sleeping gently, and on their faces there was the look of long years of peace and contentment. Haridi looked on in pity and fear — and in envy. Sheikh Dessouki must have been right, when he used to say that rest and peace came only with death. Haridi then searched the dark room but found nothing but some stones of different sizes.

Until suddenly he found something shining in the dark. This must be a treasure, he thought; and he quickly put it in his pocket.

The opening had been widened and the workers above were able to see clearly into the pit. In an hour the foreman was there; several hours later the engineer arrived. That evening there was no digging anywhere, and Haridi lay there beside the opening — under guard. The lights brought by the engineer had made the darkness of the night as bright as day and the whole area was surrounded by armed policemen. Haridi felt depressed. He was sad at this unlucky end of the job. This must be a treasure owned by the government, or the grave of the forefather of one of the men in authority. Haridi thus spent the whole night thinking of what he was going to say at the enquiry in the morning. He would say that he never meant to do it but it was the *effendi*, the engineer, who had ordered him to dig there. At dawn, out of sheer exhaustion, Haridi fell asleep. In the morning he was suddenly awakened and was dragged to a tent which had been hurriedly set up by the policemen. On his way there, he stealthily put his hand in his pocket, took out the yellow lump, threw it in the sand and trod it in with his foot. In the tent, he found a young officer, with the engineer and several other gentlemen like himself. Some were taking snapshots. Others were writing things down on paper. These must be the investigators, thought Haridi, and he was about to kneel and kiss the engineer's shoes, and beg him by all that was sacred to him, to have pity on him and spare him. But the calm smooth voice of the officer sitting at the other end of the tent reached his ears.

"Were you the first to go into the Pharaoh's tomb ?"

"I swear by God Almighty that I am innocent, sir."

But the officer went on heedless of Haridi's words.

"What time was it ?" he asked.

"I swear by God Almighty I am innocent, sir. We are poor people and we don't carry watches, sir."

When those sitting in the tent laughed at these words, Haridi thought they must be making fun of him: that is what men are like — they always laugh when a misfortune comes to someone else. The enquiry ended quickly, and Haridi was out of the tent, free and unharmed. But he spent five long useless days scouring the desert sands around the tomb for that yellow lump which he had thrown there. The day before yesterday, Haridi was paid all his wages — and was given a reward of ten pounds more. Then they told him to leave, if he wanted — those stupid fools. Haridi could not believe his ears. He went to the market and bought the melon, the oke of rice, a packet of sugar and started the journey to Tema. Here it was, now — Tema station, where he would be getting off. Nobody was going to trample over him any more, for it was his turn to tread over those who were still sitting there.

Haridi then felt the twenty pounds in his pocket and opened the sack once more to see that everything was where it should be, including the paper he bought for a piastre because it carried his own photograph, standing by the pit. He was going to show it to his wife and all the men in Bahada.

Now Haridi was down on the platform and the train had moved away, but when he looked at his feet, they were both bare. He had left the second shoe behind on the train — it had gone the way of the shoe that had fallen under the train at the start of the journey.

It occurred to him to run after the train to recover the shoe but the train had disappeared into the dark. Haridi lifted his sack onto his shoulder and trod the soil of the good earth with his huge bare feet, and hastened along on his way to Bahada.

Translated by Mohamed Kaddal; revised by Lewis Hall.

THE THIEF AND THE WATCHMAN

Soliman Fayyad

SOLIMAN FAYYAD is among the younger writers who are beginning to be appreciated. He is a teacher in a Cairo school, and graduated from the Islamic university of Al Azhar.

This story, dated 1960, is from his collection published in 1961 under the title *'Aṭshān yā sabāya* (the opening words of a traditional song, meaning *I'm Thirsty, Girls*). There is a study of this collection in Ghali Shukry's *Kalima min-aj-jazīratil-mahjūra* (*Words from the Desert Island*), Sidon, 1964; Shukry entitles his study of Fayyad (pp. 206 ff.) *Legend and the Short Story.*

The lorry hooted three times : the sharp low sound echoed along the narrow side-street. A front-door bolt was drawn and out emerged a shadow. The door closed softly, and the shadow glided towards the lorry-driver who was leaning out of the window of his vehicle. The driver and the lorry together formed one thick patch of darkness.

"Seems as though you were waiting right behind the door," said the driver in a low voice. "How is she tonight ?"

"Worse than ever," replied the shadowy figure, standing so close to the driver that he could feel his breath upon his face. "I woke up some time ago and sat behind the door, waiting — and thinking."

"Look !" said the driver, staring upwards.

The glimmer of a lamp was moving behind a window which grew brighter as the light approached.

"I was sure she was watching me when I woke up. She never sleeps".

"Come on," said the driver, holding open the door of the lorry." Get in before she shouts to us and wakes up the whole neighbourhood."

The shadowy figure sighed and shoved his foot up between the seat and the steering wheel, his head turned upwards.

"It's no use. With one eye she's watching me, and the other she keeps fixed on the photograph."

The shadow got into the car and sat down. The driver cast a glance backward: there she was, glued to the dingy window-pane, her forehead and nose pressed up against the glass, and her clothes forming a dark blur. The driver slammed his door shut and started up the engine. The truck sped along the street and turned left twice: this brought it out on to the open road.

"Strange," said the driver to his companion." She didn't call out this time. What's wrong with her ?"

"I don't know. She hasn't opened her mouth for two days now. And whenever I go out, she stands at the door: and if I look back I find she's watching me till I'm out of sight. And when I come home, I find her waiting up for me. Oh, I'm fed up with it all. Anyway, if it's got to be like that, okay !"

"I can just see her without going into your house.. You sitting beside her, dozing or smoking — and her eyes, as you say, one on you and the other on him, God rest his soul."

"Ever since he died — since he was killed, she does nothing but sit on the prayer mat, sleep on it, eat beside it and pray on it. And the whole time there's her glance fixed on his picture on the wall. She doesn't burst into tears any more, but she's in a kind of daze the whole time."

"The important thing is, though, that she musn't go to pieces. Doesn't she speak.. cook.. sweep the floors.. ? Still, after all, she was his mother: and it's only normal that she should mourn. But she'll forget him. You'll make her forget him."

"What ? Me ?" mocked his companion. "I wish I could. For two whole days she hasn't spoken a word. She only looks at me and never opens her lips."

"Don't you speak to her ?"

"I do my best. But she never answers. Sometimes she just sighs. Sometimes she goes and brings me something to eat or drink. I've come to be frightened of those eyes of hers and if it weren't for — oh, what the hell !"

"To-night's haul should be good..should keep us nicely for several months."

"Tell me, how was my brother killed — that night of the raid on the camp ?"

"What a time we had tonight! never known anything like it.. Hashish like you've never had before.. don't you think so ?"

"Tell me, how was my brother killed ? .. Come on."

"My head's still in a spin," continued the driver, "and there's blue and red waves curling themselves all round it."

"Tell me, how was my brother killed ?"

"I've already told you a hundred times," retorted the driver angrily.

"But I've forgotten. Please !" pleaded his companion.

The driver accelerated and, in a sharp tone, he began, impatiently:

"It was at Tell el Kebir, in the English camp. After we'd put the landmine out of action, he began to clip the wire fence with pincers and to pull the strands aside. Then we got into the storehouses with nothing but the starlight to show our way. What a haul that was ! Over two thousand pounds' worth of stuff: socks, vests, blankets, even soap."

"It was a cold night, wasn't it ?" broke in his companion.

"No, it was still summer."

But his companion sharply retorted, "But it was cold, all the same, and then..the searchlights were turned on.."

The driver was silent while the other continued:

"There was shooting. My brother got a volley of machine-gun fire right at him, and he fell flat on his face. Why didn't you shoot at their searchlights ?"

"It would have been the death of us all. We were in the dark. We had to make a getaway while we could."

"Leaving him behind ! Alone !"

"There were three others with him." protested the driver.

"Dead..like him." muttered his companion, bitterly.

"It was a martyr's death he had." said the driver consolingly.

"What ! In the act of stealing ?" mocked his companion.

"He did what we all have to do. Sabotage all their efforts. Force them out of the country ! Besides," added the driver after a pause, "we were trying to get hold of enough to make both ends meet."

"And tonight ? Whose work are we going to sabotage ? It won't be the English we're robbing tonight."

"You're being awkward tonight. You can't have slept well."

"Slept ? I haven't slept a wink all night."

"Hadn't we better go back ?"

"No" replied the robber firmly. "Take the truck if you want to go, and I shall go on my own."

The driver smiled and was silent. He accelerated. The lamp-posts on either side of the road flew by. Out of the corner of his eye, the driver watched the wide sandy plain on his left while the thief stared fixedly through the windscreen at the distant stars. After a while he began to watch the lamp-posts. On their left there now loomed out of the dark the walls of the Institute and on the right they could see the workshop like a solid block of darkness behind its stuccoed walls.

"We'll stop here," said the driver. He turned off the headlights of his lorry and the engine spluttered to a standstill.

"We'll leave the car here," whispered the driver to his companion.

The driver got down first and his companion followed.

"Look," whispered the driver, "there's the watchman standing on one of the trucks."

"He seems to be alone," he added.

In a hoarse voice the thief said:

"I feel the cold in every part of my body."

"This isn't the time for it..besides it's summer."

"What do you say," went on the driver, "if we creep up behind him ? There doesn't seem to be any other guard on the train.. I've got a bayonet — let's finish him off with it."

"Kill him !" gasped the robber full of consternation.

"No..no, that won't do..Besides he'll never see us."

"Okay," said the driver with an exasperated wave of the hand. "Come on, give the car a shove from behind. Do you know where the wagon is we're going to raid ?"

"Yes. Over there..past the third lamp-post starting from this one right in front of the Institute gate."

The driver placed his left palm on the edge of the front window and with his right hand he very skilfully steered the car forward without a sound. Slowly the truck moved ahead, at the thrust of both men, until it came to a stop by the sidewalk at the foot of the wall. The guard had his back to them and the whole station was plunged in darkness; only the twinkling light of the stars peeped down like a myriad eyes.

"Go on now," said the driver to his companion, "and take this with you. Lovely tommy-gun."

"I'm scared tonight."

"Be a man. Besides you have this machine-gun. Or would you rather we went back ? Go on !"

"I'm not fit for business tonight."

"But it was you who told me about it," protested the driver. "You fixed everything. Why did you make me take this truck ? And me in the police force ? Anyway I don't feel a bit scared myself."

"Give me the gun," said the robber after a moment. "No. I don't want to go back to selling lupin seeds for a few coppers in the Sharia Abbas."

"Go on then," laughed the driver. "This isn't the first time. Go on."

The robber peered over the wall. He saw the watchman. His face was turned the other way, towards the station, staring up at the stars. The thief smiled to himself at the sight of the watchman standing there, gazing at the sky. In a moment the thief had vaulted over the wall and slowly, very slowly, he began to climb up the slope, over the heap of coal-dust, with both eyes steadily fixed on the guard. He thought he would fall on his belly if the guard should happen to look his way.

But the watchman never looked. He kept on gazing fixedly at the stars. Then the light from the street lamps went out at their usual hour, and a more thorough darkness prevailed. Libra with all its stars twinkled as usual and the thief and the watchman shared the same thought as they both looked up at that constellation.

"Oh, if all that's in these wagons were mine !"

And the watchman, looking into the muzzle of his machine-gun added:

"Then I wouldn't be a watchman."

"I wouldn't be a thief," said the thief to himself, looking at the wagon.

The thief stood in front of the door of the wagon. He sighed gently. The guard couldn't possibly see him now. Gently he felt along the door with his hands. Yes, there was the chain. His fingers touched the pin of the skewer-bolt at its tip; he lifted it carefully out of the eyelet and let it hang at the side of the door. He pressed the chain against the side of the wagon with his right hand so that it wouldn't swing backwards and forwards. With the fingers of his left hand he pushed the door. He was afraid of making a noise that might give him away to the watchman. The door slid back in its groove without a sound and when it was half open the thief peered inside the wagon. It was pitch dark inside. He thought he could hear someone in it, but the sound of his own heavy breathing was all there was to hear. There was no one there. Softly he chuckled to himself:

"Strange I should be frightened !"

"Bales of cloth," he mused to himself. "If I had them all, I'd open a shop and become a draper. A draper's never naked or hungry."

At that very moment the watchman was thinking:

"All these piles of wood under my feet. If they were mine, I'd build a house to live in — and I'd also let part of it and the rent would be enough to keep me."

The thief jumped nimbly into the wagon; his foot loosened a pebble which hit the wheel of the carriage on the other side and then dropped down. To the thief it sounded like a bomb; he held his breath and stood there listening. Gradually he calmed down and all he heard was the sound of his own breathing, regular as his heart-beat.

It was so dark inside the carriage that one could see nothing, but he knew what was in it. That afternoon he had peeped in through a slit and had seen that it was filled with bales of cloth. He had also collected various other pieces of information throughout the day; for example, he knew that this goods train was bound for Sinai and then for Syria.

His hands speedily ran over the bales..bales of cloth, piled high on all sides. On the left, there was a row consisting of a single line of bales laid on the floor. The thief stopped there and began to lift the medium-sized bales one after the other with his strong hands and to place them besides the open door. He stopped for a while to recover his breath, then he lay face down on the bales and let himself down out of the wagon till his feet touched ground. Carefully he stepped on the pebbles and drew out of his pocket a couple of iron hooks which he quietly passed through the two metal straps that encircled the first bale. He turned his back to it, his tommy-gun hanging close against his right shoulder. He took hold of the two hooks and by means of them he lifted the first bale on to his back. Slowly, he made his way down the coal heap, back towards the waiting driver. When he came to the wall, he turned his back to it and, while the driver on the other side of the wall got hold of the bale with another couple of grapples, the thief at the same time freed his own hooks.

"How's it going ?" whispered the driver.

"Fine," answered the thief not wasting more than a single word. To himself he muttered while re-mounting the coal-heap:

"Work makes a man forget everything, even his fear."

At the same time the watchman was musing to himself:

"There's nothing to beat a good night's sleep."

The guard was standing on top of the fifth wagon, which stood not far from the workshop. That wagon was loaded with planks of wood, piled up high, and held together at the sides by iron bars standing vertically at regular distances. The watchman was leaning his shoulder against one of these iron bars, his head cast down, and his back to the wall.

"It's the first of the month tomorrow," he thought to himself. "In the morning I shall cash my wages and take them home to the wife and kids."

With the third bale on his back, the thief was wondering:

"Who knows what's in this bale ? Cloth ? Wool, perhaps ? It's pretty heavy."

"That's enough for tonight," whispered the driver, as, with their backs turned to each other, the thief was lowering down to him the fifth of the bales. "Come on, jump over I'm getting nervous of the watchman."

"No," the thief whispered back stubbornly. "There's still one really easy bale for the taking..And that won't be for sale."

"That's enough..forget that..easy..bale," implored the driver.

Sticky sweat bathed the thief's back and his armpits, and ran down his forehead and chest.

"This one'll be a present for my mother and the family," gasped the thief with persistence.

The driver did not utter a word. He moved away from the wall. The thief began his difficult ascent of the coal heap. He trod on the pebbles without any great care and then climbed into the wagon. He tried to wipe away the drops of sweat from his eyelids. At that very moment, the watchman was saying to himself:

"What if a thief should try to rob the train ? What would I do if that happened ?" Within him he heard a voice very much like his own replying:

"Why not share the goods with him ?"

"You should kill him..Isn't that what you're paid for ?" said another voice, also very much like his own.

The thief was struggling hard to lift up the bale, but it was extremely heavy. He could feel the trembling of his fingers sending a quiver right up his arm. He tried instead to shove at the bale, using the weight of his whole body, and push it towards the door of the wagon. Like lightning a sudden strange fear flashed through his head :

"What if the guard should see me ? I shall have to kill him," he said to himself. He found himself hesitating at the thought of murder. "*His* mother too will hang his picture on the wall. And it will have been because of me."

By now, the bale was by the open door. He sat down beside it.

As he did so, his tommy-gun hit the iron floor of the wagon with a terrific clatter. He felt as though his heart had stopped beating.

"Who's there ?" came the voice of the guard, close to him in the gloom of the wagon.

Waves of fear swept over him and the drops of sweat on his skin seemed to turn to iced water. At that instant he heard the lorry starting up: he watched it gathering speed as it rushed down the road.

"The tyke ! He's let me down."

He heard the watchman fire at the receding lorry and was overwhelmed with terror. There he was, at bay, left to face the watchman alone. Without thinking, he found himself firing into space in the direction of the guard's-wagon. The watchman turned his head and saw where the spurt of bullets was coming from. From his hiding-place, the thief saw the guard turn his head — with a jump he was on the coal heap, crouching there with his finger on the trigger of his tommy-gun. Specks of coal dust, raised by the frenzy of his breathing, filled his nostrils. The watchman was still standing there in front of him, on the truck. Now was the time to get rid of him — this was his chance. And yet at the same time he thought he could make a dash for it in the dark, jump over the wall without the guard noticing and without having to kill him.

"It's the other one I shall kill ! Running away and leaving me !"

Quickly he rose to his feet, but he remained stooping, with his back to the wall. The watchman's eye caught the moving shadow. He flung himself face down on the pile of wooden planks and pointed his machine-gun at the robber's back. His hand went to the trigger and in his ear sounded the voice of his superior officer:

"Today, it's promotion for you. And a rise."

A volley of bullets pierced the back of the thief who had not yet got to the wall — not even yet reached the bottom of the coal heap. Dazzling lights of different colours flashed on in his head. He turned round. The gun dropped from his hand. He wanted to see what his killer looked like, but he fell forward and his face sank into the coal heap, beside the wall. His feet were on the upper portion of the slope and in the innermost recesses of his head there were still cells which could make things out, and which were able to go on thinking. The watchman nimbly jumped off the wagon. Crouching, he made his way carefully but swiftly to that part of the coal heap where the robber lay. From far off, there were guards coming towards them along the tracks.

Still at work inside the thief's head were those mysterious cells, lulling him to eternal sleep. They gave him a strange dream. *He stood pointing his gun at the watchman, ready to fire. The world was entirely grey — it was a cloud. He let the gun drop from his hand and with his finger, he very gently beckoned to the guard. "Come," the finger said. He wanted to take him home, to offer him some milk, to offer him a glass of coffee. The watchman followed him. Affectionately they gazed into each other's eyes. Hand in hand they went off together — and yet they did not budge from where they stood. Quietly, he lifted his hand and knocked at the door. No sound, no reply. . no watchman beside him; even the house had disappeared. He was utterly alone, with nothing left but repose.*

The guard climbed down the coal heap; out of his hand gleamed the strong beam of a torch. There was the thief lying on his face, head downwards. The watchman shoved his foot under the thief's shoulder, level with his chest, and angrily turned him on his back. The thief's face was covered with damp black coal-dust. The guard caught sight of the tommy-gun lying by the wall. The thief's eyes stared upwards, and the watchman's said to them:

"If I hadn't got you, you would have killed me."

By the light of his torch, the watchman saw the open wagon door, and, at its edge, the bale of cloth standing, discarded. He turned to the thief, and contemplated his open, senseless eyes. A tenderness filled him:

"So this is death," he said to himself. He stretched out his hand, and with his finger-tips closed the dead man's eyes. He sat down beside him on the coal heap, and gazed long at the thief's face and its closed eyelids. Even as he watched those eyelids, drops of dew began to gather on them. Then he pulled out a whistle from his pocket, put it to his mouth and blew for help.

Translated by Azza Kararah; revised by Lewis Hall.

STILL ANOTHER YEAR

Samira Azzam

SAMIRA AZZAM (1934-1967) was, as may be deduced from the subject of her story,a Palestinian refugee. She lived and wrote mainly in Lebanon from 1948 until her death in a car accident last year, and was married to a national of Iraq, a country in which she had worked, as a broadcaster, for a short time.

She wrote two novels and published four collections of short stories, of which the last was *Al-insānu was-sā'a* (*Man and the Clock*); she also translated Ray West's *Fifty years of American Fiction*.

This story (originally *'Amun 'ākhar — Another Year*) is from her second collection, *Aḍh-ḍhillu-l-kabīr* (*The Great Shadow*), published in Beirut in 1955. The author deftly weaves humour into her melancholy theme. The setting of the events is, of course, the annual visit of Christian Arabs from Israel to the Holy Places in the Old City of Jerusalem; until more recent events, the Mandelbaum Gate was the focal centre for temporary reunions of divided families and friends.

In one of the cars filing up for inspection at the Customs Office at Daraa, there sat a woman huddled under a grey woollen blanket. She was evidently disturbed, Her anxious look through the rear window caught the fair-haired Syrian inspector who, after a sweeping glance over the luggage, was now fingering one bulging bag which could have never been kept closed except for the rope tied around it. The old woman tapped the window with her fingers, and the driver came up to her.

"Tell me, my son, what do they want from us ?" asked the woman.

"Nothing," answered the man, "They're just doing their job; they'll let us go soon."

"Have they disturbed the basket ?"

"They asked me what was in it, so I said only hard boiled eggs, pastry stuffed with dates, and pine kernels and.. and.. Haven't you counted the contents a hundred times in front of me ?"

"But, my son, you've forgotten the coffee. You know, over there coffee is something precious; more valuable than gold. I am taking two kilos for Mary; she loves coffee. Every morning as soon as she'd opened her eyes, her hand used to reach for a matchstick to light the primus stove, and put the coffee on to boil. Then she'd hand me a cup, and give one to each of the others, And then she'd drink what remained in the pot."

The old woman's words were followed by a sigh and with the edge of her black shawl she rubbed away a tear that was trickling down the deep lines of her face.

When the inspection was over, the driver returned to his seat, adjusted his felt cap and started the motor. The car sped along the road which crossed the desert that stretched out between them and the frontier of Jordan.

With shrivelled fingers the old woman crossed herself over the face three times over and then asked, "How many hours before we get there ?"

She heard the driver answer her without turning his head.

"It's one o'clock now, we might reach Amman by six o'clock in the evening. That is, of course, if everything goes smoothly and we are not detained by the Jordanian Police Inspection at Ramtha."

"Are they too going to go through our things ?" asked the woman.

"It's their duty."

"Then will you try, my son, not to let them open the basket. Tell them that all I'm carrying to Mary is hard boi-"

"Hard boiled eggs, pastry stuffed with dates, pine kernels and coffee," the man hastened to complete.

"There are also some apples and some clothes for the children: a suit for Karim, another just like it for Elias, and a red jacket for Abdul Nur. I don't know why, but Abdul Nur is the nearest to my heart. Is it because he has his grandfather's — Abboud's father's — name ? He was born the year before last, at Christmas time : we learnt of his birth through the Family Programme over the wireless. A friend of mine got the message, it wasn't I that heard it. I kissed the ground twice in thanks to God for Mary's safety. Three times Mary has been through childbirth — all alone, with no one to help her. Her mother-in-law is dead and I — her mother — was far away. Seven years have gone by since we were parted. She was a bride then but now she has Karim, Elias and Abdul Nur. Seven years.. a good slice of your life. She never was able to leave Nazareth for Jerusalem to see us: each time she was either pregnant or in childbed. Her husband came over once and my boy Abboud went to meet him in Jerusalem. He told Abboud that Mary had become so lean — and you can already see some white in her hair. Poor girl ! she is still too young to age like that. How old is she ? Many girls of her age have not yet married. She is only twenty six, or even a little less. She is two years younger than my son Abboud. Abboud is not yet married, but Mary.. She has three sons, Karim and—".

"And Elias and Abdul Nur — and the last of them has his grandfather's name.. and —"

"God bless you, my son, you have a good memory," the old woman said and went on, "Young people have good memories. It is youth. When I was young and before my back was bent, I used to memorize the dates of birth, marriage and death of the sons of our community. People used to call me the Register. But now, aren't I too far gone from those days ?

"Sorrow, my son, dims the mind and exhausts the body. We used to live in Jaffa. You know the place ? We lived in the Darj el Qalaa. We had an orange plantation; its oranges glistened like gold and were known for their sweetness. Our people had been there a long time. Our house was open to all — my husband being the head man, what we used to call the *mukhtar*. And according to custom, it was he who used to receive strangers. We were cooking constantly — always puffing and blowing at the oven — and our home always echoed with visitors' voices.. you know, the day Mary got married, more than twenty persons stayed with us overnight.. no lack of bedding, and plenty of food.. The copper pots which Abboud's grandfather had brought from Damascus.. Now everything's gone: house, orange-grove, bedding, pots — all ! All I have now is two mattresses and two sets of bedclothes, and two pots and a table — which Abboud himself made before going off to the desert.. And I live in one room — that's the way the world goes, my son. Don't drive in such a rush..you're making my bones ache. Arrived, are we ? What are these houses ? Not Amman ? It's Ramtha.

''Ah ! an inspection here ?''

The car stopped and the driver jumped out with the passports for inspection. The old woman tinkered with the window until she managed to open it and, pushing her head out, she took a deep breath. She called the bronze-faced policeman wearing a red head-cloth and started to talk to him in a half-whisper.

''My son, the basket at the back of the car, the basket is mine.. I'll save you the trouble of inspection. All I have in it is boiled eggs and..''

''Boiled eggs ?'' asked the man.

''Yes,'' she answered,'' for I am going to meet Mary, who is coming from Nazareth to Jerusalem. I thought that boiled eggs..''

''But why boiled ?'' put in the man. ''Mary might prefer them fried.''

An aged smile covered the woman's face as she went on, ''Ah, I did a bit of thinking: I said to myself, fresh eggs would crack with the shaking of the car, and spill over the cakes, pine kernels and clothes. They say that over there clothes are expensive: have you heard anything of the sort ? No eggs at all there, my son. This I came to know from some people who went to Jerusalem last year. And meat too, they say is scarce. How I wish I could have brought her some meat.. but I was afraid it'd go bad. One can survive on a meagre fare. And as long as Mary and her husband and her sons are in good health, then my thanks to God know no bounds. We're better off than others and there are others better off than us.. Lost money you can regain.. houses we can restore as long as we have our men safe around us. The unjust will have their day. And when Abboud comes to see me, well, that's enough to make me forget the tears, the suffering and the long cares.

But there's nothing grieves me as much as my separation from Mary. Seven years now, my son. She was only just married when I left her. Now she has Karim, Elias and Abdul Nur."

When the old woman saw the driver approaching, she swallowed her words, and withdrew from the window.

She then arranged her blanket and fell to nibbling at a cake which she had pulled out of her bag. "Gracious God !" she muttered. And the car resumed its journey.

"My son, do you know where Jubran el Sayegh lives in Amman ?"

"No I do not."

"Then how can you say that you go to Amman frequently ? You should know the place. Jubran has a drapery store in .. oh ! I forget the name of the street now. Wait son, I'll look for it. Abboud wrote it down for me on a piece of paper. Yes, here it is.. read it. Will you take me to that place ? For that's where I'll be spending the night. The man is a distant relative of ours, and his wife has been a friend of Mary's since they used to go to the convent school together.. they were in the very same form. Do you think the man will keep the shop open till we arrive ? Why don't you answer ? You look tired.. I don't blame you. One single journey has left my bones broken. I don't know what I'd do if I had to make it three times a week like you do. I never thought I'd make this journey, but I have to. I couldn't let the opportunity slip this time.. I'd have made it on foot. If you were a father you'd know the longing a mother has for her child. Nothing is dearer to you than your child, unless it's your grandchild. I can't contain myself.. wish for nothing more than for this night to be over. For then I'll find myself in a car carrying me to Jerusalem and another driver, as kind as you are, taking me to Mary. Then I'll never stop kissing her; I'll be savouring the smell of her flesh, and never have enough of it. I'll talk to her till my mouth grows dry. I'll ask her about Jaffa; she might have visited it. I wonder what's become of our house ? Is it still standing ? which of my people are still left there ? And our orchard — has Mary tasted its oranges ? And the church, is Father Ibrahim still the parish priest ? And my friends Sarah, Um Jamil, and Mariana ? Are they still alive ?"

Then Um Abboud started to tell stories of those three friends of hers. She had hardly finished the story of the last when her eyes closed in deep sleep and her head bent down upon her shoulder.

When they reached Jubran's drapery, the driver shook her awake. Taken by surprise, the woman opened her eyes. She looked at the back of the car to make sure that the basket was still there.

* * *

In Jerusalem, before the Mandelbaum Gate, sat Um Abboud squatting on hard stone. The place was filled with the shouts of sellers of rosaries, of hawkers crying their wares, and of the press that had gathered there. She was almost lost in the crowd of faces, the heaps of baskets and holy pictures.

Faces wrought by longing passed before her, but to her they all looked one and the same. The place was crammed with eyes filled with a searching look and necks craning up to look over intervening shoulders. It was at that moment that there began to appear those who came from the land which had been wrested away, arrived upon Jordanian soil, there to be welcomed by people who had waited anxiously for them, embracing them with sighs of relief. And Mary ? Where was the face that the old woman expected to see ? Who was going to show up first ? The ones from Jaffa or those from Nazareth or from Haifa ?

Mary was indeed taking too long to show up and the old woman was beginning to lose her patience.

Her feet ached, her throat was parched and she started to feel hungry. She tugged at the hem of the gown of a peasant who stood before her: "Man" she said, "would you move aside a bit ? I want to see Mary, Mary my daughter who is to come from Nazareth. If you hear anyone calling for Um Abboud, show him to me, will you ? It is the basket that holds me here.. I'd have gone through those crowds.. who can bear the waiting, when Mary — Mary and her husband and her three children are there beyond the barrier." But the words of Um Abboud were swallowed up. For a multitude of voices calling for one another rose and intermingled while many pairs of eyes roved in search of a loved one; all round there were tears, kisses, sighs of happiness. "But Mary has not yet appeared. What could have delayed her ? Haven't they allowed the people of Nazareth through ? When was their turn to come then ? If anyone has seen Mary, will you tell her that her mother is waiting ? — Has anyone seen her ? She is not particularly tall or short : she is fair and has light brown hair. There's a man and three children with her. Mary ! Mary ! Mary !"

* * *

The old woman woke up from her faint to find a man from Nazareth, whom Mary had sent, standing before her. He carried to her the greetings of Mary who also asked her to try to bear her absence easily, for her husband has been taken ill. But she promised to come next year.

The old woman mumbled as she wiped her tears with the edge of her black shawl: "Take the basket then, my friend. The dresses are for her and the woollen vests for her husband. The rest for the children.. the red jacket for Abdul Nur.. Take the basket.. kiss her for me on the crown of the head. And when you've greeted them, tell her if I live another year I'll come.. I'll come crawling on my knees. But if God's mercy should take me sooner I'll die with just two griefs: a grief for my country, and my grief for Mary and the kiss on her cheek that I never gave her."

Translated by Safia Rabie; revised by Peter Callaghan.

A JAILHOUSE OF MY OWN

Ihsan Kamal

IHSAN KAMAL is an Egyptian woman writer, whose first collection of short stories appeared in 1965. The collection is named *Sijnun amlikuh*, after the title of this present story, with which it opens. Other stories in the collection show a wry sense of humour. A film scenario is being based upon this story, which provides an interesting contrast with the one which follows it here. There is a review of her collection in the weekly *Al Kawakib* for June 7th., 1966.

I do not know why every time I passed in front of the Hadara prison, when I was a child, a tremor ran through my body, and I was filled with pity for the inmates shut behind those high grim walls.

Perhaps it was a foreboding of the twenty years I was to spend in another prison, later on. I had committed no crime, unless it is a crime to marry, for which the penalty is a life sentence. For that had been my only crime. I had married, and so found myself living behind bars. Thick heavy bars of convention harder and far more unyielding than bars of iron. Only my husband, who was at the same time my jailer, made it tolerable by his kindness and love, so that I did not once try to break out.

He was my father's partner in business in Alexandria when I first came to know and admire him, and he occupied the flat facing ours where we lived in Ramleh. What first made me notice him was his consideration towards his neighbours. For instance he would never embarrass my mother by remaining on his balcony when she was out on ours. Also, when he came to visit my father he would acknowledge the sacrosanct nature of the home, and always made a point of choosing a seat from which he could not see out of the drawing room into any other room; before leaving, he would wait until my father had cleared the way. If my mother or I happened to run into him, and greet him, he would return the greeting courteously, keeping his eyes respectfully averted. He impressed me by these ways of his, so different from those of our other neighbours and acquaintances. In my imagination, he became a merchant prince come from a distant land, not only to trade, but perhaps also to seek a bride from amongst us. Would I be the one ?

It was no wonder then, having let my fancy run away with me in this way, that I consented to marry him when he proposed. I was only sixteen, while he was about twice my age: my father had left me in complete freedom to make my own decision.

The first couple of years went by like a dream from which I was rudely awakened by the sound of the auctioneer's bell. A bad speculation left both my father and my husband ruined: their shops were sold by auction, and their business liquidated. We had lost everything.

My father then moved to Cairo where he found a job working as an agent for a number of dealers, many of whom had, at one time, worked for him. But my husband, Hag Ahmed, decided to return to his native village where he intended to live on the income of a few feddans which he still owned there. So it was that I came to live in that village I had heard so much about. I had not been there a month when I wished I had never laid eyes upon it. For soon I discovered that living there was no different from living in a prison — the same high grim walls cut one off from the rest of the world. No matter what I tried to do, a wall of conventions loomed high before me: a wall invisible to all but myself, against which I alone banged my head.

I was astonished at first to find that none of the other womenfolk complained. I should have known that, to them, this was a normal pattern, for, as I came to realize, they lived their whole life confined to their homes, never doubting that within them lay the entire universe. But it was different for me; I was born beside the open sea and its inviting beaches, I was raised in the bustle of the public parks, the crowded cinemas, large avenues, big department stores, busy traffic and hurrying crowds. How could I regard my new life as anything but imprisonment ?

Conventions in Upper Egypt are more rigid than elsewhere, but they were more so than ever in the particular village where we lived, near Girgeh. The people were never tired of boasting that there, a woman left her house only twice in her lifetime. Once to leave her father's house when she married, and finally to go from her husband's house to her grave.

'Home' consisted of a number of small buildings standing around a large courtyard. They all opened out on it except the one with a frontage upon the street: this was called the *dawwar*, and it served as a guest-house, where the men of the family gathered in the evenings, to receive callers from other families and officials from town. From the outside the homestead looked more like a huge fortress, with scarcely a way of ingress. There were three such households in the village belonging to the three branches of the family which ruled the region and to which my husband proudly belonged. The rest of the village consisted of the mud huts of the peasants, or 'serfs' as they were called. The womenfolk of one household were allowed to visit one another after sundown. But they could go to the other two compounds only to perform their 'duty', that is to say, when there was a death to condole upon. Venturing outside the village was a privilege reserved for those lucky enough to be afflicted with a malady for which the local doctor was insufficient, and which needed the more specialized services of the doctor in Girgeh.

The days dragged on at a crawling pace. Long, tedious, empty days. Life itself came to a halt and remained still and stagnant as the putrid water that covered the rotting marshes. It was as if the wheel of time had bogged down, and needed a jack to lift it out of the slithery mud of the damp, heavy days, in which it could get no grip. I felt as if a great weight was round my neck, stifling me.

I decided to rebel. I tried to rouse the other women to rebel too and free themselves from their thraldom. I did not imagine that they would blame me for this. I thought I was championing a noble cause, and that I should enter the annals of history as the liberatress of the women of Upper Egypt. But their mockery and derision damped my enthusiasm; and they proceeded to carry tales of my subversive activities to their husbands, who did not fail to report them to mine, adding their own reproaches.

I decided to avoid them in the future not only because of my husband's rebukes, but because an evening spent with them only added to my boredom, with its petty gossip. It would be unjust of me to blame them: how could they have tried to talk of international events, or the current trends in literature at home and abroad, or the latest film, or the trend in fashions ? I even began to dislike the reading from which, at first, I had derived consolation. Books and magazines spoke to me of a world beyond my reach. The only respite from this depressing atmosphere was in the few moments when Hag Ahmed came home to our own quarters, after an evening spent in the *dawwar*. Gentle and understanding, his solicitude made up for the father and friends whom I missed. He felt what I suffered, and assured me that things would change when I had a child to occupy me. The child did not come until two years had gone by. But it was a girl-child. I had not wanted to have a girl; not because I had any prejudice against girls — for, on the contrary, I am very fond of them, and I grew especially fond of Salwa, indescribably so. But I thought it would be more merciful to her if I did not breast-feed her, if I let her die. I could not bear to think of the life that awaited her in this prison-house. But my resolution only lasted half an hour.

Time went slightly faster now. Salwa was growing up: my boredom and frustration seemed to shrink as I watched her grow. I began to feel more cheerful. The feeling of being in a prison did not vanish, but it came at intervals — no longer gnawing at me every moment like a bad tooth.

During all the years I was Hag Ahmed's wife, I visited Cairo only twice. The first was to attend my father's funeral. There, for the first time, I met my younger sister's husband and saw her children. I also saw my only brother again, now nearly a man. When I wept on returning to the village, Hag Ahmed promised to let me go back to Cairo as soon as circumstances allowed. But this did not happen until, weighed down by illness, Hag Ahmed was advised by his doctor to go to the capital for various tests. By now Salwa was a grown girl. And when it was time to go home again, we both cried as we stood in Cairo station, and said goodbye to my family and to some of Hag Ahmed's relatives in Cairo, who had come to see us off. Two promises were made to us then. One by my husband, that we would return to Cairo soon. The other by my brother, who said he would come and visit me at the village. Only my brother was able to keep his word, for a year later my husband died, and my brother had to come down for the funeral.

After the traditional three nights of mourning were over, my brother came to me in order to discuss my future plans. "I suppose there is no need for you to stay on here any more. You'll come back with me to Cairo — and bring Salwa ?"

"Of course," I replied.

When the decision was announced to the family, the uproar it raised subsided only after my brother left — without me. Aboul Magd, my husband's nephew, who succeeded him as head of the family (as he was now the eldest member), undertook to explain their views to my brother, not hiding his indignation that such a possibility should have been considered at all.

"It's a disgrace, sir, the greatest disgrace there can be among us ! To have the girl brought up in a strange house ? We'd send heads flying off their shoulders rather than agree to that. If it weren't that we knew that you're not familiar with our customs, and that you mean no offence, we wouldn't have let it pass. The girl stays among us, and she'll wed among us. Why there's no one in the family — not me or any one else — who can allow her to go to Cairo now, not even on a visit. Not until she's married. As to her lady mother, she's free to go if she chooses. However, if she chooses to stay, this still remains her home, and we are all her devoted, servants."

I could not now even bear to think of my original intention of going away. To leave Salwa was impossible. She was the sole object of my life. Bereft of her father, I could not now abandon her.

"Perhaps when Salwa is married.." said my brother to give me hope before he left the following day.

I could not answer.. could not tell him that when I saw Salwa married in this village of hers, I did not know whether I would be at ease about her, or whether my real worry about her would only then begin. God, would I never be out of this jail ?

I have not seen my brother since, and I do not know if I shall ever see him again. For two years later, I learned from my mother, in one of her letters, that he had gone to Syria in connexion with his trade, married a Syrian girl, and settled in her country, where he thought his prospects were better. I did not even see him to say goodbye, and now he finds it difficult to come to Egypt. I never went to visit my family at that time, although I might have gone to Cairo, for I could not bring myself to leave Salwa at all, even for a few days.

She had been acting strangely of late, and I was worried about her. Sometimes she would be gay and full of life.. then suddenly she would lapse into a long silence. Sometimes she would create a pretext to step across and call on some of her relatives; at other times she avoided all such visits. I longed to penetrate that little head of hers, to know what it was that tormented her. Many times I thought of asking, but refrained, for fear of seeming to intrude. Then one day she told me.

We had just returned from a visit to Aboul Magd when suddenly she threw herself into my arms, and laughing and sobbing, and stammering incoherently, she told me. I could hardly believe it, when I had caught hold of her words, one by one, and strung them together to make sense. It was not believable, but it must be true, since it had taken place. The high ramparts, the cruel conventions, could keep out pleasure, learning, progress, merriment, perhaps sunshine and air, but they could not keep out love.

She had fallen in love with Fuad, Aboul Magd's son. It had happened more than two years earlier, during our second visit to Cairo, when he was there at the same time, studying at the Faculty of Engineering. A hundred things came back to my mind now, that explained what I had not been able to account for then: the trouble he had taken during the whole of two months of our stay, to be constantly with us —

for instance, when we went to consult a doctor, or when we went to the zoo or to the cinema — always obliging and reliable. She had sensed his feeling for her, and loved him in return. Now I knew why she wept so much when we left Cairo that time, why she had her strange moods, why they always came upon her each time Ramadan, Fuad's servant, came up from Cairo to see his wife and children every month or two. The man used to bring us parcels of goods we had asked for, and which Fuad had bought for us; taking back in exchange poultry, pies, and butter.

I little suspected the secret messages smuggled inside the skeins of wool Salwa was continually ordering from Cairo. It was inside one of them that Fuad had first openly declared his love — until then only guessed at. Nor could I have guessed that Salwa had hidden two of the skeins, when she claimed that she had miscalculated the amount she needed for her jumper, and must have some more to get on with. What she wanted to get on with was her love story. One day she had insisted upon our sending to Aboul Magd's household some of a particular kind of Turkish sweetmeat which I alone in the whole village knew how to make. Fuad had tasted it once in our house in Cairo: he had told her in his letter that he realized that she could not answer it, but that he would know that she returned his love if he found that particular sweetmeat among the goods in the hamper his family would send. She had known that Ramadan was leaving that day to return to Cairo. When Fuad had sent his mother some skeins of wool, and asked her to make one of his relations knit them into a pullover for him, he had had her in mind. She had wept when his mother had handed the wool to another cousin. And so it had gone on. She told me all this; and I listened happily. I was happier still when she showed me the message she had received that day inside the box of chocolates he had bought her. Fuad's mother had handed it to her when we went to pay her a sick call: he too had come home to the village to visit his mother, bringing quantities of presents for his family — there was even one for me. In the message he told Salwa that he had spoken to his father about his wish to marry her, and that his father had consented.

I was even happier than she was. There would be no more need for worry. Fuad was to be an engineer: he would not be living in the village. Even if they were to set up house in hell, I would be at ease, for I knew him to be a fine boy. Above all, he was marrying her for love, and she was in love with him.

Together we planned for and dreamed of the future. We built up hopes that soared higher the next day when I went to see Fuad's mother. I met his Aunt Bahana there: both women spoke to me of Aboul Magd's wish to have Salwa as a bride for Fuad, and to announce the engagement the following week. But our hopes were built on weak foundations, for at the first ill-wind of adversity they crumbled to dust. In this case, it was Azrael, the angel of Death, who blew the wind. He carried off Fuad's mother, and brought our hopes tumbling down with the same breath.

When the prescribed nights of the wake were past, Fuad went back to his college. When the forty days of full mourning had passed, Aboul Magd sent his sister Bahana to me to say that he was asking for Salwa's hand — this time for himself. I could not believe my ears. I thought the woman was raving. But I finally understood that it was the plain truth, and that the message was a mere formality to inform me of what was to be, and no more. I turned upon her and told her that it was impossible. It was her turn to look at me as though I were out of my mind.

"What do you mean, impossible ? Aboul Maged is her first cousin and therefore has priority over everyone else in the family. You have no right whatever to interfere."

"Priority !" I shouted, outraged, "You're talking as if the girl were some legacy to be divided up."

"That's our convention here. Priority goes to first cousins before others, and to the old before the young."

"Conventions !" I found myself shrieking, "God blast your conventions."

Desperately, I tried every way I could to prevent this marriage. I appealed to Aboul Magd, by sending him messages directly, and by asking the older men of the family to dissuade him. I stormed and threatened. It was no use. Salwa's unhappiness moved me so deeply that I had thoughts of murdering Aboul Magd,and would have cheerfully faced the gallows as a price for the knowledge that Fuad would thereby take his place, as the closest of Salwa's unmarried male kinsmen. Finally I asked to see Aboul Magd: I insisted until an interview was granted. It was a strange meeting. We sat in separate rooms with an open door between us, through which we spoke. I appealed to him again while he argued about his 'rights'. At last I could bear it no longer, I rushed in to him with my hair uncovered, and my face unveiled —except for the long strands of my golden hair which fell over it in my confusion.

"How can you marry a girl who is two years younger than your own daughter ?" I implored, "You ought to be ashamed of yourself. Surely you don't really think that you can make her happy ? You don't really think she'll make you happy if she's forced into living with you against her will ? She and Fuad are the same age, and they're suited to each other. Maybe you have a prior right, but if you were to waive your rights, it would be more noble of you. Please, Hag Aboul Magd, I beg you."

I stepped towards him and threw myself at his feet. I seized his hand to kiss it, but he pulled it quickly away, muttering the usual formula which protests a person's unworthiness, — but not before I had left a tangible sign of my appeal upon it in the form of a kiss and of several tear-drops. I was ready to do anything, to humiliate myself in any way, even to offer up my life.

He helped me up as I staggered to my feet; I would have fallen if he had not supported me with his arms.

I spent the next few days in bed, too worn out to be able to stand on my feet. Then one day Bahana came in to announce that her brother Aboul Magd wished to see me. She lent me her head veil and I draped it around my face. Aboul Magd stepped in. He told me he was there to carry out the ceremony of giving Salwa her engagement present.

"There's nothing to be done then ?" I asked faintly, as if talking to myself. He shook his head and laughed.

"I'll present the bride with her betrothal gift now, although her bridegroom is away."

I looked up. He nodded in a kindly way.

"It's Fuad's engagement present to Salwa."

I was so dazed, I could think of nothing to say. His daughter now entered, and called out for Salwa.

"I have been thinking over what you told me," he said in a soft voice, "you were right. Salwa is too young for me. I need a rather older woman, someone with a lot of good sense, a good housewife."

The implication was evident and my heart sank. "Is that your price, Hag Aboul Magd ?" I asked sarcastically. He drew back, obviously offended.

"Price, Madam ? We set no prices upon things here."

Salwa came in just then. When he had put the bracelet round her wrist, he said, "Tomorrow is the last day of Fuad's examinations. I'm sending him a telegram asking him to come down as soon as he has finished. We'll sign the wedding contract a week today."

On that day I felt Providence had compensated me for all the things it had denied me before. No words are strong enough to describe the happiness I felt.

After the wedding Aboul Magd came to congratulate me.

"I did not want to discuss things with you before the marriage,' he began, "because I did not want you to feel I was pressing you. But' now you are free to answer *yes* or *no*."

"I'm sorry, Hag. Please forgive me.."

"As you wish then, if that's the way you feel about me."

"Please do not misunderstand. I have the highest regard for you, and I have every reason to feel thankful to you; but I have lived in this prison house for twenty years; I've got a clean record as a prisoner for my good conduct, so I think it's time I was released. With your permission I shall leave for Cairo in the morning."

"Won't you even wait to join us when we celebrate the seventh day of their marriage ? Have you forgotten our obligations ? Why such a hurry ?"

And so I chose freedom. In the train that took me north I began to breathe freely. Now I could enjoy liberty, enjoy living. All those years had been a long death: life surely meant movement, change, and not stagnation: but at the very best, those years had merely seen me marking time. Nothing worried me as I sat in the train, not even the thought of leaving Salwa behind. She was not to be away from me for long: in three months' time she was due to come to Cairo with her husband, who still had a year's study ahead of him at college.

A few weeks later, happiness began to slip out of my hands again. In Cairo, I lived with my sister and my brother-in-law. With my father dead, and my brother away, this was the only home I had, and my mother lived there too.

Gradually I came to realize that Adly Effendi, my sister's husband, was not particularly fond of my mother. In fact it turned out that he was not fond of anybody, and I suspected that he did not take very kindly to my mother and me living with them. It was only a vague feeling at first, but I had no doubts left when I overheard him remark to his wife one day:

"Have you no more stray relatives to take in ? I'm allowed four women by law. There are only three of you so far; plenty of room for one more !"

I winced. The next day I dropped a hint to my sister of her husband's irritation with my presence, and told her to announce to him that since I was to live with them permanently I would be happier if they let me pay for my board. This time I went out of my way to eavesdrop on the remarks he would make in answer to her announcement. I received a second slap.

"I don't intend to run a boarding house," he said sarcastically.

I could not get over his retort. It hung before me over their dinner table: every mouthful of their food tasted bitter. I took to cutting down on it, and would get through a meal with my appetite no more than a quarter satisfied. Every time I walked home to their flat, I felt myself dragging my feet, as though they were weighted down with sandbags, even as my heart was weighed down with humiliation and disappointment. That was hardly the paradise I had promised myself.

Soon his hints became open words to my face. One night, my niece, who was barely fifteen, answered me back with a sneer and with wounding irony. This was not the first brush we had had. She had, I think, never liked me from the start, for although I never interfered in her affairs she was annoyed to feel I could not disguise my look of disapproval at her staying out late unaccompanied, and making free use of her mother's make-up. So, taking her cue from her father, she never missed a chance of bringing home the fact that she disliked me.

On this occasion, her mother scolded her; she left the room in a tantrum. Adly Effendi protested.

"She didn't say anything wrong. It's your sister who's crazy to take offence at anything a child like that might say."

"Let her learn her lesson. She's getting too spoilt."

"At least *she*'s in her own house. Why shouldn't she do what she likes: *she*'s not in someone else's house."

This was more than I could stand. Next morning, the others had calmed down, but I had not. As I was on my way out, my sister called me to breakfast. I said I had no appetite. Adly Effendi then flew in a rage.

"I'm sick and tired of these scenes," he roared, "Are we to be given one every day by her ? Am I to put up with them forever ?"

I closed the door behind me and did not listen to the rest. His question echoed in my ears. Suddenly an answer flashed into my mind: I had come to dry land after a struggle in the waves. I stopped and bought a sandwich of *foul*-beans: it was the first time in weeks that I really enjoyed my food. I was not away for long: the telegraph office was not far from our home — from Adly Effendi's house, I should say. The message Aboul Magd received was brief, "RETURNING TONIGHTS EXPRESS."

The only reason I could think of giving Aboul Magd and Fuad — who were waiting for me at the station — for my return, was that

I was longing to see my daughter. But I obstinately refused their invitation to stay in their living-quarters.

"I have my own house: that's where I'm going. Why inflict myself upon others? Salwa can come and see me in the morning."

My pretext was a lame one: Salwa was leaving for Cairo with her husband in a fortnight. But I could think of no other excuse.

The fortnight flew past. On the eve of their departure I went round to her house. After dinner, Fuad went out to see some of his tenants, and Salwa went to her room to finish packing, so that I was left alone with Aboul Magd. There was an awkward silence for a while.

"Do you intend to go back to Cairo with Salwa?" he asked at last.

"Well, I was thinking.."

"If you'll allow me, I'd advise you to remain here for a while. Cairo does not seem to have suited your health. You do not look too well. The last time I saw you there were roses in your cheeks."

I found this last remark rather forward. I tried to look offended, as indeed I ought to have been, but the smile in his eyes was so undisguised that I was disarmed, and my frown turned into a smile of my own.

"As a matter of fact I was intending to stay for a while," I said, "unless, of course, I am not wanted."

"You must not say such things, there is nothing I desire more than having you here, especially if you stay in this house." I kept silent. Taking courage at this he went on ".. and whenever we miss Salwa and Fuad, we could go to Cairo to visit them."

"But, Hag Aboul Magd, it would hardly do for me to marry again."

"But you're still in your prime," he objected, "and Hag Ahmed would be happy in his grave to know you have a man to serve you and take care of you, unless you still look upon this village as a jail."

"Oh, not at all, not at all. I never meant to say that. The village is a fine one, and the people are a splendid lot. No place where one can breathe freely and live with dignity can be a jail." And I added softly as though to myself, "And if it were, well, at least, it would be a jailhouse of my own."

Translated by Wadida Wassef; revised by Lewis Hall.

STREET WALKER

Ghada el Samman

GHADA EL SAMMAN (b. 1942), although she is a Syrian, is representative of a movement which has the Lebanese capital, Beirut, as its centre. She is one of the several young women writers who have made their name there in the writing of fiction, two others being Colette Suhayl and Laila Baalabaki. All are regarded as unusually frank and daring.

Ghada el Samman's mother, Salms Ruwaiha, who died when her daughter was only five years old, was herself a writer. Her father is a scholar, and is a former Rector of the University of Damascus. Miss Samman claims that until the age of four she knew French only, and that, at that age, she began to learn to speak both Arabic and English simultaneously. After a brief attempt at studying medicine, she changed over to English literature, in which she graduated in 1961. She has worked as a civil servant, as a journalist, and as a university lecturer: she is at present carrying out research in English literature in London. She has published three collections of short stories, and has completed an as yet unpublished novel, *As-suqūt ilal-qima* (*The Fall Towards the Summit*). In her stories, with a sensibility formed to a great extent by her European education, she explores the tensions which can be felt in her environment between tradition and modernism. Her heroines contrast sharply in their sensibility with the heroine of Ihsan Kamal's story.

This story appeared in her collection *Lā Baḥra fī Bairūt* (*There Is No Sea at Beirut*), published in 1963; its original title is *Ghajariyya bilā marfa'* (*A Gipsy Without a Haven*). An article by Galal Ishri, devoted to Ghada el Samman, will be found in the May 1967 number of the Cairo periodical *Al Fikrul-Mu'aṣir.* A study of Laila Baalabakki and Colette Suhayl forms Chapter 8 (pp. 257-300) of Ghali Shukry's *Azmatuj-jinsi fil-qiṣṣatil-'arabiyya* (*The Sexual Crisis in Arabic Fiction*), Beirut, 1962.

Your face speaks to me of vagrancy once again. It brings with it the tang of rainfall on beaches, tender with its sadness and warmth.

Your face. Anguish in the green of your eyes, the lusts of Rome behind your stern features. How long will the beloved curse follow me ? When will you no longer appear in the gloom of my room when I put out the light to go to sleep ? For it is then that your strange laugh, which smells of your cigarette smoke, comes to me and then I long to dissolve in its scent, disintegrate like a cloud that nobody regrets.

Midnight. The comic programme on TV has just finished, and the innocent, unforced laughter of my grandfather and young brothers and sisters has come to an end. I gaze at him, laughing among the children,the expression on his face as naive as theirs in spite of the traces left by the slow, forceful gliding of the vipers of Time. I am deeply fond of him: I long to bring back to his lips the smile that was buried with the body of his only daughter, my mother.

He, too, watches me, with contentment in his eyes as I sit there beside my fiancé, Kamal; his glance steals to my hand lying lifeless in that of Kamal. Lying there only so as to bring a smile to that dear face at any cost.

My weary, broken-down grandfather never once complained of me and my brothers and sisters. Not once did he show any sign of irritation from the day my father left to go to a distant country with a woman who was said to be very beautiful; he left my sick mother behind to die soon after.

In spite of his annoyance at my passion for singing, my grandfather never once tried to stand in my way, though he could not conceal his pleasure the day Kamal, a well-to-do engineer, offered me his heart and fortune. Will I have the strength to go through with it ? wearing, for his sake, the mask of an innocent girl ? Will I have the strength to go on for the sake of my grandfather's smile ?

Your face is a dearly-loved tale of vagrancy; it lures me towards itself, it draws the lost gypsy within me. In your laughter I hear the ring of golden anchor-chains when a vessel strikes landfall. Your arms are my haven, and how can I escape ? Night imposes its routine. My grandfather and my brothers and sisters have retired to their rooms;

my fiancé has left and every one of my masks has fallen away. I lie in bed and suffer my nightly agony.

I plunge my face under the pillow in search of sleep, for it might be lurking there, but I only find your face — so near.. yet so far.

I open my eyes and contemplate the curtains. Sleep might be hiding there. My mind searches behind them..behind the picture.. behind the dressing-table..with my eyelashes. I shut out the faint beam of light that steals in through the small window and casts a shadow of bitter reproach over everything — over the image of your face which I see in all things.

It is a procession of faces that I watch in my room — images merging one with the other in my head, thrown up into it by my sleeplessness .. a score of incidents, a score of scenes — your face, adored in spite of everything that has happened..yes, in spite of everything. I feel you waking up within my veins as you wake up every night to become one with me, your smile on my lips and the smoke from your cigarette coming out of my mouth.

Those faces, angry vindictive faces, sad faces that scream at me, others that have not yet learnt how to scream. I curse the hallucinations of insomnia. I curse the city of fears it awakens in my head, this weary life of mine torn into shreds of memories..broken up into scattered whirlpools..

There's nothing left for me but to remember..re-live.

The sea lay indolent, glistening, naked and bored, heavy with the rays of the sun on her. You were so considerate, so charming that I quite forgot it was our very first meeting: you, the great composer who could make the city laugh and weep, and I, the young girl who longed to be asked to sing one of your songs.

"This is how I love the sea," I said. "Solid and naked, lazy and bored, and not shrouded in the masked veiling of moonlight. Groaning under the weight of the sun on her bosom, the sun that she loves so much."

"Yes, the sea loves the sun when the sun is far away. Have you noticed the sea by night ? She has the face of a person in love, all shadows and fears and sighs.

"And when he is near ?"

"She loves him all the more, knowing that he will soon leave. That's what true love is: it's longing, it's the search for security; it's the way to an end, not the end in itself. It reaches its climax the instant before the moment of meeting, then, after a few seconds, it is over."

"What a tragedy. To spend one's life reaching out for a cup that will be the death of us if we don't drink from it. And yet once we take it, and sip from it, we die even so. First it's love and longing that kills us, then it's the lack of love. It kills us simply to know ourselves."

"But you're still so young. Do you really believe what you're saying ?"

"I'm afraid so."

"Sing me something ! Anything !"

And I sang. I sang of the virgin depths that no man has ever penetrated. I sang of the loneliness that no person has ever escaped.

Every one of us lives isolated in a glass case..each of us talks but not one of us listens. Our life is spent wandering in woods, on seashores, in and out of islands, without haven or retreat. Even when we sight a harbour in the distance, we realize it is not for us.

"There's a strange agony in your voice; there's a bitterness that is deeply stirring. You'll go far. I can understand you so well."

Happy. Happy with our tale of vagrancy. Why do the faces attack me so ? Wretched sleeplessness, peeling away from my eyelids the shreds of the happiness we knew. Faces springing out of my weakness and my cowardice, faces that I love and hate. I know what you are. You're part of me. Just as his face is part of me. And like some fabulous beast with two heads, each facing a different way, I'm torn apart. If only sleep could quieten the whirling city within my head. If I could only forget.

Once, when the night was a shimmering fairy tale flowing from your eyes and jetting itself into the sea in front of us, you stretched out your hand, and your palm held a thousand tales of loss. I didn't hesitate. My hand clutched all those tales of deprivation and for the first time I knew the joy of the clouds that moan out thunder when the ecstacy of their meeting rends them. Lightning sprang from our eyes and I felt the fire moving from my hand to my throat. I found it difficult to breathe. But I would not have needed to do any breathing to stay alive, if only we could have stayed like that. I made as if I wanted to pull my hand out of yours, only so that your grip would hold it tighter, so tight that my fingers would knead themselves together and become one single new finger that could join itself to your hand for ever. The delicious battle continued for a few moments, and like a fish that is delighted at being caught, my hand finally relaxed in yours, and you were gentle with it: you took it tenderly by the fingers and brought it close to the red candle on the table we were sitting at, whose soft light crept up the side of your face. I felt its kindness like a book filled with warm words, rich with the glow of harbours basking in the exciting magic of oriental evenings.. and I, a tramp in search of a warm harbour.

You pretended to read my palm. You held my hand in yours and your look sank deep into the wilderness of my eyes. You tried to read the unending misery that you saw in them, to smell the tang of the sad rains that pursued the vagrant tramp and to hear the creak of rusty doors that had remained closed too long and round which thorns and creepers had grown, making the place desolate and unattractive.

"I see a bored gypsy," you said.

"Who loves her boredom."

"Who has no home.."

"And who does not wish to have a home because she hates masks. The city is a mask on the face of the wild forest. She is still the daughter of the wilderness."

"There are two men fighting for her. One wants to give her a home.."

"And her mask loves the home; and she wears her mask to bring a smile to the faces of those she loves and feels obliged to."

"As for the other man, he has nothing but a new tale of vagrancy to give."

"That is what she wants. Because a home is a transitory thing, while exile and sorrow are the real truth of human existence."

"She is like a child, searching for fame with her sweet singing voice, but no one knows the deep sorrows she has to bear; she goes on living a life of indifference, of vagrancy, of longing for a tenderness she knows she will never find."

"That is why she loves the man who resembles her, who carries in his face a tale of indifference and vagrancy and tenderness. In loving him, she is idolizing her own self."

"It's an admission of her own artistic narcissism."

"What else do you see in my eyes — my palm, I mean ?"

"I see a tramp who loves her quest for a haven more than she loves the haven itself. She will hate it if she finds it — if she has to drop anchor among its rocks."

"I'm sorry for this tramp who drags her anchor and her sorrow along, lost and at sea."

"No you're not: you envy her. Because to you she represents the truth of life: she is a naked totem of human reality. You would be miserable if you let her go."

"What else do you see in my eyes ? — I mean, my palm ?"

Maybe you saw the truth, for you kept silent.

But why do I go on brooding over everything ? This sleeplessness opens up old wounds and with its sorcery raises from their graves old tales, revived with the warm blood gushing from their wounds. What a wasted life ! How can I forget ?

Your face was aglow with hope when you said to me, "Let's go away together — anywhere."

A splendid plan. Not to have to suffer agonies of jealousy every time I think of your wife lying next too you all through the night and robbing my bosom of your breath, sucking it in from the pillow you share. Always together, tramping about together; your breath would belong to me only and your arms would be a haven for me alone. I saw you out walking one evening, you and your wife and children. I watched you from a distance. I walked behind you like a wolf that had made up its mind to snatch the shepherd away from the fold. Quite simply I longed to tear your wife to pieces — to devour her. I did not hide myself from my own eyes behind a mask of false pity and tenderness. I hated her. Then one of your daughters tripped and fell. I heard her crying, as you bent down to pick her up — so tenderly.. and then it was I who wept..cried in the street..cried because of the many times I had fallen down and found no one to lift me up, no father to take hold of me, for he had run away with a woman as lost as I am.

That evening, Kamal offered me his life. I would not have to rob someone else in order to have him. That evening I accepted him, not because of your wife, but because of the little girl that I had once been. I consented so that your daughter would not grow up like me and become a tramp without a haven.

But I cannot believe myself — how can I leave you and go away ? What about our happy moments spent together, and the people I used to sing to with your voice in my throat, with your melodies in my heart..the courage you gave me to face them..the sweet taste of conquest, the great success I had when I was able to make strangers respond to the feelings in my breast. I was able, then, to create for myself a huge unknown family with whom I could share my loneliness, my sense of being lost..And you..and the little trifles we shared..and our laughter..

Once when I was sitting beside you in your car which was littered, as always, with the things you kept strewn there, I looked at the streets, the passers-by and the gay shops, and suddenly cried out, "How marvellous !"

"What ?" you asked. "Is it some attractive young man ?"

"If it were an attractive young man, I would have stifled the sound in my throat."

"A pretty girl, than ?"

"If it were, I would have kept quiet and stolen a glance at your face to see if you too were looking at her."

You burst out laughing. You are mine alright. You will look at all faces and still only see me. You will hug dozens of bodies to you, but it will be my hand only that you will feel in yours. You are mine.. You were mine. Why do I torture myself so ?

What then you sleepless, night, that is tearing me to pieces? This bed feels heavy to me, as though I were carrying it on my back. I must escape from this bedroom.

I get up..wander through the rooms of the dark house like a murdered ghost that had not been avenged..and the shabby ribbons of my life trail behind me on the floor.

I was sitting in a café with a few friends. The discussion grew heated, one of them addressed the visor-face of the stern-looking girl.

"Tell us," he said. "What shall we do ? How shall we distribute the leaflets ?"

Full of enthusiasm, the silly fool planned and acted.. like an automaton that is under some ideological hypnosis.. a city girl with many parts to play and many masks to slip over her face.

But this is my true face, the face of the gypsy who makes fun of other people's idealism. The noise of argument sounds like the buzzing of a gnat in the ears of eternity. Nothing can move the street-woman from her dark, deserted beat as her footsteps stumble along over the rough pavements.

She loves goodness and truth and freedom and the principles that all parties call for; but she does not feel responsible for anything or anyone in this wide world. No one is really interested in anyone else; we are individual grapes that have dropped off an unseen bunch and no legislation or belief or order can put us together again. Why do I contradict myself ? How can I explain this overwhelming desire to bring a smile to the lips of my grandfather ?

Why is it I care about your daughter and do not wish her to become like me if you were ever to leave her— a gypsy without haven..? Why do I pretend that no ties bind me to anyone ?

But this is no pretence — I really do live the life of a comet that loves its loneliness. Maybe it is only my mask that clings to them, the mask of a well-brought up girl which has now moulded itself to my face. Who knows what I would find underneath, if I were to pull it off? Has the gypsy's face decayed with time? If I were to fling off my mask would I find I had any face at all?

The image frightens me and I escape from it on to the balcony, with the bubble of feverish faces still pursuing me.

Yesterday morning, the rain washed the windows of Kamal's car as it carried me to view the new house he has prepared for us..the rain wept and wept and the streets and the faces appeared through it, strange and far away like the tearful memory of a tale of cherished vagrancy.

"You've made me so happy," whispered Kamal. "I just can't believe that you'll really be mine in a few days."

I did not tell him that I too could not believe it. I felt like a puppet bound with invisible cords to the finger of a madman who delights in moving us whichever way we do not want to go, thrusting us in directions we do not wish to take, snatching from us all the things we love.

Your face dissolved in the rain..your face and our tales, your melodies and the gypsy who missed her haven when she lost her face.. and who lost her face when she realized that the haven was not for her.

"From now on you will sing for me alone," Kamal whispered.

The mask laughed with the joy of a young bride on the threshold of a new life. Your face dissolved in the rain. The day after tomorrow I shall go away with him. When will this night be over? Tired and alone I am, as the gods and the demons are. I go back to my room. I dress, not knowing what I am doing. I go to the street door..I open it to go out..where to?

I go back to my room..exhausted, I fling myself on the bed.. The world of insomnia crumbles over my head..the faces leap around, turn, howl, laugh, scream, closer and closer. I fall into a bottomless pit. I give myself up to this indescribable torture — not a pain in one part of the body only, not one that is caused by any one particular idea, but an all-consuming pain, which is tearing at my whole being..

I give way.

With difficulty I open my eyes. The grey dawn comes in at the window. Out of my coma I rise, my pain purified like a rock washed clean by the wind and the rain.

I must go out for a walk, alone; this newly-acquired peace needs to be strengthened. I have to resign myself to the fate I had no hand in preparing.

I softly open the street door; my grandfather and brothers and sisters are still fast asleep.

Alone in the street — in the long sad road, where the darkness creeps into corners while the metallic dawn spreads itself over the pavements and shines down off the windows that stand here and there above me, dispersed and staring.

No one is awake: the city is still deep in slumber, enjoying its limited span of death.

And I, a lost tramp in a brazen city of legends weep for a lost haven..weep for roads I am forced to tread and strangers with whom I have to keep company on the journey through life..pretending I am happy and making believe I enjoy being with them.

I see a man in the distance. He is walking slowly at the end of the road. He comes towards me. Nearer. With a stick he taps the ground. My companion in the deserted street .. my companion in the brazen city, the companion of my wanderings at dawn..in a dawn that will not brighten. He comes nearer. Lost, he wanders towards me, he does not see me..He is blind. My companion is a blind man, who taps the ground with his stick, walking along unseen ways. Dawn and dusk are all one to him. I feel a strong link between him and me..I walk beside him..He does not hear my footsteps..

I walk beside him and feel my way along with my glances as he feels his with his stick. He walks and talks to himself — it does not matter what he is saying. I also mutter and talk to myself. We walk on and on and at a distance we look like two friends.

A fearful satisfaction fills me. Together we represent the closest of human ties.. no pretences, no forced conversation..

Beside the blind man I walk. each one of us talking to himself. The sun rises, people pour out on to the street, a stream of bubbles which are faces fizzing up all around me. I lose my blind man in a side-street.

Translated by Azza Kararah; revised by Lewis Hall.

THE CROWD

Youssef el Sharouny

YOUSSEF EL SHAROUNY was born in 1924 in the Delta governorate of Menoufia. After studying philosophy in Cairo, he worked as a teacher in the Sudan, then for the Supreme Council for the Arts, Literature and Social Science in Cairo, and has also been on the editorial board of a cultural periodical. He has produced critical essays (mentioned in our Arabic reading list at the end of the volume) and several volumes of short stories. *The Crowd* appeared in the literary pages of the daily *Al Ahram* on February 15th., 1963, and a version of this translation has been broadcast on the European language service from Cairo. His work combines the assurance of the established generation with the experimentalism of the younger writers, and achieves a balance between the qualities of both.

You might describe me as a human being who has been pursed up. When I was an adolescent, a third of a century ago, I was extremely fat. And so was my father before me. (May his soul rest in peace !) My mother too remained fleshy to the last, for they both grew up in the country, where the world is wide and open to all, fat and thin alike. As for myself, I had to get rid of my fat to find a place for myself and make room for others in the city.

I've been waiting at the bus stop for twenty minutes, trying to clamber on to get to the terminus to take over my shift. I'm a conductor in the City Transport Company and my shift starts in twenty minutes. A bus hurtles by without stopping. It's crowded to suffocation. Another stops. Those who want to get off, and those who are trying to get on collide and stand to, holding out; not budging. Finally the bus disgorges one lot of arms and legs and sucks in another. I try to push my way into the middle of the battle of the Getters-off and the Getters-on, and hardly find a toe-hold with my right foot when the bus pulls out. I sway backward in an effort to keep my balance; someone butts me in the chest and I fall on the ground. I get up, slapping the dust off my clothes.

My name is Fathi Abdel Rasul, bus conductor and poet from Kom Ghorab in the markaz of Wasta, Province of Beni Suef. I grew up there in the middle of boundless fields and unlimited horizons. My father used to take part in the *zikr*[1] of the Sheikh Sharani. His corpulent body would sway rythmically right and left as I, awe-struck yet happy, watched him and tried to imitate him. I still remember — in flashes — the long evenings when he read by the pale light of the oil lamp the legend of the Sayyed el Badawi, or the Supplications of the Sheikh Metwalli. They were proposing him as the next head of the order of Sheikh Sharani, for he was loved and honoured by all. People used to kiss his hand reverently and bend down playfully to kiss my cheek.

I'm terrified of crowds. When I was a small boy, my father took me to the *moulid*[2] of Sidi Ahmed el Nouti, where he led a circle in a *zikr* and forgot all about me. I'd hoped to have a turn on a swing. I stood breathless in front of a sugar horse carrying a young horseman of about my age. The paper-hat seller passed, and I followed him for a while. Suddenly I realized I was lost in the crowd. I ran here and there among the circles of the *zikr* looking for my father, several times mistaking another of the worshippers for him. I wept, running and bumping into people, trying to get away from them in their very thick — frightened, in a panic. If I'd been in the fields with him, I would have seen my father at a distance far greater than the stretch of the whole *moulid.* In the end, a man from our village recognized me. "Abdel Rassoul's boy, in tears ?" I heard him say. "What's the matter, boy ?" He took me to my father. Since then I've been afraid of crowds.

When my father left the country and moved into the big city in search of a livelihood, I was an adolescent. Signs of inherited corpulence began to show on me, and my voice began to break just as I had entered the town school and learnt to browse through the books that my father

(1) Communal act of devotion, performed by religious fraternity.

(2) Celebration of Saint's day.

read : *The Fragrance of Meads, In Praise of the Beloved Who Intercedes;* and *The Traveller's Delight, For Company on his Pilgrimage towards Effulgent Light;* and *Fine Firstlings of the Flock, An Offering to the Lord of Life.* I was particularly fascinated by the stories in *A Garden of Aromatic Shrubs, being a Legendary of the Holy Ones.*

The big city, teeming with people, dazzled me. It was like a million *moulids* all on at once. It was clear that we had come too late, for there was no room for any more people. I saw the tall many-storeyed buildings, and wondered how houses could be perched on top of each other in that way. I had a terror that they might crumble down under their own weight and crush everyone in them. For the first time, I saw buses and trams, crowded with people and, in turn, themselves jamming the streets of the city. Every one, men and women, old and young, seemed to be dashing towards something, as if they were a herd of sheep driven on the homeward track, down at our village at sunset; each pushing along, separately, alone in the middle of the crowd. A huge wave of depression broke over me, greater than the one that had overwhelmed me at the *moulid*; for if ever I got lost and cried, there would be no one to ask me: "What's the matter, boy ?" Here you know no one, and no one knows you.

Father (it was probably one of his miracles) succeeded in finding work for himself and a roof for us. He opened up a small grocery shop and rented a room into which we all crowded; my father and mother, my sister Saadeyya and I, and the furniture and books we had brought with us. The room stood in what was a cross between a ground floor and a basement. A dim light penetrated through barred windows, like those of prison cells. But no sunshine. We lived in a cold, damp, grey twilight.

In the tenement the rooms were close to each other. And in the rooms the bodies of men and women were also close to each other. Whenever the darkness of night brought them together, they begot children; like rabbits. If balked, desire would turn into a loud quarrel; if desires matched, passions flared up. Screaming was the only recognized language on the floor where we lived. Words did not matter; as if there was a great distance between a man and his wife, a father and his son, or a woman and her neighbour.

Father and Mother used to sleep on a bed; my sister and I on a rush mat on the floor. My mother gave birth seven times. Three of her children died before they were a year old; one before the age of two; the seventh time, she died. She had a hemorrhage and the midwife didn't know what to do about it. That night our neighbours didn't sleep. They offered whatever help and sympathy they could : a word of encouragement, a piece of cloth, sighs, a washing pan, a bed sheet, a wail. And in the morning she was dead. The men lent my father whatever money they could to cover the cost of dying. The men who carried her coffin staggered under the weight. People said that her fatness had brought on her death. My father wept over her, and so did my sister and so did I.

A month later there was a new bride in our room occupying my mother's place in the bed. Awatef was not a stranger. She had lived with her family in a room close by, though they had recently moved away to another room at a little distance from us. She was twenty and my father was then almost fifty. I treated her at first with some reserve, but she was so kind with me and my sister, and so beautiful, that she won me over. Within weeks she had become indispensable to us. In the month that had followed my mother's death, before Awatef appeared, we had been utterly helpless and disorganized. The neighbours did our washing, and my father bought ready-cooked food; the room had become filthy. When Awatef took over, order was restored; in fact our lives became even more orderly than in my mother's day.

At that time I had taken my Preparatory Certificate and my father tried to enroll me in a Secondary Technical school. We were told everywhere that there was no place for me. My grades were low. The classes were filled with schoolchildren who had managed to get better grades. My father heard that there were still some places in the Physical Training Institute where high grades did not matter, and he took me along. As soon as the registrar saw me, and my father too, he told us that we didn't have a chance: "We've only got one place," he said to my father, looking me over with a smile, "and your son needs two !"

"But your exercises will take care of that."

"Let him lose weight first. A slim figure is required here."

Ashamed, I went back, dragging my weight as if I were crawling. My breasts were like a woman's, or the udders of a milk cow in Kom Ghorab. My belly had fold over fold of flesh. My buttocks drooped heavily. I swam in a sticky, jelly-like sweat. I joined an inexpensive sports club at once, and started on some strenuous drilling. When I had got my weight down a bit, it was too late for admission. Schools were closed to me, and I realized that I would have to get a job.

To save himself the bother of finding me a job, my father decided to let me help him in the grocery shop. He accused his assistant of swindling him over the customers' accounts, and dismissed him; there was no room for both of us.

At the beginning of every month, the customers pressed together in the shop for their rations, with their grubby coupons in one hand and their equally grubby paper currency in the other. Whenever there was a shortage of anything in the market and people heard that Abdel Rasul had some, they would rush to us, pushing and fighting. The brand would soon be sold out, but they would still fight. I had quite a time keeping them out of the store in case our stock should tumble down on their heads, or any of them lift something.

I had more admiration and respect than love for my father. I admired his courage and was afraid of his severity. He had given up being a religious leader, as the shop took up all his time. Whenever he caught me reading, or writing a song, he would sneer:

"Why didn't you succeed at school, then ? Why don't you earn your living as your own people do ?"

But I kept on sending lyrics to the broadcasting station without receiving an answer. I wrote in secret about the love and anguish that other songs dealt with, but also about a new emotion that was kindling in my blood.

At night, when we were all clustered in our room, when the lights in the neighbourhood had been turned off, and the uproar turned into whispers, I began to notice strange things.. Movements and unusual sounds coming from the bed reached me as I lay half-asleep. With a mixture of curiosity and disgust and excitement, I became gradually aware of what took place in their world. In summer I chose to sleep in the entrance hall. In the winter it was too cold. Before the end of the year Awatef had her first child. She had him at noon.

The hot sun is scorching my head. My head which has gone bald. The heat has wilted the freshness of the women. Their perfumes have evaporated and the smell of sweat spreads from under their armpits. There hasn't been a third bus yet. I ask a man standing beside me what time it is. "It's a million o'clock !" he answers, puffing. A woman is shifting her baby from one shoulder to the other every two minutes, very regularly. An old man stares at the sun for a moment, then asks me about the number of the approaching bus. Once in a while a man leaves the bus stop, in resignation, raises his hand and hails a taxi..

In the grocery shop my father raised the knife, wanting to strike me:

"What are you doing, you son of a bitch ! Still writing love songs ? Is this what you've turned out to be after the trouble I've taken with your education ? I wanted you to be Dervish leader and you've ended up by becoming a devil's disciple !"

The customers came between:

"Leave him alone, Abdel Rasul; all boys are like that !"

"I'll show him ! The good-for-nothing ! Even here he's a failure !"

They got the knife out of his hand, but he tore himself away from them and hit me in front of everyone. Some bars of soap fell on the floor. I thought of flinging one at his head. This was not the first time; I decided it would be the last. It was not the last; it takes time to get another job.

Finally a friend of mine took me along to the transport Company. I stood in front of the personnel manager and thought of the registrar of the Physical Education Institute. He too didn't like my weight (most of which has now melted away).

"Our buses are crowded, I *mean* crowded. There are even people of your size among the passengers. How will you be able to push about among them ? We need conductors slim as sugar cane. But you..

you're more like an elephant or a porpoise !" he laughed.

I laughed, not wanting the man to think me heavy and dull as well as fat, and he went on:

"Our company likes crowds. The more crowded our buses are, the more money we make. Our conductors get a bonus of eight piastres if the takings reach ten pounds, and four piastres after that for every other pound. Your size will prevent you from ever getting the bonus."

"I promise you I'll lose weight," I pleaded.

"Why do you eat so much ? Leave something for the others !"

"Don't think I'm a millionaire," I joined in the laughter, "I promise you I shan't eat any more."

"Good. I'll take your application, but it's up to you to convince them at the interview."

Back I went to the sports club and paid them to take weight off me. There were dozens of men doing vigorous exercises in the hope of losing weight to find a place in a school or office. The exercises were more like torture. I had to bend and raise myself; sit down, stand up, lie down; to stretch one arm upward and the other down; to twist right and left; to bend forward and backwards as if I were in a *zikr*, sweating floods and panting like a runaway dog.

I drank little water. I never slept in the afternoon. I had one meal a day. My body like that of our omda's unruly horse, I broke, or rather I broke in, so that it would take me into the thick of the throng. I never looked like a sugar cane; still, I satisfied the board at the interview. I sang them some of my own songs to borrowed tunes. One of them laughed. Another smiled. This was the first appraisal of my art. They made me a bus conductor in the 'City Transport Company'.

Crushed into the bus, I feel as though I'm in our ground floor room. The bodies of men and women press together, blazing with sex. The ones getting on and those getting off collide and trample on one another with loud arguments. Everyone has the same idea — to get a seat; a vacant seat becomes the main aim in life, as though the whole future rested on it.

"Excuse me, lady."

"Move on. Who's stopping you ?"

"You're in the way. How can I go on ?"

"Where do you think you are ? In the Continental Hotel ? This is a bus. Huh ! Thinks he's in the Continental. 'Excuse me' he says ! Huh !"

"Very well, I'm to blame !"

"She certainly wants a man to look at her ! He's in the wrong alright !"

"She may be in the mood !"

General hilarity.

"Oh, my foot ! My foot !"

"If we find the crush unbearable now, what'll our children do in the future ?"

"Ah ! That's why I'm still a bachelor ! Sensible, isn't it ?"

"Huh ! That's the crowd's own wisdom ! It carries its own cure in itself. It cramps people up so much that they no longer want to reproduce."

"In a way it's as good a solution as plagues, famines and wars."

"Ah ! It's a war alright ! I feel really sorry for my children ! What future'll they have ?"

"They say in a few years people will find only standing room on the earth."

"Take your hands off me !" shrieks a woman's voice from the second class.

"Take a taxi if you don't like the crowd !"

"You're dirty and obscene !"

"There's nobody obscener or more dirty-minded than *you* !"

"Calm down ! We'll be there in a couple of minutes !"

There are only two minutes left for my shift. My bus will be waiting, packed. They'll be clamouring for the conductor. The inspector will cut my day's pay. I can't stand being on my feet so long. My joints are giving way.

One morning my father complained about his joints, about his right knee in particular. And in the evening he was complaining about both knees. He had a high temperature and was covered with sweat that smelled of vinegar. He took some aspirin and went to sleep. In the morning he refused to rest.

"Stay in bed, father, "I said to him. "Awatef will go to the shop."

His eyes flashed like a tiger's.

"I know," he shouted, "you want to get everything while I'm still alive !"

"I only want you to rest a bit. I'm worried about you. You went out in the morning with one knee aching and when you came back both knees were bad."

"You want to sell my shop !" he screamed as he leapt up and tried to grab me. "And buy paper and pencils ! I know you ! Awatef is not leaving this room !"

The neighbours appeared at the door, driven, as they usually were, partly by curiosity and partly by a desire to make it up between my father and me. They broke up the fight.

He went to work, as strong as a bull, ready to fight death itself. Suddenly he collapsed and we put him to bed. He couldn't stand anyone touching his limbs. His joints swelled and filled with liquid. The doctor said that the disease had reached the heart. He was exhausted by fits of coughing and vomiting. Whenever he coughed his inside was torn apart; and my heart with it. His eyes goggled in alarm as his screams pierced the air -- the nightmare of it still obsesses me.

At night, after the funeral, after the mourners departed and my sister Saadeyya returned, still weeping, to her husband's house; after my young brothers — Awatef's children — went to sleep, Awatef was still crying. I couldn't shed a tear, but my heart wept silently, bitterly.

I had truly inherited my father's belongings: the small, famished mouths, his books, and his shop, and also Awatef. I tried to comfort her. I who was in greater need of being soothed. Her skin seemed whiter against her black dress. I had never realized how white it was before.. or how soft.

The night after my father's death, I discovered that her nose was beautiful. The nose decides the beauty of the whole face, of which it is the centre. If it is big, or long, or snub, it makes the other features ugly. But her fine nose gave beauty to the lips and chin, and even to her eyes. I longed to kiss the tip of her nose. I put it down in a song.

I dreamed that I was carrying my father and that he was groaning. He was too heavy for me, for I had become thin. I fell, and dropped him on the ground. I heard him moaning piteously:

"How can you let me fall, you cruel harsh son !"

My heart melted with love and compassion for him as I saw myself responsible for his agony. I rose in alarm and saw Awatef lying in bed, breathing quietly. Her thigh was uncovered; it was whiter and softer than I had discovered the night before. I got up and covered it gently, feeling her warmth.

On the night that followed I made up my mind to go home late, after Awatef had gone to bed. I asked for a night shift; at least there would be no rush hour.

On the fortieth evening after my father's death, we received the mourners again, and I had to be at Awatef's side on this occasion. That night I discovered her voice, strangely enough, for the first time. Her broken tone was like a call; it was husky, as though with desire. That night I slept on the floor right beside her bed, and not, as I had so far, with her children lying between me and her bed. That was at the beginning of the night. In the middle of the night I found myself in the bed, in my father's place. It was then that I discovered her feet, her toes and her toe nails. We devoured each other until we had our fill, then she slept and I slept too.

I was in the *moulid.* The *moulid* was in a bus. The procession was heading straight for me. They were murmuring prayers and incantations, carrying flags and torches and drums. At the head was my father, riding a sugar horse and wearing a dervish's tall cap, his sword out of its sheath. His horse's hoofs were trampling over me, his sword struck me. Behind him the people pushed and pressed as they did when they fought for their rations, or when they tried to get on the bus before the others could get off. They pushed and pressed and trampled over me. I shouted but no sound came out of my mouth for it was full of dust. I was crushed under their boots as they trampled over my joints, until I lost my ticket block, and the money in my pouch was scattered while I tried to hang on to what was left. Oh, they'll give me the sack ! *There are twenty seconds left for my shift. Their shoes and their feet have left their traces in my joints. My right knee has been split open by my father's sword. My body is covered with sweat; sweat that smells of vinegar. The flood will spread to my heart.*

I'm Fathi Abdel Rasul, conductor and poet and lover. We are all in the one room. Her elder son is beginning to notice. He gets up in the middle of the night as if he wants a drink of water from the jug. And he looks towards the bed. I move away from her. Does he want her for himself, I wonder.

"What do you want, Saïd ?"

"A drink."

"Ah ? A drink, is it ?"

Awatef woke up :

"It's night and the walls have ears. Do stop."

"What does the boy want with you ?"

"Do you mean my son Saïd ? Are you mad ?"

"I'm not mad. Why does he get up every night ?"

"To drink or go to the lavatory."

"Oh no ! I know what he wants !"

I slapped him. His mother screamed. The neighbours woke up. Awatef shrieked :

"He's mad ! Keep him away !"

At dawn I saw my father in a corner of the room wearing the inspector's uniform. He squatted on the floor leaning to the right, then to the left, reading the daily bus report in his hand, reciting as if in a *zikr:* "You harsh son, you cruel son. I'm your father, you ungrateful son !" He went on with his chant, until I remembered the *Fateha*,[1] and when I recited it to myself, he disappeared. But he came back again, and again. At first he came at dawn. Then at all hours.

I had fits of depression and fright in the crowded bus as I bent over

(1) The brief opening chapter of *Koran*, regularly recited as a prayer.

the passengers, and tore off the tickets. I lost all interest in life: I simply went through the motions of living. I lost my appetite for food and sleep and my desire for Awatef and my capacity to write songs.

"Tickets please, lady."

"One moment..Oh ! My purse, where's my purse !"

"A pickpocket must have taken it. Thief,..thief..ief..iefief."

"Stop the bus !"

"Hey ! we've got work to do !"

"Search the passengers !"

"There was a little boy standing next to her. He jumped off two stops back."

"Was there a lot of money in it ?"

"It's no use crying over spilt milk."

The woman curses the crowd while everyone touches his pocket.

"What did you give me ?"

"Five piastres."

"And how much change did you take back ?"

"Nine piastres."

"Now, was that the correct change !"

"I don't know what a ticket costs in your bus !"

They laugh.

I long for the smell of green fields; to breathe the moonlight spread out over a crop of maize. All I smell now is sweat and bad breath. At night the moonlight is strangled by the clustered houses. They've chased the moon out of the city. (*I put that into a song.*)

Awatef looked after the shop. She left the house in the morning and came back at night. I dropped in unexpectedly more than once to see if she was flirting with the customers; the shop was more crowded than ever. Saïd helped her after school. She never gave me my share. I want to bite her nose off. My father's face stands between me and her son:

"What's the boy doing here ?"

"Helping me as you used to help your father."

"He's pinching my share of the takings."

"I'm feeding your brothers with your share."

"Then it's your nose I'll have to eat."

"Isn't your pay enough for you ?"

"The tip of your nose is enough for me !"

"There's no share for you !

"Your nose is my share !

"Help ! What are you doing !"

I sprang at her and grabbed her hair and hung on to it trying to pull her face to me and bite her nose. She scratched my face with her nails, and broke into loud screams. I banged her head against the wall. The crowd pressed together as in the bus. I told them she would not pay her fare and that she must get off at the next stop. "Tickets please! I know your sort. I know how you hide in the crowd to get off without paying your fare. But I can tell very well the face that has paid and the back of the neck that has not paid !"

The crowd dragged us to the police station. She said I was mad and pointed to her bitten nose. She asked for protection against me; asked to have my head looked into. The sergeant drew up the report. He took my name and address, wrote down my age and occupation.

Since that day I've been expecting them to put me in a straight-jacket and take me away. I try to hide and at the same time to be prepared. Every pay-day I think to myself, "This is the last time I'll cash my wages before they transfer me." Every time I have a hair-cut I say to myself, "This is the last haircut before they take me away." Every time I take a bath I say, "This is my last bath here, before I'm shut up in a cell".

"Tickets, please !"

"Official of the firm."

"Your card, please !"

The man presents me with an identity card that certifies he's just left the asylum. I ask him why he doesn't want to pay his fare and he laughs:

"Oh ! Oh ! We're both alike !"

Ha ! Ha ! Ha ! Ho ! Ho ! Ho !

I am Fathi Abdel Rasul, bus conductor, poet, lover and madman. I wrote a song about crowds. My doctor doesn't want to believe I am the author.

When you're in the crowd,
Body joins with body,
Word runs into word.
And feelings go aflying.
You don't need your conjunctions;
You cut off your relations;
No one has a use for
The 'which' and 'what' and 'who'.
The crowd's a heavy parcel;
It's weighing on my heart.
I lug it around with me, shoulder-high
And it presses down on my flesh.
In it runs a-filtering
Right inside my bones;
All through the marrow it goes,
Dancing down my bones.

I've observed the crowd and their reaction to an empty seat. I've seen dozens of people rushing furiously, greedily, towards the empty seat. Yet some people are more competent than others in elbowing along among the masses of human flesh. They are the victorious ! They occupy a seat or half a seat and sit there, a vague smile on their faces — like some local hero, to be imitated and envied. But pregnant women, and nursing mothers, the polite ones who hesitate, they stay on their feet, hanging desperately to the horizontal rod, as if they were so many carcases of human butcher's-meat, dangling in close-packed rows, and dripping with bitterness. Ah ! My joints are aching ! (This is not in the song.)

In this place I live with those who weep, and those who laugh, and those who have determined to spend the rest of their lives standing on one foot, and those who have decided to remain with one hand for ever raised. I mix with the heroes and the great. Napoleon and El Sayed el Badawi and the manager of 'The Association of Rocket Transport Companies Prior to Invention of Rockets' (that is the complete title of his trust), and also those who claim omnipotence.

I have promised myself I shall get out, every day since I came here. Tomorrow I shall get out, or the day after tomorrow, or the day after that. Every year I say, "This is the last *moulid* of Sidi Ahmad el Nouti that I shall spend here!","This is the last *moulid* of the Prophet!", "The last Ramadan..", "The last Bairam.."

Every time I ask the doctor:

"When will you decide about my release?" he answers:

"It's you who must decide. Whenever you stop seeing your father's face and whenever you stop biting women's noses."

"Is the city still crowded?" I ask. He laughs.

"You see, you're still sick!"

The doctor comes to see me every day in his white coat and silver-rimmed glasses, accompanied by a new visitor. I know what he whispers to him. The same as he whispered to yesterday's visitor, and the visitor the day before yesterday and the visitor the day before that. He is saying that my joints are intact and that the disease is in my mental joints. Ha! Ha! Ha!

He points at me saying:

"This man is still waiting for his bus. For twenty years he has been standing and waiting. Waiting for his place in the crowd."

Translated by Nadia Farag; revised by Phillip Ward-Green.

DUNYA[1]

Fathi Ghanem

FATHI GHANEM was born in Cairo in 1924, and took a degree in law from the University there in 1944. After working as a civil servant, he began to write fiction — his first published work being *Aj-jaba* (*The Hill*), inspired by his official investigations into a crime concerning the disappearance of some antiquities in a village near Luxor. He entered journalism, and became editor of the weekly *Sabah el Khair*, in which many of the works of younger short story writers have made their first appearance. He is at present editor of the daily *Al Gumhuriyya*, as well as being at the head of a state publishing house.

Ghanem's best-known work is the tetralogy *Ar-rajulul-ladhī faqada ḍhillahu* (*The Man who lost his Shadow*) in which he adopts the technical device of retelling the narrative from the point of view of different characters. As with many English and European writers and critics, the device came to him from Lawrence Durrell's *Alexandria Quartet* (one might ask how the true master of the method, William Faulkner, apparently passed unnoticed by them for forty years). *The Man who Lost his Shadow* has been translated into English (by Desmond Stewart) and into French.

Ghanem's work has become increasingly experimental, and he is attempting impressionistic and surrealist techniques. *Dunya* is from the volume *Tajrubatu ḥubbin*(1958), to which a critical essay is devoted in Shukri Ayyad's *Tajārub fil adabi wan-naqd* (*Experiments in Literature and Criticism*) as given in the Arabic reading-list at the end of this volume. Ghanem's later collection *Suru ḥadīdin mudabbab* (*A Spiked Iron Fence*) reveals his recent tendencies more clearly.

---

(1) The word *dunya* basically means *lower*, and came to be used as an adjective qualifying *life*: *al hayat-ud-dunya* is life in this world, as distinct from life in the other world, the higher world, life after death. It has come to mean just *world* or more specifically what is both worldly and temporal. It is also used as a proper name, more commonly for a girl. As an exclamation it is equivalent to *Vanitas vanitatum*, an expression of wonder at the mutability of things in general. In Egyptian colloquial Arabic, it can mean *marriage* or rather *the married state*. All these meanings are evoked and

Cairo ! A big throbbing heart. Large avenues, fine streets, dark narrow alleys. And in them the strangely assorted crowd which we call 'the public' : business-men and beggars, elegant ladies and ragged girls selling lottery tickets, foreigners from London and New York and rustics from Sahragt and Shandawil; policemen and pickpockets, healthy children with glowing cheeks and pale ones with stony eyes; dustmen and lovers.

They are all wrapt up in their private affairs, their secrets deeply buried in their hearts: a hope fondly nursed, a job long sought, a private vista of human nature, an uneasy conscience painfully pricking; instincts working blindly and fastening upon their minds. People walk out in the streets, strangers all, each a world on his own, unfathomed by any other. They exchange glances, run into one another, meet, trade, fight. When a policeman meets a thief, he arrests him. When a boy meets a girl, he runs after her. When a debtor sees his creditor, he avoids him and slips quietly away. When a thin, ragged boy sees a cigarette stub he picks it up. When a healthy boy, with glowing cheeks, sees the sweet-seller, he fills his pockets with sweets. Strangers all, their hearts are filled with a medley of emotions — love envy, gratitude, hatred, anger, happiness, understanding, or..fear: the common stock of the human heart.

This is the story of some such strangers, who walked along the same street, late one evening, looked at one another, exchanged a few words, then went their ways, strangers still, though each was to leave an enduring mark upon the feelings of the others.

There is a bridge at the top of the road, in a residential district of fine rich houses. At the bottom of the road in an old poor district, there stands a second bridge. All was quiet that night at the top of the road, but for the footsteps of the lovers, Dunya and Badr, as they walked together towards the poorer district.

---

intertwined in this short story. The girl's name is Dunya and the boy is Badr, a proper name which means *full moon*. It stands for what is resplendent and unattainable. (Translator's note)

They could hear nothing but toads croaking and crickets chirping. From time to time, the sound suddenly grew louder in their ears and as suddenly vanished. A car would tear past at a terrible speed, scaring away the loafing street curs. Another would follow at a slow pace, the sound of pop music floating out of its wireless. The dogs would rush at it, sniffing inquisitively, and bark loudly after it.

Halfway between the two bridges, a policeman, stock-still, stared across at the few lighted houses on the other bank of the Nile. He dreamt sleepily of his home, which lies among those houses. He was startled out of his dream by a car tearing past. His body came to life, he swayed slightly upon his feet, then took a few steps and stopped at a crossing. He peered up the empty street with a hawk's sharp eyes, on the lookout for a thief or a murderer who might be lurking in the dark. He gave a loud hoarse cough, repeating it till an answering cough reached him from far off.[1] He went back on his tracks for a few paces, and soon sank back into his old reverie, staring steadily at the other bank, stock-still, dreaming of his home..

Three dustmen had started sweeping the road, beginning at the bridge in the poorer district. With their long broomsticks they cleared the litter off the road, and gathered it in piles: peanut shells, maize cobs, pieces of paper stained with the oil of *falafel* and *halawa* which people of the district bring along with them, when they escape from the stuffiness of their narrow rooms and low ceilings, their homes crowded with women and children and cluttered with useless old sticks of furniture. Every afternoon at dusk, there emerge troupes of children, girls in bright pink or blue, women walking heavily, carrying baskets and bundles full of food; they invade the river-bank and settle on the narrow strip of grass running along the riverside. The fat women sit down heaving with the effort of their walk but the girls saunter to and fro, glancing sideways at the students in pyjamas and *gallabeyyas*, who make a pretence of studying out of torn books as they eat peanuts and nibble water-melon seeds in a quick and greedy way, with eager move-

(1) This is a method of siqualling used by nightwatchmen and guards.

ments of the lips. The little boys play football, their voices — and their keenness — rising with the number of goals scored by either side. When it grows late, they all go home, there is nothing left but the empty road, and the litter which Abdel Sattar, Amin and Farag, the dustmen, have to sweep off the grass.

* * *

On the grass border at the other end, the lovers were walking arm in arm. The road was clean there, the grass was long and fresh; it had not been trodden on. Lights shone in the large windows on the other side of the road. The lovers could occasionally catch a glimpse of men and women moving gracefully in the well-lit rooms.

"What shall I do ?"

Dunya made no answer; her look wandered over the river, sunk in darkness, light from the street-lamps touching only the edges. Her anger was rising. She could not bear to hear the question a second time. *What shall I do*, he asks in the plaintive tones of a child. I haven't got any money, *what shall I do* ? I'm in trouble, *what can I do* ? I love you, *what can I do* ? His mother has spoilt him; she gives him everything he asks for. He has never been hungry, never had to earn his own living. His mother provides his board and lodging. He goes in and out of the house as if it were a hotel. She knows he will always go back to her. *He* has never faced the life of the poor and homeless. His bed is always got ready for him, a clean, warm bed. Will he ever have any sense of responsibility ? Does he think I am his mother ? that I should spoil him as she does. I wish I could, but I am tired, I need someone to look after me.. I love him. I have told him so. Life would mean nothing without him. I know he will be a fine doctor some day; I have seen him at the clinic with a beautiful smile on his face, his eyes gleaming with satisfaction, puffing cigarette smoke out of his lips with self-assurance, and chaffing that old man: "Now isn't she the most beautiful woman in the world ?" The old man peered at me with weak bloodshot eyes. "May God grant her long life for your sake, doctor, and bless your children !" Our eyes met over the old man's head. Badr looked anxiously at me. I knew he felt he was deceiving the man, knew that he was on the point of confessing we were not married. That is his forte, candour ! I could almost hear the question, *What shall I do* ? shall I tell him the truth ? But he did shut up. He thrust his hand into his pocket, looking for his cigarette case. The gleam of satisfaction died out of his eyes and he was frowning like a cross child. The old man wiped his eyes with cotton wool. "When do I come again, doctor ?" "Go to hell !" "But, Doctor !" His face was transfixed with astonishment. "I'll shut up the clinic ! I'm giving up this job !" When the old man left, I went up to him; he looked at me, furious. I was sorry for him.. I love him. I sensed his weakness, his inability to be his own master, to marry me and continue to work for a living..

Her thoughts were interrupted by his insistent voice, "Dunya, what is the matter with you ?"

She looked around her at the road, the tree-tops, the street-lamps, the Nile, the opulent houses ranged along the opposite side of the road. She started, realising where she was.

"Nothing," she answered in the thick voice of one waking from a deep sleep.

"You were thinking ?"

"Yes."

"Of what ?"

"Oh ! many things."

"What are they ?"

"Oh, trifles."

"How dangerous they can be, once they find a place in that beautiful head of yours !"

"Are you making fun of me ?"

"No, but I know your love of logic."

"And you ?"

"I.. I have nothing to do with logic — I am in love !"

"In love like a boy of seventeen.."

"And you, like a reasonable woman of forty.. Couldn't we meet half-way ?"

"You're crazy."

"Yes, crazy.. the whole world's not worth one glance of your eyes. Isn't that madness ?"

"If you loved me less.."

"If this river were dry.. if this road were shorter.. if half the stars went out.. if half the leaves died.."

"Stop it, Badr."

"Dunya !"

"You frighten me."

"Are you scared of my love ?"

"You're always soaring up into a dream world of your own.."

"Love makes miracles."

"I have no wings like yours."

"How ? You're an angel !"

"My feet are on the ground."

"What are you doing there ?"

"Watching you from far. I don't like that."

"What do you want then ?"

"To be with you.."

"In my dream world ?"

"No, on the ground, with people."

"What can we do on the ground ?"

* * *

On the ground, at a point half-way along the road, the policeman had rested the butt of his rifle, as he stood staring with a hawk's eyes, on the lookout for thieves and murderers. He coughed repeatedly till he heard an answering cough in the distance. A voice suddenly rose in the dark, a man's voice shouting, "*Ya Kareem* — O Bountiful God !" On the ground the work of the three dustmen had ended: they had swept the stretch that lies close to the poorer district. Farag had hurried on in front, crying out in the night, "*Ya Kareem* !" His eyes were glowering; his face, half-hidden under his thick beard, wore a fierce scowl, so that he looked a terrible sight in the dark.

It had all happened so suddenly. He had been working with the other two. He was quiet and seemed to be listening to their conversation.

They never tried to draw him into their talk. They had an uncomfortable sense that he was a crackpot, uncannily religious. Amin used to tell people that Farag "must be in contact — may God preserve us — with the underworld of the *djinn*." Suddenly the man burst forth; he had stopped working and looked up, craning his neck to the right and left, shouting "*Ya Kareem* !"

Abdel Sattar stopped breathlessly.

"Now ! Is he going to start that every evening ?"

"Leave him alone."

"But the overseer'll soon be round. This time he'll sack him."

"Let him ! He doesn't need to work."

"How will he live ?"

"They say he's married — God preserve us ! — to a she-*djinn* who's head over heels in love with him. Every night when he goes home, she's waiting for him, with his table spread with cooked chickens and pigeons and all sorts of delicacies we've never even heard of !"

"Would she provide for him if he got the sack ?"

"Why, of course : she'd send him breakfast, lunch and supper."

"Don't talk nonsense ! We've got to shield him."

"Why doesn't he sweep the ground as we do and feel the dust that fills our eyes and chokes us even before we die ! If he lives on the earth he has to work — or else let him give someone else the job of sweeping the earth, and let someone earn a living."

"Have a heart, man."

"I haven't any tender feelings any more. I sweep the dirt other people make. I can't work on my own, and I have no time for the crackbrained ways of Sheikh Farag and all this hocus-pocus. I am fed up. O God Almighty !"

* * *

"God Almighty ! Oh, I am fed up."

"Dunya, what is it ?"

"I keep thinking of our love."

"And what is it you think ?"

"It won't last !"

"It will never end — there !"

"Badr, we are like two tram rails, running alongside each other. We never meet."

"Haven't we met in love ?"

"Love ! love ! you've turned it into a mere word !"

"You're cruel ! Have a heart."

"I haven't any tender feelings any more. I have to think of the future of this love of ours. I have to put up with people's talk, their dirty tongues, the bad feelings of my family. I have no time for your crackbrained ways.. and your fancies.. We must leave each other, Badr."

"Dunya, it wouldn't be life for me."

"You're soaring way up in your fancy, because you can't stand what lies in store for you on the earth. You're afraid of work. You're running away from it. People's inquisitiveness is drawing me down in the mud. Their chatter is smearing me with dirt. I have to sweep up all the filth they sling at me, all on my own, and then forget all about it and walk with you by the Nile and listen to your talk of love and a dream world."

* * *

The overseer on his bicycle came suddenly upon them. He went straight to Sheikh Farag. You would have thought his bicycle was a ship piercing its way along with radar-equipment. In a few moments his voice rose high. The policeman came, holding his gun tightly. Abdel Sattar and Amin shouldered their broomsticks as though they were rifles, and came running. The overseer was shouting as he tried to take the broom out of Farag's hand.

"I swear you'll never touch it again. I've lost patience with you. You won't stop this silliness. Do you think it's your father's private firm you're working for ? Do you think we run a charity for your kind ?"

He turned sharply to Abdel Sattar and Amin.

"What are you gaping at ? Get on with your work and leave this man alone."

* * *

"I've lost patience with you — you won't stop this silliness."

"What can I do ?"

"Don't do anything ! I don't know what you can do."

She turned round suddenly and started to go back towards the bridge at the top of the road. He stood there dumbfounded; *what can I do* ? he thought. Someone said:

"Please, have you got the time ?"

Bad looked at his wrist and said crossly, "Sorry, I've no watch."

It was Amin. He went his way, and Abdel Sattar came following after. They went in the direction Dunya had taken. Badr wanted to go after them but some force within him held him back. He was suddenly very lonely, listening to the toads croaking, the crickets chirping and dogs barking. The quiet street seemed to come to life: trees were waving, lights danced and moths and mosquitoes circled madly in the patches of light.

A man in a khaki uniform walked past, pushing a bicycle with one hand and holding a broom with the other. A number of dogs were following, barking at him. A tall, bearded man came after him, sobbing and moaning. The policeman walked by his side, still on the lookout for thieves and murderers. Badr drew closer to them, trying to understand. He lit a cigarette and puffed out the smoke.

"The overseer has confiscated his broom and given him the sack," the policeman explained. He lowered his voice, and glanced at Farag to make sure he could not hear. "You see, it seems he's possessed. Cries out in the street and doesn't do a stroke of work," he whispered.

Badr looked anxiously backward in the direction taken by Dunya.

* * *

"*Dunya* ! What a world !" Abdel Sattar exclaimed, in a voice as sharply bitter as his feelings were. Dunya started, when she heard the dustman calling out her name.

"The poor man must be lonely ! Let's go back to him."

"It's too late. We'll call on him tomorrow."

"No ! I can't stop worrying ! Let's turn back."

"What's the good ? There's nothing that we can do. He lives in a world of his own."

"It'll comfort him if we stick to him. It's terrible to be alone at a time like this."

Abdel Sattar turned back to where they had left Sheikh Farag. Amin followed him.

Dunya stood at the bridge, hesitating. She thought the dustmen were speaking of Badr, that they were going back to him. She shook her head in wonder, she could not believe her ears : had these dustmen descended as messengers from the beyond ? Her heart went to him. She forgot his weakness and could only think of her love for him. She rushed back after the dustmen, looking for Badr, to look in his eyes and see them gleam with pleasure and hear him ask again, *What shall I do*?

Translated by Fatma Moussa; revised by Phillip Ward-Green.

THE FORTUNE TELLER

Alaa Deeb

ALAA DEEB is prominent among the younger generation of Egyptian writers. He is on the staff of the weekly *Sabah el Khair*, in which some of the most interesting new ventures in fiction have appeared: his own contribution should be reckoned among these. *Qāri' ul-kaf* (*The Palmist*) appeared in his collection *Al-Qahira*, (October 1964), and takes its title from that of a long short story which forms the bulk of the volume.

The war in which the aged fortune teller became a refugee, if we are to take it at all as a historical event, seems to be the First World War, in which Arab nationalists came to Egypt from Syria to escape Ottoman persecution.

There is no change on the island; the sun's rays break on the naked branches of an old tree, and the dark surface of the water reflects the glare. The big black ducks romp about the water as they chase the cheerful little brown ones. A hum of conversation rises from the tables, the words dropping from the mouths of men and women to hang.. suspended. Nobody believes anybody else; only the quacking of the big ducks, rising from the rushes, is real and true.

The Nubian waiters thread their way between the customers who seem, like statues of wood or stone, to be unaware of them.

When Anwar Effendi el Messiry chose a table to sit at, he picked a distant one, up against the wall, with a single chair and an old table-cloth; he was wearing his comfortable brown suit and a pair of light-weight shoes bought some years before. He had had a light lunch in his little Cairo restaurant and then boarded an empty trolley-bus to alight before the garden.

He called for tea and kept his newspaper folded, letting his eyes settle on the little green hillock adjacent to the island. There was the flutter of white goose wings before his eyes and the sound of an ancient song filled his ears, till his attention was caught by the red mouth of a girl smiling lazily, stickily.

The things they put before him were not really clean; a plate, a cup, a thick white china pot covered on the outside with tiny grains, like gooseflesh.

He poured his tea over a lump of sugar, and watched it change colour till it disappeared from sight; and all the time he was looking within himself.

When he had asked to take a holiday the day before, he had really needed it; a familiar sense of balance was being threatened; four days' holiday would change everything, would put paid to the fear and anxiety that were crawling up his chest to choke him. Four days to restore the ability to enjoy an ordinary day.. the sun through the office window, the eleven o'clock chatter of officials and colleagues, the emptiness of noon, the heat of the square in town; to give meaning again to the evening conversation of Madame at the pension. Yes, four stolen days would certainly restore everything, give life to things wilted and return him to his old rhythm.

The old palmist crossed on to the island through the arches of the green kiosk — a kindly face, soft, flaccid, with eyes of a faded honey colour half hidden within dark folds of flesh; a loose-fitting collar to his shirt, the knot of his bedraggled tie covered by a multi-coloured jersey, worn at the edges, his short ill-proportioned body wrapped around in a brown suit. It too was faded.

Anwar Effendi watched the palmist, but his eyes veered back to the tea cup as embarrassment rose within him. Patches of sunlight reached his table through the branches of the old tree.

The palmist did not make for him straightaway, but strayed about the island looking for customers. A man and his fat wife, their child between them, had ordered food, and called to him. The woman sat with her obese body squeezed into a chair, her hand in the palmist's while her husband chewed on the food in his mouth, his lips glistening as he looked around him, seeming (his wife had wanted this) unconcerned and bored. He wiped his lips on the napkin and gave the palmist some coins. The palmist moved on, displaying a card in his outstretched hand, as Anwar Effendi's eyes followed him.

Three o'clock..the waiter moves; a small child, laughing, goes in search of the lavatory.

Anwar dropped his eyes to the teacup, turned, looked about him as the palmist bore down on him, penetrating his very being as he approached, the hand showing its card as it invaded the broken sunlight. He raised his eyes to the face above him and was astonished.. and relieved. It was as if he had found himself, as if the oppressiveness of the man's coming had withered, and his presence become a light, desirable thing, comforting his loneliness.

Anwar Effendi asked him with a smile: "Are you..married ?"

"No..". The man remained standing.

"Sit down."

The palmist sat down next to Anwar, an expression of gentle gratitude on his face as he took the hand extended to him and ran his sensitive fingers over the soft pink skin of the palm, sprinkled powder on it and traced over the lines with his fingers.

The sensation affected Anwar Effendi's mind strangely, and the movements of the fingers on his palm stirred obscure feelings in him, warm currents, strange and new to this old, cold, body. The palmist before him smiled, and then there was his voice, a deep broad voice coming through the old, loose-skinned neck to resonate gently in the surrounding air:

"You, who are you ?..what brought you here ?" and shaking his head in amazement, he spoke again:

"The road is long.. and all else concerning you, and on into the future..all will issue from God..We are only the balm to soothe man's soul and allay his fears. I read, and all is already written; knowledge rests with God.. and within you; may God guide us all..let us put our trust in Him, the Merciful Lord of mercy. Now listen, sir !.."

Anwar felt that his life was a pile of red bricks and that the man's words were strange, tender hands, rearranging the bricks. As though this was the effect he anticipated, the man drew his chair closer to

Anwar Effendi's.

Anwar felt able now to skim off the sorrow that floated on the surface of his life, to roll it into a ball in his hands as though it were a scum of cold ghee and to hurl it away, and so free himself for the little measure of joy that he felt sprouting within hlm.

As for the palmist, he was engrossed in observing the knotted, seemingly moving tracery in the palm before him. He wanted, this once, to read everything, to see, to test his ability and his eyes to the full. He wished the hand before him to turn into something transparent which he could pierce with his eyes. For he felt himself enmeshed in strange things from which he wanted to extricate himself; the words he had mouthed a thousand times, the daydreams he had given expression to at every table, had all become hateful to him, things to which he must never return, things to be got rid of, cast away. He wanted now to see, and to speak, to be able to look back to this one reading, this palm and the security he felt beside this man, when he was old and his eyes had dimmed.

Their nearness to one another beside the small table had become a total coalescence. In the fading afternoon light on the Tea Island, there was a shared effort driving them to meet and discover things held in common, towards a closeness in search of the warmth their cold bones so needed.

Together they recalled the 'half-deserted streets", and the "restless nights", and the crowded noisy places in which they had known loneliness. They remembered their patient despair when understanding failed.. and the empty abandoned village at noon-time, and the Nile at night when they were young.

The palmist remembered.. the sea, and the boat, and the clamour of the refugees driven by the war to escape to Cairo, with himself among them, a young man, bare-breasted, facing the cold blowing in from the sea, warmed only by his dreams as he observed the moon and felt ardent and alive.

He remembered the streets of Alexandria, the companions he had left behind on the shore. He had not wanted to look back, but felt sorry to leave them. His life would have been different had he looked back, but that is just what he did not do. He committed his crime, did violence to his better feelings, betrayed his friends and learnt the taste of treachery. . His words became imbued with its poison, it ran through his body, and he betrayed again and again. . betrayed the memory of Syria, and the image of the Syrian hillside village which struggled every night to fill his vision; he buried it alive, determined that the memory should fade; he betrayed even his very own words till they turned into the rotted carrion of dreams.

Anwar Effendi's mouth filled with the taste of loneliness as he recalled his own bitter helplessness. . recalled the dark, twisting stairs down which he had rushed when his engagement was broken, driving before him with a deliberate violence the image of the girl he was to have married, young, fairskinned, pale. He had told himself that the image would leave him at the street door; that he would not emerge into the street until he had got rid of it, he paused on the threshold — the street had been dark, lit by a single lamp at one end, and the cool breeze had struck his hot blood-congested face and the image had vanished. He could only remember today that her skin had been very white, and that she used to wear soft materials which would slide over her tender body.

Age brushed over the hairs of his legs, climbed up his body to chill it and fill it with loneliness. Oppression grew, and the bare room in the pension, overlooking the large square, became life itself. Nor was there any resistance to this, only surrender — albeit the surrender of a floating body, its ideal equilibrium upset by the slightest sudden movement.

Life then was that Anwar Effendi should remain Anwar Effendi, neither less nor more, restricted inextensibly by the very real limits set by the cut of his suit. . nor did he wish its extension into any other state of being, content to remain an old official in search of the sun on a cold day. All is settled and clear and will be consummated; only the water beneath us moves to disturb the surrender we so much desire.

"There is a soul, of your own kin, hovering over you, enquiring after you," and as he spoke the palmist remembered the lined old face of his mother; recalled the cool eyes and the sad cxpression; she knew he was about to leave them; she and the blind old man lying there inside the house; her hard-eyed look said so, as he left her that last night, though he had not announced his departure.

Her small face enveloped in a white headveil as she stood in the doorway of the house, against the darkness within, was to remain in his mind's eye forever. And Anwar Effendi remembered his lonely corner against the rails of the tiny balcony overlooking the square and wondered: "Shall I remain forever holding that stance? Will they find me there one day, a dead man looking out of a window?"

A tear or two trembled hesitantly in his eyes.

The palmist smiled as he finished his task and Anwar Effendi took money from his pocket..a ten-piastre piece shone in the light.

The fortune teller moved on. In the garden there was a boy with a large, close-cropped head and big feet, munching on a round[1] sandwich as he trod the grass.

Translated by Medhat Shaheen; revised by Peter Callaghan.

(1) Cheaper sandwiches are commonly made of small flat circular loaves.

THE FUTILITY OF IT ALL

Farouk Khorshid

FAROUK KHORSHID (b. Cairo 1914) lived in the provinces as a child, and graduated in Arabic from Cairo University in 1950. He has been a teacher and a broadcaster, and is at present a Director of Programmes in the UAR Broadcasing Service. His short stories have shown an increasingly experimental manner, as can be seen by comparing the present story, the title-story of his recent volume *Al-Kullu bāṭil* (*All is Vanity*) with earlier stories such as those in the anthology *Qiṣas min Miṣr* (*Short Stories from Egypt*) (1958). Khorshid has written studies of earlier Arabic fiction (e.g. *Ar-riwāyatil-'arabiyya — The Arabic Novel*), and has given particular attention to *sīrah* or popular prose epic in his two books *Fannu kitābati-s-suirati-sh-sha'biyya* (*The Art of writing in the popular prose-epic*) and *Aḍwa' 'ala-s-sirati-sh-sha'biyya* (*New light upon the popular prose-epic*). He has himself written a modern version of the popular traditional tale of Sayf ibn dhi Yazan, and other works deriving their inspiration from these traditional sources.

He shuddered again, supporting himself with his hand against the wall, as he stood in the corner. "O God !" he whispered. He found it difficult to open his lips; they twisted when he tried to. His left hand came up slowly to his eyes to wipe away a tear, which was too small for me to see at that distance. But I could see his right hand ! it hung there against his thigh, motionless. He trembled once again and staggered. His left foot moved forward, while his hand was still held there against the wall, helping him to move his right foot, slowly and with difficulty. My eyes were riveted to his foot as it took a step and then paused, in a desperate effort. He lowered his left hand to pick up the thin walking-stick. He tottered again, and with a lurch of the waist, his chest moved ahead, followed and obeyed by the rest of his body. He was walking forward.

"Shoeshine, sir ?"

"No."

"Lovely shoeshine ?"

"No !"

He tapped his brush against his box of equipment.

"I'll really make'em dazzle for you."

I went back to following the movements of the other man: his hand had become exhausted by its efforts, and had paused, so that he stood trembling in front of a table, at which a man sat fast asleep. He gripped the back of the sleeper's chair and stood there, shaking.

"Let's sit here, Ahmed. It's too noisy over there."

The newcomers were a long procession of people. In the forefront was a loud suit above which appeared a face with the features of a film-star — you know the sort of moustache sported by the hero in Hollywood films ? Behind him came a man with a number of loaves clutched together in his hands. Third in the group came a pot-belly with a dish in hand.

I should have liked to laugh. But my friend had not turned up, and my heartbeat had a melancholy rhythm, for last night I had spent a lonely winter's night, without any means of warming myself.

The fourth companion was a puny little man carrying a lot of large packets; the smell of grilled meat came to my nostrils.

"Oh, no, not here. It's better over there."

The procession doubled back. The white dog stared at them, its ears twitching, but as for its tail — I could not see one. Perhaps it had had a tail once, but now — I couldn't imagine what had happened to it.

The sleeper woke up and put his hand into his pocket to draw something out. Money, perhaps. *Yes, it was money, and he put it in the waiting left hand, the hand that moved; its owner let go of his walking stick, and dithered as he put the money away in the top outside pocket of his green jacket (that's right, it was green — a green with vertical stripes). Then he trembled, picked up his walking stick again, trembled once more, and moved his left leg.*

"Cigarettes !"

A nasal, sinuous cry, in an odd accent. It came from a one-eyed man who was standing in front of me, the shout emerging from his solar plexus, like a ventriloquist's words.

"Cigarettes !"

I turned back to watching the left foot as it moved. The man doddered, and leaned his hand on a wall, and his right foot started to come to life again; it was a long slow journey, as he made his way forward, shaking.

"What's that ? Green tea.. and a *hemmi* hookah..right you are."

Kamal the waiter turned round and cried out:

"One green over here. One hookah over there, a *hemmi* hookah."

A hectic cry burst over us all:

"Scarves and handkerchiefs. A nice belt. Razor blades."

The weight-lifter went past me. On his head he was carrying a box which had its lid and one of its sides open, piled high with his wares. On his shoulder, he carried some lengths of suit-material, over his arm some scarves, in one hand some belts; in the other a large bundle — and from his mouth came the incessant call:

"Belts. Razor-blades. Razor-blades."

He slowed down to look around, and his eyes fell on the man in the green jacket. He stared at him. *He had stopped by the second of the tables, where no one was sitting. He stood there for some time. I couldn't tell what he was doing. He trembled and moved his left foot forward.* The full-throated voice rose:

"Copies of the *Koran*. Works of literature. Books on science".

This was Sheikh Ibrahim, short, stocky, blind, who knew every inch of the café and every one of the regulars.

"A *Koran* complete with commentary. I've *The Arabian Nights* with illustrations ah good-morning sir how are you it's the Sheikh El Ghawali's commentary very well what about *The Marvels of the Twentieth Century.*"

"Cigarettes ! Cigarettes ! Cigrets ! Cigareets !"

Walking past with one hand in his pocket and the oblong dispay case, with its boxes of cigarettes, over his shoulder, intoning his call and feeling pleasure at the sound of his own voice, surveying the crowd with his single eye.

The man with the tremble was now making his way past the large cubicle with the sofa and the coloured leather pouffes, the one used by tourists and artists. There was no one in it excepting for a group of youngsters, chatting, and puffing at a hookah (that's right, just one hookah between all of them). *He stood in front of them, shaking. They paid no attention to him. He leaned his hand on his cane, letting it take all the weight of his body for a few moments. Then he shook, and his chest moved forward and the rest of his body followed obediently. He reached the sofa, and slowly lowered himself down on to it. He stretched out his foot, but his right hand was still asleep as it had been for a long time. His lips moved in a murmur which was lost in the press of noises.* Then :

"White semolina bread."

A little basket, hung left and right with rings of semolina rusks. But I wasn't hungry.

"Why not make sure ? It's most important to know the grammar of literary Arabic."

I glanced to my right, at the trio that sat there: a tarboush and a cap and a pedant: a blue suit and a well-pressed tarboush, holding a newspaper in his hand, his words winding round and round his mouth in a long coil before they were given forth to the people.

"For example, if you say *Daraba Ali Zayd*[1], which of the two did the drubbing and which of them got the beating ? Accidence is important. Exceedingly important."

I didn't catch the reply. I was too busy scrutinizing his features, trying to work out if I could deduce from them that the world was round, and that matter was formed of *molecules* — with a short *o*, and the stress on the first syllable.

"Grammar is not difficult, and it does not cost anything. All you have to do is to consult a reference work, on your own : you need no teacher, for you will not be confronted by any untowardly recondite

(1) This phrase is often used as a paradigm in teaching grammar. With vocalization omitted, the case endings are uncertain, so that it can either mean *Ali beat Zayd* or *Zayd beat Ali.*

matters. Let us take an example. You are familiar with the problem of how to use the word *hatta*: when to use it as a preposition governing a genitive noun, and having the meaning *until* and when to use it as a particle which requires an accusative after it, and signifies *even*."

"Step this way, Mohamed Bey; yes, come on here, and we'll smoke a splendid hookah, I promise you."

The man shook as he moved towards the next cubicle. One of the young men took out a piastre — no, a five-piastre piece. I'm wrong, it was a piastre after all. *He stood the cane against the wall, and he trembled. Then he stretched out his left hand — (always his left) and took the piastre (or was it a five-piastre piece ? I'm not sure).*

"To be comprehended, one must construct one's propositions unambiguously. Let us take an example. *Feed the cold and starve the fever*: have we here a disjunctive conjunction of corellation or a copulative conjunction of cause ?"

In a flash, I remembered how ill I had been after that party Ahmed Zaki had given in his garden. But why remember that ? I don't know. We were all there and we had a great deal to eat, but I hadn't got a cold and didn't get a fever afterwards, though I was very sick because of the drinks I had. As for Abdel Rahman, the drinks made his eyes pop out of his head, while Salah couldn't walk straight, and staggered all over the place. That evening I forgot all about the girl that I loved but didn't like (that's right: that's what I mean), with her dark complexion and her stray wisp of hair. The black cat jumped up on to the leather sofa, curled up, laid its head down with complete self-assurance and went to sleep. Black, black as night..no, why put it that way ? Nada sketched it once; he sat on one of those striped divans, with an idiotic expression on his face, and one of the boys held the cat for him — I can't remember his name — while Nada drew it, with his face lit up, and his eyes shining, and his nose shining too, that long nose. His nose is — well, odd. I hadn't realized it before, but then I haven't seen him for a long time, not since he went to Mansoura. God, I must have written a hundred letters to the Mansoura Local Educational Authority yesterday. It certainly gave me cramp in my right hand.

"Help me with a prayer for the beloved Prophet, with a prayer for his family. A prayer for the Prophet."

Said in the regulation whine, monotonously, with her black cloak wound all over her body, excepting for her face, her pale face which revealed nothing, nothing at all: it said nothing to you, not a word. Her mouth alone repeated insistently:

"Will you help me, sir ?"

One hand held out peanuts, the other carried a laden basket. I didn't answer. I don't know why: I was, quite simply, tongue-tied. She put the stuff that was in her hand down on the table in front of me. I didn't answer. *I was looking at the man; again he was shaking as he moved forward — he floundered, so that he almost fell. He let himself down gently on to the ground, trembling. Then he stood up again, straightened himself, stretched out the hand with the walking stick in it, and dragged along his lifeless right foot — I couldn't see it because it was hidden under his* gallabeyya, *a very white* gallabeyya *— perhaps it had been washed that day — that's right, it probably had.*

I raised my eyes. In front of me, hanging on the wall, was the crocodile, with its mouth wide open, although it had no intention of swallowing anyone up. Its jaws were open in an odd way, as though it were moaning, or perhaps yawning — how could I tell when I couldn't see its expression properly ? Its feet were fixed to the wall, and its bright skin was powdered over with a layer of dust. Opposite it there hung a fish. Or perhaps a shark — I don't know, because I have never seen a shark — broad in the middle and narrow at either end. Perhaps it was a flying fish ? Anyway, there it was, hanging up in mid-air. And it too was holding its mouth open — but no, that isn't the way a fish normally opens its mouth. Where's the tiger ? That's tight, that's what I asked: where's the tiger ?

"Alms for the love of God."

I looked up at him. A black beard muffled in a strip of dark cloth; strength and feverishness in his eyes. I gave him a second look.

"Alms for the love of God."

He had something strapped to his back — a bundle tied round

with a length of flimsy red string: what did he keep in the bundle ? was it something very precious and personal ? or perhaps only some cotton ? Perhaps it contained documents ?

"Alms for the love of God, sir."

There was a tigerish glare in his eyes: I don't think he really believed that any alms he was given would be destined for God. I shook my head; he smiled mockingly, and bent down to the ground just under my feet to pick up the stubs of the cigarettes I had smoked. Raising his head, he dusted the stubs against his overcoat — a worn-out coat, but it had been of good quality once, and he was carrying a stick. Oh, there was the tiger, on top of the cupboard, yellow, with dark stripes, a huge, long body — but something had torn a gash in its hide, behind its left back paw, and you could see the straw stuffing peeping out.

The actor walked in, coming nonchalantly down the single step at the doorway with his voice thundering out in a bellow of which I couldn't make out a single word. He was followed by a crowd, most of whom I knew — they were actors too. The place was filled with their uproar: everyone stared at them. *The man trembled as he drew nearer to the cubicle where the cat lay asleep on the leather sofa. There was no one sitting there: he supported himself by placing a hand on the table. He shook, and stepped backward, almost fell, then leant his whole body against the wall, and whispered, "Oh, God !" — a low whisper, far away from people's glances. He was paying no attention to anyone. His left hand rose to wipe away a tear. I felt my heart sink and my breath come faster, for the man was slipping — his stick was leaning over, and his body with it. He trembled. But then, very gradually, he righted himself.*

"The car broke down on our way here and, just imagine it, along came this policeman and actually asked —"

The actor was giving a public address — you couldn't call that a conversation — they all laughed, clustered around him in a circle. That young man there — I'd seen him in a film — played a thief in it did it very well. And the one over there: that was Ghaith — I recognized him — they say he's a man of real culture.

"A pocket *Koran. The Arabian Nights* with illustrations."

Sheikh Ibrahim felt his way past, stretching his arm out over the backs of the seated customers.

"Cigarettes, cigareets."

The man's single eye peered in among the customers.

"One *hemmi* hookah. One black tea. One green tea just right!" A pause for breath, and then he shrieked, "And let's have only thevery best — get a move on now."

Then he dashed away out of my sight. To the far right — that was a panther.. but it was worn out, dusty and torn. On its back was a little monkey. Inshirah announced this morning that a girl who worked with her was going to the Sudan and would bring her back a monkey. Pretty smile, she had. Pretty girl altogether. There was something between her and Zaki at one time..

"Shoeshine, sir ?"

I shook my head. He knocked on his box and walked on, looking down at the feet of the clientèle. The man in the green jacket drew near the group at the table next to me.

He trembled, and the literary gentleman put his hand into his pocket and gave him something. He shook and dithered, and moved on towards me. I studied him more closely. Dull eyes without a glimmer in them, taking refuge behind loose-hanging eyelids. A lower lip drooping down over his chin, a lifeless face, and his right hand clinging close to his thigh. He put his left foot forward, and started to tremble. There was pain written all over him. He muttered to himself, but I couldn't catch what he said: it might have been a prayer — it might have been an outburst of bitterness — it might have been a stifled cry of pain — or else again.. I could feel the tears welling up in my eyes. What had possessed this man to leave his home today ? He should be lying down, having a complete rest. He should get away from this place. Every step he took was at a price. There he was in front of me, trembling, with my heart beating violently, while I was wondering what I could give him. He moved slowly away, dragging himself along, leaning his weight on objects here and there. Once he let himself down slowly and sat on the ground; then he stood up straight again even more slowly.

(1) Red tea in the original, tea made by boiling the tea-leaves in the kettle.

He fumbled at a seat in an isolated corner, and sat down, whispering:

"Oh, my God !"

Then he lifted his hand to wipe something off his eyelid. It was his left hand — I'm sure, yes, his left.

The man who sold razor blades approached him. He had been standing in the middle of the café, following his movements as I had, and had just been about to move on. In fact, he had just opened his mouth to cry his wares. *The man tried to stand up; he almost did so, but he fell back on the seat helplessly. He decided to lay his walking stick on the ground, and rose in his seat to do this, but fell back once more, and sat there with his arm stretched forward. The weight-lifter rushed up to him, and put out a hand to help him up. The man got up, stood still for some moments, trembled, and shuffled on. I drew a hand up to my moist eyes. — Enough — Some people might call our age an age without any miseries — but this man was the tail-end of a long story which may have contained some happiness, a family, love, a child — and then, this end.* No, Sir, no one will believe you; they will call you an unsuccessful romantic. Abdel Ghaffar says this is the age of facts, with no place for pain in it. The actors laughed. And a voice rose:

"A leather belt ? Razor-blades. Razor-blades."

The dwarf went by: "White semolina bread."

"A *Koran* with commentary. *The Arabian Nights* with illustrations."

"For the sake of our dear Prophet."

"Shoeshine, sir ?"

"One *hemmi* hookah. And let's have only the very best !"

Translated by Mahmoud Manzalaoui; revised by Lewis Hall.

VOSTOK REACHES THE MOON

Magid Tobia

MAGID TOBIA was born in 1938, and took a Teachers' Training Diploma in 1960.He is a teacher of mathematics, and is studying scenario writing in the Cairo Film Institute. He has had one collection of stories published: it takes its title from the present story and appeared in 1967 with a preface by Dr. Saheir el Kalamawi. The first publication of this story, however, was in *Al Magalla* in May 1965. Other stories of Tobia's have appeared in dailies and weeklies. In 1964 Tobia won the award of the Short Story Club, as well as taking first prize for his story *Al-makamir* (*The Dung Heaps*) in a film scenario competition organized by the Cinema Institute.

Vostok was, of course, the name of one of the experimental Russian space ships.

"To the moon, Vostok !" The driver stood there reading it. It must have been getting on for the hundredth time in the last two days. He smiled to congratulate himself. He had got *his* slogan on the back of the car.[1] The owner had wanted to put something quite different:

O Lord Who granteth secret grace.

Save us from all we fear.

But he hadn't budged and the owner had to agree. The owner's prayer would go on the door : the driver's slogan could use the whole of the back of the car. And here was his slogan ! The words and, above, a painting. A little rocket nosing its way to the moon whose happy smiling human face beamed out from its fringe of radiant flowers..

The policeman shouted. Two snakes came out of his mouth. Their fangs sank into the driver's eardrums.

"Get a move on there ! Can't you see you're holding up the traffic."

(1) Egyptian lorry and taxi drivers often have prayers and slogans painted on their vehicles in this way.

The driver looked up. His smile disappeared. He tested the pressure of the spare tyre fixed to the back. Reaching to open the door he saw the luggage piled about on the roof rack and grumbled to the porter inside:

"Hey. You awake there or asleep ?"

There was no reply. That answered his question.

"God save us," the driver muttered as he switched on the ignition. But when the car had picked up some speed and the engine was roaring away the driver began to feel like a lonely child running down a dark empty road. And he found himself whispering the owner's prayer :

O Lord who granteth secret grace
Save us from all we fear.

And his voice got louder and gradually louder till the words tumbled out. And the car accelerated till the road shook. And the clatter was so intense that instead of dying as it rose in the air it hardened into the shape of a bottle out of which the monster sprang with hammer and dagger and a malevolent grin. To float slowly and surely down till he was slipping through the broken side-window and sitting on the seat beside him.

"O Lord who granteth secret grace. . O my God !" the driver shouted. "Here he is again to torment me. It's not enough for him to make his home in front of my house. Oh, no! He has to follow me. Every time I go out in this car he has to follow me." Turning to the monster the driver gestured to his ear drums. "Here you are," he said. "Take them. Goon. Beat on them to your heart's content!" But this wasn't enough for the monster. He gestured with the dagger. Like someone offering himself as a sacrifice to propitiate a terrible god, the driver dug his fingers in his head and pulled out some fibres. He held them out to him: the monster was delighted. He bit and tore and sucked.

The driver looked ahead and spat. The pain was tremendous. If only he had brought some cotton he could have stuffed his ears. He could have hidden his ear-holes from this monster. But no. The doctors wouldn't allow him to. Then he had an idea. He lit a cigarette and first puffed a cloud angrily in the monster's face and then jabbed with the glowing tip. But this didn't worry the monster. He just went on beating upon the driver's eardrums and tearing at the fibres while the high sun blazed down on the speeding car. And now the cigarette had burnt down and was scorching his fingers. He hurled it away and cursed everyone and everything. Then there was only the amulet hanging there. He could smile and be at ease. He whispered gratefully, "Your forgiveness, O Lord. Your will be done."

* * *

The driver looked in wonder. So many strange creatures everywhere. They had never looked like this before. The duck fluttering in the roadside canal to escape the August heat. The cows ceaselessly grazing. The buffalo roped to the water wheel. The dogs ran alongside barking, to back away and loll out their tongues in frustration. The sheep, its head bent down with anxiety like a family man wondering how to buy those clothes for his children. And people. So many human beings, doing different things. One busy with his waterwheel. Another just eating and eating. Others who followed him with curses because of the smoke from his exhaust. The sad man who sat and ruminated, his finger tracing something in the dust. The naked ones who had stripped off their clothes to swim in the canal. The driver could not express the thoughts the scene evoked: all he could say was "What a world !" All he could do was to look ahead and spit.

He looked sideways again. The monster was still there, skulking. Playing his pitiless game. "Will he never get tired of it ?" the driver wondered. There was a *fellah*[2] walking along in front, dragging a cow, making the best he could of the shade of the double row of roadside trees, as some sort of shelter from the blazing sun, for himself and his beast, in the journey they both had to make. The driver turned his eyes away: when he looked ahead, again, the car was rushing headlong

(1) A favourite custom of taxi drivers is to hang an amulet from the arm of the driving mirror.

(2) Countryman.

at the cow. It seemed bent on killing it. In a panic the driver stepped on the brake. The *fellah* shouted and cursed. At the height of his terror, the driver felt the words pelting down upon him. He turned to reproach the monster, but he was not there. He had vanished, leaving no trace except the driver's eardrums. The man swore. "The coward. He's gone. Gone back into his bottle. Now that he's helped himself to the fibres of my head —." There was the owner of the cow. The driver apologized. "Sorry," he said, "the steering wheel got out of control." The sudden braking and the loud curses of the *fellah* had awakened the porter. He got out of the car and did his best to soothe the *fellah* down, patting his cow on its back, until eventually the man and his beast did go on their way.

As soon as the car was seen to, it moved off. The porter sat next to the driver this time, yelling to make himself heard above the roar of the engine.

"Can't you hear the sound of this engine ?" he asked. "It's worse than a tractor !"

The veins of the driver's neck swelled out.

"It was already a wreck when the boss put me in charge. Do you think I'm responsible ? You think it's my fault ?"

He turned to the porter but the monster was back sitting between them. How was it the porter could not see him ? He felt very depressed. To hide this, he began to talk to himself but the porter thought he was talking to him. The driver was furious that the monster should follow him wherever he was, in his car or at home. The monster had come and settled across the way from his home in the railway yard where there was always such a constant din of hammers or trains that he and his wife and children had to raise their voices when they spoke even though they were all in one room. It was as if they were separated by hundreds of yards. But the monster was not satisfied. He even passed into the bodies of the children so that they spoke so loudly, even if there was total quiet, that he was forced, in spite of the heat, to cover his head with the pillow, not only to hide his ear-drums from this ever-persistent monster but also to get to sleep.

How earnestly the driver prayed now ! “O Lord. You have made man out of clay..er..well then.. er.. why then did you have to go and create monsters as well ?”

And he asked the porter, “Is it too much to ask ? Just a quiet home. Anywhere. Even in the moon.”

The porter thought it was a great joke. He just laughed and said, “Tell me then. If you were given a chance to get to the moon, would you take it up ?”

“Why shouldn't I ?”

“There are monsters there.”

The driver shouted in protest:

“Who told you all that nonsense ?”

“I saw it. In an American film. There was this monster. It came down to the earth. And destroyed it.”

“Whoever made that film must have been mad. Raving mad.”

And the driver said to himself, “Even if there were a monster on the moon I'd rather face him than this one here who's after me everywhere.” Still, talking to the porter was relieving him. But there was a man on the road beckoning him to stop and so he slowed down and asked the porter to get back to the back seat. He could do with the money. Even the price of a packet of cigarettes would be welcome. The cost of living was frighteningly high. It was only the low rent that had made him agree to live in that noisy flat of his across from the railway yard where the monster lived.

The car went past the man a little. So the man came running and saw the slogan on the back of the car. “What's all this about Vostok ?” he asked smiling. The veins in the driver's neck began to swell again. Vostok was the rocket which was going to reach the moon. The moon that he always saw smiling down to him from the sky. The moon that was always quiet, was always calm.

Seeing the hitchhiker so surprised, however, the driver explained hat he was a constant reader of the daily newspapers, and began to alk about politics, about Russia and America, about mankind and its ockets, its greed and its poverty. Then he remembered the present problem. For a while he was silent and then looking at the monster he nodded, reasserting a decision.

"Yes sir, yes. To me it does seem that everything is so quiet on the moon.. No noise, no bustle.. None of the din that we have down here."

The traveller laughed; and when they reached Tanta, he got off, and wished the driver the quiet life that he longed for.

* * *

Tanta was soon left behind as the car raced along, making the road vibrate with its reckless speed, and disturbing the birds in the trees with its thundering din. The cloud of stirred-up dust and the trail of thick black smoke quite hid the picture of the moon's round smiling human face. The smoke trail began to fan out, shaking, stirring, circling, ever-moving, and ever-drawing weird fantastical shapes. They looked like numbers written in the air..five..four..three..two..one..and then *zero.* This was when the accident took place and the smiling face of the moon, fringed by its flowers, overturned.

* * *

When the driver regained consciousness and opened his eyes, there he was with his head bandaged, and beside him two men and a woman, all in white. He smiled happily at the calm, quiet, atmosphere about him. The monster had disappeared. He looked up at the two men and it seemed to him they were talking.

"He's had what I thought he was in for, I'm afraid—" one doctor was saying to the other.

But although the driver could see the two doctors clearly, and distinctly see their lips moving, he could not hear one word. He wondered at the complete silence, the serenity around him.

Puzzled, bewildered that the monster was not there in front of him he asked himself, "Has Vostok got to the moon ?"

Translated by Mohamed Kaddal; revised by Keith Jones.

THE SNEAK-THIEF

Dia el Sharkawy

DIA EL SHARKAWY was born in 1938, took a diploma in Insurance in 1959, and works in a fertilizer firm. His stories have appeared in Egyptian and Lebanese magazines, and one collection in book form is to be published shortly under the title *Riḥla fi qiṭāri kulli yawm* (*A Journey in the Railway Train of Everyday*). The present story appeared under the title *At-tasallul* (*Infiltration*), in the special avant-garde number of *Al Qissa*, in June 1965.

I am not really as complicated as people seem to think. They are shocked at my restlessness, at my apparent instability, which they believe to be the reflection of a complex esoteric nature. But it's not that at all. Neither do those cravings of mine permeate my existence; my spiritual existence, that is. It's simply that I've found out very early in my life that nothing in the world is worth my care. That most things are trivial; depressingly so, in fact. Therefore, I look on things detachedly, indifferently, through vacuous eyes, like two empty pools, drained of all interest, of all hope. I remember my father, one day towards the end of his life, gave me a long searching look, and then shut his eyes in distaste, so I looked away at shapes that were floating in the sky which I didn't trouble to make out. "Listen,my boy, "he said, "you will destroy yourself very soon." He then paused, waiting for me to answer, so I said, "Yes." The lines on his face deepened, and he looked at me wonderingly. "You are a frightful individual," he said at last, and paused again, probably expecting me to say something, but I didn't bother to, this time, so he continued, "That's why you will destroy yourself.. you must.." Somewhere outside, people were running and shouting. "I'll see what it is," said my father, giving a little cry; but he shut his eyes and continued, "..You are destroying yourself.. you've got to believe in something.." Then he spat in disgust, "..a man with no convictions.. no convictions.. you will destroy yourself." And only then did he turn away.

I don't know how the clanging got to fill my head, the clanging of the train wheels. Someone was shaking me gently, and I looked up and saw her.

"Are you not feeling well ?" she asked. There was a man selling fizzy drinks in the corridor, shouting out his wares, and a child was stamping its feet on the floor.

"Here's your paper," she said, "you didn't realize you'd dropped it." She was sitting next to me, smiling, and she was quite young; she reminded me of an immature pearl. Usually when I see a statue with a Roman nose I feel tempted to squeeze it with my hand. She had a round face, like my mother's: that's why I stared at her. Then I noticed the pale yellow down on her upper lip, and I felt a sudden repulsion. It was very pale and light, but it repelled me just the same. I stretched out my forefinger like a spear; I wanted to poke it in her side; she irritated me. She shook me again, and pointed at a man standing beside me: "Speak up."

"Tickets," said the man. I gave him mine and he punched it much as though he were playing a stupid game, just punching tickets. That's his profession. It made me laugh. He looked dull and pathetic; of medium height, with an ordinary face, and a plain unprovoking nose like a potato; and his teeth were clouded with yellow. Had he looked like Hans Christian Andersen, for instance, lean and tall, with lanky extremities, he might have amused my young companion, but he was nothing like that.

"Here's your ticket," he said.

Then she began:

"It's the second year of war in Korea, you know.. funny, the way things are going, isn't it ? How many casualties until now, do you think ? A million, nearly a million.. no less than that.. Why doesn't the world do something to stop this butchery ? It's barbarous. Do you consent that this butchery should continue any longer ?" Here she paused, stubbornly waiting for me to answer. I nodded.

"Good God ! You approve of this butchery ?" she cried. All I did was nod my head, you chattering magpie. I'd rather you were a funny old hag.

"Listen to me," she went on, "Don't you know that it may lead to a third world war ? Answer me," she cried irritably. I answered.

"Very likely."

"Then why doesn't the world do something about it ?"

"Stop that," I interrupted, "this conversation is quite unsuitable."

"Unsuitable ?"

"Why don't you talk about fashions ? That would be more appropriate."

"And what do you know about fashions for me to talk to you about them ?"

Then, after a pause, she cried, "Answer me."

"..more in keeping."

"Do you know about clothes ?"

"That's right..talk about clothes."

"What do you do ?" she asked impatiently, "are you a woman's tailor ?"

"No, and I don't know about fashions."

"Then how will you know what I'm talking about ?" .. I don't care what you're talking about, silly girl, I'm more interested in your little white teeth.

"Where are you getting off ?" she asked after a while.

"Are you a student ?"

"Yes, Faculty of Arts, Cairo University. I'm going home to see my people. I haven't seen them for two months." She rattled on, "..the world's in danger..examinations are coming..I forgot to tell you, I'm in the Third Year, French Department.. a living language, French. And what are you ?"

"A plane has crashed,and all aboard have been killed except the pilot."

"All except the pilot ?" the voice, sounded incredulous.

"All except the pilot."

"Why ? What did he do ?"

"I don't know, it says so in the paper, I only read the headline."

"Today's paper ?"

"I want to sleep."

"Where are you getting off, so I can wake you in time ?"

"Port Said."

"Good, so am I."

I leaned my head back, but did not shut my eyes. The clanging got into my head again, threading its way right in, and I was beginning to drift away on its beat when the silly creature shook me again.

"Why don't you go to sleep ?" I looked at her and noted the pale down on her upper lip, and her little white teeth. She went on.

"Are you not feeling well ?"

"I'm alright, just keep on talking."

"What about ?"

"Anything that comes into your head."

"Ah.. well, have you no opinion on this question of Korea, then ?"

"So you're studying French ?"

"Well, for Heaven's sake.." she cried in exasperation, but she continued to blabber, while I nodded distractedly to each of her many questions, which I did not even make out. When we got off at Port Said, she took hold of my arm, and stood close to me, and smiled.

"You're a man with a very fine intellect," she said. "You approve of my political opinions. Most people don't. I like you. I'd like to visit you before I return to Cairo. Where do you live ?"

I gave her my card.

The same day, she came in the evening. I opened the door, and she stood smiling a moment before she came in.

"You live all alone in this big flat ?"

"All alone."

"See ? I've come. The same day." When I did not answer, she asked, "Are you annoyed ?"

"No."

"I must say, I like you very much."

"What is this 'cultural conscience' André Gide is always talking about ? I don't know what he means."

"Gide ?"

"Yes."

"Well, actually, he means a lot of things.. although I'm not familiar with the man's philosophy.. but obviously he means.." I was staring at her white teeth, and her face that resembled my mother's. The room was full of the sea air, with its peculiar smell, humid and bracing. I caught her last words.

"..and this cultural conscience, I suppose, serves the cause of peace, doesn't it ?" I wasn't following, so I just nodded.

"We have the same views on things, you and I. I'm very glad of that. It's like finding a precious stone. Everyone else.. well, not exactly everyone, but most people distrust me.. and they kill me with argument."

"I'll make tea.'

"Let me make it."

"Alright, the kitchen's over there. You'll find everything you need."

She smiled at me.

"Funny, the way I like you."

"What's funny ?"

"My liking you."

"Go on and make the tea."

I stretched myself out in a deck chair when she left the room; one of those clumsy contraptions that tilt backwards, and I turned my face to receive the fresh breeze that came in through the big old-fashioned window. I could hear the stove in the kitchen, and then I realized she was standing behind me. I didn't want to look at her, such a funny creature.

"Listen," she began in a serious voice, like a man's, "has religion anything to do with war ?" A windbag, that's what she was, exasperating me with her continuous prattle; I could have hit her. Full of queer notions too, all of them useless. There are many people like that, fond of floating round in a never-ending void. I peered through the window, hoping something would catch my attention.

"*That* is a ponderous issue," I heard her say, ".. very significant; not a question to be answered in a flash. Now, that's what I like about you. You don't answer rashly. If I'd put a question like that to any of my fellow students, the answer would have been out even before they'd heard me through. That's why I dislike them so, and they're all so conceited, everyone of them insists that only what he thinks is right."

All of a sudden, I remembered fragments from the Easter liturgy. They were Benedictions I had come across in an old book. What reminded me was a word I hadn't understood and which persisted in my memory. It came to me now. "*Evloghiai*.." That was the Greek for *benedictions*, I liked the sound.. "*Evloghiai*.." I said aloud with a laugh, "Let me see..it goes something like..Blessed art Thou, o God, teach me Thy laws.. the host of angels beholding Thy face is amazed and bewildered..counted art Thou amongst the dead, o Lord our Saviour. Thou hast defeated the power of death, raising Adam with Thee, and delivering us all from the regions of hell..blessed art Thou o God, teach me Thy laws.. the shining angel at the grave called unto the ointment-bearers, saying, Wherefore mix ye tears with ointment in mourning, o ye women, .. behold the shroud and rejoice.. for the Saviour is risen from the grave.."

"What is this ?"

"Something I remembered; I don't know any more."

"You certainly have remarkable gifts," she laughed.

"Where's the tea ?"

"I'll bring it." What's this girl after, I wondered. But I didn't really care; let her chatter on, as much as she likes.

"The tea's getting cold," she cried. I took my cup.

"In these *Evlo*.. what did you say the word was ?"

"What word ?"

"What you recited just now.. never mind the name. You said something like.. 'behold the shroud and rejoice' .. does that help the cause of peace, now ?"

"You're only a university student, I don't see why you should worry about.."

"About what ?"

"All those things."

"Do you know many of these texts ?"

"I'm not sure."

"Are they Christian texts ?"

"Yes."

Later, it was she who broke the silence.

"I'm getting damp in here." She got up to close the window, and looked at her watch, and then at me.

"It's getting late," she said. "I wish I could stay longer and talk to you, and discuss politics. You are a cultured man." She gave a startled little smile. Her face coloured. It made the yellow down on her lip glisten, and her little teeth flashed. "I must go now. I'll be back tomorrow, and we'll talk a little more..You're a man," she said in some confusion. "All the others are so childish. It's no good discussing anything with them. Listen..No.." The last word spurted out rapidly, as though it took her by surprise. She extended her hand to me, but when I extended mine, she was taken aback. We shook hands, then she was gone, and I heard the door close behind her. I stood up and opened the window, and the humid air blew in.

When the sea on the skyline broke away from the risen sun in the east, the sun stood glowing in the rosy mist of dawn and the cool morning air. I looked out, and saw the deserted shore, stretching wearily, lashed by the waves. There was no one there, so I got into my bathing trunks and sneaked out. A little boy saw me as I went downstairs. He stood staring at me for a moment and then laughed. I walked to the sea, shivering a little and I remembered what I knew about the water being warmer at daybreak..What I knew ?..now how should I know that ? ..I stopped, puzzled..and the same at sunset too.. People were beginning to come now, and a man stood watching me swim, and when I looked up a second time, he was gone. I was still shivering, and for no reason I thought of the ferocious fish living in the sea. When I started to come out I turned back and dived in again when I saw an old woman wrapped in a black coat, trudging along the shore, and holding a coloured parasol above her head. When she had gone, and I could see her as a mere shadow rolling slowly off, I came out shivering even more. It was warmer now, as I walked back home. I had a shower and the water trickled down on my body like frozen threads of ice, I remembered the girl as I drank my tea, and the yellow down on her upper lip flashed across my mind. She'll come again today, I thought with a laugh, and make my head ache with her chatter. I wish she'd sit quietly somewhere behind me so that I wouldn't have to look at her. Her little head is full of strange notions. Why does she have to worry about peace ? The idiot. It's almost as if she wants to guarantee peace and security to the children she has not even conceived yet. An old tic of the human mind, which would appear again and again — why hadn't I put the cup down yet : I had finished the tea that was in it some time ago. I didn't feel any warmer after drinking my tea: my teeth began to chatter. I looked out of the window and saw the yellow sands on the beach shining dazzlingly. The sun was well up in the sky by now. Something in the middle distance by the sea glistened like a diamond but I couldn't tell what it was from where I was standing. It was peeping out from among little hummocks of sand. I was so cold, I put an overcoat on, and closed the window. Then I had breakfast and stretched out in the deck chair. I'm rather fond of that chair. When I woke up, I realized I hadn't slept for more than an hour, and my face had a light perspiration on it. I thought of the girl again, as the sun slithered down westward and while the sea was swallowing it up. Now it must be peering down at the other side of the globe. They must be waking up now, over there, just when we're getting ready to go to sleep. Then there was a light knock at the door and it was she.

"Why didn't you ring ?"

"I didn't realize there was a bell." Her white teeth flashed through her smile as she settled down in a chair facing mine, as though we were old friends.

"Why are you wearing an overcoat ?"

"I went swimming at dawn this morning."

"Swimming ? At this time of the year ?" she said in surprise.

"Yes."

"That's unusual."

"It was cold: I shivered."

"And why today in particular ?"

"The sea looked very tempting in the light of dawn." She stared into her lap for a while.

"Isn't it funny, you don't even know my name."

"That's true."

"I'll open the window." When she stood up, I noticed she was rather full round the buttocks, but she seemed more beautiful than the day before. The salt sea-air blew in. She'll be gone soon, I reflected, gazing my fill at her, and I shan't see her again. I felt rather sorry about that.

"Here I am again," she said.

"Good."

"You don't look very pleased." Her talk became trifling once more and I didn't feel like answering so I looked out of the window beyond her, into the darkness crouching outside. It was getting chilly, and I pulled my coat tighter around me.

"You look a hundred years old," she laughed.

"Do I have wrinkles ?"

"Ah..that reminds me.." I was getting curious about her.

"What of ? Peace ?"

"No," she laughed gaily, and with a man's vigour, "but tell me, are you forty ?"

"Only thirty."

"That's quite young," she exclaimed, as she laughed more lodly, "but you look so old and truculent and.." Her dress was the colour of the sea, and fitted her body rather tightly.

"Do you hear me ?" she was saying.

"I do."

"The truth is," she went on, "that philosophy is not good for the mind if one starts reading it too early. It should not be attempted at all until quite late in life.. don't you think ? And I believe that is the conclusion Bourget draws in that very complicated novel of his, *Le Disciple*."

"No doubt," I agreed. There was no point in contradicting her. I liked her when she laughed.

"Do you like to appear mysterious ?" she asked suddenly in a voice that startled me.

"No."

"Isn't it strange..rather a pleasant coincidence..one rarely comes across someone who agrees with all one's opinions."

"Is that why I seem mysterious ?"

"I think so..the strange thing is," she continued reflectively, after a short silence, "..no, it's a fact, that we dislike people who are full of their own importance, who continually want to assert themselves. We really come to loathe them."

Her legs were fidgeting nervously, and I could feel she was beginning to lose the balance of her thoughts.

"How do you manage here, all alone ?" she continued. There she was, blabbering, again, "..examinations are ridiculous..we, the girls of this generation are preparing a new era for the women of tomorrow.. intellectual bondage..nonsense..there's no such thing.." She stopped abruptly when the window suddenly slammed. She stared absently into the darkness outside, "..I loathe Eugène Sue; he comes nowhere near Balzac," she resumed.

"I'll make tea," I interrupted.

"There's no need."

"I'd like some."

"Then let me make it." I was relieved when she left the room and I was alone. I shut my eyes : I wished she'd go, or else remain quiet. I could hear the waves splashing on the shore, then the window slammed again and I drew my chair to one side. The electric light was swinging in the breeze that blew in from outside; it held my gaze, and I raptly followed its motions until it stopped. I was distracted by the sound of the stove in the kitchen, and I noticed there was a book on the table. Suddenly she came running in from the kitchen. "How can you live like this ?" she said impetuously. "The house is filthy."

"I know."

"Doesn't it worry you ?"

"Why should it worry you, little girl ?"

She blushed, her eyes flickered, and she gave another of her half-smiles, "You need.."

"What do I need ?"

"You need a whole battalion of women to tidy up the mess in this flat. It's disgusting." I could see she was pretending.

"Just don't worry, little girl," I laughed. She sat on the edge of her chair.

"Why do you always call me 'little girl ?' " she asked, and her cheek coloured, "I'm not a little girl. I'm twenty."

"Then why aren't you married ?" That was a question I had meant to ask her.

It took her by surprise and she looked at me disconcertedly, as though I had asked an obscene question. "What a man !" she exclaimed." For the time being, I want to continue my studies.. I don't see why you men always link the idea of marriage with death.. I ought not to marry until I finish my studies."

"That's a good sequence of ideas."

"The kettle's boiling over," she laughed, and looked at me slyly as she ran out of the room.

I heard a noise outside the flat, and I could recognize some of the voices as it grew louder. I was able to distinguish that of a young girl I'd seen several times before, and I remembered the way she wore her pitch-black hair in a pony tail that waved in the wind and shook vigorously whenever she ran along the beach. I wanted to open the door and look at it, it must be shaking furiously now.. I could hear her laughter on the staircase.. she had large eyes too, and didn't talk like my little friend here. She liked to listen, and always said 'yes' to everything and everyone. She must be about sixteen. Her only defect was her big mouth. When she laughed, it reminded me of the broad coastline, stretching lengthwise into infinity. I laughed nervously at the thought.

"Why are you laughing ?" My little friend was standing before me. I hadn't noticed before that her skin was fair.

"No reason in particular." I replied.

"Here's your tea." I thanked her and took the cup. She drew her chair nearer mine, and began to sip her tea, looking intently into it, pretending not to notice I was staring hard at her. That was an old trick — I smiled at the idea — as good as saying, "Take your time.. admire me.." I am not really quite so inane. Sometimes I like to strike hard and suddenly, although I know that this leads one nowhere.

"Suppose a man proposed to you now," I put in obliquely, "would you refuse him ?" She wasn't prepared for such a question. It obviously threw her off balance, and I gloated over her discomfiture. The silence was getting awkward, and she blushed as she groped for an answer.

"I want to finish my studies," she said, recovering her self-possession. "If he agreed to that I would accept him."

"Suppose he didn't." This was a calculated challenge to all her convictions, to her very femininity.

"Why shouldn't he ?" she said, trying to stall.

"Just suppose he doesn't."

"I'd convince him." I made no comment as I could see she was making an effort to collect her thoughts. That had been a quick round, evidently trying to her nerves. Here I realized she was nothing but a container full of the opinions of others, with none of her own.

I was rather amused by the revelation, although I didn't really care, one way or another.

"You know, I think you're cunning," she said.

"Why ?" I looked at her out of the corner of my eye.

"You think in a roundabout way."

"What do you mean ?"

"Well, I don't know, exactly," she replied hesitantly "You rather depend on taking your opponent by surprise. You disarm him, and then you force him to fight with unfamiliar weapons."

"I still don't understand..yesterday's tea was better."

"And do you prefer the educated, or the uneducated woman ?" So ! She was hitting back, the vicious cat. I stared hard at her. I could have slapped the girl. Now her real face was revealed, stripped of every mask.

"Take a doctor," I replied slowly. "He would not be considered fully educated if he knew all about mathematics for instance, but he would be if he knew all about medicine."

"What do you mean ?"

"I mean that education is a matter of adjustment." She pondered over that for a while, trying to look as if she understood.

"I don't understand," she said suddenly.

"Do you think prolonging the span of man's life would affect cultural values ?"

"You're being mysterious again," she cried.

I laughed. I could see a light glimmering out to seaward.

"You're a mischievous little creature,"I said. She moved her chair closer.

"But, tell me — what do you think of a man who asks a girl to give up her studies in order to marry him ?"

"What I think ?"

"Yes."

"Any woman would know what to think in the circumstances."

"Sheer slavery."

"Not at all."

"What do you mean, not at all ?" She was indignant. I knew I ought to say, "Alright, yes, certainly it is," so I said it. She was pleased and her smile returned.

"You're beginning to mutiny," she said.

"That's hard on me."

"I like you."

"Thanks."

"An uneducated girl, now, could never have said such a thing to a man. Education has given us freedom, and everything else that it takes for the complete emancipation of women.." I looked at her narrowly, and she shifted uneasily in her chair. "You'll never be any good as a wife." That was a direct hit. I could see she was struggling within herself: there was a storm raging beneath the calm surface. She stood up abruptly and looked at her watch.

"I'm going away tomorrow," she said.

"Oh, well then, so long."

"So !" She stared at me for a moment. "I don't know". She paused, then went on, "Listen..I want to tell you that I'm.."

"I said 'So long'..I may come.." She put her hand on my shoulder, and looked into my eyes.

"Have you nothing else to say ?"

"There's a light over there, shining across the sea.." She leaned with her face towards me, and brought her lips close to mine, but I turned my face away.

"Pitch it all into the sea."

"You're trying for the umpteenth time to be mysterious !"

After a silence she asked with pique:

"Why won't you let me kiss you ?"

"There's no point in it. What for ?"

"I love you."

"But I don't love you."

"Thanks," she said angrily between her teeth, and gave me her back as she turned to go. I followed her quickly, and held her roughly by the shoulders, then turned her round and kissed her lengthily on the mouth.

"Why did you do that ?" she asked coyly. "You said you didn't love me."

"We have different concepts: that's all."

Then my father's words came back to me, rising out of a distant past, like a chant from primeval times, ringing in an ancient sanctuary.

"..a man with no convictions..you will destroy yourself..surely."

When I came back into the room, I stood looking out intently at the sea. I couldn't see it, it was engulfed in darkness. I only heard the waves rise and fall, and beating furiously upon the shore. There was a storm, and it was restless, agitated..it, too, had surely no convictions.

Translated by Wadida Wassef; revised by Phillip Ward-Green.

VANITY BOX

Mohamed Hafiz Ragab

MOHAMED HAFIZ RAGAB (b. 1935) is a self-taught writer, who, some years ago, was peddling nuts in the streets of Alexandria. His usual stand at the suburban tram terminus was next to the newboys who sell current books as well as newspapers and periodicals. It is by reading the books and magazines that were on sale there that he acquired the urge to write. His father had been a street vendor before him, and Hafiz Ragab was the only one of ten brothers and sisters to have survived. His formal education ended with the primary level, and, at his father's insistence, he married at the age of seventeen, and was a father himself at eighteen (his family at present consists of two daughters).

He has worked as a clerk in the Ministry of Culture, and in the Alexandria Municipality, and is at present on the staff of the Graeco-Roman Museum of Alexandria. He hopes to start a literary magazine in his home town soon. Ragab claims to be entirely uninfluenced by western literatures, which he has not read, and states that his blend of reality and fantasy derives its inspiration from Czechoslovak cartoon films, with their composite use of the photograph and the drawing. His stories have been published in magazines in Egypt, Lebanon and Kuwait, and have been broadcast from Cairo. His earlier stories, written between 1952 and 1959, were of a more conventional type than the recent ones; some of them appeared with the works of six others in the collection *'Aish wa malḥ*: ***Bread and Salt*** (1959), with a preface by Yehia Hakki.

The present story originally appeared under the title *Aṣṣābi'ush-sha'r* (*Fingers of Hair*) in the special *avant garde* number of *'Al-Qissah* (June 1965). A collected volume of his more recent stories has recently appeared under the title *Al kura wa ra'su-r-rajul — The Ball and the Man's Head* (1968).

It is difficult to pass literary judgement on this work, which sometimes makes statements of narrative realities, and, at other times, puts them in metaphorical terms. (For instance the heroine's youngest son, who has not run away from his mother, is sometimes a child in her room, and sometimes a small severed head kept in the plumber's box). The chronology of the events in the story starts in p. 392, proceeds to the end, and *continues* at the opening of the story, to reach a final point on p.402. This story is included as the most extreme case we know of the exploitation of the non-realistic technique, and it is doubly interesting that it comes from a writer without a conventional background of education and of literary influences, Arabic or foreign. The writer says of his stories that their main theme is man's entanglement in life, and that he calls upon his readers to supply their own interpretations by their taking the initiative themselves.

Hanna lays her head on the cushion. She stretches herself out on the violet padding of the divan, inside the vanity box on the dressing table. She pulls the coverlet over her. She leaves the door ajar purposely to draw the man in: she yawns. Not that she is succumbing to sleep. She is repulsing it. Soon the Hair is slipping in after her. Hanna stretches her fingers out. They embrace. The Hair winds around her, covers her. She is his prisoner.

The fingers fall asleep in the box interlocked. Neither of them pays any attention to the lipstick, the powder-compact, the scent bottle and the little handbag mirror — the creatures of the vanity box — even though they have helped to get Hanna ready for the happening.

A few moments before she lay down in the box Hanna had picked up the lipstick: it passed over a pair of chapped lips, its softness absorbed by their dryness. She reached for the powder compact. The grains of powder swept over the rough ground, turning it to smooth ice, for the fingertips of the Hair to glide over.

Hanna is prepared for the encounter. She puts the vanity box languidly down on the dressing table, close to the mirror. There are two images: the reflexion in the shade, of a woman not truly present; the other, in the hot zone, there in the region of the fallen, Hanna who only lived within the being of the man who wore his hair long, did exist.

Below the vanity box, beneath the dressing-table, in a silent corner which gave away no secrets although the consternation there almost screeched, there stood a grim iron box, obedient — almost servile —

to its master. In the box lay delicate instruments and latent fire; a blow lamp belonging to the master of the box, the master of Hanna; sticks of tin, short-lived fingers which the blowlamp would cut off. The blowlamp stood on the box, guarding it for its master who possessed Hanna's body — thin fingers of tin used by the fingers of men, to solder leaks in pipes and oilburners, fissures in old women, worn out by time and distance. Hanna was such a time-ravaged body full of cracks. Next to the grim box is a little head sunk in dreams of suffering. The head is shuddering beside the box. The box shelters it from the blind draught that rushes in from the half-open door. The box knows the meaning of suffering. It has experienced it, being a slave to the man — a despised means for him to carry the tools of his trade around the streets of the city. The head: a boy, an unfinished human being, and yet suffering has come of age within him — the youngest of Hanna's children, a piece of flesh that she had vomited, thrown from a window. And now there are two heads missing from the room, lost in a strange, unseen land: they disappeared when the outsider, the Hair, burst into Hanna's existence, stretched out on the soft couch inside the vanity box. He turned up, bringing the box with him, and she took her clothes off, stretched herself out naked, kissing the nails of the Hair, rubbing her skin against him. The children saw her at this: two of them were struck with horror; those two ran away. But one sleeps; the youngest of them sleeps. He was too young to know clear fear. He stayed.

The two Heads got out of the house by a way which her breasts had so far kept closed. Out into a land which caught them in its fangs. Not a finger, not an eye is left of those two Heads to comfort the people. They are forgotten.

Inside the skull of the night, beside the continuing silence (while a vanity-box, with pleasures in it, shakes with ecstasy, blended with the exhausted sighs of Hanna, which tell that the frightened woman has given herself up into servility), next to the box stuffed full of short-lived sticks of tin, and also housing the little Head which has not been able to join the two vagrant Heads, (the box was made out of the skin of a dead snake, and it keeps prisoner the fingers of the Hair, which play with what lies underneath the dressing-gown), while her two chapped lips show cruel lines brought out by the thick lipstick, and while Hanna's hands stretch out into the Hair, while she buries in it her body and heart and the whole of her life, as she tries to shrug off the weight of the price she has paid, *inside the skull of the night*, punctured by sockets, a voice — (while Hanna is hugging the Hair close) comes up the steep stairwell, daylight robbery carried out by blind burglars.

Now a man with a limp is climbing up the stairs, a man with a stump. "Hanna ! Hanna ! I'm sitting here at the foot of the stairs, keeping off the tramcars so they can't come up and snatch you away, keeping the tram driver away so that he can't come up and slit your throat. Hanna, I'm so afraid they'll hang you from the trolley-pole of the tram, and your clothes'll hang down and leave your body uncovered, Hanna."

She cowers under the attack of the nails that are scratching her. This punishment comes from somewhere far down, an echo of the past — scattered flesh and the absent shadow of the man who has left his fingerprints on her neck, the man who collects all these old memories. She jumps up in fear and hits out angrily at her memories. She strips off the past and throws it down. It rolls down the staircase. She rushes naked to throw herself into the Hair, to scatter the echo of the Voice in fragments, and puff away what is still left of the chaff of the two children, and tread her memories in the face.

At the bottom of the stairs there is a man with an empty brain-pan. The wheels of the Ramleh tram have passed over his face and altered his features, while a blind tram-conductor was trumpetting into his whistle, so that the wall fell upon the boy's head.

Before the busmen and tram teams took the lid off the man's brain-box and ate his brain, he had worn a white jacket and carried a tray with bottles on it, which he had served out to Neckties and Spectacles. The Spectacles and Ties stretched out for the bottles and glasses and scampered off with them into the recesses of desk-drawers; in the darkness there they sipped their drinks, their eyes scanning the columns of the *Ahram* newspaper line after line; every so often they took a nibble at a sandwich of *foul*-and-salad.

At two o'clock, when they creep out of the drawers of their desks, Mahrous leaves the office buffet and throws up a grapple on one end of a line inside the neck of a lemonade bottle (the buffet caterer has put him in the bottle and pressed the stopper down) — and he climbs up the rope; he knocks on the bottle-stopper and the caterer prises it off. At this moment the last office-worker skulking in the recesses of the drawers has gone, and the cortège of the crowds shuffles hurriedly through the streets. Mahrous walks at the rear, wanders around the town, and turns up again as evening is falling. The moon floats over the Mahmoudieh Canal and the tin shanties of Ghorbal swim up, lit with pressure-lamps, and lifted up in the wind upon a magic carpet, on which a genie rides, floating on the white cloud where Mahrous is sitting, with his feet dangling down over Ghorbal.

With the day's taking he buys himself some *hashish*, places it in the bowl of the hookah, buries it in the ropy treacled tobacco. He puffs at it, and dreams rise up yawning, bracing their shoulders which have been lying relaxed and rounded. Mahrous braces his own shoulders but they instantly relax: he no longer has a pair of shoulders which will obey him and help him to face the dogged thing that blocks his path. He hurries to a table laid with grilled meat, pigeons, plums and Syrian grapes. He chuckles inwardly. His heart is dead, but it goes on chuckling, chuckling at the glasses and neckties, his laughter seeping out of unseen cracks: Mahrous is a man full of cracks, cracks that the smoke comes out of, leaving no trace behind. When all his laughter has leaked away so that there isn't a chuckle left in him, he drags his feet along — heavily, because of their weight — and on his head he carries the tray that belongs to the office-buffet, with the buffet caterer stretched out upon it at his ease, shouting out orders to him. "Stopping to get your breath back ? Don't you dare stop for a moment. For the sake of the ties and the spectacle-lenses. . the legs of the office desks. Make a round of every drawer. You're to bow to every drawer: ask it what it'll have to drink. Get a move on ! Remember, the customer's always right. You're to rush and answer every call you hear." Mahrous starts to run around, he screams, and throws tray and caterer down to the ground, "Hanna ! Help me, Hanna ! The boss is after me. He wants me to run to every single call that's made."

Hanna makes him stand still. She hugs him. She takes his feet off for him, and stands them in salt water. His feet drink in the restfulness; they relax.

At midnight Mahrous turns into a magician. He lights a brazier and throws frankincense and sticks of Javanese incense on to it. He calls up genies, orders them to raise up volcanoes out of which flow streams of liquid flame. He hurries to the lemonade bottle and prises off the stopper, clambers out of the neck, seizes hold of the bottle, and dashes it to pieces against the ceiling. He flings the stopper right in the face of the caterer, and of the whole wide world. He runs to an office close-by to the buffet; there is a civil servant there, dreaming of forthcoming promotion and a rise; he creeps up to him and snatches off his glasses and throws them down underfoot, tramples on them, until they are in tiny fragments which he scatters in the faces of the office-workers: "You've all got glass eyes, you Neckties. I've pounded your eyes to smithereens. I've trampled on them, and I'm flinging the bits and pieces in your faces." The morning comes. Hanna gets up, refreshed. Mahrous has rubbed off all his degradation on to her: she wipes her flesh dry of the dripping bathwater, wipes her body clean of her husband's day-long humiliation. It does not take her more than an instant to fly back from the long night journeys she makes into the landscape of magic with the night-time enchanter, the day-time waiter, the family man, chief prop of the buffet of a government office.

At seven o'clock, when the whistle blows at the spinning mill across the canal, three Heads leave the room, carried along on three pairs of legs. They are Hanna, Mahrous and Harby.[1] Three heads stay behind, held daylong in a single moment of expectation, until the other three heads come home.

Hanna stretches out her hundred fingers, washes the wide world's

---

(1) An unusual name, meaning *Warchild*.

laundry in a large basin. Some of the world's creatures give her their cast-off clothing: a silk brassière in which a cockroach has eaten a hole, a blouse that has lost a sleeve — they give her the left-overs of their meals (these come from single men who live alone in solitary rooftop rooms). She carries off the world's gifts in a sack, and when she gets home, she empties everything out of it into four open mouths.

Every morning, when feet firmly set out to walk, and boats laden with blue saucepans are ferried across the Mahmoudieh Canal, Hanna, Mahrous and their son Harby leave the house. Harby is a hundred years old. He wears a beret which his mother has rifled out of the laundry of an aging foreign gentleman who once made passes at her with his fingers and his fumbling palm — the man had long since stopped trying to satisfy his urges, and this pawing of a woman was all he could do instead.

Harby works as a servant in the home of a foreigner and a she-foreigner. He digs his teeth into the stone floor of their flat in the hope of pleasing the Hat who might then give him his reward at the end of the day: half a tin of corned beef that his brothers and his sister would stare at avidly. For in the evening they rummaged under the beret in his basket, and in the basket there would be one banana finger and an orange and a delicious slice of meat. The women eye him, *so clever just the way his Mum and Dad are, all earning a good living they are, Mahrous and Hanna and their son — all three of them — every one of them — they've got luck, they have.* Every eye in the quarter pierced into his basket. And what they wish for Harby is this: that his hands should be cut off, that his mother should die under the surgeon's scalpel, and that his father should go crazy with grief. Life strides on, with these six beings clinging to its neck. It carries three of them out every morning, and drops the other three behind — an unbearable life, but they put up with it. When it strikes them hard in the eyes, they laugh. Every evening, they greet life with chuckles. But with a stutter too. The mother comes home from caverns where she has seen melancholy men wearing masks. She is pursued by house-porters all the way down to the washing-rooms in the basement; she slips free of their hold, only to be clutched to their breasts by strangers with a fiercely burning eagerness that she has to fight off. Danger smouldering in close-lipped civil servants — it's in their silence that the danger lies. They hope to use her to lift off the weight of the silence of their loneliness. But she escapes them. She slips free. So far she has slipped free.

The father comes home, wearing a turban, and he lifts Hanna and carries her up, shows her a land where no human foot has trodden. He protects her from the roof-top males who, patient, and fawning, keep on the look-out for their homeward flight. But they do not return until the dawn is there, standing and crying out, a rooster on a rooftop, without a minaret to make its call from.

One day the foreigner, the man who wears the Hat, says to Harby, the son of Hanna, "Kharrpi ! Kharrpi ! You go fetch for me one pottle peer." Bottled fever settles the boy's fortunes. The woman in the bathroom peers through the holes of the shower-head: her eyes glare down out of two of the holes: "Kharrpi ! I also you bring for me one pottle of peer." Bottles of amber water, bottles of the water of pain.

So, two bottles it's to be. The master has asked for one, the mistress has asked for one (who told them to ? what made them ask for them ?). Harby runs down to fetch the two bottles (— and how ? why ?). He picks up the beer bottles, and halts: he notices that the beer is red. The warning is inside. Each of the bottles has a severed neck inside it, dripping blood (how is it then that he isn't frightened ? that he doesn't run away ? what makes him pick them up and walk on ?).

The man who sells the beer is astonished to see the blood dripping out, drop by drop. But he wants to sell his bottles, and he hides his astonishment; he gives the bottles to Harby and says nothing, though his mind is at one with the covert warning. A bottle of what the Hat fancies (if only every desire had shrivelled up inside that Hat long ago!). A bottle for the eye-sockets of the shower-head, for the smooth flesh of the bath-tub (if only the bathroom had tumbled down over the woman in it !).

Ten fingers and ten toes on their way back. Terror on its way with nothing to stop it. Ten fingers held up, dancing higher than the four wheels: if only wheels could be stopped at will by pedestrians who don't make use of them. And there are more wheels, and they dance higher than the ten toes. The double-decker tram lumbers on. On the top deck the passengers are asleep, waiting for the scream that is to wake them up, for them to start up in a panic and fling themselves out of the windows.

Harby looks at the beer-bottles; he notices that the contents are completely red. *Drop them and run away now..run away*, the warning says. He is astonished, swathed in astonishment, muffled by it. Inside each bottle is a head, its severed neck dripping blood. He stops still, rigid (why does he ?).

(Why is he so astonished ? People are always astonished at the moment of defeat — why is he struck helpless ?).

People scream. The passengers on the top deck wake up, rub their eyes, yell, and throw themselves out of the windows. And the tram continues on its way. But everything is over. It is all over. Two heads sink from the necks of the bottles down to their bottoms.

The two bottles fall on to the rails. They are smashed. The splinters of glass scatter. Harby has been cut in two. The bus scoops one half up and hides it, keeps it all to itself, and the other half is swallowed up by the wheels of the tram. A swindle: he has been here, now he isn't (has he been ? *has* anyone ever seen him ?).

(Do the wheels of the tram stop ? Do the wheels of the bus stop ? and the people ? and the wheels of cloud above them ? does the water freeze in the bath-tub — does it stop showering down, in its astonishment ? does it stop spraying down out of the holes in the shower-head ? Every one of the wheels turns, turns.)

The woman screams out of the bath, "Kharrpi ! Kharrpi ! You are zere, Kharrpi ? Where my pottle of beer is ?"

The master shouts, "Where my bottle of peer iss, Kharppi ? You goot-for-nozing boy !"

Harby answers the call. He comes in suddenly, carrying the two bottles, his hands bloodstained. He smiles as he stands the bottles on the table. His foreign employer opens his mouth to ask the boy about his bloodstained hands, but he jumps back in terror as Harby's flesh scatters into gobbets, and lies around the room. The *khawaga*[1] runs into the bathroom to tell his wife what has happened. They come back into the room together, and find nothing: the wind has blown in from the open french windows; it has swept up the morsels of flesh: it scatters them all over the people.

Hanna comes home, but Harby does not. Mahrous comes home. But Harby does not. Mahrous comes home in the evening with his magic carpet, and joins his little family. Hanna whispers, "Harby hasn't come in..yet."

He pulls his belt off. He drives the genie away, and throws the magic carpet out of the window. "I shan't come back unless I've got Harby's hand in mine."

He gives up his bed and spends the night on the floor. Hanna goes to the *khawaga*. The *khawaga* says to her, "Kharrpi never come back wiz the bottle of beer. Lady, I'm fond of beer. And zere's my wife in the bathroom over zere, waiting for the beer. Kharrpi's a good-for-nozing boy."

Hanna does not climb into the washbasin and fly up in it over the washing-lines stretched out on the rooftop. She does not hang the laundry out in the clouds. She and Mahrous make the rounds of the police-stations. "Try the morgue," a neighbour says to her, "You try the deep-freeze ice-chest, love. That's where you ought to be looking. Put yourself out of all this suspense. And that'll put your mind at rest."

They lift off the sheet from the first corpse for them. Mahrous and Hanna say nothing.

They lift off the sheet from the second corpse for them. Will his firm hand, which carries hundreds of orders on his tray of sorrows, be able to keep firm now ? It hangs down by his side, proclaiming surrender in the face of the stretched-out corpse which stares up at him.

When they lift the sheet off the third corpse, Hanna falls forward on her face. She has seen enough. The men who run the morgue

(1) In Egypt, a foreigner, especially a westerner.

dismiss the man and woman. But something unknown is tugging at their hearts: Hanna notices drops of her own blood rolling along on the ground. She screams, "My blood. There are drops of it on the ground."

Mahrous, too, notices a piece of his own flesh, clinging to his leg, nuzzling into it. He recognises it at once. "A piece of my own flesh. They've swiped it. But how ?"

They go back to the men in charge. The men stand facing them, and the chief official steps out of the crowd, shaken at heart. "*They want to look at death. They're craning forward to look at it.* Show them the icebox, men. Just a look at the boy's head will be enough. And you pull yourself together, woman. I won't have a single word from you. There isn't to be the ghost of a shriek from your lips, d'you understand ?"

The man sews their lips up. His men draw them forward by a thin thread attached to their lips, and they fling the sheet off the corpse, Harby.

His eyeball has burst. His liver is gashed in two. Put to death with a beer bottle. The tram wheels have ridden over his bones. The conductor has trumpeted his horn over the boy's flesh. Not a single word. Not the ghost of a shriek. One tear and the men will pull her away by the thread they hold her by. The stifled scream tears her skin, tears through everything that lies under the skin, makes its way into her heart, the bottom of her heart, the very end of things, the ultimate end of the finish of all things.

At the bottom of the staircase now a man stands silent. He is silent because the things he has met with have terrified him; he stumbles on the steps, wounded and bleeding. He does not know how he can get to the top of the steps and call out, "Hanna ! ", when she lies naked, bathing in water that gushes out of a tangle of black hair, hair that is growing into her flesh, while nails are clawing at the inner folds of her breasts, tearing at them, leaving bloody scars on them.

Hanna's son has been butchered. She wears black. She turns herself round and round on live embers, in order to hide her secret: that Mahrous no longer takes any journeys into the landscape of enchantment. Hanna has grown used to the night voyages. He would knock on her door, an elephant's ear in his hand. "Bring your things with you. We're off on a journey from now until the morning." She would pick up her things, run wildly to him. But now he comes back to her in the evenings with a gravestone for his head, heaps his bones upon the rushmat on the ground and lies there all night with open eyes, thinking of fortune, of the unexpectedness of the end. A father who's not been able to save his son: how can he go back to his smoke-clouds and climb their slopes ? The son is a wretch. The father is a wretch. One of them works as a servant. The other cringes to people's orders. The world snatches his son away — wheels that reason does not control — one second, and a person's being is annihilated. Hanna is fond of the smoke-clouds. She has danced on the stairway they formed. That is her logic. Will the son come back ? It isn't possible. Only in a world purged of all cruelty can Harby ever come back to her. She tries to draw close to Mahrous, but he shies away from her in panic; he stands up in front of her and pulls a skull out of his sack. "See this, my dear ? My own head. Your own head, Hanna. My head and yours, they're one and the same. You and I together: we're a skull. I found Harby's head inside the skull. There's the whole world inside. Strange, isn't it, my dear, the whole world being a skull ?"

He picks up the heap of bones, heaves them on to his shoulder, and leaves the room.

Long ago, when night-time was safe, there was a thing which passed from Hanna's tongue to Mahrous's tongue, a juice that came from them both when the night-time had been tenderness. Now Mahrous crawls under the wheels of the tram looking for hands, severed hands strewn here and there, a stray toe or a foot that the days had hidden away — busy with hashed-up flesh, gathering it in, piling it into a coarsely-spun sack, heaving it on to his shoulder, and making off with it to the cemetery in the shadow of Pompey's Pillar: he buries it in the dust there and gains a little merit for a pious deed. Hanna screams at him, asks him to throw the sack away and take her up on his shoulders: couldn't they both take a strong puff at the hookah, at a perfumed cigarette stuffed with wads of aromatic Indian leaves ? Couldn't he fly off with her, away above the rooftop, the washing-lines, the students who make passes at her, the porters she has to shake off ? Mahrous does not listen. Silence.

On the second-storey landing in the building that Abul Badr owns, Hanna crouches in a washbasin wringing out her clothes, and her children's clothes. Mahrous's clothes are not in the washbasin. "You see his clothes, girls ? Just as he left them. They're just as they were — I haven't touched them. It would be a shame for me to bother with them. Full of sores from the sack of bones and the walking among the graves by the Pillar all day. The man never touches me now. He never has a bath. He's been scared off me. The miserable creature's afraid of me. He's afraid of the holes in the shower-head. The man's turned into a block of wood, girls. I shan't wash his clothes for him, it's a waste of good work." She tosses them out of the window.

Hanna's words fly above the chattering of the women and come to their menfolk in the night-time, turning into giggles and pettings and kisses. And the story of the scared Mahrous spreads. And spreads. It is dragged about by a fifty-year-old woman who was snatched away from her husband and children. She tells it to the man who snatched her away (he is her husband now), tells it to him in the folds of the night when the breathings of people have burnt themselves down — her husband, the owner of the box of secrets, who repairs primus stoves, makes the rounds of the town and spends lavishly upon his woman's flesh (and if a woman has a husband, well, then, he'll steal her away from him) — he will stay awake right through the night, with his blowlamp lit, and the fingerprints of the previous man upon it — and that is his pleasure, stupid and stolen. His fifty-year-old tells him about the crushing of Mahrous, gives him all the details, so that he can use the story to crown himself: Mahrous is crushed, and he is still a champion.

Two days later. The man comes to Hanna's room while Mahrous is away looking for a new sack to hold the scattered bones he has found on the down-town tram-lines. Hanna's look falls on the Hair, and she stiffens. "Right there. That's where I shall spend the rest of my days: every moment that's left to me."

He pats her on the shoulder. She leans on his breast and burst into tears.

Next day. He comes back with an expensive vanity box. And inside it Hanna stretches herself out comfortably on the violet upholstery of the couch.

Translated by Mahmoud Manzalaoui; revised by Keith Jones.

SUGGESTIONS FOR FURTHER READING

In European Languages:

Abdel Aziz Abdel Meguid, *The Modern Arabic Short Story: Its Emergence, Development and Form*, Al-Maaref Press, Cairo, 1955. This is a commentary(149 pp.) in English, with a collection of thirty-four short stories in their original form.

William R. Polk, editor, *Perspective of the Arab World: An Atlantic Monthly 'Supplement'*, 1956. Contains commentaries and translations.

Vincent Monteil, *Anthologie bilingue de la littérature arabe contemporaine*, Beirut, 1961.

Louis Morcos, trans. (with Introduction), *Modern Egyptian Short Stories*, Anglo-Egyptian Bookshop, Cairo, 1961. Includes further stories by Yehia Hakki and Youssef el Sharouny.

Raymond Francis, *Aspects de la littérature arabe contemporaine*, Dar Al-Maaref, Cairo, 1963. Includes studies of Youssef Idris. Youssef el Sharouny, Tewfik el Hakim, Soheir el Kalamawi, Soliman Fayyad, Yehia Hakki, Naguib Mahfouz, and Mahmoud Taymour.

Hermann Ziock, ed. and trans., *Der Tod des Wassertragers*, Hernalp, 1963. Contains stories and extracts from novels.

Raoul and Laura Makarius, *Le roman et la nouvelle* (vol. I of *Anthologie de la littérature arabe contemporaine*); preface by Jacques Berque. An excellent collection of extracts, with commentaries upon authors and trends.

Gaston Wiet, *Introduction à la littérature Arabe*, Paris, 1966.

Denys Johnson-Davies, trans. (with preface), *Modern Arabic Short Stories*, London, Oxford University Press, 1967. Introduction by Professor A.J. Arberry. Excellent selection of twenty stories, one half from Egypt, the other half from other Arab countries. Coverage could not be bettered, and translation is outstanding.

In Arabic :

« ألوان من القصة المصرية » مقدمة للدكتور طه حسين . دراسة لمحمود أمين العالم . دار النديم – القاهرة ١٩٥٦ .

« قصص واقعية من العالم العربى » تقديم أمين محمود العالم ، وغائب طعمة فرمان ، القاهرة ١٩٥٦ .

Stories from Syria, Lebanon, Jordan, Sudan, Morocco, Egypt and Iraq.

« ١٥ قصة مصرية » كتب للجميع عدد ١٢٤ ، القاهرة يناير ١٩٥٧ .

« ١٥ قصة سورية » تحوى مقدمة لأحمد حمروش ، كتب للجميع ، عدد ١٢٧ ، القاهرة ، أبريل ١٩٥٨ .

« قصص من مصر » مع دراسة بقلم عز الدين إسماعيل ، القاهرة ، ١٩٥٨ .

Contains stories by Soheir el Kalamawi, Shukri Ayyad, Abdel Rahman Fahmi, Farouk Khorshid and three others.

« من الشاطىء » مجموعة قصص قصيرة ، الاسكندرية ١٩٦٥ .

Contains twenty-six stories by Alexandrian writers, and critical essays by Professor M. Khalafallah and Gazbeyya Sedky.

Short stories appear regularly in: *Al Magalla*, *Sabah el Khair*, *Al Hilal* and the defunct *Al Qissa*, Cairo, *Al Adab* and the defunct *Hiwar*, Beirut, and the defunct *Aswat*, London.

I have not seen W.M. Brinner and M.A. Khour, *A Selection of Readings in Modern Arabic* (I) *The Short Story and the Novel*, Leiden 1967, a students' reader with notes and glossary.

Al-Thaqafa (Cairo) no. 732, for 5 January 1953, is a special number devoted to the short story; *Al Qissa* No. 18, June 1965, and *Al Magalla* no. 116, August 1966, are special numbers devoted to *avant garde* short story writing, with contributions by young writers, and comments upon them by established critics. *Al Magalla* no. 134, February 1968, is also devoted to the short story. It contains eight new stories by different writers, including Sharouny and Kharrat, and an essay by Sabri Hafez on the rôle of Mohamed Taher Lashin in the development of the short story in Egypt. This number appeared too late to be made use of in the present work.

عمر الدسوقى « فى الأدب الحديث » القاهرة ١٩٥٣ .

محمود يوسف نجم « القصة فى الأدب العربى الحديث » (حتى عام ١٩١٧) ، القاهرة ١٩٥٣ .

محمد حامد شوكت « الفن القصصى فى الأدب المصرى الحديث ١٨٠٠ — ١٩٥٦ » القاهرة ١٩٥٦ .

محمود تيمور « محاضرات فى القصص فى أدب العرب ، ماضيه وحاضره » ، جامعة الدول العربية ، القاهرة ، ١٩٥٨ .

Pp. 75ff. contain bibliography covering early fiction.

شاكر مصطفى « محاضرات عن القصة فى سورية حتى الحرب العالمية الثانية » ، جامعة الدول العربية ، القاهرة ١٩٥٨ .

583 pages: too detailed and undiscriminating, but includes lengthy illustrations.

عبد القادر القط « مشكلتان فى القصة المصرية القصيرة » فى مجلة « الشهر » العددين ١ و٢ القاهرة ١٩٥٨ .

سعد الدين وهبة « فن القصة القصيرة » فى مجلة « الشهر » العدد ١٣ ، القاهرة ١٩٥٩ .

يحيى حقى « فجر القصة المصرية » العدد ٦ من « المكتبة الثقافية » ، القاهرة ١٩٦٠ .

Covers the short story from the beginning of the First World War to the mid-thirties, concentrating upon five principal writers. A short work, far above most other Arabic studies in critical depth and analytical accuracy.

يحيى حقى « خطوات فى النقد » ، القاهرة .

Contains the author's views on the past and the prospects of the Arabic short story (pp. 190-20), as well as studies of Abdel Kuddus (pp. 169-79) and Sharouny (pp. 264-78).

محمد الصادق عفيفى « القصة المغربية الحديثة » ، الدار البيضاء ، ١٩٦١ .

غالى شكرى « أزمة الجنس فى القصة العربية » بيروت ١٩٦٢ .

Contains chapters on Yehia Hakki (pp. 127-40), Ehsan Abdel Kuddus (pp. 181-208) Youssef Idris (pp. 231-255) and the Lebanese female short story writers (pp. 257-300).

غالى شكرى « فى أزمة القصة القصيرة » باب (ص ١٠٥ — ١٢٣ من كتاب « ماذا أضافوا إلى ضمير العصر ؟ » القاهرة ١٩٦٧ .

عباس خضر « القصة القصيرة فى مصر منذ نشأتها حتى سنة ١٩٣٠ » القاهرة ١٩٦٦ .

صبرى حافظ « مستقبل الأقصوصة المصرية » : ملامحه واتجاهاته » فى « المجلة » من أغسطس إلى نوفمبر ١٩٦٦ .

Detailed account of very recent short stories, including those of Mohamed Hafez Ragab.

يوسف الشارونى « دراسات فى الرواية والقصة القصيرة » القاهرة ، ١٩٦٧ .

Contains studies of Naguib Mahfouz, Yehia Hakki, Edward Kharrat, Ala' Deeb, and Sharouny's own fiction. Refers to study of modern Iraqi fiction by Abdel Kader Hassan Amin, and to the following unpublished works: a study of modern Egyptian fiction by Dr. Abdel Hamid Younes, a thesis on the Egyptian short story, 1910-1933, by Sayyed Hamed el Nassag, one on the Syrian short story, 1870-1964, by Naim Hassan el Yafi, and one on the influence of the *maqama* by Mohamed Rushdi Hassan.

فؤاد دوارة « فى القصة القصيرة » ، القاهرة ١٩٦٦ .

Contains studies of Hakki, Sharouny, Fayyad, Abdel Rahman Fahmi and Kharrat.

شكرى عياد « تجارب فى الأدب والنقد » ، القاهرة ١٩٦٧ .

Contains several essays on the short story, including studies of Fathi Ghanem, Mahfouz, Abdel Rahman Fahmi, and Youssef Idris.

شكرى عياد : « القصة القصيرة فى مصر : دراسة فى تأصيل فن أدبى » ، جامعة الدول العربية ، القاهرة ١٩٦٨ .

An important study, which appeared too late to be made use of in the present work.